Secrets Mothers Keep

A Novel by Linda J Bettenay

ISBN: 978-0-9922967-0-4

This book was first published in 2013 by:

The Roleystone Courier

1 Taree Place, Roleystone

Western Australia, 6111

www.roleystonecourier.com.au

Purchase copies of this book and others in the Secrets Series from the author direct:

www.lindasbooks.com.au

All rights reserved. This book is sold under the condition that it shall not be lent, hired out or otherwise circulated in any form other than that in which it is published. No part of this publication can be reproduced, stored in a retrieval system or transmitted by any means (electronic, mechanical, photocopying, recording or otherwise) without the prior written consent of the author.

Text Copyright © Linda J Bettenay, 2013

This is a work of fiction based on historical fact. Some actual events did occur: the murder of Harold E. Smith, the assault on Mrs Smith and her children, the trial and the subsequent execution of Clifford Hulme are real events. Some real names and real events where they have been documented in the historical record have been used. However, their characters and other incidents in their lives have been fictionalised.

Mrs Parrott/Smith's name has been altered deliberately. The characterisation of this individual in particular has been significantly altered. From relatives' testimony, the character in this novel in no way represents the real person.

Many of the names, characters, places and incidents included in this story are the products of the author's imagination or are used fictitiously. Any resemblance to persons, living or dead, is entirely co-incidental.

For My Husband Mike,
whose patience, support and everlasting love has kept me going when it would have been easier to give up.
And for his grandfather Harold E. Smith,
whose life was cut short far too soon and who has lain alone and rarely visited for far too long.
We now remember you.

SMITHY

In affectionate memory of the late Harold Eaton Smith who was familiarly known to us all as Smithy.

S'long old pal, across the great divide;
You've solved the greatest problem parson's preached;
And though we had no chance to say goodbye;
Here's hoping that the long sought goal you've reached.
It's hard old pal to think you did your bit;
And like a true Australian faced the Hun;
And then to come back home to sunny Aussie;
To meet your fate beneath a murderer's gun.
You had no chance - the coward saw to that;
This fiend who dealt out death, relentless, grim;
And even struck down helpless little children;
The hangman's rope is far too good for him.
S'long old pal - there's one great consolation;
Far down the ages rings the angel's song;
That God will surely comfort all your loved ones;
And heal their broken hearts - old pal so long.

Fagan

Prologue

Present Day

Peggy lay quietly as her death day approached, her eyes staring at the hospital white ceiling and slowly revolving fan. The clack of the fan revolutions counting down the years of her existence, as her life force gradually seeped away. Her son sat close to her in companionable silence, holding her hand and staring at her aged face. Her days were now numbered in single digits and no longer in multiples. Peggy was at peace - just the last few clockwork breaths to achieve, automatic after nearly a century of habit.

Her body hung on but her mind was locked, vague memories swirling, of events far away in time. Was she conscious that, at last - the ghastly story would now be heard. The truth hidden for so long would now be colourfully told, embellished and embroidered as a tale of long ago. But would the story tellers understand how lives had been lost, innocence taken and childhoods ruined. Perhaps those who heard the tale would be interested, fascinated, embarrassed and perhaps even ashamed but for those who had actually been there, the reality had been life altering. Shame, pain, loss, unwanted public notoriety, financial ruination - the day the laughter left her mother Lillian and her family lost faith and trust in God and their fellow man.

Lying with her last Will and Testament was the letter, that would outline the events; 'not to be read until my death,' the instruction that would guide the telling.

Locked in her moribund body, her eyes were the last to have witnessed the gruesome events of June 22nd 1928. She was 'just the baby' to all the actors with major parts in the main event; she was still just a week off her first birthday, a milestone that she so nearly didn't achieve. And now with all the actors gone, as the very last she would tell what for so long had stayed hidden.

Her innings was one to be proud of, with all but one of the years granted as an addendum; a reward for surviving the killer blows that should have snuffed out her life at 11 months, and three weeks of age. Her life had not been sad; she had recovered well from the early setback. The eyes of a baby, even when unbelievable horrors are witnessed, do not register lasting shock. She had lived a great life, she had loved and laughed and was satisfied. Peggy's mind didn't register how events decades before, irrevocably altered her family.

Her sisters also recovered - but their scars went deeper, their eyes had seen more. They registered the pain and horrors in that deep place where hurt children store up resentment and grief. However, the sisters' memories were vague, explanations never given and all three shared an unspoken belief that Lillian had kept some parts hidden away from them. Some things are just too private to share.

Three Lives
Cliff Hanger

January 26th, 1910

Beeston Hill, Leeds, England

On the 26th January ten year old Clifford Hulme was perfecting the art of being invisible. He wanted not to be noticed, so that afterwards when asked, people just couldn't recall whether he was there or not.

At school this was really important. If he was invisible then he wouldn't be bullied. No-one would tease him or laugh at him or cringe when they were told to go and sit next to him. Plus Mr Robinson, his teacher and expert tyrant, wouldn't ask him any questions and get really cranky when he didn't know the answer.

At home being invisible was critical. If he wasn't there he couldn't see what his Da did to his Mother, Mami. He couldn't see the brutal fights. He couldn't get punished when he couldn't get his clumsy body out of the way of his Da's flailing fists. He couldn't hear his Mami wailing. He couldn't feel the gut wrenching guilt that rose like bile in his gut after a fight when he had not been able to protect her from him - again.

On the 26th January, Clifford had had a better day than most. School had just gone back after the Christmas break. He was now in fifth form, tall and gangly with what his older brother Albert called a 'permanently dopey look on his face'.

Clifford had managed to stay out of everyone's way nearly all day. He had answered 'present' when Mr Robinson had called out the roll but otherwise he had not said a word to anyone. He hadn't looked at any other person and he didn't think anyone had looked much at him. Except when he got the cuts before recess because he hadn't copied the sentences off the board. But this was normal, and the other kids didn't laugh at him so much anymore because he had also learnt not to cry. Mr Robinson only hit him five times over the knuckles today and this was bearable - far better than when Da hit him.

He hadn't even been kept in at lunchtime because he hadn't got any of his sums right today. And his lunch hadn't been stolen, so he had actually got to eat it all - and his Spanish mum had made him chorizo bologna and cheese. The other kids couldn't stand the stinky smell so they had left it alone. Yep, this had been a pretty good day.

So he was a bit stunned when Mr Robinson asked him to stay back after school.

Mr Robinson waited until all the students had left. It took a while because Maisie and Emily wanted to clean up their desks first. Right little teacher's pets they were. Always trying to please.

And now they were alone. Cliff kept his eyes down - it was always better that way. Look someone in the eyes and they start talking to you and prying into your business. Cliff assumed his dopey, smiley mask face.

'Clifford why do you come to school?' Mr Robinson asked, his tone steady and with just a hint of sarcastic malice which was totally wasted on Clifford.

Cliff just stared slightly away from him - focus on the wall he thought. He stood in front of his teacher with his shoulders stooped - he tried to make his big frame fit into the least space available. Tried to fold in his bits so he was hardly even there.

This was a stupid question! Mr Robinson knew the answer so why would he ask such a dumb question? He had to go to school! There was nowhere else to go.

Home was not an option - he wanted to get away from there as much as possible. The streets were not safe - every time he had truanted in the past he had got caught by the bullies or the police. No sir, he would far rather be in school. And the school room had a fire and this meant warmth. This was the only chance he had of any heat in a bitter January in Leeds.

'Well answer me boy. I know you are dumb but you are not totally stupid! Why do you bother to turn up? You haven't learned anything since you have been here. You still can't read. You can't write and your maths skills are nonexistent so why are you here? You just take up space.'

As Mr Robinson got going into his tirade his lips started growing in size and spittle came out of his mouth. He always had fat, full lips. They seemed to be too big for his skull like face and they started to move really fast quivering up and down. Clifford put his head down, he started to panic. Mr Robinson was starting to look like the Blue Cod on the fish monger trolley in the high street. The one that wasn't quite dead yet, mouth opening into an 'O' before the fat, blubbery lips snapped shut. The cod that was Mr Robinson was starting to thrash about - he was even starting to smell fishy.

But Clifford was having a good day. Mr Robinson is not really a fish he thought. Don't get panicky, don't show any fear - put the dopey smile back on your face and look away. Be invisible.

'It's useless,' the cod-like Mr Robinson yelled, hooking Clifford back into the moment and reeling him ever closer.

'I am wasting my time and your place in this class can be given to someone who wants to learn. A child who is polite and respectful. Are you even in there?' he shouted.

Mr Robinson grasped Clifford's head and roughly forced it around to face his own.

The cod's face was far too close for Clifford. Fishy eyes swivelled, probing his private thoughts and staring into him - the pain of this invasion was huge. He felt revolted and nausea waved across him.

Clifford gulped and Mr Robinson let out an outward breath that came out with a hiss: the steamy, tropical breath was a concoction of his lunchtime snack of sardines, mixed with cigar and a whiff of medicinal whisky imbibed just a few minutes before.

Clifford put his hands over his face to black out the unwanted sensations but not before his lunch came up and projectile vomit flew out all over Mr Robinson. The cod was now covered in Clifford's vomit. Two hours ago it had been chorizo bologna and cheese - now it was a reeking, brownish goo.

Mr Robinson roared and stepped back.

'You little bastard,' he screamed. 'You did that on purpose. This is my best suit - ruined and you've covered me with your foul spew. I was trying to help you, you're an ungrateful whelp.'

'Get out of here,' he roared. 'This will be the last day you ever come into my classroom you stinking little dago whoreson.'

Clifford was not only good at being invisible, he also knew just when to disappear. And this seemed like the perfect time. He was only ten but he bolted from that classroom like he was trying out for the Olympics. He didn't stop to retrieve his jacket or to say a fond goodbye to his desk, his inkwell or even the stove (the only thing he had ever really liked in that room).

He tore from the room and then out of the front entrance of the school with its bleak Georgian facade that had been built on the site of the old workhouse.

No he didn't stop to reminisce about his 'good old school days'. In renovating the Holbeck Union workhouse to become the Beeston Hill School, little in the way of improvements or comforts had been incorporated. Lives were still being ruined in that place like they had for the last two centuries.

Clifford left and did not go back.

He knew of a little nook in the back of the bakery that retained its warmth throughout the day, long after the morning loaves were cooked. It had been a great hidey hole when he was six. Now at ten he did not really fit but this was a time for being as small as possible so his gangly legs were pulled in and he cowered down as the daylight hours faded. He waited while the anxiety drained away and the madness left him. Clifford stayed there until the darkness came, the last vestiges of warmth had fled the bricks and hunger pangs gripped his body. It was time to go home.

As a ten year old slinking down the lane, Clifford was proud that he thought he had not disturbed much air in getting home. No-one had seen him, no one had noticed him, he had been like a ghost moving through the cold night with just his warm breath leaving a vapour trail to show where he had been.

The door of his family home loomed in front of him and he listened keenly for raised voices behind the barrier. Not yet, just the gentle rise and fall, burble of his brothers and his mum. Da mustn't be home yet. Clifford eased himself inside and slipped unnoticed into the back of the room, away from the light.

'What are you doing, skulking in at this time and where have you been?'

This was his older brother Albert, at 12 he was nearly the size of a man. He sounded gruff but he was the protector in the family. He picked on Clifford, but everyone did, but he also stood up for him when he was getting pummelled by bullies. Cliff could turn his back on Albert and know he wouldn't be hurt. This was Clifford's measure of trust. He only trusted three people Albert, Mami and his baby brother William. (Well, he was only six so hadn't had much time to develop yet but Cliff liked him.)

Albert told Clifford this was his Triangle of Trust.

'Look mate, you're a bit dim and in life folks are going to take advantage of you,' Albert had explained. 'For some weird reason you are not too good with people. Some will pick on you, some will cheat you - but there are just a few people who you need to let in. You will know who they are. They will feel good to you. These are the people who you can rely on.'

'How will I know who they are?' Clifford had mumbled.

Even with Albert he didn't look straight at him. But there was good air between them when Albert talked to him. He was not so anxious when Albert was there.

Albert had put his hand on Clifford's shoulder. Cliff did that involuntary twitch thing that occurred whenever anyone touched him. But then it was good - he relaxed. The hand on his shoulder felt warm, but it didn't burn. It felt strong and his shoulder felt safe.

Albert had explained things to him:

'It feels like when you're sitting with me or Mami. It's like when you are playing around with Young William. You know we are not going to hurt you. You can feel that things are good. You know you can turn your back on us and when you turn back we will still be there. We will protect you. This is trust. It comes when folks love you. And they will - if you let them in. We are your Triangle of Trust. You will always need some people, just a few. Choose well. They will keep you safe.'

Albert was the only one in the family who had ever faced up to Da. This had started last June; there had been a terrible fight. Da had come home blind drunk and so angry. He usually took it out on Mami and then on Clifford but Clifford had learnt to become invisible so it just wasn't so much fun to beat someone up if they don't even let out a whimper. And Clifford had learnt how to not make a sound, no matter how much it hurt.

Clifford thought Mami was a bit stupid - she always answered him back. Whenever he was apologizing next morning for her black eye or broken lip or whatever injury he had inflicted on her the night before, Da would justify the violence because 'her nagging annoyed him'.

But Mami just didn't know when to shut up. She had been born free, she'd had aspirations and she felt she had been sold into the slavery of a loveless marriage. Mami still wanted to live life on her terms and Da just wanted her to obey him.

On the night of the big fight, Mami had missed the lot. Da had knocked her out cold after she yelled a Spanish obscenity at him, which was silly because he didn't know what it meant but by the look on Mami's face it was really as rude as she could go. Now she was comatose but he was still keen on hurting someone else, so he turned on Young William.

This had never happened before; six year old children are meant to be safe in their own homes. William has the looks of a cherub, all smiles and dimples with black, smiley eyes and curly black hair. He is up to laughing, playing peek a boo and doing somersaults not being punched in the face by a screaming pig, masquerading as a father.

Da had punched Young William in the face and both of his front teeth had come out. Blood spurted out; William screamed; Clifford faded further back into the wall; Mami was still out cold and Albert went berserk.

Clifford had never seen anything like it. Calm, placid Albert, ever the peacemaker, just lost it. He roared and went at Da like an enraged bull. They wrestled and screamed, smashing up all the furniture and blood was streaming down Da's face. When it was over Da was just a bloodied pulp. He was whimpering, coughing and spitting out blood and bits of teeth. Albert stood up straight, he hadn't even been scratched.

He turned to Da: 'Don't ever lay a hand on any of them again.'

It was Albert's voice alright but it did not quiver and sounded all grown up, it was probably the voice Mr Robinson talked about when he would say 'read it with gravitas'.

Then Albert turned to Clifford and said 'Fix up Young William and Mami Cliff,' and then he turned on his heel and walked out.

Since that horrible fight when Albert had punched Da back, Da didn't pick so many fights when Albert was home. The physical violence had got less - but he still yelled abuse and tried to slap Mami whenever Albert was out.

Big bully fights little bully; little bully takes it for just so long then little bully fights back and big bully's days are numbered. And that was just what was happening in the Hulme's little happy family - the leader of the pack was changing.

On the night of Albert's fight back, Da had gone into a convulsion of coughing after the fight. Ever since then Da had coughed and spluttered his way through life.

Two weeks before, Da had found out that he had Tuberculosis. The family had suspected this, what with the angry bouts of coughing and phlegm clearing and they'd had to have spittoon bowls around the house.

Now with Da sick this had meant less money. Da had worked for the leading Leeds Boot Makers: Mason and Family. He had worked there for twenty five years. But this had not mattered when they sacked him as soon as they heard about his diagnosis. Apparently the letter of dismissal, still open on the cabinet, had said that they were having to let people go as orders had dried up, but Da was sure it was because they knew he was soon going to be a corpse and they may as well train up a new young bloke now.

Clifford wasn't sorry his Da was dying. Mami had said he should be but Clifford found it hard to feel for anyone, let along someone who had been brutal to him since birth.

'He is a Buen Hombre - a good man,' she explained. 'He gets frustrated with life and when he drinks too much this frustration comes out with his fists. He has done his best for us. Life could have been a lot worse.' Mami was stroking Clifford's hair as she said this.

Mami was in Cliff's Triangle of Trust, she always had been and her touch didn't make him jerk, it made him purr.

He looked at his mother seeing remnants of her beauty, stunning coal black, curly ringlets, dark eyes that danced and glinted with light but this was marred by the black hole left by the lack of a front tooth. Deep, jagged scars near her eyes showed the cruel blows she had suffered. The most obvious thing was that her skin was yellowing and starting to wrinkle on her once flawless face. Mediterranean skin needs sunlight to be healthy. Her Spanish glow had been all but extinguished by the damp, dank climate of Leeds.

So the end of the abuse had come a bit too late for his Mami. Her loveliness nearly snuffed out already and she was not yet 30 years old. The photo on her mantelpiece shows her as she was 12 years ago, a wild haired, dark eyed 'Castilian Princess'.

Mami, whose real name was Rosa Kujawski, and her sister Estrella, had been brought from Spain as continental servants by Lord Lascalles from the Manor. They had been lured here with offers of a fine salary and a wonderful life free from the persecution Spanish Jewesses suffered in their home country. The girls' father had fled the programs in Poland and had landed in Spain as a twenty year old. There he had met a stunning Sephardic Jewess and together they had dreamed of a life free from discrimination for their family. But Spain was not a safe haven for Jews, so a new life in England had seemed filled with promise.

Clifford loved that photo. Most folks in 1910 didn't have any photographs but this one had been taken in 1898 for Lord Lascalles to show off his pretty new maids. Mami was dressed in Spanish clothes with big earrings and castanets held high. The photo was sepia toned but Clifford knew that his Mami's skirt was blood red, the top was emerald green and the jewellery was real gold.

'They had dressed us up to look like Spanish Dancers,' Mami recalled. 'The skirt was red silk, it had so many different hues and colours when the light touched it. It was cool and smooth to touch and felt wonderful on my skin - so exquisite. I wanted so badly to keep those clothes. They told us that we could have lots of fine clothes when we got to England. We thought we were going to capture their hearts and both marry English Lords and live in fine castles.'

Their fine Lord had paraded them like peacocks - a fad to have foreign servants in your employ. His friends had been impressed. This had created quite a stir and for a while everyone in society was getting 'their help from the continent'.

The girls had played their part, working just hard enough, flirting with the men and filling the house with Spanish music and mirth. The Lord thought it was quaint to have a pair of prattling Spanish maids in the manor house but the dream didn't last too long. The Hulme boys knew the story well. The sisters had been sacked and Mami's sister had 'gone looney' and had been locked up in the asylum after some unwanted attention from three blue blood Lords celebrating after a hunting party.

'Estrella was really roughed up,' Mami said. 'She never recovered and just screamed whenever she saw men. Even today she sees visions when she is awake and the old Estrella is lost to us. Lord Lascalles was good about it though, he had made sure she was taken care of - she was admitted into a quality asylum, somewhere up north.'

What Mami didn't say was that Lord Lascalles had hosted the hunting party but things had gone horribly wrong. The hunt was enjoyed, the drink flowed, the ladies went to bed and the men got more raucous. Lord Lascalles had asked the two Spanish girls to do some provocative dancing for his friends.

Estrella was so excited: 'Really try your hardest to please Rosa. This is our chance to snare a Lord. That Lord Milbourne is so handsome and he is almost down the aisle with me already.' She had laughed with eager anticipation.

They had dressed up in the costumes and done the Seguidilla, as well as they could without music. Beguiling, flirtatious both evoking Carmen. The intoxicated guests were impressed, the girls flirted. They were demure and charming, the Lords besotted and very drunk. Mami and Estrella were so proud. They were young, they were beautiful and they were admired by great, powerful and very rich English Lords.

Lord Lascalles had collapsed into a drunken stupor. He snored while his three friends kept drinking, got louder and things turned a bit rough. They grabbed Mami and Estrella kissing them roughly and fondling their breasts. Mami struggled, broke free and ran from the room.

The drunken men then set out to ravage Estrella Kujawski - the 16 year old virgin Spanish Jewess, full of innocent hopes and dreams of a better life. Mami had crept back and she watched the whole thing from behind the curtains. She was mortified, terrified and rooted to her position as a reluctant voyeur. Powerless to help because if she was discovered this was to be her fate too. The men kissed Estrella roughly, bit her breasts, held her legs open and then forced themselves into her. All three had their turn and then they raped her again. When she screamed they hit her. She stopped screaming and just cried silently throughout the ordeal.

The men then all stood up wiped themselves off and went upstairs. Mami could hear them laughing and slapping each other on the back as they readied themselves for bed. It had been a great day of hunting and then they had taken the spoils of the hunt as was their divine right as English Lords. Of course they never mentioned it to their ladies next morning.

Other silent, judgemental, servants came in and cleaned up the room and helped Lord Lascalles up to his bedchamber. They did not go anywhere near the near naked, ravaged, weeping body of Estrella. Mami went in and carried Estrella to the room they shared. She bathed her, soothed her wounds and put her to bed. Estrella never recovered. The other servants didn't speak about it to Mami. They looked away from her, they despised the sisters for their lewd and provocative behaviour. They thought they had brought the attack on themselves and had brought shame on their Lord. Rosa was ashamed.

Lord Lascalles had been really embarrassed. Not about the attack but about Mami. He did not really want her around anymore - what is the use of a pair of Spanish maids if one just jabbers and the other one just skulks around. Plus Mami kept pestering him about why he didn't do something about the assault and his criminal friends. She was Spanish and she just didn't understand that servants just shouldn't question their superiors.

So Lord Lascalles had asked 'His Man' to fix up this messy situation. 'His Man' came up with the perfect settlement - Estrella would be placed in an asylum and looked after for the rest of her days. Mami would be handed over to William Hulme.

William was a 36 year old single man, who had a good steady job in Leeds working in a factory making boots. He was also a mean spirited drunkard who had a tendency to violence. William was very keen on having a free home for life in one of the Lord's buildings on Beeston Hill and a dowry of 100 pounds plus he would score a lovely, young, Spanish wife to boot. Lord Lascalles was pleased, William was happy and Mami learnt that dreams do not come true.

This was the same house Clifford Hulme aged 10 years had sidled back into at 7pm on a bitterly cold night on the 26th January 1910. The accommodation was better than most, two rooms in a back to back, red brick housing tenement. The lower floor had a central table with four rough chairs and a wet area for washing and cooking - the toilets and laundry were shared with other tenants. The top room had rude cots around the perimeter, with a curtained off 'room' for Mami.

Mami used to share this with Da but after the birth of young William she had 'denied her husband his rights' and she kept 6 year old William in the bed to keep him away. Da would bellow about this from time to time: 'That Castilian Witch should know her place and succumb to her husband's needs.'

Da had realised that his lovely Spanish wife had an untamed, indomitable spirit and this just added to his mean spiritedness and general life misery.

The Hulme home was warmed with a fireplace but the family could rarely afford the coal at night - this was more often lit in the day when Mami boiled the kettle or prepared the soup for supper. Tonight the coals were glowing red and the room was filled with the wonderful smell of Sopa de ajo, Castilian garlic soup. Mami found it very hard to get the ingredients and often had to substitute but when she made Spanish food it was always appreciated by her boys. It also meant that Da was not expected home. Da hated all that 'Spanish muck' and preferred good, solid English stodge.

Candles on the table glowed their welcome. Clifford had a warm feeling that the room really felt like a home tonight but he wasn't too sure he should trust this feeling just yet. Mami was at the stove stirring the pot. The scent of the food, reminiscent of Spanish sunshine, filled the room.

Rosa Kujawski's dark eyes settled on her second son.

'Where have you been Clifford? I have been worried.'

'What have you been doing?' yelled Albert, 'you have spew all down your front!'

Clifford looked down at his shirt. Brown curdling spew, dried out now, had made a river and some tributaries down his shirt. Clifford peeled his shirt over his head carefully so the vomit didn't get on him or drop on the floor, he dropped it in the laundry bucket and went to grab another from his clothes chest.

His loose framed body was now revealed. He had grown two or three inches over the last year and his body had started to fill out. Clifford had the musculature of his Castilian relatives, he shared little resemblance to the skinny, wasted, pale white body of his Da. This was revealed here because he was not scared and he occupied his body proudly. Cliff was becoming a man.

'I vomited on Mr Robinson and he threw me out of school. He said school was wasted on me 'cos I can't read or write or do sums,' Cliff blurted out. He had discovered that silence only works for so long. When you need to speak, get as much out as quickly as possible. Everyone else will fill in all the blanks.

'Serves the old geezer right. So did you vomit on him before he said this or after? He is a vicious, despicable child molester,' Albert said with laughter and a broad smile. He was really proud - his little loony brother had got one back on one of his worst tormenters.

'I vomited on him after he said it because I thought he was a cod fish. His breath stank and I just couldn't stop it and it all came up all over him,' Cliff explained. 'Mami, I ran out without getting my stuff. I am real sorry. I have lost my coat and I can't ever go back there again to get it.'

The three people in the room were his Triangle of Trust. They could handle the fact that Mr Robinson was a cod fish. He could tell these people about his thoughts. They translated his visions into a workable reality and they guided him through the crazy maze of life.

'Fishy, fishy very slishy,' chimed in young William.

'Oh mi amada hiyo. (My lovely son). You do not have an easy life,' enthused Mami. 'Well do not worry. You will be a man now and you will go to work. You are growing large. We will just pretend that you are 12 and not 10.'

'Da is not needing his job any more so there will be a position for you at Mason and Family. The foreman at the boot maker's factory will be pleased because he was a bit afraid I might agitate a bit and threaten to take Da's sacking to the union.' Mami was on a roll, she had it all worked out. She was friendly with the foreman Joe Blootle, who the boys believed had a bit of a crush on her.

'Albert you can come with me tomorrow early in the morning. We will go down and convince them that it will be good to take on young Cliff.'

Mami turned to Clifford:

'You will be good at that job and the work will be good for you. Da's job was just punching holes into boot leather for the bootlaces. You don't need reading, writing or sums for that. Just concentration and hard work. You'll be warm and safe and the pay will help us now that Da's salary has gone.'

'Don't worry about the jacket. It was too short for you anyway and I will save some off cuts from the clothing factory and make you something new, a working man's jacket. You will need to borrow Da's for tomorrow - you have to make a good impression.'

Mami was into organising mode. Her face took on a youthful expression as she flicked her ebony locks from her face; the candle light didn't show any hint of grey, her eyes glinted and the beautiful Castilian lady was back.

'Where is Da?' Clifford asked tentatively.

Mami put her eyes down, a ghost of a smile crossed her face. She moved across to the table and served four plates of hot, steamy Castilian garlic soup, complete with chunks of ham. Already on the table Clifford could see crusty bread with some real pats of butter. He was salivating in anticipation.

Albert's smile wasn't hidden - it spread across his face. He answered: 'The neighbours complained about Da's constant coughing. Mami had a visit from some bloke from the West Riding County Council's Public Health and Housing Inspectorate. He said Da couldn't stay here coughing because his sputum had TB germs in it and everyone would get the disease. So they took him away in a big ambulance wagon.'

'Da was real mad. He was yelling and screaming but there wasn't anything any of us could do. He is in the West Riding Tuberculosis Sanatorium, it has a chest clinic and he will get some good treatment but he will not be coming home again.'

Clifford supposed he should have been sad. Da had gone for good. But he was filled with golden, bubbly happiness. Everywhere the happiness flowed up and out of him - like a fountain. It frothed out of every limb and Clifford was floating. He didn't need to be absorbed into the walls anymore, he could move into the centre of this safe, cheery place. He would be safe from Da, he would be happy in this home, he would have a good job, he would bring home money every week to help out.

On the 26th January 1910, ten year old Clifford Hulme had really had a very good day.

Three Lives
A Flock Of Parrotts

January 26th, 1910

Perth, Western Australia

On the other side of the world, by the time Clifford Hulme started out for school on the 26th January 1910, Lillian Margaret Parrott was having a day of extremes.

In the morning, Lillian, who was 13 years old, lived in Leederville, an inner suburb of Perth, Western Australia along with her mother Frances Gurtrude Parrott, her brother John Ardley Parrott (known to everyone as Jack) and her father Thomas Wilson Parrott.

By the afternoon there was one less person at this address. Her father, the esteemed architect, strong patron of the arts and quite rich fellow, had died at the ripe and venerable age of 71.

Lilly was contemplating her lot in the morning before she arose from her bed, luxuriating amongst the sheets just a while longer. She was considering her impossible family situation and how she was going to manipulate things to be able to see the boy she had developed a crush on.

Firstly Lilly considered her Father. Although he didn't realise this was the day he would die, Thomas Parrott had been on the verge of death for a long time. In fact, her father had been sick for her whole life. Each day he was to be found sitting in the same place, in the drawing room with a blanket on his lap and hushed tones around him.

As she entered to say good morning his rheumy eyes would follow her, struggling for recognition. Did he know her? Frances, Lillian's mother, would gently whisper to him 'this is little Lillian, your youngest daughter'.

His face would crease up into a smile, well a grimace really, as the last stroke had frozen the facial muscles on the left side. This side of his face stayed totally impassive, frozen for all time.

Lilly would smile back politely, and curtsey saying: 'Good morning Father'.

Lillian's insides would be churning, she thought he looked so ugly. Would she one day be as repulsive as that? What about if her husband grew to be a hideous caricature as he aged. Would she be able to be with him, smile sweetly and even kiss him lovingly like her mother did? These thoughts horrified her.

'Come over and give him a kiss dear,' her mother would urge.

Lilly would walk the 5 steps needed and bend down, forcing herself to remain poker faced despite her revulsion and plant a dry kiss on the leathery, parchment skin of his immobilized cheek. He smelt like 'old person'.

That was it - she was free to go. This was the daily father/daughter interaction. From this five minute ritual, loving bonds were supposed to have developed. Jack at least remembered when there used to be a human inside the zombie-like carcass that was now Thomas Parrott.

Her mother would fuss about the place, dealing with his every need, ministering to his every whim. She was the perfect nurse, the flawless wife. Her mother Frances was known by everyone, to be a saint.

'She has given up her youth to nurse him,' they said.

'What a wonderful person, so caring, so giving, so unselfish.' The good people of Perth thought her mother was next in line for deification.

Well this morning Lillian Parrott was having decidedly uncharitable thoughts. She didn't think Frances Parrott was doing such a wonderful thing. Lilly believed her mother was a martyr and had sacrificed Lilly's and Jack's chance at happiness, youth and adventure for a life of financial security. But had she truly measured the weight of the strings that were attached to this union?

Well today, Lilly decided she would not go in and say 'Hello' to her Father. She wondered if anyone would notice. Father certainly wouldn't care. Mother might get a bit angry but she was sick of being nice to an old person and pretending to care.

Today she had other more important things to do - and one was to fantasize about the return of James Nelson, Jack's school friend, who had been in England playing tennis for Australia! James was wonderful at tennis and had been chosen to play at the Junior Tennis Championships that had been played at Wimbledon in early November.

Lilly had read in the papers that: *'he had played admirably well and showed extreme sportsmanship in the three narrow losses.'* They had gone on to say that: *'if he had the benefit of good coaching he may reach a high standard and compete at the top level'.*

So she knew someone who was famous; his deeds reported in the papers. Thirteen year old Lillian Parrott wanted more than anything to be famous and to have her deeds reported in the papers. She fancied a large smiling photo of herself on the front page; she just wasn't too sure yet what she would be famous for!

Lilly had often watched Jack and James play tennis and once when there was a 'no show' in the mixed doubles, she had been invited to play to make up the team. She partnered Jack and they had been soundly beaten by James and his more experienced partner. She hadn't had any tennis shoes and she had slipped all over the court, once landing on her backside much to their amusement.

Lilly had tried hard. She was a gifted sportswoman and tried hard to support Jack but she had only been 12 then and she was clearly outclassed by the older players. Lilly was mortified. Her chance to impress had dissipated.

Her recollections of James, had improved with time. For most of her life she remembered James to be an unpleasant pest, who partnered with Jack to make her life miserable. They pulled her hair, played tricks on her and called her names. James had been gawky, with spiky, carrot coloured hair, freckles and had angry pimples on his chin.

Now that she was 13 and he was 15, when she thought of him the image was far more flattering and she had set her mind on making him notice how she had grown up too.

Lilly jumped out of bed and, like every other summer morning, she went to the window and looked out. The dawn magpie choristers were still trilling, the click, click of the cicadas just starting. She could see the heat haze blurring the distant hills and a hot easterly wind was already blowing hot inland air over the city. It was going to be a really hot one, over 100 degrees she guessed. School would be like a furnace. It was ludicrous that, to be a quality young lady in Perth in 1910, one needed to wear full Edwardian fashion in a climate that was made for running around naked!

Perhaps Mum would allow her to go with Jack after school - she was sure he would be heading over to the Nelson's to welcome James home. Now that she was 13, her Mother should be loosening up some of the restrictions. She would just have to invent a really plausible reason why she needed to go with him.

Lilly went to look at herself in her hand mirror. Her face was pretty enough she supposed. She had good teeth, a fine clear complexion and her eyes were deep brown. She would love to have swapped her colouring for blue eyes and fair hair - girls with these accoutrements always seemed to be the ones that 'did well' in her experience.

This face was framed by her burnished, copper brown hair with blonde highlights, the legacy of the West Australian sun. Her Mother was always telling her to 'keep her bonnet on and to use her parasol' but Lilly's sporty nature made her want to run and skip; hats and parasols just got in the way. Now she was a young lady of 13 she would need to curb this boisterousness and hopefully her complexion could still be saved.

She looked down at her slim body. She felt the budding of her breasts and wondered how large they would grow. She was still very short, the shortest in her class, and this was a constant source of annoyance to her. Lilly's vision of herself was that she would be tall and willowy.

'Hurry up Lillian, you will be late for school,' her mother called. 'Your breakfast is ready and your Father is waiting for you in the drawing room.'

Lilly grabbed her underclothes and uniform. 'Yuck,' she thought as she put on the clothes of her school girl servitude.

The starched pinafore of Subiaco Senior School, dark blue pleats with absolutely no shaping, was designed to make everyone look drab and unattractive. One thing was for sure, she would make certain she wouldn't be dressed in this horrible outfit when she saw James Nelson. White stockings, black lace up boots ('ouch' they were a bit too tight) topped off by her boater and she was dressed and ready.

She raced into the kitchen where her breakfast was already made. Jack was already there grabbing the toast and slathering it with heaps of butter and marmalade.

'You slept in this morning Lilly,' said her mother handing her a steaming cup of tea.

'Sorry Mother I was up late last night planning my oral presentation for literature and elocution.'

Lilly was proud of her report on the jailing of suffragette Lady Constance Lytton. Now there was a lady who had followed her principles, defied the restrictions placed on her by the men in her life and was becoming rather notorious for it.

'What are you making a big thing of a stupid suffragette for?' Jack guffawed, crudely stuffing toast into his mouth. 'She is probably just a spoilt, bored little heiress. I don't know why they even bother to educate girls let alone let them have important rights like giving them the right to vote. How can women make important decisions like that? We all know that their brains are smaller than men's. Let them stay home, have babies and look after the household, I say. My wife will never be allowed to have an opinion. And she will vote the way I tell her.' Jack liked the world just like it was. He was a man and it suited him just fine.

Lilly gave her brother a venomous stare: 'Your attitudes are so old fashioned Jack. I pity your future wife.'

'Do you realise that the only reason that women were granted the vote in Australia is that our smart male politicians wanted to minimise the 'no vote' regarding Western Australia's succeeding from the Commonwealth. The politicians knew that most of the woman were in the towns in the East and they would vote 'no' - because their husbands would tell them to. Good women do what they are told.' Jack was on a roll, his chest puffed and full of his own importance.

'Well dear it is a man's world and women who want to succeed in it would be well advised to not annoy the men who feed, protect and clothe them,' her mother demurred. 'I certainly ask my husband's advice before I vote and Jack don't talk with your mouth full dear.'

Lilly despaired. Her brother wanted to keep things as they are with men firmly in control, her mother was a happy pawn and her father was, well he was too old to matter.

'Come on Jack it's late and we need to get walking to school. That's unless you want me to piggy back you like a beast of burden. It sounds like you want all women around you to be oxen, dumb but able to carry heavy things.' Lilly shouted her retort over her retreating shoulder.

Lilly was up and out of the house before anyone could answer. Her mini act of defiance had been achieved. She had escaped the house without going through the horrible ordeal of greeting her Father.

Jack raced up behind her, breathing deeply from the sprint up the road. 'You didn't go in to see Father, Mum will be angry when you get home,' Jack huffed.

'I'll deal with it. I am 13 now and it is time to start living life a bit - my way.' Lilly replied rebelliously.

'Have you had any word about when James' boat will dock today?' she enquired gently, steering the conversation to something that really mattered.

'Well the paper this morning said it was due at Fremantle early this morning. I'll head over to the Nelson's place at about 5pm after I have done my chores. I bet James has some corker stories to tell,' Jack said, his eyes misty with mild envy. He would dearly have loved to have swapped places with his friend.

Lilly was still no closer to coming up with a strategy so that she too would be invited. She really wanted to go and see James but she reasoned that if she looked too keen, the contrary Jack would just exclude her on purpose. He was such a rotten brother.

Lilly stayed silent. As she walked along she kicked honky nuts into the bush at the side of the road. The black cockatoos had been busy, the brutalised nuts where scattered everywhere. Her feet hurt as she walked, she really did need some new boots.

The Parrott siblings walked in single file as the road was quite busy at this time of the morning. Spring carts from the Perth markets passed them by, stirring up the bulldust of a dry summer as they went. Shopkeepers loaded up with their early morning purchases and farmers with empty carts and full pockets having unloaded their produce.

The pair crossed over Thomas Street and the traffic flow ceased; for the last mile to school they followed a narrow bush track. Lilly kept her eyes peeled for snakes. These were often found sunning themselves on the track. She had trodden on one last year, although the snake seemed just as surprised as she was and had vanished into the bush without trace. Lilly was nervous not to repeat this experience.

Jack broke the silence. 'The lawyer came over last night to talk to Mum about money again. She is getting really worried. I've been eavesdropping over the last few months and I think I finally have the background behind what is going on.'

'Well tell me,' Lilly said, exasperated that Jack would have information denied to her. 'There are too many unsaid bits and I can't work out why she married Father in the first place.'

They both knew that Frances had been employed to nurse

Thomas Parrott when he had become ill on a trip to the West when he was 57. But Lilly and Jack had only ever had vague hints and innuendo about the history of their Mother's union with his Father. From listening into the lawyer's conversations with his Mother and a bit of sleuthing, Jack now thought he knew how things had developed up to this point.

This is the more complete version Jack revealed to Lilly as they walked to school in the early summer heat of January 26th, 1910:

Thomas Parrott had travelled to the West in April 1894 to contribute to the debate that had been raging on the establishment of a University in Western Australia. He had been charged with the important task of ensuring that no faculty of Architecture would be included in this proposal, thus protecting the monopoly in this area of study for his beloved University of Sydney.

Thomas Parrott felt that he was more than suited to the task. His work in the field of architecture, although he could not make claim to greatness, he believed had been sound. However his greatest skill in this endeavour was that he was considered by all, himself included, to be a persuasive and eloquent speaker. He was a fine figure, born and educated in England. He had refined and maintained his upper class accent, he dressed immaculately and he listened attentively, knowing exactly when to interrupt the debate and put his point across. He was deemed by all to be perfectly suited to this mission.

Sadly none of this came to pass. Thomas was struck down with his first debilitating stroke on the evening before the talks started. After two days of doctor's ministrations it was declared that he must not travel for at least six months but with attentive and careful nursing he should be able to fully recover his health.

Frances was 21 in 1894 and she answered the advertisement to nurse Thomas Parrott back to health. She had arrived at his rooms and found an enfeebled man but the surroundings and his possessions screamed 'luxury'. The more she discovered about his life back in the North Shore of Sydney, the more she wanted that life for herself. His mansion had a view of Sydney Harbour!

The house had fifteen bedrooms, gas lighting and a flushing toilet! She wasn't a gold digger but her prospects up to that point were not dazzling and she definitely moulded herself into becoming indispensable to the ailing Thomas Parrott.

Frances thought of Thomas Parrott as a King and she had her sights on becoming a Queen Parrott.

Thomas was a widower who had married his two daughters off some years before. Both had made excellent alliances. His eldest son Thomas Junior, was now a rising star in the Bank of New South Wales. Thomas Junior was also, very kindly, looking after his father's affairs. In light of Thomas Senior's illness and incapacity, he had taken up occupancy in the North Shore mansion overlooking Sydney Harbour and was ensuring that it was being efficiently and capably cared for. What a good lad!

By October 1895, Thomas had recovered enough to decide that the Florence Nightingale of his life was also his dearly beloved. He wrote to his three children to tell them of his intention to remarry. He invited them, and their husbands (in the case of Amy Maude and Ada May), to come west at his expense, to meet his betrothed. He was sure they would fall in love with sweet Frances, just as he had.

The engaged couple thought they would meet with the children and then travel as a group by sea to Adelaide and then overland by rail to Sydney. There they would be married. They had wonderful plans to include all of the dear children in the wedding party. Thomas even thought he might like Thomas Junior to be his best man. Thomas had told his 'future bride to be' all about his beautiful children, Frances was so excited, the daughters would be more like sisters to her.

But the jubilant and excited replies to the invitations did not arrive. In fact the very considerate and wonderful good lad who was Thomas Junior, had gone immediately to his Father's own Sydney solicitor and had slapped caveats on all of his realty, invoking the 1890 Property Act.

He had then issued an injunction - questioning his Father's mental capacity and applying to be the guardian of the estate, in the eventuality of a successful legal challenge. He was sure this threat would bring his father to his senses and scare off the Western Australian imposter.

Frances listened sympathetically and then quietly made plans for a low key Western Australian union. She also arranged for their Western Australian lawyer, Mr Hardinge to extend the lease on their home at 606 Newcastle St, Leederville. She also asked him to explore an option to buy the property.

Thomas Senior was devastated and enraged in equal measure. And this may have been the impetus which caused the second stroke to occur, so fortuitously, just two days after their quiet registry office wedding and the consummation of the wedding, of Thomas to Frances.

Luckily this stroke had not affected his sexual prowess and under the allure of a 21 year old bride, the old stallion had performed admirably. Nine months after this wedding John Ardley Parrott, aka Jack, was born.

The old war horse, was really chuffed with his abilities and thought he might sire a new dynasty as the old one had let him down so disastrously.

Another herculean effort, this time from the stroke ravaged 58 year old patient now showing early signs of dementia as well, produced Lillian Margaret Parrott.

The birth of these two children made the Eastern States relatives even more estranged and doubly determined that these interlopers would neither inherit nor become legitimately part of the esteemed Eastern States branch of the Parrott family.

Lilly hadn't known all of the details before Jack's revelations. Just vague rumour and innuendo had seeped through to her as a child innocent. As she conferred with Jack they both agreed in adult tones, that the Eastern States Parrotts may prove to be a problem in the future.

Lilly knew of the half sisters (who were older than her mother) and the existence of the half brother who seemed to be always stopping payment on something or other. She also knew that they had remained incommunicado by choice.

One tricky thing was that Thomas Senior seemed to be getting a bit confused about his family situation. Sometimes when she skipped in to say good morning to her Father, if her Mother wasn't nearby to whisper that she was 'little Lillian', his dementia ravaged brain sometimes mis-guessed that she was either Amy Maude or sometimes Ada May. Lilly answered to all names with the same wooden smile and rapidly applied kiss.

As Lilly Parrott entered the school grounds of Subiaco Senior School it was 8.30am and these serious thoughts were filed away. All problems for another day she thought.

She headed to her classroom with no backward glance at Jack who was two years senior to her and so was educated in a different block.

Although the school was co-educational, on Tuesday mornings the girls in her form were engaged in feminine subjects: Letter Writing and then Literature and Elocution were scheduled first thing while the boys did Geometry and Design.

Lilly settled herself at her desk as the teacher, Mr Hobson, called the roll and led them with a sombre voice through the Lord's Prayer. Mr Hobson then asked them all to rise as they sang the National Anthem, 'God Save the King'. Lilly sang with gusto and enthusiasm. She loved to sing but had been told on many occasions that her voice, although loud, was not melodious, so she had realised that she would not become famous as a songstress.

Mr Hobson then went out with the boys and the hopelessly and permanently single Miss Pringle came in to guide the girls through Elocution and Literature. Today the ladies were to present: *'an oral presentation on a case from the newspaper with a personal view attached'*.

Lilly dug out her report from yesterday's West Australian. She was ready and sat with arms folded. An emboldened stare challenged any other girl in the class to be ready before her.

'Lillian Parrott would you care to go first?' asked Miss Pringle with just a hint of nervous anticipation. Young Miss Parrott had a tendency to overreach herself and often presented most unladylike opinions.

'Certainly Miss Pringle,' Lilly replied and launched immediately into her presentation.

'My case was from the newspaper and is entitled:

THE SUFFRAGETTES - LADY CONSTANCE LYTTON'S CASE.

It was published in London on January 24, 1910.'

Lilly read the extract to the class in her best plummy voice, being certain her diction was exact:

'A woman calling herself Jane Warton was on January 14 last, sentenced to a fortnight's imprisonment for having taken part in the suffragette disturbances in Liverpool. The gaol authorities have just discovered that the prisoner is Lady Constance Lytton, who gave the police an assumed name in order that she might have an opportunity of ridiculing the Secretary of State for Home Affairs (Mr Herbert Gladstone).

Previously she had pleaded that she had a weak heart but when she was arrested she attempted a hunger strike. Mr Herbert Gladstone immediately ordered her release from prison rather than forcibly feed an Earl's sister.'

Lilly then started her oratory:

'I think the ladies of the suffragettes movement are immeasurably brave. They are willing to risk prison and even death in the pursuit of attaining the vote, a principle they strongly believe in. They are often ridiculed by the press and the community. Sometimes they are denounced by their own male relatives and still they continue.'

'I am in awe of people who are so certain of what they believe in that they will risk their lives and safety. I hope one day I will be shown to have such resolve. The freedom to speak what you believe, whether or not it is the accepted wisdom of the society you live in, is the most important right of man. And of woman. In the words of Voltaire: '*I disapprove of what you say but I will defend to the death your right to say it,*' as quoted in S.G. Tallentyre in his biography 'The Friends of Voltaire'.'

Lilly looked around the class to see if her words had made the expected impact. Many of the young ladies looked down or checked their nails. None of them met her eyes. Her arch enemy, Emily Mattersen smiled meanly as she muttered: 'More squawks from a wounded Parrott.'

There was no polite applause. 'Oh no,' thought Lilly, 'I have gone a bit too far again.'

She sat down, her ears were red and tingling and she felt the hot blush of embarrassed scarlet creep up her neck.

'An interesting choice of article and a very elucidating opinion Lillian!'

Miss Pringle uttered these words in a clipped manner, whilst looking over the top of her thin glasses. These were perched precariously on the bridge of her very aquiline nose. There was no hint of warmth or approval in her voice. Lilly knew that she would not score well in this assessment. The other girls from the class chose far safer passages and gave opinions more in keeping with the times.

For the second subject of the day Miss Pringle was to give instruction on letter writing to the girls. But because it was summer and it was hot, she had decided not to force a formal style of letter writing onto the young ladies. Instead she gave them the option of writing an informal letter to a friend. She sat at the front desk fanning herself, overcome by a hot florid flush and with rivulets of perspiration cascading down the sides of her corpulent face.

Lilly was pleased, she could escape. Her letter was addressed to her dear friend and pen pal Chrissie Ayres. Chrissie had been in her class up to a year ago but her father was a blacksmith and they had gone to live in the wheat belt in a place called Wubin. Now Chrissie was doing her lessons by Correspondence. Lilly missed her companion and had not found anyone to replace her.

Dearest Chrissie

How lovely this is - we have been given some free time in class to write a personal letter. I think Miss Pringle is feeling the heat. Her complexion today is quite florid and she keeps fanning herself. Not that I think this is doing much good. She makes a lie of the old saying that women do not sweat - she is soaked in perspiration.

It is so hot in here today. But I bet this is nothing compared to you out in the wheat belt. How do you stand it? Although you probably do not have to dress in such an absurd thing as this uniform. I do hate it so.

Guess what? James Nelson is coming home today. His ship has already docked this morning. Can you imagine being one of the poor immigrants on the ship coming into this country today - they will have come from the snows of England right into this! They will be regretting their decision to come, I bet.

Now back to James. You may remember I wrote to you that James had been selected to go to England to play tennis. Jack was a bit envious as he did really well in the selection trials too but James' parents have loads of money and they could afford the cost of the fare.

James did pretty well considering. I saw him when he left and he looked really handsome. He has certainly improved with age! His hair is not so red now and his ears don't seem to stick out so much. Now I know he was horrid when you last saw him but he has grown up to be quite charming.

He looked at me and gave me the sweetest smile. Those buck teeth seem more in proportion with his face now that he has grown. He also gave me a wink and whispered to me that he'd like to catch up with me when he came back. I went really red of course and my heart jumped right into the side of my chest. I was sure James would see how flustered I was. I must practice looking coy when a man gives me a compliment.

Jack was really mad at him and told him to stop flirting with his little sister and reminded him that I was still only 13. It's great to have a brother who protects me but I wish he had stayed out of this one. I will be quite happy to see the charming Mr James Nelson when he returns. You never know, one day he might be a famous tennis player and I could be on his arm.

Perhaps I could even have some tennis games and perhaps I could be famous at sport. It would be great to see an Australian Lady win at Wimbledon.

Jack is going over to see the Nelsons today. (I am hoping I can go too). He is going to organise that James comes with us on Monday. Of course Monday is a declared holiday for Anniversary Day. There is a big fun fair organised on Subiaco Oval and our family will be going - hopefully with the Nelsons. It will be such fun. I wish you were here to come too.

Do you celebrate Anniversary Day out there in Wubin?

Mr Hobson said we should all take a moment on the holiday to bless our new nation and the realm. He is just enamoured with Mr Dawkins, our new Prime Minister. He thinks it is great that we joined the Union of Australia. I do not think I share his views in this. The only people I know from the Eastern States are my half sisters and brother and I really do not want any union or reunion with them!

At this stage in the letter Lilly suffered from a mental block. Her mind wandered but she did not know how to express these thoughts on paper.

What she wanted to explain was that she was having trouble at home relating to her Father. The trouble was she was sure she loved her father but he was so old. He had always been old. Her earliest memories were of him hunched over, leaning on his cane. He was already old when she was born. It was like living with a grandfather - or even worse living with a great grandfather.

Her friends all had young, vibrant, active fathers, men who were involved in life. Men who you could tell stories about because they did something. Chrissie Ayres had a father who was only just

36. The Ayres family got to go on picnics and holidays and they joined in with local community events. Chrissie's letters were so interesting.

In contrast Lilly had a bit of a secret; because she had no life sometimes she had created an illusion of how life should be. Sometimes her letters to Chrissie just could have blurred the truth between Lillian's real life and the exciting one she imagined. Like the bit in the letter about them going off to Anniversary Day. The reality was that they would not be going - they never went anywhere as a family. Jack would probably go with the Nelsons and she would stay at home and mope.

Her life was so monotonous and she believed that this was because her father was old and sick and her Mother was always nursing him. Having an old sick man in the house really had limited what her and Jack could get up to.

She felt a breeze and looked up as Miss Pringle came to stand by her elbow. She instinctively covered the writing, not wanting her to see the bit about her being florid and sweaty.

Miss Pringle's face was full of concern as she stared down at her. Lilly realised that she was looking at her and not at her writing. Lilly looked past her and there was Jack and Mr Hardinge the lawyer standing in the doorway of the classroom. Jack looked ashen faced. Mr Hardinge looked like he always did - lawyerish.

'I have some sad news for you dear, your Father has passed away,' Miss Pringle said, with a compassionate edge to her voice Lilly had never heard before.

Tears welled up inside Lilly and started their slow trickle down her face. Whether it was grief or relief or guilt or a combination, either way Lilly just started to sob. They led her out to where Mr Hardinge had brought his sulky to pick them up. It was 12 noon.

By the afternoon only three Parrotts were left alive at 606 Newcastle St. Thomas Parrott had died in his seat; he just slumped forward and departed the world. He was now lying in state in the bedroom and visitors were starting to arrive to pay their respects.

37

Their mother Frances was already in black - in full mourning attire. She had had 16 years to get ready for this day and was intending to do it with all of the ceremony the occasion warranted.

Frances Parrott held herself with immaculate detachment, accepting condolences, acknowledging other's grief. As the afternoon wore on Lilly was stunned how many across the Perth Community had loved her father, admired his generosity and had wonderful stories to tell about him and his exploits. Lilly wondered where she had been when this side of her father had been revealed.

Lilly was now all dressed in black and sitting demurely next to Jack with her head bowed in the sweltering room. The bereft children. Both sat very still, their eyes were red, they accepted hugs and dry kisses from all. They silently nodded thanks to the mourners; those they knew and those they had never even met. They were all playing their roles to perfection.

Food arrived, sent over by well meaning neighbours and friends. A bountiful supply, enough to feed the mourners for weeks.

Flowers came in and wilted as soon as they were delivered. Lilly noticed the appropriate use of Arum lilies and wondered who'd had the wonderful job of collecting these lilies from their watery home down on the river bank on this unbelievably hot day. More guests passed respectfully through, viewing the body. The undertaker had done a fine job. Even before the children had arrived home from school, the undertaker had used his skills and his cosmetics to paint on a face. This was far better than the original Thomas had worn daily for the past ten years. Lilly thought the red lips were a bit much to take but at least the frozen left side now fitted well with the right - a mask forever immobilised.

As the day wore on and the temperature finally dipped below the century, guests started to leave and by 8pm every non Parrott had left except for Mr Hardinge. Even the corpse had gone. In light of the very hot temperature the undertaker had returned and removed the body: 'unless putrefaction starts,' he had said to their Mother as he left. Lilly felt that this was exceptionally lacking in both tact and sensitivity but perhaps there was little call for such attributes in his profession.

When all had left and quiet had again draped itself over the house, Mr Hardinge asked them all to come into the drawing room. Lilly could not remember this room without her father in it. There was no sign of his chair, his blanket or any of the refuse left by the infirm. His shadow had been erased, he was definitely departed.

The three Parrotts sat and looked at Mr Hardinge. He started to speak solemnly, the words he had practiced so many times. Delivering pronouncements of great import was definitely his favourite part of the job. 'I have before me the last Will and Testament of your late Husband and Father, Mr Thomas W. Parrott dated 15th January 1906,' Mr Hardinge announced, in a voice just right for reading wills.

'I declare that I am in sound mind when making this last Will and Testament. In the event of my death I leave all my worldly possessions to be divided equally and in three parts to my beloved wife Frances Gertrude Parrott, my youngest son John Ardley Parrott and my youngest daughter Lillian Margaret Parrott. I have loved you and I thank you for allowing me to have the pleasure of a new life, after my first family were shown to be faithless. The children of my first marriage have already been well provided for and are in no way to benefit from any inheritance.'

Mr Hardinge looked up at the three bereaved Parrotts.

'There is more but this is the section that pertains to you and I felt it judicious to let you know that you will be cared for,' Mr Hardinge said with a gentle paternalistic pat on Lillian's Mother's hand.

'The will is legal, his intentions are clear. Unfortunately there may be some unpleasantness while the Eastern States Parrotts come to terms with this reality. I am sure the estate has sufficient funds to fight off any counter claim they may have against the enactment of this will and the disbursement of your inheritance.' And with that he left and the Parrotts' life, post Thomas Wilson Parrott, commenced.

Mr Hardinge did prove to be right - there was unpleasantness, over 6 years of it. The West Coast Parrotts were finally shown to be the legal beneficiaries of the will and there was sufficient funds in the estate to pay the lawyers' bills for six years of legal wrangling. The East Coast Parrotts were very nasty, right until the end.

Sadly there was not a lot to spare at the end of the six years so the West Coast Parrotts never did become very wealthy. They ended up owning their home in Leederville and having sufficient funds to live modestly.

However this was all to be in the future and as Lillian Parrott, 13 years old, went to bed on the 26th January 1910 she was over all of this. She was again plotting to see Mr James Nelson. Perhaps as an heiress, she thought, she would have a better chance of capturing his heart.

Three Lives
Harold's Australia Day

January 26th, 1910

Fremantle, Western Australia

At six in the morning on the 26th January the R.M.S. Orvieto, flag ship of the Orient line, arrived at the Port of Fremantle in Western Australia from London, stopping at Marseilles, Cairo, Port Said and Colombo. It had been two long months at sea.

Although it was early in the morning, a large number of eager passengers lined the deck all craning their necks to see the town of Fremantle emerging in the distance from the morning shadows. For many this was their first look at the land that was to become their home country and the mystery of what their new lives would be like here was hidden in the mists of the future.

Most of the enthusiastic throng had been up since before dawn as the ship had entered Gage Roads, the safe anchorage and channel for Fremantle Harbour. The ship had arrived at 2am and had waited at anchor until first light to make their way safely to the quay.

Listed on the passenger list and marked as disembarking at Fremantle were Harold Eaton Smith (16 years old) formerly of Ipswich in England (immigrant) and James Nelson (15 years old), Western Australian by birth and returning home after a successful sporting sojourn in England.

Harold and James were on the deck that early morning - in fact they had not gone to bed the night before and had secured a fabulous front row vantage point. James was in his element, pointing out places of interest and regaling the enthralled passengers with stories of his home that may or may not have held a grain of truth.

He told of the terror of shark attacks for anyone who entered the water, how the place was teeming with venomous snakes that often found their way into people's homes (and even into their beds according to James), how traffic in the city was often held up when kangaroos hopped down the main street and even how the good people of Perth thought it was *de rigueur* to drink beer with their breakfast. Harold smiled to himself as he listened to James' tales hoping that the listeners would not be gullibly seduced by James' exaggerated yarns.

The gentle wind ruffling their hair that morning was the same breeze that Lillian Parrott was sensing 8 miles inland in her home in Leederville. Both Harold and James noticed the early heat in the air, but to James it carried a special message, the distinctly Australian smell of his native land in summer. The two young men were also looking east, past the skyline of Perth and Fremantle towards the distant grey brown, hazy hills of the Darling Scarp.

'Is it always as hot as this?' asked Harold. 'I know I thought Colombo was warm but this is like a baker's oven and I feel like a well roasted loaf.'

'Yes it is going to be a hot one all right, when the easterly is hot at six in the morning we know we're going to be in for a scorcher. But don't panic it will not always be like this. It is midsummer you know. When it is June or July and you are enjoying one of those magic winter blue sky days and you remember your England summer sleet, that is when you are going to appreciate this climate. Trust me you do get used to the heat and at least you can cool off. When I am in England I can never get warm, no matter how many layers I put on,' replied James.

These two passengers had spent the two months on board almost exclusively in each other's company. They had shared second class cabin 223A and, although they had never met before embarking on the trip, they were now great chums (if you ask Harold) or best mates (if you asked James). They were also very different characters.

Harold Smith was tall and stockily built with well defined

musculature. He had dark brown eyes, thick slightly wavy brown hair, a square jaw and if he had but known it, movie star looks. He was quick to smile and his smile showed straight, white teeth - his smile lit up his face. He was tall, dark and handsome and many of the single girls (and some who were not single but wished they were) aboard R.M.S. Orvieto had tried from day one to capture his attention.

Harold had a gentle nature, exceptional honesty and integrity and, rare in someone so well endowed with great looks, extreme modesty and total lack of egotism. Harold Smith was also hard working, determined and blessed with natural intelligence.

The immigration clerk back in London last March, when assessing Harold Smith's suitability for the new continent, took less than three seconds to assess his claim but had padded out the interview, as to have conducted such a short assessment could have been considered presumptuous.

His cabin mate James Nelson had fewer of these natural attributes but he was a lovable larrikin and whatever positive character traits he lacked, were soon overlooked. He was just so likeable. James was tall and slim with the body of a natural born sportsman. He had tawny, red hair (this had faded from the carrot top of his childhood) and his fair complexion had a small button nose, sprinkled with freckles. His smile revealed a crooked front tooth but his teeth were good and the smile never left his face. James was always happy, jokes were his calling card. Deep thinking was not something he did often. He was not always scrupulously honest but those whom he diddled nearly always forgave him. James' sporting prowess was based on speed, endurance and agility not brute strength - he was a natural at Athletics, Cricket, Football (Australian Rules of course) and Tennis.

James was returning to Perth having represented his country at Junior Wimbledon and, the way he told the story, he had successfully won the trophy (once again, this was not entirely true). James Nelson's parents loved and doted on him and as an only child and heir to their not inconsiderable wealth, he had a charmed life.

The pair on board the R.M.S. Orvieto had created quite a stir amongst the ladies. James was quite content to charm 'Harold's leftovers' as he called them. The ladies that had been attracted by Harold's good looks had then been seduced by James' wit and charm and by the end of the voyage James boasted many more hearts than Harold had snared. In fact Harold had shown a total lack of interest in the attention of the ladies. As he had explained to James one evening after James had given him a bollocking over not bothering to chat up the very desirable ladies from cabin 201B:

'I am a monogamous chap James. When I was a boy I used to go down to Suffolk and watch the annual mating of the Marsh Harrier. Every year they came and every year they set up their nest with the same mate - they were content. That is what I want to do. I will take my time to choose but once I have decided on a lady she will be my partner for life.'

James immediately returned the verbal volley: 'Well that may be alright for Marsh Harriers; one female Marsh Harrier probably looks the same as the next. I bet if a really attractive, dolly bird Marsh Harrier was to cruise into Suffolk one mating season, all the previously happily content Marsh Harrier bloke birds would be squawking, preening and carrying on trying to get her attention. The Marsh Harrier Divorce Courts would be overflowing.'

'So tell me, why would anyone settle for one lady when there are so many out there?' asked James.

Harold smiled at the analogy of sexual fission in the Marsh Harrier community. The Marsh Harrier, a proud, regal bird of prey, seemed hardly likely to behave in the way James had described. But he stuck to his guns, this principle was just too important to him.

'You only ask that because you have not yet found your true love yet. When you do, the others will just not be so important anymore.'

James was young, feckless and carefree but he did listen to his friend and although he had made many shipboard conquests he had been sure to keep all of the interactions frivolous so no hearts were broken. And he had started to think about what he really did want in a sweetheart. After his talks to the resolute Harold, he had decided that he too would become a little bit more selective.

'So Harold, what is she going to be like this woman of your dreams? Blonde, brunette, tall or short, sporty or bookish, demure or boisterous, you must have some criteria that you will use to decide,' queried James.

Harold cogitated on his reply and was slow to answer. He lit a cigarette and drew the smoke of the first breath in deeply before exhaling the pungent smoke. Only then did he respond.

'I just don't know. I don't think I will know by looking at her. It probably will not be linked to any physical attribute but I am sure it will be just some form of wonderful heart/mind connection. Then just watch out because I will go after her and do anything in my power to win her.'

'And what will happen if this Miss Perfect is already married to someone else before you come along?' chided James with a cheeky grin as he imagined the hanky panky of an illicit affair.

One again Harold hesitated but was deliberate when he did respond. 'Well I will just have to go away, leave town, join the French Foreign Legion or do what you call 'go bush'. I will not be able to stand living close by and not being with her. But to me a marriage vow is forever and I am not prepared to break a vow made before God, no matter how much my heart would want me to.'

'Struth you are such an honourable bloke,' said James, 'and much more admirable than me. I must admit if I fell hard for a girl I don't think a husband and his army would keep me away.'

'It is sounding like you are thinking more like me now,' Harold said. 'You are starting to think that there just might be one special girl of your dreams, one worth fighting for. I just hope that you and I do not fall for the same lady that is all. It could be the end of a fabulous friendship.'

This conversation had happened as the ship sailed out of Colombo just over a week before. It was typical of a multitude of conversations in cabin 223A that ranged over many topics. Serious discussions on love, loyalty, patriotism to King and Country, would be interspersed with lighter topics like whether mutton or beef was superior meat and whether the motor car would replace horse drawn vehicles in the future. It didn't matter who raised a point, the other would have a different opinion and off they would go, discussing the pros and cons.

Other passengers would be astounded to see them striding down the promenade deck going for it, hammer and tongs or sitting in the smoking room arguing the toss with a brandy and a good cigar. (Both had assured the purser that they were 'over the legal age' and entitled to enjoy such pleasures.) James and Harold had formed a strong bond - long before they came gently steaming into Fremantle Harbour.

James had first set eyes on Harold when they both hit the gangplank at the same moment on a freezing day, with a forty knot gale blowing airborne snow into eddies of chill, at London's Royal Victoria Dock on November 15th 1909. Ever the gentleman, even in this foulest of weather, Harold had stood back respectfully and James had seized the opportunity to race ahead with his luggage with an offhand 'thanks mate' thrown out as an acknowledgement to British good manners.

Strangely once below deck they had both taken different routes through the intricate bowels of R.M.S. Orvieto and once again had come to the door of 223A at exactly the same time. Once again Harold stood back and James entered the cabin first.

There was a very good reason for James' display of crass impoliteness. On the way over James had come late to his cabin and as the 'second in' had had to accept the unspoken rule that the passenger in first had first choice of bunks. His roommate on this trip had been extremely overweight and had opted for the top bunk with a porthole near his bed. James had graciously settled for the lower bunk. This had proved to be a huge error. James not only had to suffer every time the gargantuan grunted and huffed his bulk into the top bed but he also had to endure the man's bodily excesses every night.

The top bunk occupant belched and farted his way to England. Because of the angle of the porthole the putrid and smelly air had all been directed straight past big boy on the top bunk, right down to poor James' assaulted nostrils pleading for clean air on the bottom bunk. He had been asphyxiated and had spent the long months of the journey seeking to sleep anywhere but in his cabin. (Of course later James embroidered this story enormously and it was to become one of his favourite after dinner yarns - so all was not lost about the whole affair.) Still when he first met Harold, he was determined not to let this happen to him on the return journey.

Imagine James' surprise when he entered their quality second class cabin and found that the advertising had been truthful, there were two 'proper beds' in room 223A. The advert had read: *'This accommodation is commodious and comfortable. Special care has been taken to secure every possible comfort and convenience for passengers.'* It was worth every bit of the 40 pounds with a non refundable 10 pound deposit!

The quick thinking James saw this in a moment. He had one chance to reverse the impression his roommate must have already formed of him as a rude, boorish yokel. James turned to him with his most disarming smile: 'Sir please make your choice of sleeping arrangement.'

Harold was impressed with the politeness of the young man whom he had thus far summed up as 'a colonial with little breeding.' Sadly, even Harold with all of his great attributes, still carried the prejudices of his upper middle class upbringing.

'Well thank you. I would like to take the bed on the right if that is alright with you. I am Harold Smith and I am immigrating to Australia,' he replied shooting his hand out for the polite handshake between gentlemen.

James responded directly while he grasped the hand in friendship:

'Pleased to meet you Harold. That is a good choice sleeping on the right. I will be happy with the left. I am James Nelson and I have been in England playing tennis. And now that I have won heaps of money on wagers on the dogs and horses, drunk all of London's stout reserves and captured the hearts of all of the best looking English ladies, I am off home to Perth, Western Australia to repent my sins.'

And with some wit, humour and a heavy slather of politeness the foundation of their firm friendship was laid.

By 7.15am on January the 26th 1910, the ship had entered the Port of Fremantle and was gliding slowly across the dead calm waters towards the Passenger Terminal. Many of the folk who were choosing to leave the ship here, had already left their vantage points to ensure that their luggage had been collected and to do those last minute checks one does when one is leaving one's residence of two months. Of course many passengers were staying on board. The R.M.S. Orvieto was travelling to the east coast of Australia and the final destination port was Brisbane. But this was the home port for James and Harold.

Harold looked over to the small roped off section of deck where the steerage passengers were gathered in an unruly mass. They were packed in like spectators at a football game. Once again Harold thanked his Mother for her generosity and recalled her words as she pressed his second class ticket into his hand. 'Now I understand you have to go dear but I don't want you associating with those folk in steerage. There will be a better class of chap in Second Class and this will enable you to meet people who can help you out when you get to Australia.'

'Thank you Mother,' he said silently to himself as he looked at the gathering of assisted immigrants heaving and surging for a look at their new land.

James picked up on his thoughts, a habit of people who have

spent a lot of time in each other's company.

'When we get to the Port it is going to be bedlam. All passengers are treated the same when we get to immigration. It will be all right for me, I'm an Australian Citizen but you will get held up for hours. And it will be super hot in the Arrivals Hall.'

Harold felt his elation at arriving here start to ebb, he was dispirited at the thought of what was coming next. His trip had been wonderful but he had not really thought much about what he would do when he arrived in Australia. All of his energies had been expended on getting here and while on board he had spent the time conversing with James and chatting randomly with other passengers. He had not spent it wisely making connections as his mother would have hoped and advised. Plus he did have some limited funds but he would need to find work quickly or he would be destitute. He estimated that he had enough for perhaps two weeks without help.

Harold was admonishing himself for not having made better plans.

The ship slowly slipped past wharves laden with large containers packed for export. This young nation was already producing more than it needed. It was feeding and providing for the rest of the world thought Harold.

'Yes! Yes! Yes! I have an idea!' exclaimed James.

Harold was jolted out of his malaise and turned to James to see what he was so wound up about. He looked like an animated puppy as he jumped up and down with excitement.

'Look at those crates,' James was pointing at some large freight boxes with bold red writing. Even from the deck they were clearly labelled: *'Sandalwood For China by Agency Nelson and Co'*.

'That is sandalwood from my Father's company. The ship lying at berth is the Brand and it is currently unloading the ballast and will soon take on the produce in the crates,' James went on eagerly.

Harold watched the burly men shouldering bags of what must

be ballast from the hold of the ship and lugging it back onto the wharf. He couldn't see where this was heading but let James keep going.

'Now I do not want to wait in the stinking hot Arrivals Hall and for you it will be three times as long BUT if we were to stay on this side of the line and go down to the loading dock with say, the pretence that we needed to check out the shipment of Father's sandalwood, we could avoid immigration altogether.'

Harold's cautious nature was not completely sure about this idea but he too did not want to hang about in a long, sweaty queue. He was pretty sure that it wasn't really legal to take up residence in a country unless you had gone through some form of immigration check. But he was feeling pretty carefree plus he wanted to keep the illusion and adventure of the voyage and his friendship with James going for as long as possible.

'Well if you think you know what you are doing?' Harold said, still somewhat hesitantly.

'Well I have been down to the wharf heaps of times and no-one checks entry and exit over there.' James pointed back to the commercial wharf they had just passed.

'We will just need to make certain our luggage is safely on its way. Without luggage we will fit in as young chaps with business on the wharf.'

'My folks will not be picking me up until about ten anyway. They know about the hold ups that happen when large ships dock, so we can do some exploring while we wait.' James had decided.

The boys were already walking back to the cabin and James was still formulating the plan as he went. Harold could imagine the wheels spinning in his brain - faster than he could get the words out.

'We will have to have a good story to tell them, so I will say that you are the new overseer for Nelson and Co and I have been asked to show you the Port side of the operations.'

They had entered the passage leading to their cabin and James called a harried porter over: 'Can you arrange for the trunks for Harold Smith and James Nelson from room 223A to be delivered to the front of the railway station at Fremantle for pick up at 10am this morning please?'

The porter wrote these instructions down and then scurried away down the passage where other passengers were keen to make similar requests.

'Now for the whole trip we never talked about any mundane things before did we?' went on James, 'so do you have somewhere to go now that you are here?'

'Well no I don't actually,' said Harold. 'I do not know anyone in Perth and I have no idea about where anything is or how to get anywhere. I thought I would just get some lodgings and then try to find a job when I arrived.'

As Harold was saying this he reflected on how pathetically naive this sounded. He was ashamed. Everyone always complimented him on his good common sense and maturity and he had lobbed up in a new country with absolutely no idea what he was doing.

'Excellent,' said James. This pattern of 'planning by chance' was perfectly aligned to how he lived his life. 'You can stay with us for a while and Father can offer you a job.'

Harold was speechless. It looked like his young friend had thrown him a life line. At this point Harold just gave up; he was in a storm that he couldn't control so he thought he would just put his trust in his young friend.

'I am in your hands and it seems like if this all works I will be deeply in your debt,' Harold said.

'And don't think I will not keep reminding you of it,' James replied with his cheeky grin crinkling his face up into a jumble of laughter lines.

With their day packs on their shoulders, carrying their personal documents and effects, and after hastily saying goodbye to cabin 223A, James and Harold now headed to the area of the ship where the gangplank had just been fitted.

A large group of first and second class passengers were gathered sedately and politely waiting for instructions and permission to start exiting the ship. James was neither interested in instructions nor permission or politeness. As soon as he saw things were safe, he grabbed Harold by the hand and bounded down the gangplank.

He did hear an irritated call behind him: 'Excuse me gentleman you need to wait for .....'

Sadly he was gone before he heard just what he was supposed to be waiting for. At the end of the canvas covered gangplank there were some hastily erected barriers with signs saying: 'Arrivals this way'. Once again James showed his inability to follow the most simple instruction: the sign showed to go left and he pulled Harold to the right.

'Now just walk along nonchalantly chatting to me and look like you have a right to be here,' James instructed.

Although it may have seemed that James had no idea what he was doing, it was soon clear he had an excellent sense of direction. Soon he had left the passenger wharf and they were heading towards the commercial wharf which they had passed earlier this morning.

It was now just after 8am and the white singleted wharfies had nearly finished unloading the ballast. Harold watched, astounded at their strength, marvelling that these men could carry such heavy loads. The apparently effortless action was obviously an illusion as he watched the sweat staining their clothing and streaming from their strain creased faces. The temperature was already obscene and he could well understand why they were stripped to the bare essentials.

'Why are you blokes here?' called a foreman, the only one present in business attire, who looked far more uncomfortable than any of the hard working navvies. He was carrying a board with official looking paperwork and marking off items as they were carried onto the ship.

'I am James Nelson of Nelson and Co,' responded James, 'and this is Harold Smith. He has just started working with the company supervising the transport of the sandalwood from the wheat belt to the Port. My Father, John Nelson thought it was important for him to come and see this side of the operation.' James made the story sound amazingly plausible. His voice was modulated just right and his body stance gave the impression of nonchalant confidence. Superb acting thought Harold.

'Is it OK if we come aboard and watch?' James enquired.

'No problems Mr Nelson and nice to meet you Mr. Smith. You are more than welcome.'

The harried foreman shook the hands of both men, tucked his pen behind his ear and ushered the pair up the gangway, slotting them in between the assembly line of workers carrying their loads, who did not falter in their movements or even look up.

'You will excuse me if I do not show you around though - things are a bit busy while the load is happening. Oh, can you take this back to the office? It is the cartage note for the sandalwood. This will save us a stamp.'

The foreman hurriedly put his scrawl on the paperwork and passed the official form to James and he was off.

James and Harold continued onto the boat and looked over into the hold. Whether it was enhanced by the heat or it was always like this, Harold was suddenly blown away with the strong, thick heady aroma of the sandalwood. Free from its container the aromatic wood smell filled the air. Harold was enthralled.

'This is amazing,' he uttered. 'What is it used for?'

'The Orientals burn it in incense or you might have smelt it before in church. This lot is off to China - so it will probably be used in joss sticks.'

'Is it farmed here?' asked Harold.

'No it grows wild in the bush. It is everywhere across the wheat belt. The early settlers used to chuck it on the fire late at night to make the place smell good. We've been involved in it for about ten years and it has made us filthy rich. Now it is a thriving industry and Father can't keep up with the demand.'

'Come on Harold, we need to get out of here,' said James.

James looked around, he was already bored with the sandalwood and was moving onto the next part of his plan.

Harold was reluctant to leave. The heady aroma was amazing and he felt a powerful pull to learn more about this amazing product. However, he let James lead him down from the boat and away from the passenger wharf towards a security gate. A guard saw they were holding some official paperwork and waved them through onto the street.

And with that Harold had entered Australia. No customs, no immigration and the officials had no record of his entry but he didn't care, he was 16 and he was 'in'. The Australian way was to bend the rules and he had. The 26th January would forever be his Australia Day. Harold felt elated.

The two friends now had two hours to kill before James' parents were due to pick him up.

'What next?' James asked.

'Food please. I'm starving!' Harold requested. They had missed the shipboard breakfast as they had been too involved in the docking process and they were both famished.

So James took Harold for a very welcome Australian breakfast at a cafe on the High St. Their order was taken by a swarthy looking Italian waiter called Luigi who assured them the food was 'Magnifico'. They ordered a cooked breakfast of eggs, sausages and bacon and a pot of Robur tea to follow.

While they waited Harold had a chance to look around. The cafe was fairly full. Most customers were workers from the wharf having finished their shift. Sitting opposite the pair were two 'ladies of the night' still in their work clothes with low cut décolletage and painted faces. They talked animatedly with each other. No one else in the cafe gave them more than a glance. The ladies had obviously 'knocked off 'and no one paid them any notice. Harold watched as a society matron waltzed in with her daughter in school uniform. They took a table near the street and while not facing the other customers they still shared the establishment. Harold was astounded at how different this was from the society he had just come from. It seems that in this town social class distinction is not as important as getting a good breakfast.

After imbibing in an exceptional (yes Magnifico) breakfast the pair then caught a tram to Obelisk Hill which had just been created as a Park for the town of Fremantle and afforded them a great view.

The two friends stood near the obelisk and looked west at about quarter past 9 in the morning. The beautiful Indian Ocean was azure blue and on the horizon, Rottnest Island could be clearly seen.

James, the tour guide, took over: 'Well below you is the great Port Town of Fremantle,' he explained officiously. 'To the north east of us is Perth. You can see the buildings over yonder. The river you can see is the Swan and we are pretty proud of our beautiful blue river. Our home is on the Swan and I just love it,' James enthused.

'Below us is Fremantle. Over there, that round shaped dome, is the Round House and that was built by convicts over seventy years ago. You British sent us your prisoners and we set them to work, transformed them and they became our model citizens. The Nelson family has some convict ancestors and we are quite proud of it these days,' James joked.

'And look that way,' he pointed out a flat limestone building to the south with turrets and walls covered in wire. 'That's the state's prison where we lock up the convicts of today. A good place to keep away from I reckon.'

Harold looked around. This place had such bright, vivid colours and such huge horizons. He felt it was a place of vast possibilities and where anything was possible. He was bursting with the colossal potential for him in this place.

'Now we better get going or we will be late,' James said, grabbing Harold's arm and pulling him down the hill. As they ran, James suddenly stopped and tugged Harold downwards. They rolled and somersaulted down on the fresh mown grass. At the base of the hill they collapsed into each other's arms laughing and giggling like 8 year olds. Harold was ecstatically and unbelievably happy.

As they laughed they spotted the tram coming around the bend. The lads sprang up, and jumped onto the vehicle not waiting for it to slow down. In only half a mile they had reached the railway station and James was excitedly pointing, there was the sulky and his parents waiting by the front entrance of the station.

'Hello Mother, Father. It is so good to see you,' James called as he sprinted across to meet with his parents.

Broad smiles spread over their faces as they both enveloped their son in hugs and kisses in a wonderfully unabashed show of affection.

'We have missed you so much James,' his Mother gasped out through happy tears as she grabbed James' face and gave him another hug.

'And who is this, Son?' asked his Father, looking welcomingly at Harold.

James pulled himself up and in a controlled voice he gave the introductions: 'Please excuse my rudeness. Mother, Father this is Harold Smith, my companion, cabin mate and simply wonderful Englishman soon to become Australian. Harold has looked after me on my trip, made certain I did not get up to any mischief and I have taken the liberty of inviting him to stay awhile until he gets established.'

'Harold this is my Father, Mr John Nelson and my Mother, Mrs Ada Nelson.'

Harold answered in his best voice: 'I am delighted to meet you both and may I say how wonderful you must be as parents, as your son has not stopped singing your praises across the expanse of ocean from London to here.' Harold gave a slight bow and with his natural charm and exceptional looks, accentuated with these fine words, he instantly stole the Nelsons' hearts and they accepted him into their home and family like he was one of their own.

The family took no time to locate their trunks, load them onto the sulky and the group were on their way home. The trip was fascinating. James and Ada prattled and pointed out sights as they drove. Mr John Nelson did not allow himself to be distracted from negotiating a safe passage home as the road was quite rutted and exceedingly busy with traffic.

The Nelson family's home was in Nedlands, just off Broadway. The home was not extensive but was comfortable and roomy and had the great advantage of being right on the Swan River. Built on a small cliff, it was safe from floods and had a wonderful view and great access to the river, which James had used to full advantage when he was growing up.

A slight breeze off the river meant that the home was cool. Harold felt instantly relaxed. He stared out the window at the wide blue river and was once again taken aback at the vivid colours - when God had created this country he had used a very colourful palette.

Upon entering the home, Harold was shown the guest room and told that he was able to stay as long as he wanted. Harold looked around his room. The furnishings were not expensive but the family was obviously well to do. Everywhere he looked Harold saw comfort. However there was no opulence. This was the home of a family who had come into money fairly recently and were still coming to grips with having disposable wealth. James had accepted it more readily than his parents, Ada and John still carried the lifelong lessons of thrift learnt from years of hard work and slog.

While Harold was in his room, James had immediately gone to see his Father to request that Harold be given employment. Mr John Nelson paused for a while before deciding. Although his son was sometimes a bit hasty and was of course a bit young to make astute business decisions, he was inclined to trust his instincts on this one. Harold had the demeanour of a mature person. But Mr John Nelson was professional in all things and he resolved to give Harold the application form and let the board make the decision.

The family sat down to luncheon at 12 noon. Harold looked around at the dining room. The maid had set the table and laid out before them cold cuts of ham and corn beef with a salad of tomatoes, cucumber and onion.

'I am sorry there is no lettuce today Mrs Nelson. The grocer said it has been too hot,' commented the maid with no hint of deference in her voice.

'That is all right Mavis. We have all been too hot lately,' laughed Mrs Nelson.

Harold marvelled at the comfortable manner and banter between servant and master. This was a land where years of humility and servitude had not created a divide between the classes. He would need to be aware of this if he was going to be successful here. Obviously banishing snobbery and living in a classless society was a great thing but for a young man raised in Edwardian England this would take some getting used to.

'My son has indicated that you may be looking for employment. Is this correct?' asked John Nelson opening the lunchtime conversation.

Harold was a bit taken aback. Except for some general conversation in the sulky on the way here this was the first time Mr Nelson had addressed him. And the question was very to the point, almost brusque thought Harold. Generally he was more used to people making some polite, if superficial conversation before coming to the important issues but he thought this is refreshing and will certainly save time and unnecessary verbiage.

'Well yes I am as a matter of fact. James showed me some of your sandalwood at the Port and I must admit I am intrigued with this industry and I would like to learn more about it. I would love to be able to work with this wonderful product,' answered Harold as directly and to the point as his host had been.

'Well here you are then,' replied John Nelson and he handed him a small jagged piece of paper.

Harold hesitated. Once again he recalled his Mother telling him to: 'never read at the dining table while he was eating,' but he was in a new country and he took his lead from them.

'When in Rome do as the Romans do,' he thought.

He took the paper and noticed it was a job application cut from the local paper.

Advert: Men Wanted. Clearing 8 acres a day; burning, scrub cutting, sandalwood cutting or contract, also general work. Transport supervisor wanted. Need reading and writing skills and need to be good with people. Apply to J Nelson and Co. 65 St Georges Terrace, Perth.

'I was thinking you might be good for the transport supervisor. I think it might be a bit hot to put you on an axe straight out from an English winter. Sorry, but you would not make a day I reckon,' laughed John Nelson.

'Of course I cannot just give you a job but if you fill it out I will take it in this afternoon and I will talk to the board. I will tell you their answer this evening.'

'Thank you so much Mr Nelson. I will go and fill out the application immediately. And I agree about putting me on an axe. I think I am strong but I doubt I could last doing manual labour in this heat,' said Harold very relieved.

Harold turned to his hostess, 'Lunch was delightful. May I please be excused?'

Ada Nelson nodded. 'Thank you Harold. After lunch John is heading back to work but I want both of you boys to have a sleep. James has let it slip that you didn't sleep at all last night so you both must be exhausted'.

The boys both did as Ada Nelson suggested and it was late twilight when Harold's eyes opened in his unfamiliar surroundings. He was jolted awake with a loud crescendo of raucous laughter coming from outside his room. For a while he was confused and then he realised this was the laughter of a kookaburra - its hilarity just adding to the bizarreness of the day he had just experienced.

Harold looked out of the window and saw the expanse of the Swan River, lazily meandering its way to the sea, now navy in colour, with the shadows of evening creeping across his adopted land. He rose from his bed, washed his face and, unaware of the conventions of the Nelsons' household, he changed into more formal attire before joining the family.

Harold could hear the muffled tone of conversation. All three voices could be distinguished but not the words. He entered the room and the three turned to him with sombre looks on their faces. James face was suffused with red and he immediately turned away looking obviously troubled.

Harold was suddenly worried that something was terribly wrong. 'It looks like I did not get the job and perhaps the offer of accommodation is also about to be taken way,' Harold thought. He felt crestfallen.

Ada smiled at him and walked forward grasping both of his hands.

'You have slept for so long Harold. I do hope you are refreshed.' She was being polite but superficial. There was obviously something of greater import on her mind.

'Are you all right?' Harold inquired, 'I heard you talking and it sounded like there has been some bad news. Please tell me if it is something to do with me being here?'

Harold was learning that in Australia, holding back is not the best approach.

'Oh no Harold. It has nothing to do with you,' Ada crooned. 'James' friend from school, Jack Parrott has sadly lost his father this afternoon. We were just discussing the best way we can send our condolences.'

Harold felt a surge of relief flood over him. He was unaware that there was some irony that the death of Mr Thomas Wilson Parrott should have caused another person, this time someone who had never even heard of him until that moment, such elation.

James turned to him and it was immediately apparent from the look on James' face that he also wasn't upset about the death of Mr Parrott. James was just angry. Obviously things were not going his way.

Before James could speak, Mr John Nelson held out his hand to Harold and in an officious and commanding voice announced: 'The important thing to let you know, my boy, is that we have accepted your application. Congratulations. You are now an employee of the Company and you will be starting work on Tuesday, February 1st.'

There was no time for Harold to digest this information before Mr Nelson went on:

'So I will want you to come with me into the Perth office over the next three days to get to know us all and find your way around the business. And then you will need to be trained and this means getting you out to Northam by Tuesday next. Now there are a few problems here as Monday has been declared a holiday for Anniversary Day so you will need to travel on the train and the only one available is late on Sunday night. I was just explaining to James that, as a British citizen, you will not mind missing out on the Anniversary Day Celebrations.'

'James was keen to take you with him to meet his friend. But as you are going to be leaving, Jack Parrott will obviously be in mourning for his father and James will be getting ready to return to school, celebrations are now not in order. I am sure you will have ample opportunity to meet James' friend on another opportunity.'

And with that the discussion was over.

Mr John Nelson may have been a doting parent but as a father in 1910 his word was iron and when he made a decree it was enacted.

So that is why James looked angry. Three blows at once: his school friend's father's untimely demise meant Jack was unavailable, his friend Harold was leaving immediately after all James' manipulation to get him here and to top it off he had to go back to school. Life wasn't fair to James Nelson.

Harold, however, was elated. For him this date, 26th January 1910, had been very auspicious. He had landed on his feet in his adopted new country, he had been offered a new job and his whole life was stretched out before him and looked very promising indeed.

War Comes To Australia
A Blue Sky Day

Saturday September 4th, 1914

The Jarrah Forest, Western Australia

On an amazing day, with just a hint of the warm weather to come, Harold Eaton Smith looked up and saw a 'deep blue sky day' and he was transported back to a conversation held over four years ago with his friend James Nelson about blue sky days and how only then would he really appreciate the climate of Western Australia. Harold had lots of time to contemplate this as he was a passenger on a spring cart, stacked precariously high with sandalwood, moving slowly down the Canning Valley in the dense jarrah forests southeast of Perth.

Harold was catching a lift with a sandalwood cutter, Old Tom Wesley. They had travelled in from Brookton for over a week and were now only hours from their destination. Harold had not been in this area before. His job had led him mainly around the wheat belt and the outer agricultural regions where the sandalwood was being harvested. The wood was more common out there, being felled by the settlers as they took up great holdings of land and turned it into sheep pasture or wheat fields. There the vegetation was sparse, with the scrubland consisting largely of stunted, spare eucalypt trees known as the mallee. Harold was impressed with the mallee, he liked the sunlight and the smell of the heavy red brown earth especially after rain. The northern wheat belt had a secret too, a range of surprisingly colourful wildflowers. Strangely these flowers appeared on the ugliest of bushes and after a good rain the whole area became a dazzling display.

But this trip was different. He was now travelling through dense forest where the trees, massive stands of jarrah and red gum, stood impressively above the thick green undergrowth. This bushland took Harold's breath away. He was looking up at these trees with their huge canopies, when he saw the wonderful blue sky day and he felt euphoric - his adopted country kept giving him these wonderful new experiences.

This was the area of Western Australia where timber cutters had flourished, felling these great, giant trees and exporting them across the globe, when it was discovered how hard, durable and sturdy the timber was. To service the timber cutters, rough tracks and railway lines had been constructed 'across the hills' and one of these tracks was now giving Old Tom Wesley a clear and unobstructed passage back to civilization.

The travellers had been bumping along bush tracks since they had left the town of Brookton eight days ago. Old Tom Wesley had passed many forks in the road but he had not wavered - he knew his way home. They had seen other timber cutters pulling enormous jarrah trees behind teams of oxen but had not stopped for any idle conversations. Just the customary wave between isolated groups alone in the enormity of the deep forest.

On this last day of the journey Harold was relaxed, reflecting on his new surroundings. The deep undergrowth was not a monocolour. The green was set off by the deep purple of the native wisteria Hardenbergia, the red coral vine, little white cross flowers of the Clematis and everywhere the stunning yellow fluffy balls on the low lying Acacia bushes. This was not the deep emerald green of the forests of Harold's childhood in England. The beauty of the Australian bush was different.

The bird life in the jarrah forest was also amazing. The loud raucous screeches of the red tailed black cockatoos involved in their endless destruction of Marri tree nuts. Other bright parrots darted passed the cart, letting out their cries of '28 28' that had led to their local name the 28 Parrot.

Harold was just starting to reflect on the plants and animals he had learnt about on this trip when a voice uttered: 'We'll soon be coming to my house.'

Old Tom had been silent for most of the trip but as he approached the end of the journey the sluice opened and he started to speak. Harold was jolted into consciousness, as he had seen no sign of any habitation for at least seven days and had also not heard Old Tom mutter a whole sentence before.

'In about a mile we'll come to the first orchards. That'll be Karragullen which has a railway siding, school and a hall. Then we get to Roleystone and that's where my wife and kid live,' said Old Tom in a matter of fact fashion.

Harold nodded and taking up the conversation he inquired: 'That is lovely, will we be going close to your house? How many children have you got?'

'We only have the one. That'd be little Martha. She was born late to both of us but we really cherish her.' Old Tom was becoming quite garrulous. After days of near silence this was the first time Harold had heard him mutter more than a single word of instruction. Harold had had to work out that 'tea' had meant 'would you like a cup of tea' and by 'camp' he intended Harold to realise that 'this is enough travelling today, I think we will make camp here'.

Old Tom continued: 'So when we get home I'll get off and you can take the cart down to the Mill. They'll get the sandalwood unloaded. I'll get me own way there to pick up the cart on Monday.'

'But I don't know where I am going,' protested Harold. 'I really would not feel confident driving a fully loaded cart I am not used to, in an area where I have never been before.' He felt panic rising in him, fearing where he might end up without the old bushie beside him.

'Don't worry about it. The horses know where to go. Any fool can drive this and they won't take any notice of you anyway if you tell them to leave the route. They want to get home safe as much as you do.' Harold started to protest but Old Tom had finished this conversation and silence came again to the cart.

Just as Old Tom had predicted, the cart then entered a flat cleared expanse. The dense bush had given way to orchards. It was early spring and many of the trees were fully covered in blossom, bright pink nectarines and peaches and stunning white flowering plums. The stark deciduous trees just waking up from the winter sleep.

'Pretty hey?' Old Tom said.

'They grow good fruit here in the hills.'

The orchards stretched for many miles, orchardists taking advantage of the fertile soils, good rainfall and benign climate of the hills area close to Perth.

As the horses plodded along Harold saw an older lady up ahead waving to them. She had a young girl on her hip.

'That'd be the wife and little Martha now. Move over lad, they'll need a lift for the next few miles.' He slowed the horses as they approached and up climbed 'the wife' and little Martha. Old Tom smiled at them both and Mrs Wesley said as she climbed onto the seat: 'Good to see you home Tom'.

Mrs Wesley said nothing more, but her presence spoke volumes. She had walked miles with her daughter to welcome her man home from his travels. Like thousands of Australian wives she lived her life in an isolated, challenging rural location. She was the only adult so had to do the man's jobs as well as her womanly chores. She bore all of these hardships with stoic acceptance and still greeted her man with a no frills welcome.

Harold was in awe of her calm and capable manner. He reflected that these traits were so much more admirable to him than any of the stilted airs and graces affected by middle class women in the country of his birth.

Mrs Wesley carried a basket and she produced a plate with sliced up orange quarters. 'Navels from the orchard on the way,' she said. Harold savoured the sweet and flavoursome taste of the freshly picked citrus. When they had completed this, Mrs Wesley opened the basket again and revealed slices of rich fruit cake and poured each man a small canteen of tea, pre-sweetened with condensed milk.

Martha put her arm about Old Tom, planted a kiss on his leathery cheek and then prattled to her Daddy about school, the sports day and the flotsam of kid's chatter. Martha with her swinging legs and bouncy curls was all full of her life, her world and her Daddy. Suddenly she turned to Harold and said pointedly, 'Who are you and what are you doing with my Daddy?'

He answered her: 'I'm Harold Smith and I'm just catching a lift'. This was a short but sufficient answer. Harold would have a chance to ponder Martha's question in far greater detail in less than five minutes because as they came around the next bend Old Tom said:

'This'll be us then'. In one action he stopped the cart and handed the reigns to the reluctant Harold. The Wesley family got off and before Harold could catch his breath, Old Tom let out a 'Whoa' and flicked the horses' rumps and the fully laden spring cart lurched forward with Harold in reluctant control.

After a few moments of terror Harold realised that he was not in control, the horses were, and he just let them have their way. They plodded steadily to their destination where their horse brains no doubt pictured some lovely oats and a chance to get the harness and the cart off their backs.

It was now apparent that the cart was moving along a major thoroughfare and although Harold didn't know it, they were heading down Old Albany Lane. The cart passed by some other horse drawn vehicles and Harold greeted each other person with a polite 'How de do,' which seemed to be the customary greeting.

Harold gazed about and when he realised how useless he was in controlling the cart's movements, he took time to reflect on Little Martha's question; so exactly who was he and how had he got here?

Physically he had changed little over the last four years. His shoulders had broadened and he now had the physique of a fully grown man. His skin had tanned and his hair had lightened a tad

- the legacy of working outdoors in the Australian sun. He had an extra scar or two and he had lost the last joint of the little finger on his right hand but these he put down to the battle scars of life. Although he saw very few ladies, those who did see him were still taken aback by his exceptionally good looks.

Harold had taken the job with Nelson and Co and although he had been given a helping hand in the beginning, his hard work and innate abilities had led to all promotions from that time on. He had risen in the Company and was now in charge of transportation of sandalwood across the state. This meant that he travelled continuously around the sandalwood harvesting areas and checked that the transport corridors were working well.

Recently he had started to see the need to forgo old transportation methods and to make more use of the new machines starting to arise in the catalogues. He was keen to have this conversation with Mr John Nelson when he returned to Perth. Harold felt that expansion in this state meant taking some risks, spending some capital and he was convinced that the way ahead was mechanization.

Harold had turned twenty on the 15th May 1914 and the Sandalwood men of the Midwest had given him a rousing party. They toasted his good health, with some sly grog, of dubious origin. He blushed at this reminiscence as the normally abstemious Harold had become horribly drunk that night and had woken up next morning feeling very ill and very worried about what he may have got up to.

His 'friends', realising that he had little memory of the events of the evening, had told him lurid tales of himself and his extraordinary exploits in the local brothel over the evening. Harold prayed vehemently that none of these anecdotes were true.

So at this point of time he was Harold Smith, 20 years old, formerly of Ipswich, England (still retaining strong traces of the Suffolk middle class accent of his youth) and now most definitely resident of Australia. He was heading to Perth for his first real break from his work in four years.

After he had unburdened himself of this cart and its cargo he was planning on spending Sunday at the foothills resort of the Narrogin Inne (in Armadale) along with his great friends James Nelson and Jack Parrott. And after his plans for Sunday, Harold had no firm arrangements as he would be on holidays. He would let things take their course.

While Harold was having these meandering thoughts, the horses concentrated on the job at hand and had steered the cart and Harold, down the Canning Valley to Buckingham's Mill. They were entering the gates when Harold awoke from his daydream and sat up straight, looked attentive and pretended to be in control.

'Whoa,' he instructed as he pulled sharply on the reigns. But Old Tom Wesley had told him the horses knew what they were doing and they totally ignored his shouted instructions and remonstrations. They plodded on until they were deep into the mill area. Then they abruptly stopped. Harold looked around and could see the mill activities were all continuing as normal except for a massive bulk coming out of the shadows of the mill interior and bearing down towards the cart.

A burly, giant of a man, bearing a grotesquely disfigured face, came towards Harold. One eye was closed and an angry scar travelled from somewhere under his hair line to the point of his chin.

Harold was just starting to shake in his boots when the man said politely, but with no spark of true welcome: 'G'day Mr Smith, I am Charles Martin and I will be taking you into Armadale. We have had a note from your head office to take you to the Narrogin Inne immediately you arrive.'

'We will deal with the cart and the horses. If you wouldn't mind coming with me we can transfer your trunk to the sulky and we will be off directly.'

Harold was confused. The voice sung with the lilt of the Irish but although the information conveyed was pleasing to Harold, he sensed no friendship from the badly scarred man. Charles Martin went to the horses and fondled their snouts with familiarity, giving both a titbit of some unknown origin from his hand.

Harold dismounted from the cart and stretched after his long trip. He went to get his trunk but the large Irishman had beaten him to it and was already heaving the large case across to the sulky tethered in front of the office.

'Please get up sir and we will get you to the Inne,' instructed Charles.

Harold was confused. Generally he believed he was a good judge of a person but this man had looked like everyman's nightmare, a monster who you would not like to see late at night in a dark alley, but he spoke politely and was obviously skilled with animals. Sadly little of this kindness was directed towards him. Harold understood immediately that his looks belied him.

'Please excuse my looks Sir,' started the man reading his thoughts as the sulky moved off. Once again in Australia Harold was struck with the thought: 'Why make polite and superficial conversation when you can plunge straight in and speak about the thing that everyone is thinking about.' And in this case it was the giant man's disfigurement.

Charles put his left hand to his face as his right held the reigns:

'This is the calling card of the British Army. Back in 1901, I was caught up with a small group seeking Home Rule in Northern Ireland. We thought we were protesting peacefully. My face bears witness to how a group of four British soldiers tried to persuade me to change my mind. Three days of torture I went through. The bastards who did this to me found it amusing. I was big even then and making me cry, wet my breeches and scream with pain amused them. I was only 14 and terrified out of my wits. I'll never be free of the pain or the nightmares.'

'When the bastards let me go my family decided that Ireland was no longer safe for me. They gave me a new name, I was Seamus Martyn once and now that has been anglicised to Charles

Martin. I have come to Australia and forged a new life but I will never forgive your country men for taking away my childhood innocence, my life and my country.' The lilting voice had changed and menace and profound sadness came into it. Charles stared straight ahead - his one good eye was misty with tears.

Harold was overcome with sympathy for this giant of a man, dealt so cruel a hand. He felt the urge to apologise, not only for himself but for the lack of compassion of humanity.

'I am so deeply sorry Sir and apologise unreservedly for my countrymen. I cannot say how much I detest what these bullies have done to you. I am British by birth and still retain a great love for my King and country but your story makes me ashamed of the actions of those thugs.'

Harold spoke with such vehemence and he put his hand companionably on Charles' shoulder. His words broke the tension and Charles gave him a crooked smile.

'Thank you. Your words are a comfort but I cannot keep blaming everyone I meet of British origin for what was done to me. There are lots of you who show exceptional mettle and I feel you are one of them. But look at me! I will never have a sweetheart. None of the young ladies can get passed my ugly mug. I will bear the outside signs of my torture until I die but inside me there is hatred and I will carry this for all eternity,' Charles continued, bitter and angry. But Harold no longer felt the barbs were directed towards him, more at the world in general.

'And now Britain is going to war with Germany and they are calling for all loyal subjects to come and fight under the Union Jack. I for one will never go. Given the chance I would sign up tomorrow in the Hun army and spend years killing every last British soldier I could find, just in case I managed to shoot one of those four miserable bastards.'

Harold could see Charles' point of view and under similar circumstances he may very well have shared it.

'We Irish have a lot of resentment. We've had centuries of being dominated and beaten. England has stolen everything of value from our land and left us to starve. It's not just me, everyone in my village before I came out had seen the cruelty of our British lords and masters. And this has happened all over the world.'

'So I cannot understand why anyone from another country would help the British. Why do Australians want to assist them? Do they really feel the British will say thank you or share their wealth with them after this war is over? I truly doubt it!'

'Well I hope you choose to stay here in Western Australia and let others fight the war. I certainly intend to,' Harold said as the sulky pulled into the parking area in front of the Narrogin Inne.

'Thank you for driving me. I wish you all the best in your adopted country,' Harold said with a slight bow as Charles unloaded his trunk.

And with that the sulky left. Harold paused to think of the deeply wounded man and his yawning hatred. Harold reflected again on the coincidence of peace, prosperity and turmoil, his country had created in the world. Britannia did rule the waves and definitely had risen to become the greatest colonial power in the world. But at what cost?

Of course this power meant it was a great advantage to be British. He had seen this when he had started to travel overseas. Being British, one has such benefits; civilized, privileged and elite. Harold accepted all of the trappings of his birth, but would he fight to keep them?

The interaction Harold had just experienced revealed that there was an underbelly to British domination. Those who have been cruelly subjugated develop intense hatred. Down-trodden men fight back. And if they lashed out at him because he was British and his country or his countrymen had subjected them to a past injustice, he might have no choice but to fight back.

Look at what the British settlers, and those who now called themselves Australians, had done to the aboriginal peoples of this land. Every Aboriginal he had met since he had been in Australia was living in total poverty either locked in some camp or forced from their traditional lands. Do all strong invaders force slavery on those who were here before them? And can you expect such slaves to like you and fight for you when you call on them to do so?

As Harold entered the Ye Old Narrogin Inne reception he was keenly looking forward to meeting up with James Nelson and Jack Parrott. He thought this would be a superb discussion topic for them. See what the two colonials might think of the divine right of the British and whether this war was important in maintaining the status quo. He had missed great conversation.

It was fourish when he entered into the reception area. An attractive, middle aged woman welcomed him with a beaming smile and the efficiency of someone who had done this many times before.

'Welcome. It is Mr Harold Smith isn't it?' she enquired, 'I am Mrs Kate Wilkinson. My husband Charles is the Proprietor of this establishment.'

'I believe you are booked in for a week's stay. Two of your company are expected later this afternoon, Mr James Nelson and Mr Jack Parrott. We have put all three of you into the Sunrise Suite upstairs. It has a great view of the hills and of course the sun peaks through at dawn. It is a favourite room for hunters, adventurers and of course honeymooners and I am certain you will be very satisfied.'

'The costs for your stay including all food and drinks, are being covered by Nelson and Co so you can be quite free to indulge your every whim while you are here. Please accept the following guide that shows you when meals are served and the services we offer. The evening meal is served after 6pm in the dining room. We do expect guests to dress for dinner,' Mrs Kate Wilkinson continued with her well rehearsed introduction speech.

'My son Eustace will take your trunk and I will organise for a bath to be drawn for you. After you are refreshed I suggest you may like to wait for your friends in the smoking room. All of the last week's papers are in there as I expect you will be keen to catch up on the news. You have been travelling upcountry for a while I believe?'

'There is such a flurry of excitement about the declaration of War and there is so much news from Europe. Things are changing daily over there I understand and we need our English brothers to know that we stand with them in their time of need.'

Harold squeezed in a brief, 'thank you,' to his hostess and he turned to follow his trunk being carried to the stairs by the efficient Eustace who had opened the Sunrise Suite, left the bags and hastily made his departure. The young handsome youth seemed none too keen on engaging in any polite conversation with the guests.

Harold entered his room and was very pleased to see the opulence of the surroundings. He would be more than pleased to lie in a soft feather bed after his many years of roughing it. Most of his nights were spent in campsites or low class boarding houses. Harold determined to leave the choice of bed until James arrived, smiling with the memory of the beginning of their friendship when they shared cabin 223A on the R.M.S. Orvieto.

A knock on the door disturbed his reverie and a delightful young lady entered: 'Excuse me Sir, your bath is ready. I am Marjorie Wilkinson and I will be the maid for you and your companions. There are towels in the bathroom and please feel free to use any of the fine soaps, oils and creams we have collected for your pleasure. Tomorrow morning after 9am, we will be happy to arrange for a barber to give you a haircut and shave if you wish.'

The young lady was certainly a great beauty with curly blonde hair captured into a bun but escaping from the bands. She too was struck by the attractiveness of the tall Mr Smith but she was aware of the severity of the punishment that would be metered out to her if she was caught behaving too familiarly with any of the guests.

The memory of her sister Elizabeth, who was spending six months at the Sisters of Mercy Convent because she had been caught stealing a kiss with a wayward guest, kept her firmly in check.

Harold took off his travel-soiled clothes and entered the bath, submerging his body in the piping hot water, luxuriating, soaking away the months of grime and exhaustion. And as he savoured the watery pleasure he reflected:

'I love my new country. I want to stay here, build my life and get rich. I want to find a wonderful wife, marry her and have children. Together I want us to own a farm of our own and make it productive and beautiful. I want to grow old with my wife at my side and grandchildren at my feet. So why on earth would I put all of this at risk and go off to fight in a war? I'm not that crazy!'

War Comes To Australia
Starry Starry Night

Saturday Evening, September 4th, 1914

The Narrogin Inne, Western Australia

After his long soak Harold felt most relieved. He took time dressing in his formal dinner attire but as it was still only just after 5pm, he decided to accept his hostess's offer of going to the smoking room.

'I need a cigarette first,' Harold thought and walked out to the verandah at the side of the Narrogin Inne. He lit up and dragged deeply on the rollie, admiring the golden tones of the late afternoon sun filtering though the trees of his adopted bushland.

At the sounds of approach he turned and found that he had been joined by the Wilkinson's young son Eustace.

'Would you like one?' asked Harold, holding out his tobacco pouch in a gesture of welcome.

'Thanks Mate. I'd love one,' said Eustace conspiratorially. 'I'm just escaping before my Mother or Father give me any more chores.' Eustace expertly took the paper and a pinch of tobacco, rolling the cigarette with the obvious enjoyment of a frequently stolen pleasure.

'Your folks run a great establishment here. It's a delightful place. I notice most of the work is done by your family. Do you enjoy it?' asked Harold.

Eustace looked to the west and let the smoke ease out slowly before answering.

'Look, this place is lovely and Mum and Dad are as keen as mustard that I should take it over. They have this dream of me being the Publican and settling down with a local lass. They have been here for 15 years and would love to keep it in the family.

Sadly for them though, this is their dream and not mine.' Eustace paused letting his words settle. It seemed that he was speaking words to Harold that really deserved a different audience. A patient impassive listener was all the encouragement the young Eustace needed.

'My sisters also want to escape. They want to see something more than just the inside of this place. The girls' heads are full of meeting a handsome young fellow but Dad is hell bent on stopping them and watches them like a hawk.' Harold nodded as the young man continued to pour out his heart.

'There is a downside to working in a place like this. It isn't just the monotony of the work, it is meeting other people and getting grand ideas. Listening to their stories is great but you are left bereft, the travellers all move on and I'm left stuck here. Most of our guests seem to have far more exciting lives than I do.'

'You know what I would really like to do, is to tell some of their stories. To be an author would be great. Or even better to be a newspaperman. To travel to exotic places and tell wonderful yarns to all of the people with boring little lives back home. Now that would be a life worth living. But even hinting that I would like to do this would make my parents really angry.' Eustace's eyes glistened. He was animated and enthusiastic as he sucked deeply on the cigarette, then exhaled a trail of smoke. Obviously this had been a dream he had frequently revisited.

'So what are you going to do?' asked Harold, empathising with the young man's predicament.

'Please don't whisper a word of this but I'm going to join up. I'm nearly 16 and cannot enlist without my parents' permission. They'll never give it. We've already had a huge barney about it. Mother is full of the glories of the battle and how we need to fight alongside the soldiers of the motherland but this does not extend to allowing her only son to go. So I'll just bide my time. When I turn 20, I'll no longer need their permission and I'll be out of here. I am patient. Either they'll give in or I'll just pack up and leave.'

Eustace's eyes were already dreaming of living a life far away from this idyllic location. Even if it would be four years before he could leave.

'But this would mean going to war across the other side of the world - it is dangerous you know. You could die or be maimed. Doesn't this worry you?' Harold asked.

'I don't think of that. I think of escape and new worlds and seeing things not even conceivable to a young bloke stuck in Armadale. I want a life away from here. It is better to go and get killed than never to have gone at all I reckon.'

Harold let his words sink in and they had a profound impression on him. This young man was serious and was prepared to destroy his family's harmony to achieve his dream.

'Thanks Mate, for the cigarette and the opportunity to talk. There is something about you. I just feel that I can share something with you and that the confidence will remain safe. You must have trusting eyes or something. Now I must get back to work or my Mother will show you her not so very nice side.'

With that Eustace left the verandah and Harold went back inside and moved towards the reading room. As he entered he noticed many aspects of the room's luxury. He walked around the perimeter taking in the decor and furnishings. Heavy red drapes locked the daylight out but the room was well illuminated by lamps. Harold took in the well-made jarrah furniture and comfortable damask covered chairs. High tables were spread with newspapers. The far wall was covered with testimonials from many satisfied guests.

One section caught his eye under the title: *'History of the Ye Old Narrogin Inne'*. It told the story of a previous proprietor, Mr William Foster, who was murdered by the cook John Gill on December 14th, 1874. Apparently Mr Foster had complained to the cook about the quality of the meat and John Gill had shot him. Mr Foster had died of his injuries. The locals had convened a 'kangaroo court' and John Gill, with no lawyer appointed to mount a defence, had been declared guilty and summarily hung.

Harold determined that he would not complain about the quality of the food, just in case this spirit still prevailed.

Harold then turned his attention to the last week's papers. As Mrs Wilkinson had said, the War was the only news item.

On Thursday 2nd September 1914, The West Australian had reported: *German Troops Advance on Paris. People leave the city in droves.*

Reuter's Paris correspondent reported:

Numbers of people are leaving here. They are mostly provincials and men removing their families in order not to hamper the defence. There is no reason to be unduly alarmed by the German advance or by the French leaving, as the German troops there are quite insufficient to besiege Paris. The Germans are believed to be at the limit of their effort.

On Friday 3rd September 1914, The West Australian announced: *The enemy menaces Paris. German troops approach the city. Grave fears are held for the defence of Paris.*

An article entitled: *Further German Outrages,* highlighted, *the animalistic behaviour of the German troops.*

Another article showed how well some fronts were going. On the Eastern Front the headline screamed:

Russia's irresistible advance. 70,000 prisoners captured and two hundred guns were taken.

Friday's West Australian papers also showed what was happening back in England: *The British Army calls for all able bodied men to enlist. Over 280,000 men have enlisted over the last week in August.*

Harold stopped, shocked at the enormity of that number. He reflected on what his homeland would be like today. Alive with frenetic activity. The War could be ignored here, especially in the bush, but there it would now be all encompassing.

Over the past month he had discussed with many people from his new land about the inevitable progress towards war. Around campfires in the bush, discussing issues from far away with men who had no close association with Britain, these matters had seemed to be someone else's problem. They were academic debates, sterile opinions of no real consequence.

Everyone was an expert. Even in the most isolated outpost in the Australian bush, all and sundry seemed to know about the shooting of the Archduke Ferdinand and most sided with the British idea that this had been a Serbian plot instigated by Germany to de-stabilise Europe. But none of these people really cared.

What did it matter to Old Tom Wesley whether Ipswich was invaded or not. To some, the war had re-kindled desires of vengeance and retribution. To Irishman Charles Martin, such news only flamed old hatreds. Even to Mrs Kate Wilkinson, with all of her patriotic utterances, her beautiful daughter who dreamt of true love and her young son who yearned to escape - would their life change tomorrow if Paris fell or if Germany invaded London?

Harold doubted if life would be much different for anyone here if Britain fell; lives in Perth, Western Australia would be the same.

But if Eustace enlisted and was involved in the fighting, the Wilkinson's lives would be very much affected. With a loved one heavily involved in the affray, people had a vested interest. That foreign war would soon become their war. Harold believed that the reasons for Britain's involvement were flimsy and revolved around the self interest and pride of those in charge.

He could see that the imperialistic desires of all of the major players, including Britain and Germany, were equally questionable. But whether one believed in the reason for the war was not the question for Harold. It was whether his conscience would allow him not to go and fight.

Harold was a moral man and he felt a fundamental responsibility to protect those he loved. At present his England and those he still loved in England, were being threatened.

Prior to this afternoon Harold had thought that the war was far removed from him. He had told Charles this just two hours ago. He had thought this way while luxuriating in the warm suds not half an hour ago. But these stories in the papers brought these issues home.

Plus his mother was still back in Ipswich in England and her life was being affected - seriously affected. This war had just got a lot more personal.

Harold read on:

Announcement from Australia's War Office:

We will not let England fight this alone. Australia's War office announced today that an additional Infantry Brigade and a Light Horse Brigade would be sent to aid the war effort with expected disembarkation in December.

And at this moment Harold determined that he would be with them. Harold would go to war!

Loud bellows behind him broke his reverie and he turned to see the smiling face and open arms of James Nelson. They fell into each other's arms in a bear hug embrace. Breaking the hold he turned to welcome Jack Parrott with two outstretched hands. He had now met Jack on at least five occasions and although he didn't share the deep bond of brotherly association he had with James, he was still a warm friend. He had missed the camaraderie of equals.

'We've just arrived and were told you were in here. My gosh it is good to see you,' enthused James. 'Now come out the front and see our new conveyance. It's my Father's pride and joy and it's a wonderful form of transport. You should have seen us driving here, tooting the horn at things in front of us on the road. And the admiring looks - I felt famous. I swear I'm never going to go back to the horse if I can drive a motor car.'

'It's a fabulous form of transport,' added Jack, just as excited as his friend, 'so smooth and much faster than a horse and buggy. It still took us 5 hours from Nedlands but that is due to the shoddy state of the roads!'

The trio was full of the excitement at their first up close and personal experience of an automobile. Parked out the front was their gleaming dark red, Ford Model T Touring Car. Already a crowd of interested onlookers had gathered. This was still a real novelty in this location.

'Just take a look at this piece of art,' said James, his hands caressing the bonnet. 'Do you know that they are selling one of these cars every day in Australia at the moment?'

'Father waited until the price dropped and he picked this one for the reasonable price of only 480 pounds. It is so great to drive, very easy after you get the hang of it and so comfortable. These all terrain tyres just take the ruts and bumps so well,' James sprouted, obviously he was well acquainted with the manual.

The lads peered inside the side opening bonnet, marvelling at the magic machinery that had been assembled. Harold was ecstatic and was like a little boy at a birthday party.

'Do you know these are produced in a factory in Detroit by an industrialist called Henry Ford. He uses a method called the mass production line. One worker just does the same thing all day, perhaps being involved in the building of up to twenty of these a day. They say that one day we'll all have one,' said Harold. This was his passion and he was eager to share his knowledge of it with his friends.

Harold slipped into the driver's seat and felt so at home. His hands naturally found the steering wheel and the throttle, his feet felt for the pedals. In his mind he was already driving with the wind in his hair.

He admired the look of the car and sudenly he experienced a profound feeling of destiny. Harold could feel its potential, this was an indication of how the world was changing and he was excited to be part of it.

'You can both have a drive tomorrow when we explore the hills,' James promised. 'We cannot go out again now, the lights are not good at night and Harold is in his dinner jacket - hardly touring clothes!'

Reluctantly the trio left the touring car and re-entered the Inne.

One hour later they were seated in the dining room. The stunning Miss Marjorie Wilkinson had just served the lads their main meal of roast beef, vegetables and gravy. The three were sampling a sweet, white wine produced locally by Derry Na Sura vineyard, and moving towards the very pleasant stage of post dinner conversation. They were not wine connoisseurs but the intoxication from their second glass of wine to folk who are not seasoned drinkers, added to a hearty well cooked meal, meant they were seeing the world in a very positive light. Plus they were on holidays. All three declared that the wine was excellent and Jack Parrott shared with his friends his intention to swear his undying devotion to the lovely Miss Marjorie Wilkinson.

'I will have a kiss from that lovely little lass by the end of the evening,' vowed Jack, looking with longing at the lovely girl as she disappeared back into the kitchen. 'If you were my real mates you would be plotting to get me alone with her.'

'You are on your own with this my friend,' said James laughing.

'I very much doubt it will work,' agreed Harold. 'Have you seen how her father watches her? You'll need to separate her from her father, brother and mother and I will not protect you if they come after you with a shotgun. Don't forget this place has a history of murderous acts.'

Harold had regaled his friends with the story of the Publican murdered after criticising the cook. James and Jack had agreed with great mirth that they would be certain to compliment the chef no matter how poor the meal.

'But this is a very strange thing,' said Harold looking directly at James. 'Here is a stunning young lady. Jack is showing red blooded interest in the pursuit and you James are just handing her to him on a platter. I have never seen this before. Are you well? Why are you not going after her too?' enquired Harold.

'Oh haven't you heard? James is spoken for - he has a sweetheart,' laughed Jack.

James' face was slowly mottling to a pinkish hue. 'It's true. I am bespoken,' said James. 'This wonderful gift to all ladies has met his match. I am now attached to the delightful Miss Lillian Parrott.'

'So James has fallen for your little sister?' stated Harold. 'This is wonderful news but I cannot believe it, you were so keen on conquering every lady you met. It is wonderful if you have settled on just one, however I find it very difficult to believe. She must have bewitched you with charms and spells or else she must be an exceptional lady. So tell me all about her.'

'She is everything I was looking for but I didn't know I was looking,' confided James. 'As Jack's sister, I have known her since we were children and those things I used to tease her about before, I now find really endearing. She has beautiful brown eyes and glistening hair but it is her mind that I like. She is an independent thinker. I am in love Harold.'

As James turned to his friend his face had taken on a dreamy look, 'I think this is it. Although I must confess I can still see the great merit in appreciating the beauty of the wonderful Miss Wilkinson, I am content to let Jack try his luck. I am satisfied to dream about my Lilly.' The three friends now fell into a long discussion on the relative merits of love and single life while they had dessert, apple pie and cream and finished the meal with a strong cup of tea.

An hour later the three lads had retreated to the verandah off the smoking room and were staring into an inky black sky. They had opted for a Madeira and had brought the bottle out with them to make certain that their glasses would remain full. The three friends stared towards the southwest as a faint sickle moon dipped low on the western horizon. The stars of the Milky Way stretched across the sky and the Southern Cross was clearly visible low in the south. All three had lit their cigarettes and were slowly sipping their drinks when James cleared his throat to get their attention.

'The Southern Cross is a signal of our new nation,' said James seriously - obviously about to launch into a serious and profound conversation. 'It is the country Jack and I were born in and it is your adopted land Harold. I think we are just coming to the crossroads of our nationhood. The threat England is facing and the situation across Europe is dire. I wanted to share with you both that I have decided that I want to enlist. I want to go to war.' James made this sternest announcement to his two best friends, letting the importance sink in before he continued.

'My dilemma is that I am leaving my wonderful parents behind and they have nothing except me and now I have found Lilly. I don't want her left without care. I am going to sign up but I want you both to look after them while I am gone and to be there to support them all if something was to happen to me.'

Jack was immediately involved speaking loudly and with great insistence.

'I feel exactly the same as you do James. I want to go and fight the Germans too,' said Jack. 'At present I have no real career and my sister and my mother will be all right without me. I just can't abide how I would feel if others were taking on this burden and I was shirking. Plus, I think it will be a great adventure. Even more so if we go together.' Jack took James' hand in solidarity.

'That is wonderful news,' said James with a warmth to his voice, 'it'll be such an adventure. We'll get to see new lands and life here was getting a bit deadly dull. The story is out that we will be home by Christmas anyway. I am so happy you will be coming with me Jack. I was hoping to join the Light Horse Brigade. They are looking for people who are good on horseback and I think we West Australians fit this bill perfectly.'

'So Harold, how do you feel about looking after everything and everyone for us while we are gone?' asked James. Two sets of eyes looked at Harold, seeking his mature approval of their plans.

The starlight glinted in Harold's eyes and he was once again slow to answer.

'Isn't it strange how momentous decisions often come together. I had resolved, not ten minutes before you arrived, to go and enlist myself. I was going to share this with you over the next few days of our holiday,' Harold said smiling.

'I am British by birth, some of my family members are still in England and to me this war threatens them. It also endangers everything that we Britons stand for. Germany is being an aggressive bully and I do not want to stand by and watch, allowing them to get away with their belligerent actions. I don't think it is going to be much fun or a great adventure. I think being on a war front will be my worst nightmare. I am not looking forward to giving up my wonderful life here for that. It would be so much easier to stay here and leave the fighting to people in Europe,' Harold continued solemnly.

'But here is the rub - I do not think either of you should go. My Father was a soldier in the Crimean War and he always said *'war is hell and do not let anyone tell you otherwise.'* Plus, I do not think it is your war! I do not think this war is the responsibility of anyone in Australia or New Zealand. It is an honourable thought to protect Britain but I do not feel that this is a real obligation and it is certainly not worth you young men dying for. And to tell you the truth, if either of you was to die or be maimed over there, fighting a war that is just not your war, I would feel totally responsible if I had not done everything in my power to convince you not to go. I'll say this again to you both, it is not your war.'

James and Jack were a bit taken aback at the vehemence of Harold's retort. The night had been spent in such wonderful camaraderie and Harold's stern and serious words had put a dampener on their high spirits. Here was their chance to all go off to war together and Harold was saying they should not go. Both started to protest at once.

'Harold we are both over 18 years old, we're old enough to make our own decisions,' said James.

'I do want to go,' said Jack. 'You say it is not my war but I consider myself only one step removed from being British as my Mother was born there. Your King is my King, your customs are my customs. It is time for Australia to stand up for our motherland. This means being prepared to fight and if necessary die. Also I will be honest, I couldn't stand it if I was given a white feather accusing me of being a coward and too scared to go and fight.'

These words were from the heart and with that Jack put his head in his hands.

Harold pointed into the night sky.

'Do you both see that? It is the Southern Cross, the symbol of this new land. Do you know that you cannot even see that if you are in the Northern Hemisphere? Can you imagine lying in agony, removed from all of those you love and without even the comfort of your own night sky above you? Please do not go!'

Harold looked at both of his young friends. They stood resolute. Their faces showed their grim determination, their minds were made up. They were proud and extremely brave he thought. They don't know what they are going to do but they want to do it anyway. And he really didn't know much more than them and was only just a bit older.

Plus it really wasn't his business to stand in their way.

Harold looked at both of them, and he sighed, accepting their decision.

'All right, tomorrow we will take the Model T. Ford down to the enlistment office. Boys we are off to war.' And with that they upended their glasses of Madeira and headed up to the Sunrise Suite.

War Comes To Australia
Farewell To James

Thursday November 1st, 1914

Perth and Fremantle, Western Australia

The next door neighbour's rooster obviously had an error in its body clock mechanism when it awoke Lilly two hours before dawn but once she was awake a jumble of thoughts and emotions crowded in. Any chance of more sleep now was gone.

All of these thoughts were variations on the theme: 'This is the day I say goodbye to James'.

James Nelson was off to War and his sweetheart Lillian Parrott was proud and bereft in equal measure.

The three friends had set out to sign up, back in September. Lilly knew the story of what happened next by heart, having heard it over and over again, in frustrated rants from her dispirited brother Jack.

James, Jack and Harold had all been chock full of confidence and bravado as they approached the enlistment office. Harold Smith, whom Lilly had still never met but certainly knew all about, had been sailing though the series of tests, when he failed his eyesight test. He had been devastated at the news. It came as a complete surprise to Harold as no-one, himself included, had ever identified his short-sightedness before. Harold had never failed anything in his life.

Harold was destroyed to discover that he was not, 'able bodied enough' to go and fight. After all his soul searching had convinced him that this was what he should be doing, this was a devastating blow. He had apparently left the enlistment office with a face as black as thunder and had immediately gone back to work, cutting short his holidays and returning to the wheat belt. Neither Jack nor James had seen him or heard from him since that day.

James and Jack had both breezed through the medical and the aptitude testing. They also both fudged past the page of 'essential permissions' required from family or guardians. These needed to be appropriately filled in if the applicant was younger than 19 years old. The enlistment clerk was not into asking too many questions and they certainly didn't go out of their way to reveal the truth. On this auspicious day that marked their transition into manhood, neither boy had thought to ask anyone's permission. They were going off to war and nothing was going to stop them.

Pte Jack Parrott and Pte James Nelson accepted their pay cards and promptly fronted up to the quartermaster to receive their uniform, kit and rifle. To cap off their decision they both went to the army barber and ordered him to 'give them the full treatment, short back and sides if you please sir.' This hair cut was considered essential for the modern infantryman soldier. (Both had decided the infantry was more their calling as neither of them was really confident enough of their horsemanship skills to risk an application to the Light Horse Regiment.)

In full regalia they returned to their respective homes that evening. When their families saw that the deed had been done, despite any regrets or reservations they may have had, they accepted that the lads had made a decision. Jack and James were jubilant.

Lilly saw the boys as they drove the Ford Touring Car down the street to her house. James was driving and Jack was waving his soldiers' slouch hat proudly and hooping with joy. They both looked ecstatic. Lilly could instantly read their story; a joyful smile spread over her face as her eyes devoured the lads with honour and pride.

'How do we look? Model soldiers?' Jack asked Lilly with a mock bow and a sweep of his hat. James gathered her into his arms and spun her around on the verandah in a frivolous embrace.

'Your sweetheart is a soldier boy,' he crooned nuzzling her neck.

Lilly stepped back and looked both men up and down with a

critical eye.

'The Germans will take one look at you and I predict they will be in retreat immediately,' she laughed.

'My gosh you boys look grand,' she pronounced.

Mrs Frances Parrott came to the door and she too took in the scene immediately. A surge of emotions rose in her. The thought of losing her son was suppressed as she also smiled benevolently at the boys. Her boy had grown up.

Jack and James were eager to be off, there was too much excitement about this new turn of events to stay in one place for too long.

'Come on Lilly - let's go to my place and show my parents how their young fellow is now a handsome soldier boy!' James said. Lilly jumped into the backseat of the Ford. (This was the first time she had ever been in an automobile so she was trying to cope with this emotion as well. What excitement!)

Mr John Nelson and Mrs Ada Nelson were proud, sad, excited, scared and could almost feel the loneliness coming into their lives that the absence of their only son would bring. That night, every one of the people involved in these events was in a turmoil of emotion. Disturbed sleep and restlessness was the norm across both the Parrott and the Nelson homes.

The next step should have seen both lads turning up to Blackboy Hill Training Camp on the 12th September to commence their basic training. But fate has a habit of stepping in where it is least expected. Pte James Nelson was the only one who made it.

The very next day after enlistment, Jack complained of a headache, sore neck and a general feeling of listlessness. Frances, who had nursed his Father for 14 years, immediately convinced him to stay in bed putting it down to too much excitement. She saw the rash and surmised that he had contracted one of the many measles diseases, not good but generally light in their affliction.

'I think you may have German Measles,' she concluded after the examination. 'It looks like the Hun have sent a pestilence to strike you down even before you get over there,' she joked.

By the next day Jack was extremely ill, nauseous and with a high fever. The light streaming in through the louvres hurt him so much that shutters had to be fitted to the windows. By noon Jack was lapsing in and out of consciousness, he was delusional, and was running a high fever. The doctor was called and immediately identified that Jack Parrott was suffering from 'brain fever' or more accurately termed meningitis, a disease with a mortality rate of 90%. He announced to the frightened Parrott women that their much loved son and brother may very well not survive; there was no known cure.

The house was immediately quarantined and Lilly and Frances become full time carers, administering to Jack's every need, sponging him to keep him cool and making certain they kept his fluids up. The atmosphere in the house, so jubilant and hopeful the week before, became sombre and full of dread.

Luckily Jack was a healthy Australian lad. His nutrition and general health before the infliction of this illness had been excellent. This meant that he was one of the very few in this era who survived this disease and he emerged with no serious long term effects.

By October the 10th Jack was through the worst - the spectre of death had left and some vestige of colour had returned to his face. The Doctor came and declared that the quarantine could cease and that Lilly and Frances could leave the confinement of their home.

For Jack, worse than the sight of his disease ravaged body, was the pronouncement that he would not be able to join the army now or into the foreseeable future. The Australian Army had extreme paranoia about meningitis and all such contagious diseases. Jack was distraught. On the 12th October Jack received his army discharge.

'What is this - the most distinguished and shortest army career in history!' Jack said bitterly as he read the officious letter.

Jack then refused to see anyone or speak to a soul and for the next two weeks he was in voluntarily imposed, solitary confinement.

He didn't suffer in silence though, he ranted and grieved at his rotten luck and the evil turn of events that had befallen him.

Jack had been in the depths of his illness, when James had been granted his only two leave passes while involved in basic training at the Blackboy Hill Camp. Lilly had been unable to leave the house while Jack was ill and the lovers were starting to get fractious.

On October 27th, James had decided that this would not do and, with rumours flying around the camp that the departure date was set, he had stolen out of the camp and caught the train into town. James turned up on the verandah just as Lilly was about to go to bed. Mrs Frances Parrott had retired, tactfully, leaving the couple to say their goodbyes in private.

'Hi Lilly. I am so sorry to spring this on you but I had to see you before I go,' James said as he swept her into a friendly hug.

'Oh James, thank you so much. I was beginning to think I would not see you again until this war is over. Are you likely to get into much strife?' Lilly asked. Her eyes glistened with happiness tears as she stared at his face, burning his every feature into her memory.

'Not too much I don't reckon,' he said. 'Lots of blokes have been doing it. Most just get docked 10 shillings and are told not to do it again. The officers are fairly reasonable. They know we've been training really hard and that this is just the last chance we have to say goodbye to those we care about. It's not like we are going drinking or gambling,' James said.

They sat down on the top step of the verandah with their heads touching and their hands intertwined. The gas light on the street flickered, casting shadows over them as they sat close, savouring this moment of stolen companionship.

'Now I will not have very long. But there are some special things I need to tell you. Firstly I care for you, a lot, but I am not going to hold you to staying as a couple. If you meet someone else while I am gone I want you to tell me - no secrets. We do not know what the temptations and pressures will be on us,' James started.

Lilly began to object but James had thought carefully about what he had to say and this was the only time he would have to say these words.

'Secondly, take good care of my Mother and Father please. They are being really brave but I am their only child so this will be hard on them. If there is anything they need or you and your family need, I want you to get a message to Harold Smith. He is like a brother to me and he will do anything for the people I care about. Trust him, he is a good man.' The normally flippant James was speaking earnestly to Lilly. He had thought hard about the things he needed to say.

'Now this one is important, I want you to give this note to Jack. It tells him I love him and I will be fighting for both of us. I know he is taking this hard but he wanted to go and tried to go. Getting ill wasn't his fault. I will do the fighting for both of us.'

James gave Lilly a note for Jack and she slipped it into the bodice of her dress. Once again she started to speak but James held up his finger to her lips, impressing on her the need for silence for a little while longer.

'Now this is the most important one of all. I want to be able to write to you and I need to be able to tell you as it is. Lots of blokes are only going to tell the good parts. I want you to know exactly what it is like, what I am feeling. I know you are an intelligent woman and I think that is what I like most about you. I feel like we are equals. The only reason that you are not going off to war is that you have the body of a woman. If I am scared I want to say it to you, if I find glory in killing, or if I am in pain, I want you to know. This is because I care about you, I trust you and want you to know what makes me a human.'

Lilly was stunned. She had expected words of endearment perhaps even some physical passion but James had just revealed to her words from the depths of his soul. Their relationship had previously been built on fun, flirting and good times and she now saw how shallow this had been. This was a side of James that she had never seen before and she did not know if she was totally comfortable with it. The war was forcing them apart and like millions of couples separated by other wars, James needed to know he had the love of a woman back at home.

'Will you promise me these things?' he said with raw emotion cutting into his voice.

Lilly thought carefully before she replied. James was going off to war and he was filled with all of the confusion that this must bring. There was no chance for the gradual, steady development of their relationship. Lilly felt his desperate need and spoke words of reassurance to him:

'Yes I will do what you ask and James, I am your sweetheart and fully expect to remain so. But I too realise that we are both young and that this separation may put us both under stresses we know nothing of yet.'

'Now my wish for you is to be safe. The thing I know for sure is that wars are not good things - people get hurt and people die. The words written in the papers may not be telling us the whole truth. I fear things are not as rosy as they pretend. I do not want a dead sweetheart - even one with a posthumous medal.'

Lilly let her words sink in. Despite her own feelings of confusion she knew James needed her to sound certain. These were the most serious words they had ever spoken to each other and both felt the profound importance of this moment.

Sadly the visit now had to be cut short. There was only one more train east that evening and James knew if he didn't catch this one he would not be back at the Blackboy Camp before dawn.

They hugged again and he left walking backwards up the road.

He called to her: 'I will look for you on the wharf. Wear something bright red so I can recognise you.' He blew her a kiss as he raced up the road towards the station. As James faded from sight out of the glare of the gaslights, Lilly felt the enormity of their discussion and anticipated the despair of a long separation. Tears coursed down her face.

And now here she was two days later planning to go down to the wharf to wave farewell to James. She very much doubted that she would have any chance to say a proper goodbye. The troops had been kept at arm's length from the public the whole way through the basic training stage. At least they'd had that one chance to say farewell.

The Defence Department had kept everything under wraps but everyone knew that today was the day. The troopships were already lying in Fremantle Harbour. Lilly had arranged with the Nelsons to go down with them. They would be picking her up in the Ford Touring Car so she would travel down in style and of course Mr Nelson had special privileges at the wharf, so at least she knew she would have a great vantage point.

Now James' leaving day had dawned. Lilly had arisen from her bed and looked east out of her open window as she did every morning. There had been rain overnight, at around the time the rooster had started to crow. The plants in the garden were covered in diamond drops, glistening in the early morning sun. Lilly's mother had covered the backyard with plants. The Parrotts had a cottage garden with many English flowers flourishing in their new colonial environment, at their peak in the middle of a balmy spring. Lilly breathed in the heady scent of stocks and roses. The north easterly section was devoted to vegetables and the back corner with an outhouse, subtly covered in honeysuckle and jasmine, in an attempt to mask any less than pleasant aromas.

As Lilly stared out she saw Jack emerging from the outhouse. He was at least upright, and she thanked the Lord he had survived but his emaciated body made her heart ache.

Lilly had given Jack the letter and he had taken it without saying a word to her. She knew he would have read it and she was fairly confident that she knew what James had written. She resolved to get dressed and go straight in to see Jack.

'It's time,' she whispered to herself. 'It's time for Jack to get better. It's time for him to go and say farewell to his Mate.'

Lilly strode down the stairs, knocked once and then entered into Jack's room, full of resolve. She was about to utter the words of stern encouragement when Jack turned and said to her:

'I'm coming with you. I cannot leave this festering any longer. My best friend is going to war and I must do everything I can to do the right thing. He needs me to be strong again. You all do.'

Lilly went over and put her hands on Jack's shoulders. No words from her were necessary. Jack had made his decision and she was proud of him.

Lilly went back to her room and dressed carefully. Her skirt was grey wool and she put on her best blouse with silver trims and at her throat she wore a cameo tied with a red ribbon.

'Every bit the reserved sweetheart farewelling her man,' she muttered to herself with smug satisfaction.

'But James wants me to wear something red so he can notice me,' she recalled in exasperation, nearly forgetting his last minute request.

She got her summer hat down and removed the subtle black band replacing it with a red silk scarf that she tied around four times, still leaving two long, banner like red silk tails. Then she went into the garden and picked a mass of red roses - these she would carry and throw at the ship as a symbol of farewell.

'Perhaps he will notice the movement of the scarlet blooms,' she muttered to herself.

At 8am Jack and Lilly were both standing ready when the Ford Touring Wagon pulled up. John and Ada Nelson sat primly in the front, their emotions perfectly in control. The group travelled in style to the Port but it was a slow journey. It seemed that everyone else in Perth had the same plan. The roads were packed. Despite the secrecy of the Defence Department not announcing anything official, it seemed that everyone did know that the troops were off today.

The Nelsons were able to get their car right onto the private loading section leased by Nelson and Co. But they could soon see that if they were to get a real view of the troop loading they would need to be further to the right. This was the very route where James Nelson had steered a bemused Harold Smith away from the Arrivals Hall four years ago. This group were unaware of this fact but as they hurried to the better vantage point, they ran into someone who was clearly aware of it.

A tall, bronzed and amazingly attractive man gazed out to sea watching the docking of the first troopship - the SS Ascanius.

'Harold!' yelled Jack.

'Why it is wonderful to see you my boy,' said John Nelson.

'I have missed you so,' gushed Ada Nelson.

All three spoke at once and the handsome man turned to the group, a spectacular smile lighting up his face.

'Well James is leaving and we can't let this event go past without all of his friends being here to wish him well.' Harold's words were addressed to his dear friends but his gaze lingered on Lilly. He was clearly taken aback by the sight of this little beauty with her slash of red silk and her arms full of red blooms.

'Come along,' said Jack, 'we need to get closer or we will not see him when he arrives.'

Already the first troops were passing from the train to the gangplank and they were marching on board. So tall and proud they were, smart in their uniforms and all carrying their full kit. The soldiers wore their slouch hats and heavy overcoats even though it was warming up but 'better to wear it than carry it,' they had all thought.

The soldiers' legs marched in time but their bodies swivelled about, waving and searching for familiar faces in the crowds. Armed sentries with rifles at the ready and bayonets fixed were stationed to prevent any real contact but the adoring crowd was able to watch them as they passed from the loading yards where the train had dropped them, all the way up until they were safely aboard.

When their group arrived, Companies A, B and C of the 11th Battalion were already on board. James Nelson was part of D

Company so their timing was perfect. The group was in the third row back and were all fairly content except for Lilly. As the only short one amongst them, she found herself peering around between the bodies in front of her.

Lilly kept her silence until Jack yelled: 'It's him, look second from the back, marching slowly. Look he is doing a salute to the crowd.'

'Over here, over here,' Jack yelled, his skinny arms waving akimbo.

Harold yelled out: 'Yoo-hoo. James look this way. We're over here.' He too was raising his arms up and down in a wave to attract attention.

'He's looking over towards us. He can see us,' screeched Jack.

At this stage Lilly could not contain herself. She was aware of movement and cheering but all she could see was waving arms and pulsating bodies.

'I can't see anything!' she protested stamping her foot.

At her angry words Harold turned to her and said, 'I am so sorry, how rude of us. You must be Lilly.' And with that he leaned over and picked her up and placed her high up, perched on his shoulder.

Lilly felt a shock of emotion go through her from his touch. She hadn't ever been lifted up like this before. The pose was precarious but she felt safe with the 'Rock of Harold' below her and she could clearly see the whole scene. The troops marching and the crowd calling out but more powerful than it all to Lilly was the heady sensations of Harold's smell, his touch, the closeness of their bodies.

Lilly had figured out which one was James. She waved and he looked over at her. He kissed the air and blew it to her. Then his group entered the gangway and he was lost to them. More troops arrived and companies D, E and F were loaded before the SS Ascanius was full and the gangplank removed.

By now the deck of SS Ascanius was a mass of khaki clad humanity. They waved and cheered and sung marching songs but any attempt to differentiate one khaki coloured soldier from another was impossible. The troopship now started to pull away from the wharf.

Harold still had hold of Lilly and had not tired and she waved furiously.

The soldiers on the deck clung to any positions of vantage to get a last sight of the adoring crowd and those they loved. The group was still debating about which one was James when Lilly thought: 'this is the time for my little demonstration.'

She leant down to Harold and whispered: 'Excuse me but this could be a bit uncomfortable for you. It is just a bit of a promise I made to James.'

She started to take the rose blooms and throw them with all her might towards the boat. Her best throws were not spectacular. None of the blooms made the troopship, most fell in the water in between. The crowd before her parted to allow her better aim and still she was supported by the strong arms of Harold. With her last rose she hoisted it as high as she could and with all the effort she put into this magnificent fling, her hat band broke and the wind caught it pulling it from her head. The hat with the trailing red silk scarf was caught by the breeze, lifted in a thermal it went high into the air, spiralling over the ocean separating the departing boat from the cheering crowd. Many arms reached out from the deck of the troopship and it was finally caught by a khaki soldier. Lilly felt a connection and hoped that the soldier was James. The crowd roared in appreciation. Her red tasselled hat became a symbol for everyone on the wharf that morning, a bit of home would be going with the boys.

The SS Ascanius now swung gracefully into the river and then gradually turned her bow and steamed slowly out to Gage Roads. The group who were farewelling James Nelson now turned to leave.

They didn't stay to see the second troopship, the SS Medic be loaded with troops. They didn't witness the giant ships stay at anchor overnight before sailing next day to a rendezvous in the Indian Ocean with the rest of the fleet that had already left Albany the day before.

They had to wait for newsreels to show them, some months later, the 46 vessels, with 37 troop ships carrying 55,000 men away from their homes. These first ships were taking away the pick of the young men from Australia and New Zealand. These soldiers would establish the ANZAC tradition. These young lads were going abroad voluntarily to assist the mother country in upholding the cause of the King and Empire. How many would return and how many who would return would be able bodied, unscathed? This moment in history would change Australia forever.

The group walked silently, heads down, back to the car. All were wrapped up in their private thoughts, private grief and the outpouring of emotion had left them drained. As they approached the car Lilly realised that she was still being carried by Harold. Harold had known he was carrying Lilly the whole time, he just didn't want to let her know. He was enjoying it far too much.

War Comes To Australia
Absence Breaks The Heart Asunder

December 1914 - March 1915

Egypt

The flotilla of troopships carrying the fine soldiers of the 1st Australian Imperial Force including James Nelson, a Private in D Company of the 11th Battalion, landed in the Middle East on the 4th of December 1914. James was excited to exit the close confines of the ship. Nearly six weeks of slow sea travel, cooped up with hundreds of other men, was not an existence he relished. The draining heat of the tropics had made the daily routines of drill and army chores, a trial for many of the soldiers.

From day one James enjoyed army life. He was a natural in places where camaraderie was important. His good humour and friendliness meant that most young men related to him quickly. He was not keen to be an official leader. He did not like following rules himself so was none too keen on enforcing them on others, but his natural attributes made him an unofficial leader. He was laconic, a larrikin and of course his sporting ability made him popular; if you had James on your team you often won. And there were loads of sporting opportunities in army training camps. Long before company relationship experts invented team building activities, armies had worked out that groups bonded well if they played competitive team games and this is just what happened on the SS Ascanius. Besides the daily routine of drill, the soldiers wrestled, boxed and kicked their way across the ocean and James was in the midst of it all.

By December, James, like everyone on board, was now keen to be free of the vessel and have his feet walk firmly on dry land. The trip had not been without incident and two interesting events gave the soldiers something to write home about. (Giving the censors a field day unless confidential material be relayed.)

Firstly the progress of the fleet had been stalled for a while when word had been received that SMS Emden, a light Cruiser in the Imperial German Navy, had been spotted. The Emden had been creating havoc in the Indian Ocean shipping lanes. Discovering it in close proximity to the fleet was a major coup. Firstly, if it had discovered the flotilla first it could have wrought extensive damage and secondly, the flotilla had armed ships as part of their contingent equipped to engage the Emden in a fight.

Immediately, the light cruiser, The Sydney, left the convey and went in search of the enemy vessel. On the 9th November a battle ensued, that was later known as the Battle of the Cocos. The Sydney inflicted ruination on the Emden. The damage included extensive loss of life (134 were killed and 69 wounded, compared to only 4 killed on the Sydney), and the remaining German sailors were captured.

When news of this successful sortie came back to the fleet, the spirits of the soldiers in the troopships were buoyed. This was Australia's first success of the 1st World War. James like everyone on board drunk champagne to toast their good luck and the good aim of the gunners on board The Sydney. Each man, whether admitting to being superstitious or not, took this as a good omen for his own war outcome.

The second major event occurred on James' own ship. At 4am on the 26th November an alarm sounded across the boat. The soundly sleeping men had not needed the alarm, they had been rudely jolted from sleep (and some from their bunks) by the impact. Then a second violent crunch, with many later recalling the horribly chilling sound of ripping metal. The SS Ascanius had collided with the SS Shropshire. It was a dark night and the Captain had been negotiating a passage under very stormy conditions. Although they all felt extreme panic, this was their first real test as soldiers and none of the young lads was prepared to show even a glimmer of fear.

The Western Australian soldiers were ordered on deck, all donning their life belts and awaiting their instructions. Most thought their boat had been struck by one of the major new advances from the German Navy, the torpedo. They were all tense, anticipating the call to abandon ship. James was in turmoil, his thoughts swirling around, how the ocean would feel and whether there would be sharks or a large swell. He remembered that he would need to swim rapidly away from the boat before she went down to prevent the suction pulling him down with her. He pictured himself swimming in an oil covered sea and thought out how he would need to avoid the fire that would be burning over the surface of the ocean. James said a prayer and thought of his Mother. On the outside, James, like all the soldiers, showed no fear.

Thankfully this was not needed - tragedy had been averted. This had been a traumatic and potentially life threatening situation and although none of the lads would later admit it, they were all petrified. The ship had suffered a 20 foot gash and the decision that she was unseaworthy had seen many of the soldiers re-allocated to other troopships. Thus James found himself on the deck of the SS Euripides as they steamed across the Red Sea to the Port of Aden.

It was in Aden on December 4th, that the soldiers received their first mail from home. James immediately tore open his letter from Lilly. Before he devoured the news of home, he noticed that it was dated five weeks ago.

November 2nd 1914

Dearest James

You have only just left and I am already putting pen to paper. The Defence Department has said that any letters we post before the end of the week will be waiting for you when you arrive. It is funny to think this letter will be on a ship that will pass you on your journey. So at least you will have some correspondence from home when you get there.

Today was the most exciting day of my life. If it was like this for me it must have been unbelievable for you. The wharf and the road to

Fremantle was crowded. The papers are full of the excitement of it all and they say that crowds lined the railway line and cheered you all at every point along the way. Western Australia surely put on a wonderful show to say farewell to our finest young men.

From our spot on the wharf we could see you marching, you looked so proud. It is funny but being so short I couldn't see much so Harold Smith lifted me up. That is why you could see me above the crowd. Did you see me throw the roses and my hat get taken up by the wind? The hat thing wasn't meant to happen. (Mother was a bit cross as now I need to buy a new one.) I know someone on board caught it and my heart tells me it was you. I just wanted you to know that we were there for you.

Jack came along too - did you see him? Ever since your letter to him, he has been so much improved. I think he is over his sulking and he is ready to start living again. There are so many roles he can perform here that will help the war effort. Whatever you said to him really worked.

Now about those words on the verandah; I think we both need a few weeks to consider what we said. That moment is fixed in my mind and I have never felt such a connection with anyone before. I just need some time to sort out what I feel and whether we want to be tied by promises. At the moment my feeling is definitely YES. No definite promises but I could become Mrs James Nelson when you return.

But, I am being a bit presumptuous as you may want your freedom. After some months away, some lovely foreign lady may catch your fancy. Just remember our vow to each other is to let the other person know.

You said you wanted honesty and this letter does give you an insight into what I am feeling. Please write as soon as you arrive. I want to know everything.

Your devoted friend

Lilly Parrott.

James felt the warm glow a sweetheart's letter often brings to a homesick soldier. After only a few hours on shore he had returned to the ship which then moved to unload the troops at Alexandria. The soldiers had then been transported over the desert, a long, hot, dusty trip of 140 miles to Cairo. The trip had taken three days and it was only now, in the late evening, that James started his reply to Lilly Parrott.

December 12th 1914

Dearest Lilly

I have just had mail from home and I was overjoyed to receive a letter from you and one from Mother. Yes I too loved the send off - how exciting it all was. No, I couldn't find out who caught your hat. I saw it and thought how typical of you to make a statement like that. I wish I had caught it - then it would be my talisman and I would have cherished it. Still some lucky blighter has your colours. From now on I will always think of you as 'my lady in red'.

I hope you received my previous correspondence telling you about our trip and I do hope the censors do not slash it too much. We are now in our permanent camp in Egypt and I must tell you all about it. It is an extraordinary place.

Our tents are actually sited amongst the ruins of the pyramids. It is exceptionally beautiful. I lay down to sleep near the burial sites of the kings of the world's oldest civilization. In the afternoon my tent is actually in the shadow cast by the Giant Pyramid. The place is called Heliopolis.

Despite loads of rumours, there is no word about any Turkish advance upon the eastern frontier of Egypt. We thought that the enemy might be here to meet us but it seems that the Germans and Austrians have retreated from here like they have from so many other war fronts. They don't seem to have much stomach for any real conflict. This may turn out to be a very easy war.

Your fondest friend

James

James did not tell Lilly that he knew perfectly well who had her hat in his keeping. The 'Rosie Red Hat' yarn had developed into a famous story across the ship. A large number of the men on board had seen it and marvelled at how the hand of God (or some divine force in the case of non-believers) had steered the hat from the head of the lady with the red roses across the watery passage and into the arms of the ANZACs. True love will be triumphant over tyranny and distance. The story had now become folklore on the ship and across the fleet. They all translated this to be a sign that those who loved them at home would keep them safe.

James was very sure that the hat was Lilly's. He had watched her throwing the roses and when the hat had soared into the air, his heart had lifted. 'Something red,' he had asked and here she was sending him the strongest message: 'Come back to me - I love you'.

On the night while the SS Ascanius was still at anchor in Gage Roads, James had tracked down the lucky blighter who had caught the hat.

Pte Archie Smoots was a mean spirited bully before he enlisted and nothing had changed. All of a sudden he had been elevated to a status he had never been before. He was loving it. Quick thinking Smoots had soon spread the rumour that the lady of the red roses was his 'dear beloved Alice'. He was milking this for all that it was worth.

When James approached him that evening with his story and a request that he hand over the hat, Archie Smoots and his clutch of unpleasant little weasels gave him short shrift.

'Prove your claim or back off,' said Archie belligerently. James was more than a match for most single blokes in a sporting contest but he was more about speed and agility. Archie Smoots was a lug of a man; brute strength and not too much intellect. James had no chance of winning and so he did the smart thing, he retreated with honour (well at least with his nose unbroken). So the legend of the 'Rosie Red Hat' was entrenched with Alice being the lady and her true love the unpleasant, undeserved Archie Smoots.

Two weeks later, with no letters received from home, James tried to recall Lilly's face. He had the details right but the actual clear memory of her face was becoming a bit blurry. He was homesick as he sat down again to write:

December 25th 1914

Dearest Lilly

It is Christmas Day and we have all been given the day off - no drill and no training. Our Christmas dinner was exceptional. We had roast duck and loads of vegetables (some of these were a bit strange but they had managed to find some quality potatoes and the gravy was superb). This was followed by cake and fruit with pudding for dessert. We had a message from the King and all kinds of official messages from home. The spirit in the camp is excellent. We finished off the celebrations with a toast to absent friends and I of course thought of you and the family back home.

We are training really hard from 6am - 4pm every day. I think we are now a well trained and highly efficient fighting unit and I am sure we will convey ourselves excellently when we are put into battle. I am getting somewhat frustrated at not being put into action yet but I am sure it will come soon enough.

Last week we received an edict that we are all to cultivate moustaches! They said that this will give us a more 'Military Look'. So your soldier boy is now sporting a very impressive moustache - and yes it is tinged with red. I think I look very handsome.

I must tell you a bit more about this place.

The smell is amazing, it is so overpowering, spicy, rich and pungent. Some parts of the City look almost normal but you wander down little side streets and you are plunged back into a scene reminiscent of thousands of years ago. Artisans plying their trade, ladies wearing full Arabian dress riding on donkey carts - it all looks very biblical. It is like one long ceaseless picture show. Last week I saw the main street filled with camels as a caravan entered town after a trip across the desert. What a sight. The Desert Arabs, part of a tribe known as

Bedouins, were wearing colourful robes, had large curved swords on show and looked most fierce. Luckily they are on our side.

Mostly the Arabs seem to like the Australians, I think they like our money really as we have replaced the old tourists. They smile and greet us so politely but they are only too keen to rob us blind.

The first Sunday I was here I climbed to the top of the Cheops Pyramid and stared down at the lush, fertile valley of the Nile. The surroundings of the Nile are so emerald green and it snakes through the Sahara Desert which is brown and dry. Such a contrast. It is a great view from the top but it's very windy and dangerous. Some lads have lost their footing on climbs so I was very careful.

Last Sunday I joined with about half a dozen friends for a bit of a lark. We went wandering casually through the Temple of the Sphinx, each of us had a giant water melon. We had employed an Arab guide (Mustapha of course) who was patiently re-telling us his rote learned speech. Each time he said something impressive one of us hacked off a piece of melon, stuffed it in our mouth and then shouted some truly Australian utterance like: 'Strike me dead!' or 'Cor blimey!' We were saying these things while red mushy watermelon was gushing from our gobs. He did not know what to do. It was hilarious.

Anyway, I will finish this and get it in the mail this afternoon. I hope to have a letter from you in the next mail batch.

I remain your fondest friend

James Nelson

Nearly two weeks later James again wrote to Lilly:

January 12th 1915

Dearest Lilly

I do hope nothing is wrong. In this morning's mail despatch I received letters from Jack, Harold and my Mother but nothing from you. I can only assume you have been engaged in other activities and have been too busy to write. So I will just write a short note to let you know how things are going. We have been in Egypt for a month now. The drill is getting very monotonous and I just wish we were involved in something real. We've had some practice night raids, and had some amazingly long marches through the desert but now I think we are all ready for a battle. The Soldiers of the Australian Expeditionary Force are now tough, sinewy soldiers ready for combat. There is still no news about where we are to be sent though rumours abound. The top brass are getting stricter about censorship so I will just keep this light-hearted.

Last Sunday our company had organised a Melbourne Cup Camel race. It was very amusing. Now you have to know firstly that these beasts are not easy to ride. It is very uncomfortable and their gait is queer; you have to hold on for grim life. I have had a ride and this was only at a slow pace. I do not intend to get on one again.

We had 20 camels lined up with their skinny little riders perched on top. These boys look to be no more than about 7 or 8. It was very well organised and we had betting and sweeps. I put my money on 'Bag of Bones', a nasty looking brute, but he looked like he was capable of a good turn of speed if pressed. The bell went and these animals tore off around the hastily erected race track.

The young jockeys hit them with little leather hide whips and urged them ever faster. Huge clouds of dust came up all over us. They were so fast - the race was run at a flat out speed. We all yelled and called out encouragement to our respective beasts and I vow it was easily as exciting as a race at home. 'Bag of Bones' came second so I made a tiny sum on my wager.

So we do have some fun - but mainly it is drill and repetition.

I trust everyone at home is well. I miss you all terribly, please write soon.

Yours faithfully

James Nelson

The next batch of letters was not received until the first week of February 1915. James opened the letter from Lilly with excitement but also with some trepidation. It had been so long since he had heard from her.

December 30, 1914

Dearest James

I trust you are keeping well. I have only now received the letter you sent when you first arrived in Egypt. The delay does make it a bit tricky doesn't it? But we are hearing a lot about what is going on in the papers.

I am well and keeping very busy with war work. This seems to be the least I can do as they do not welcome women into the AIF. I have been seriously thinking about training as a nurse, this would mean that I too could do something real and tangible to help the war effort. You said that the only thing keeping me from enlisting in this war is that I am a woman!

This is a very difficult letter to write to you. I have wrestled for some time with my conscience and now I have determined to let you know the truth of my feelings. You did ask me to let you know what I was thinking at all times. I agree with you that I do not feel we should try to remain sweethearts while we are separated. That night on the porch I was touched. The profound emotion of that night overwhelmed me. But I just feel that I am not really ready for true commitment with anyone yet.

While I remain very fond of you, I no longer feel that we can be engaged or married which had been my plan prior to you leaving. I do wish to remain a loyal friend and to this end I will be sending you parcels of gifts to make your life as a solider as pleasant as possible. I also want you to feel that you can write anything to me - this is the mark of true friendship.

Please understand that I am as genuinely fond of you as ever - I just do not want either of us to be restricted by the bonds of promise.

So please accept this parcel I have prepared for you. I have included some socks and a balaclava that I knitted. I have also roused up some special gifts including some real Robur tea (your mother tells me that this is your favourite). I have included some jelly crystals so if you have some hot water you can make jelly and as you may be able to find this I have also provided some bonox soup for a cold night.

The chocolates are special ones and I have put in some cans of your favourite tobacco, Lucky Strike and some wonderful soap I purchased at the church fete last weekend. I also thought you could use a draught board and some playing cards to while away the lonely hours when you are not soldiering.

I have been very busy lately helping out at the Women's Church Auxiliary, packaging up gifts for soldiers at the front. You should have seen the sight at our receival centre in Murray Street the week before Christmas. Thousands of gifts all labelled up and ready to go. I believe that these (along with my package and letter to you) will be loaded onto the RMS Morea next week so hopefully you will receive this by late February. It will be a slightly late Christmas for you. At least the soldiers will have some understanding of how much we admire the brave boys who have answered the call to serve.

Are you enjoying Egypt? Have you had any time to go and see some of the sights? Are you remaining there or will they be sending you to the Western Front?

Did you receive the Christmas message The Women's Auxiliary sent to Egypt by telegraph? We had a reply yesterday reciprocating the greetings, so I trust you foot soldiers were all told about this. We were all thinking of you having Christmas, in a foreign land. I was so chuffed thinking that this message was going half way around the world and that you would hear our greeting on the very next day after we sent it.

Do they even celebrate Christmas in Egypt? Of course our saviour was from the Holy Land, close to where you are now so it must be a blessed land.

Your parents are keeping well. I went for a picnic last weekend with them, my brother Jack and Harold Smith. We had such a time together. The boys are such great company and get on so well together. The business side is causing your father some concern. With all of the ships diverted because of the war, commerce in the East has slowed considerably. The men were talking late into the night and saying they felt that we could just weather the storm until after the hostilities.

Harold has become a dear friend (and to think I only met him when you were leaving). You were right to tell me to trust him. He is stoic and so dependable. He speaks of you in the most revered tones - he holds you in great esteem.

Harold is still quite ashamed that his application to go to war was rejected. He is still determined to go and has resolved to re-apply to join the engineers where his myopia may not be such an issue. I think he will join you as soon as he is able.

Jack has recovered well from his illness and has finally regained some of his energy. He has now started working for your parents, in the sales side of the Sandalwood business. He has a real head for figures and he does enjoy the whole accounting side of the trade. He is talking about going into business himself in the future as a shopkeeper!

Harold Smith is still in the bush, currently working around Wubin and Dalwallinu. He is still arranging for the sandalwood to be transported down to Fremantle. He is still in love with the wide open spaces of the Australian countryside, so different to the township of Ipswich where he spent his childhood.

Harold is becoming fanatical about some of the new machines - he showed me a catalogue the other day with all kinds of tractors and engines in it. He believes after the war, bullock drays and horse drawn methods of transport will be a thing of the past. How the world is changing.

Please keep safe and don't let the Hun get too close. You are a very brave man to be doing this in service of your King and Country.

I remain your loyal and devoted friend.

Lillian Parrott

James was profoundly affected by Lilly's letter. In the stark loneliness of his tent, late in the night, he let the quiet tears of rejection flow. Silent lonely tears, home sick tears, heart sick tears.

Before he had left, James had spoken from the heart to Lilly; he had made certain not to tie her down, not to put restrictions on her, he had set her free. But that was meant to have bound her to him more strongly. Now she had accepted his words and she was taking him up on the offer. This was not how it was meant to happen.

None of his mates in the Army would have been able to guess that James was heartbroken. He retained his larrikin personality and his jovial approach to life was still there in spades. Perhaps if Harold or Jack had been there they would have been able to see - the perception that comes with true friendship. Perhaps with them he would have opened up and told them what he was feeling.

In Egypt there was no-one for James to share his pain with. Even in his letters he did not share his anguish at a love lost but there were some hints about his changed behaviour when he penned the following to Harold.

March 11th 1915

Dear Harold

Hello my friend. I do hope you have recovered from your disappointment at not getting into the Army. A rumour here is that the first lot were pretty rigorous in their selection and they have now become less stringent about things, so do have another go. You will get in I am sure. It would be great to have you here. I have not really developed true companionship with any of the mates I have here. They seem more like good time friends. Perhaps it needs battle and adversity to develop this - if so I am sure to have some before the end of this conflict.

I have spent the last few months in Egypt doing training. It is now getting really monotonous and I confess I am bored and itching to get into a real battle. The rumour around is that we are going to be shifted out soon to fight the Turks. Thank goodness.

Now a bit about Egypt. This place is hot and horrible. The Gypos are a nasty, thieving group of scoundrels. Every time you want to buy anything they try to charge you three times what it is worth. The food is inedible - it smells great but if you try to eat it, your mouth burns up. The whole place stinks too. They treat their animals and their women so badly. It is nothing to see a Gypo man laying into his wife with a stick!

The Australian troops are not too good at following orders and some blokes get up to all kinds of mischief. Now I have a bit of an admission - not something I am proud of but I had better come clean to you. Last week I joined with some of my mates to go into Cairo to find a bit of excitement. It is about ten miles into town and we were lucky enough to hitch in and we had the whole evening in there. The place was swarming with Allied Soldiers. Our crew went to a whorehouse and one of the blokes got into a right old argument with the pimp about the value of his whore. She was ancient and he wanted to charge 50 piasters. She had only been thirty piasters last week and hadn't been much good at that. The prossies and their pimps are always over charging and cheating. Plus most of the prostitutes are old bags full of syphilis and gonorrhoea. These blokes think they can charge what they like. Anyway this bloke gets really angry and starts throwing punches.

We were a bit liquored up and we started throwing stuff out of the windows. The Gypo pimps were screaming at us and trying to hide their money and valuables, the prostitutes ran for their lives. It was so funny. Most of them are really fat and have their blubbery stomachs on show (so they can do the belly dance more provocatively apparently). Their bellies were bouncing up and down as they ran passed us.

Our blokes then moved downstairs and trashed all of the shops in the vicinity, throwing all of their possessions into the street. Before we knew it, everyone was in on it and we had created a riot. Every whorehouse in the street had beds flying out of the windows. And then we all just went on a bit of a stealing spree. It went on for a couple of hours and I scored a couple of great souvenirs - a beautiful necklace and some wonderful silk scarves.

This is some compensation for all the times these thieves have cheated me since I have been here. What a lark. But we got into such trouble for it. They docked me three weeks pay and I had hardly any role in it. The English brass were mortified about our behaviour but I thought 'good on them'.

It just seemed like the right thing to do at the time. The Egyptian press wrote some pretty rude things too. Please do not pass this onto the others that I was involved. I am afraid they would all be a bit disappointed in me. I am so ashamed letting you know about this. You have been such a good role model to me and now I behave like this. But I do think the Egyptians deserved what they got.

The only good thing about Egypt was seeing the pyramids which were great. You can see this may have been the cradle of civilization but there is no sign of it now in modern day Egyptians. They couldn't build a brick outhouse let alone a pyramid!

So I must go now. Hopefully we will actually be in a real battle zone when I write to you next - not just a battle in the main red light district of Cairo.

So hopefully you are keeping well and in good spirits. Thank you for looking after my parents so well.

Your friend,

James

A whole letter with not one mention of Lillian! Subtle and slow changes had occurred in James and good friends would have seen that James was now a bit less compassionate, more ruthless, his heart had been broken and he had toughened up. James had lots of army mates and they may have noticed he was more keen to engage in some of the less reputable after hours activities. Suddenly instead of sightseeing, James was visiting the seedier side of town. He visited the brothels, started betting his wages and was more keen to be involved in the sly drinking sessions. He even enjoyed the 'hubble bubble pipes' in the Hash and Carpet shops of the seamy, non postcard part of Cairo.

James Nelson took a long time to get over the rebuff and slowly his memories of Lilly changed too. Memories formerly full of the emotions of love and nurturing were now tinged with a heavy slab of animosity. He had been rejected and that is not a nice feeling.

He did not write again to Lillian Parrott until he had left Egypt.

James did what blue blooded Australian males do with rejection; he took it inside himself and he hid it.

War Comes To Australia
At The Going Down Of The Sun

March 1915 - August 1915

Anzac Cove

When no official statements are made, censorship is strict and men are eager for news, then this is perfect for the incubation of rumours. And rumours were rife around the makeshift camp 10 miles from Cairo in late March 1915. The men were tetchy.

One of the most persistent rumours was that a large press of men was soon to be sent to the Dardanelles, an isthmus in Turkey. This theatre of war was seen as important as the Turks were locking in the Russian fleet. A huge multinational force of the allies was being gathered together for a full assault.

James Nelson was very keen to be part of any action and was overjoyed when the orders came through, with the message: 'we're off,' spreading like a bushfire across the camp.

By April 15th James Nelson was on a vessel steaming towards the Greek Island of Limnos, on the Turkish side of the Mediterranean Sea. There the vessel was to put down anchor and await further instruction. On their arrival, James was stunned to see the massive contingent of allied troopships waiting at anchor. Large British battle ships were already in action, unmercifully shelling the Dardanelles. To James, the might of the Allies was unassailable.

By the 24th of April all soldiers on board knew their instructions; all now knew they were going into action on the Turkish Peninsula and the attack was to occur at Gallipoli. It was scheduled for first light with the soldiers approaching the land using amphibious landing boats.

In the fading evening light, James used the adrenaline rush of pre-battle nerves to write his much belated letter to Lillian Parrott.

April 24th 1915

Hello Lilly

Thank you for your kind gifts, they were appreciated. Funny though the balaclavas and socks were not really that useful in Egypt or in Turkey where the weather is nearly always hot and oppressive.

My apologies for not writing over the last few months. I needed time to work out how I felt. I did receive your letter and understand that you do not want to be sweethearts any more. That was a bitter pill to swallow but it is best that you told me rather than let me build my hopes up. Perhaps when I get back I can convince you that you are wrong.

Please know that you are very dear to me, but I release you to follow your heart.

We have finally left Egypt and sailed across the Mediterranean Sea and we have come to the site of our first battle. Tomorrow at first light we are going to land on this beach. We are at a place off Turkey called Gallipoli. Apparently the Turks are holding this region and blocking the passage of the Russian fleet. It's all meant to be top secret but rumours spread really fast here.

It is beautifully calm, the sunset was amazing and there is a half moon just rising. I am writing this using the last rays of the setting sun - all lights have been strictly banned tonight so I need to be quick. It is quiet and still and so beautiful. I have a good feeling about all of this.

They reckon we should be able to clear them off the peninsular in about a week. I can't imagine that the Turks will be much good at fighting. They are probably as lazy as the Egyptians and running away will be their style no doubt. I will enjoy chasing them up the beach.

I am really excited to be finally in action after months of training and waiting around. It all looks so serene, hardly the place for a battle.

Now the sun has set, the hills have a look of menace and there is an eerie silence; somewhere within those hills lie our enemies. This boat has 3000 souls on board and I can't hear any noise. And we are only one of the troopships here. There is a fleet of us. The poor Turks will not know what hit them tomorrow.

Anyway, I must go now and get some sleep. I know you have asked to break up but I still hold your photo close to my heart. I am still really fond of you and fully intend to win you back when I return.

Yours sincerely

Ever yours

James Nelson

The events of April 25th are well documented. Many say that this day was the making of Australia. Some who knew him well would say that it was the breaking of Pte James Nelson.

James was full of pent up excitement when he lined up on the deck at 3am in the morning of the 25th April. A soft moon light revealed his companion soldiers as ghostly shadows, menacing with their rifles at the ready, all standing, silent sentinels waiting for the call.

James was mentally preparing for the ordeal. If he kept reciting the mantra he could keep the rising bile of fear at bay. Keep your rifle dry, hang on to your kit, wait for the command before firing, then run to the beach. Months of drill and steely determination meant that he was physically and mentally ready.

James' landing craft was ready to fill when the midshipman in charge held them up. One seat was broken. A last minute change was necessary.

'Pte Nelson stand down,' came the whispered instruction.

James watched as his companions entered the boat and it was lowered and launched out onto the black murky sea. The comrades he had trained with, practiced with, those he trusted and that trusted him, were off to war.

James was thrust back into the following group to clamber aboard the next available craft. As they set off onto a calm silent sea, James had the first feeling of total panic, he was going into battle with unknown and untried companions. One broken seat had robbed him of his best defence - his mates.

Up ahead the first boats in the snakelike convoy were getting closer to the dim and distant shore. Three flashed signal lights on shore gave an eerie sign that they were being watched. Suddenly some isolated gun fire indicated that the first boats had been spotted but nothing could be seen in the shadowy, early morning gloom.

'So the landing will not be a surprise,' James thought and he felt for the soldiers in the vanguard of the assault at Anzac Cove. 'They will have the worst of it, breaking through the defence,' he thought.

Now he could hear more sporadic gunfire and some screaming. But he was a well disciplined soldier. He blocked out all alarming sights, sounds and smells.

'Just concentrate on doing your part. If we all do our bit, the machine works and victory will be ours,' James muttered to himself.

As the boat crawled shoreward James took stock of his new companions in the alien landing craft. Directly in front of him someone was muttering the Lord's Prayer and sobbing gently. He looked to the right - as luck would have it he was sitting right near the bloke who had started the riot in Cairo.

'Perhaps if he had gone with the whore that night he might have been in the hospital ship with gonorrhoea and he would have missed all of this,' he thought with a wry smile. James hoped that he would hold his temper and not lose his head in the conflict ahead. Still he didn't know if he trusted such a bloke to fight well beside him in battle.

He glanced behind him and saw the unwelcome sight of the sweating, ugly visage of Archie Smoots, thief of Lillian's hat.

'Well I am certainly not surrounded by the cream of Australian humanity in this boat,' James thought to himself.

He felt the proximity to Pte Archie Smoots and knew that somewhere in his kit he carried his talisman, the hat with the long red silk scarf. The pang of love lost skewered through him, until his mental discipline brought him back to the challenge that lay only minutes away.

The roar of battle was now around him in earnest, in front of them and coming from behind too. In an instant their boat was in range. Rifle fire from Turkish snipers on the beach whizzed above their heads. James heard the whine and then felt the splash of a huge shell as it bommied into the water, so close to him he was smothered in the wash.

'That was too bloody close,' muttered the God fearing soldier in front of him.

The dawn light had finally arrived and the carnage in front was partially revealed through misted spray, gun smoke and water vapour.

'This is going to be tough,' James thought, though it is doubtful he had any comprehension of how tough it would prove to be.

The convoy was not unobserved. They were being watched, tracked and the time to pounce was upon them. Unseen and unheard by James or any of his companions, about two hundred yards from the silent ribbon of boats slowly winding towards the shore, a gunner in a submerged German submarine shouted with joy. He had launched a shell that would score a direct hit, he'd hit the bull's-eye. The shell he delivered exploded right in the middle of James' boat.

The explosion emulsified Lillian's Rosie Red Hat. It turned the whorehouse bully, the God fearing soldier and Archie Smoots into mince.

With one shot it obliterated his landing craft, killing all of his new found best buddies seated in the ill fated vessel.

The explosion also blew Pte James Nelson clear of the boat.

Regaining consciousness with the traumatising shock of hitting cold water, James quickly worked out what had happened. The explosion had deafened and disoriented him but he swum in a spiral motion to the surface.

In seconds he realised that he was being swamped. The waterlogged kit and his heavy trench coat, despite their importance, were pulling him down and he needed to go up. He wriggled from his kit letting it drop as a deadweight onto the sea floor of Anzac Cove.

'Oh my God, my rifle is soaked,' he mumbled as he struggled to right himself.

Free of the weight he found that he could swim and after twenty or so laboured strokes, his foot tapped the sandy bottom. It was shallow enough to stand. The light was clearer now as he waded through the garbage, debris and body parts that littered the water like unsavoury soup.

He pushed his way to the shore and then the enormity of the task and the delayed shock of the explosion overwhelmed him. Without the buoyancy of the water he realised his leg and foot was badly hurt by shrapnel. The leg would not support him. He dropped to his knees and then lay in the shallows, catching his breath, gradually recovering and assessing the situation.

Bodies were piled high on the beach. Bayonet fighting had been savage and Turkish and Australian soldiers lay side by side in grotesque, dirtless graves.

The beach in front of him was about 50 yards wide and then huge cliffs soared up into the morning sky. He gasped to see that the sun was rising over this foreign, unwelcoming and unfamiliar landscape. 'Sunrise ever brings hope,' he recalled but he had precious little of it here stuck in the centre of this diabolical holocaust.

He could see that some of the soldiers from earlier boats had made it across the beach and were slipping and sliding their way up the slate covered slopes. A few had reached the relative safety of a gully and were returning fire. As James lay he noticed enemy snipers were relishing the early morning light and were picking off any soldier now moving across the expanse of the beach. He could hear behind him the boom of enemy submarines torpedoing the reinforcement landing craft of the Allied soldiers following him. This had been the fate of his boat.

The landings were now to the south of him. Few soldiers passed him and those who did were too intent on survival and attack to hear the plaintive cries of injured comrades. He moved his foot and sharp pains coursed up his leg. He looked down and saw his uniform leg was ripped, ragged and stained with the bright red of a watery wound. He pushed back the torn cloth to see that a series of rat shot shrapnel wounds had peppered his leg. The boot was still intact but intense pain in his foot, told him that this was where his real injury lay.

'If I move from here, I will need to run and then climb the shale and get to the safety of the ridge,' James plotted.

'They will shoot me if I hobble. I have no ammunition, my rifle is wet and will jam if I try to shoot. So there is nothing for it but to lie here until it is safer or I can see how I can get to cover.'

James had not lost valour, he was just in an impossible situation. He lay on the beach, an immobilised spectator, as the war raged around him. He saw the valiant Australian troops storm up the beach. Three charges they made, each time more successful than the last. He saw them take the first ridge. He saw the Turks rally, coming at the enemy soldiers invading their land with fierce, patriotic zeal and grim determination.

The wounded soldier saw the incessant heavy guns of the Turks from their higher positions raining fire down on the beach and the Allies on the lower ridges. He saw death and agonised dying. He saw and felt the strafing of the bodies on the beach, time and time again particularly if any movement was detected. And he smelt and heard the foul odours and sounds of carnage all around him. He saw a lot but he was powerless to do much about any of it.

While he waited, James watched in horrid fascination as a severed eyeball rolled up and down with the gentle waves, another witness to the torment of Gallipoli Cove that morning.

James was not the only one alive on the beach that morning. He heard the agonising moans and strangled, gurgling death of a young solider not ten yards away. He wanted to call out some words of encouragement but no help was available so what words could he use? He stayed silent and let the young man die in cruel, solitary isolation, his blood staining the sand on this foreign beach.

Every hour as the sun rose higher James tested his foot; he willed it to be stronger so that it could carry his weight to safety. Shooting pains gave him no confidence that his predicament was any better.

In the early afternoon, an Allied cruiser started shelling the Turkish positions high on the cliff. James reasoned that the Turks had other things to think about and that this was his opportunity. He stood and took a step on his injured foot but immediately collapsed in pain. Frustrated tears ran down his face.

It wasn't until the sun was setting that the gunfire lessened.

'The sun's rays will be in their eyes,' he reasoned. He determined that now he must go. Silently he rose up and gingerly tested his foot. Hot knives of pain again raced up his leg but he had decided that it was not going to get any better. So he set off, loping, gorilla like, cavorting across the beach in a parody of agonised movement. His arms held him up when his foot threatened to give in.

When he hit the lose shale of the hillside he crawled, struggled and scrambled his way up until he reached the summit and collapsed into a gully. This was all accomplished as the last rays of golden sunlight passed, the daylight hours of the 25th April 1915 were done.

A welcome voice called to him: 'Hey Cobber, well done. You made it, we were all watching you and cheering your progress. Come and have a sip of water.' He had made it to safety, made it to the welcoming arms of mates. In war, it is really mates and not ammunition that saves you.

And that was James' first day at Gallipoli, he did not fire a shot, he lost his platoon and he was neither exceptionally brave nor a coward. But James survived and many others did not.

He was injured and should have received effective medical treatment. Sadly the provision of adequate medical services, like other organisational aspects, was incomplete and disorganised at Gallipoli. The top level administration failed dismally and the foot soldiers suffered from their incompetence.

Most soldiers who were saved in those first few days were saved by other soldiers and not by the medical teams who were hampered by the logistics of ineptitude. His new crew treated his wounds, cleaned out the sand and the rubbish and put iodine on the wounds. With the shrapnel cleaned and his foot wound bandaged, his cobbers told him to lay low for a while. He did and he survived.

With James' boat destroyed at the landing in the battle of Gallipoli, he had fallen, survived and arisen again. He had been adopted by another group of Australian soldiers, from the 16th battalion, part of the 4th Brigade. They welcomed him, nurtured him and he was content to stay with the new group.

He did not seek to find if any of his platoon survived or even to rejoin the remnants of other platoons in D company. There was no re-assignment to another section of the 1st Battalion after the initial carnage of the landing. This may seem unlikely to an army desk clerk in an office back in Canberra but it was very real in the mayhem on the battlefield of Gallipoli. Thus James missed the Battle of Lone Pine where his own battalion performed so valiantly. Instead he showed his bravery in other skirmishes and battles.

With no official reassigning, James was incognito in this location for some time. He was not listed as *Missing in Action* but he did not do anything to let anyone know where he was either. He had morphed into a battle veteran, a person who it seemed, had always known war and did not hanker for peace, home or peaceful pursuits. He risked his body with no thought of death or injury. He wasn't that brave, he just no longer cared that much about his life.

He made no new mates, just acquaintances in the new platoon. None of them knew him well, but they all felt that they could trust him to look after them in conflict. The Pte James Nelson on the day after the Gallipoli landing had changed but late at night James still thought of home and dreamed of a life where the scream of exploding shells didn't pierce every sleeping moment.

James did not receive any letters from home; his loved ones wrote but the letters did not find him. He just didn't want the news of the life he couldn't have any more. He had become battle hardened.

In the four months after the landing, James only wrote one letter home from Gallipoli. The evening sun was setting and, despite himself, he was seeing the similarity of this view to the sun setting over the water at Cottesloe Beach off Perth. The rays bathed the paper in a gold sheen as he wrote.

August 2nd

Dear Harold

I am so envious of you. When we both went down to enlist and I was accepted and you were rejected I was cock a hoop. I felt so glad that I was going to war, the big adventure. I saw the look of disappointment on your face and felt really sorry for you. Now this joy has turned to dust and ashes.

This place is hideous. Gallipoli is a cursed place. We have now been bunkered down on the beach head for four months and have not gained any ground. And thousands of good young blokes have lost their lives in this senseless quest. It all seems so stupid.

There are mutterings that this was a big mistake. Some say we landed in the wrong place, others say that the Turks were prepared for us. But no matter what the story from up top, the reality down here is that we are involved in a senseless war of inches. We fight and win a position and the next day we retreat and give it up. The next day we take it again. And the land we are fighting over is barren with a few straggly pine trees and some nasty gorse bushes with horrid thorns. I am sick at heart with the futility of it all.

The landing back in April was the start of this nightmare - everyone in my boat was slaughtered before we even made land. The boat took a direct hit and I was the only survivor. I was thrown into the water and soon realised I had to throw off my kit or I would have drowned. I had to swim through a sea of red; bodies, limbs and torsos all around and the continuous splash of shelling in the water. When I got to the beach I just lay there. At first I thought of moving but soldiers all around me were just being mown down. They were just using us for target practice.

I lay there for hours pretending to be dead, my leg had shrapnel wounds and I just couldn't move. Harold I was not scared but I was impotent to do anything about it. The ferocity of battle and my insignificance in changing the outcome, was a dispiriting revelation.

Soldiers coming in as reinforcements moved passed me. Some made it 20 yards, some 100 but many seemed to be shot.

Crabs crawled all over me, horrid, shiny flies buzzed and crawled over my flesh and all the while I lay there. Everywhere people were screaming, moaning and rifle fire strafed the beach.

I had no rifle and I could see everyone who was moving was being shot at.

By dusk I thought it was safe and I just ran for it. My cursed leg would not work so I scrambled along using my arms to hold me up when the pain got too bad. I made it to the safety of a gully. I do not know how but I found my way to another unit and they took me in. The new group patched up my wounds and by the next week I was ready to pay them back with my dedication.

They also re-kitted me with a dead man's pack and rifle. I now have the life and memories of a dead man. He was Wilfred Stone and was married to Violet with a young three month old daughter named May. He liked cocoa and liquorice and was an accountant from Nedlands. He had a letter to his wife in his pack which I sent off to his bride when I was able. If I ever return I will go and see Violet and thank her - Wilfred's pack helped my survival. I stole his memories, his letters from home gave me a chance to escape for a while to a happy place.

But perhaps I will not go and see her - my crime is too great and I doubt she would understand my desperate, insane need to know that somewhere life is normal.

I lost all my souvenirs; my letters, my gifts from home, even my memories have gone. I feel like the James Nelson you know is dead. I am just a hollowed out shell - the husk of a cocoon after the butterfly has long gone.

How the hell am I ever meant to forget all of this and recover even if I do get to go home? I am not wounded on the outside but my soul has hemorrhaged. Any faith I had is gone. No God I want to believe in could allow Gallipoli to happen.

I am sick, apathetic and hungry and when I sleep I just dream about blokes dying.

Tomorrow we are being pushed into the fray again to take Hill 971. This hill is so unimportant no one could even think up a proper name for it. This is horrid to say but I do not mind if I cop it tomorrow. I just think that the dead amongst us are lucky - they are no longer part of this lurid, brainless horror story.

Please do not pass this letter onto anyone else. These outpourings are for your eyes only. If those I love, knew the horror of this place it would make my ordeal even worse. Be strong and look after everyone. If I do not come home please take care of my folks.

Plus I gift you the love of Lillian Parrott. She did not say so in as many words but I can tell she has moved on from me. She wrote to me about stopping being sweethearts and I have worked it all out. I do not feel any bitterness towards you or her. She would

not want the man I have become anyway.
Sorry mate but my life has turned to hell.
Your friend
James Nelson

James did not write any more letters but one was written on his behalf. The letter from Captain Wilbur H. Eweing was sent three days after the battle to take Hill 971.

6th August 1915
Dear Mr and Mrs John Nelson
We regret to inform you that Pte James Ogden Nelson of the 16th Battalion 4th Brigade of the Australian Infantry Forces, was killed in action in the battle to take Hill 971 on the Gallipoli Peninsular.
James' death was instantaneous and he did not suffer in anyway. The Company was taking part in an attack and your son volunteered to go in an advanced team which moved against the enemy. Your son was killed in the first thrust of the attack. This group's brave action allowed for a diversion so the rest of the Company could advance.
The attack was a success and the hill was captured from the enemy.
His body was later carried from the action by his companions and he was buried that afternoon.
He now lies in a soldier's grave, where he fell on the Gallipoli Peninsular, surrounded by his comrades and other brave soldiers who have died in this theatre of war.
We are proud to announce that he has been awarded a Distinguished Service Order, posthumously, for his exceptional bravery. This has been mentioned in the dispatches from the front on the 5th August 1915.

The soldiers of the Company deeply sympathise with you on your loss. His effects will be posted to you.

Your son James was a brave soldier and always did his duty. He has now given his life for his Country and his King.

We all honour him, and I trust you will feel some consolation in remembering this.

In deepest sympathy.

Captain Wilbur H. Eweing

4th Brigade

AIF

When that letter was received and the *Killed in Action* list posted in the West Australian Newspaper of 10th August, there was sorrow across many homes in Perth, Western Australia. James was a well loved and widely admired young man with huge potential, that sadly now would not be reached.

Jack and Harold felt the lonely anguish of losing their best friend. For Jack, there was shame. If he had been there too, a comrade in arms alongside him, he would have saved him from his destiny. If only fate had been kinder.

For Harold, there was the nagging doubt that he had not tried hard enough to convince James not to go to war. When he received James' last posthumous letter he was haunted; the carefree, laconic chum of his memory had been grievously altered by his war experience.

Harold did not share the contents of this grievous correspondence with anyone.

Lillian wore black and withdrew from the world. All believed Lillian had lost her sweetheart and thus she was pushed into a role - the grieving love. She renounced frivolity, gaiety and laughter and adopted the responsibilities that come from being a lady in full mourning. However, she had not spoken about her last letters to James to anyone, so her grief was magnified by guilt that her decision had somehow exacerbated his death.

But most significant was the absolute, nightmare loss suffered by Ada and John Nelson. The gaping loss only a parent knows when their only child is taken, far too young, and they need to face the horror of the many empty years ahead.

Rest In Peace, Pte James Nelson.

All Wars End 1916 - 1918
Molly Dooker

March 16th, 1916

Leeds, England

Triangles are the basic building blocks of many structures because they can bear huge loads; they are considered the strongest shape because a triangular structure subject to strong forces doesn't collapse. Clifford's triangle gave him this support and didn't collapse many times between 1910 and 1916.

Clifford was quite content as a worker in the boot factory. As his Mami had predicted, he didn't need literacy to punch holes in shoes and he liked the repetition of the work.

He was an automaton - and could perform his role without emotion.

His immediate supervisor, the foreman Joseph Blootle watched over him protecting him from the pack of older boot makers always ready to 'give a bit of curry' especially if the culprit was weak or vulnerable.

It wasn't so much that Joseph Blootle cared about Clifford but he did fancy his Mami and when his Da's TB infested lungs finally ran out of puff, Joseph established himself as Mami's fancy boy.

Mami didn't let Joseph Blootle move into her home.

'Come on Mami, why don't you just get hitched with Joe. He's crazy about you and you need a new man,' Albert had jibed. 'You're still a bit of a looker and that Joe can't stop looking.'

Mami had a new swing to her step now that Da was dead and buried. Her hair was still glossy and black and she smiled more than frowned. She looked glowingly at her three boys with a look of whimsy on her face.

'Why do I need a new man when I have you three fine men in my life?' she explained proudly appraising Albert, Clifford and Young William in turn as she served extra large helpings of her wonderful Castilian stew to her boys.

'Now don't think I'm going to let Joseph just swoop in and take everything I've worked for all my life. I've tried the marriage thing and look what it got me, black eyes and busted teeth. No thank you very much. I did not like marriage one little bit.'

Mrs Hulme, aka Rosa Kujawski, the Spanish dancer twirled around and snapped her fingers high in the air, reminiscent of castanets. A radiant smile lit up her face.

'I am free. Why would I want a man trying to run my life? I have inherited my house and my boys are all turning out just fine.'

'I am quite happy to have a fine gentleman take me to the Malvern Picture House in Beeston or walk up to Cross Park Flatts and listen to some sweet music under the bandstand. Joseph is just right for this. But if he thinks I am going to give up all of this to marry him he is very much mistaken.'

Clifford smiled while he listened to his Mami. She was more like the Castilian Princess in the sepia picture on the dresser now than she used to be when Da was around.

Clifford had grown somewhat in confidence and although his family realised that he was not 'right in the head', with the coaching of Albert and the encouragement of Mami and Young William, Clifford was becoming a lot more sociable.

'You need to look people in the eye Cliff,' Albert had said, 'and when they ask you a question just answer them. You don't need to tell them too much. I know you don't want people getting inside you but it is good manners to just let them know a few things. And smile when people talk to you. It'll make people like you better and that is good.'

'Watch Young William. He is a natural, he charms people, gives them a big smile and his eyes watch them. He just knows instinctively how to do this. For you it is going to be much tougher. You have to learn how to get on with other people.'

Albert was a patient teacher and he coaxed and cajoled Clifford along. Teaching him the skills to live an ordinary existence.

'Coping when your triangle of trust isn't with you,' Albert called it.

With daily lessons and encouragement, Clifford had grown from an angst riddled ten year old consumed with inadequacies to a 16 year old who functioned and looked normal.

'But you're still a bit stoopid,' Young William told him with a grin.

Clifford liked routine and the boot factory gave it to him. He started at the same time every day and sat at the same bench, opposite the same men and the breaks for smoko and lunch occurred exactly when he expected them too. The smell of leather made Clifford's insides feel good. Home was good, work was good and life was good for him in the first few months of 1916.

In the boot makers' workshop the cacophony created by scores of boot makers hitting and tapping was bliss to Clifford as it stopped the need for conversation and although he had now learnt the rules of conversation, he never really saw the need for it. The risky times were the breaks. But Clifford had found that if he pretended to listen to the others, smiling at them as they talked and had a cigarette with them, he could get through most situations. Most of the others thought he was a bit simple, but they liked him well enough. Cliff was always good for a loan, he was free with his ciggies and could be trusted to cover for them if they had to leave their posts or spent a bit too long out the back.

Clifford had now worked at Mason and Family Boot Makers for six years. When he had been evicted from school prematurely, the family had pretended the 10 year old could pass as a 12 year old. And this was old enough to do a man's job. The small lie the family had told to get him into the business was now cemented as truth.

By 1916 Clifford was registered as an 18 year old on the company's official pay book. His body size reinforced this lie. He was tall and well muscled and his Spanish ancestry had come out in his lush, dark hair and his adult growth of facial hair. By 16 he had a full moustache and Clifford had a four o'clock shadow around his jaw line every day by knock off time.

He was pleasant looking especially when he smiled with brown, cheerful eyes and a naturally tanned complexion. He still frequently adopted the dopey look of his childhood but as a man this was often identified as being disinterested and aloof.

Although the war raged around them and privations and rationing were common, the Hulme household in early 1916 was quite content. The war had not really managed to sneak its tentacles into their family unit. Young William was still at school and Albert at 18, still living at home and very much the head of the Hulme family, had no intention of succumbing to coercion to go and fight for King and Country.

Albert was working at the Barnbow Munitions factory, a convenient tram ride from their home, as a supervisor overseeing a host of workers producing 10,000 shells per week for use on the Western Front.

'Better to make 'em than take 'em, I reckon,' Albert joked.

This was considered urgent war work and up to this time Albert had been able to resist all pressure on him to enlist.

'My war is right here, keeping peace on the home front,' Albert said.

The amazing appointment to the Barnbow Munitions factory had been conjured up two years before. 'Albert J. Hulme, bearer of jersey number 36,' was a talented footballer on the playing list at the Leeds City Football Club (a predecessor of Leeds United). When the Barnbow Munitions factory was established, a senior administrator at the club had found positions at the factory for some of the better players so that their talent was 'not squandered in the trenches'.

Albert was well pleased with this turn of events. As a man, in a place where young able bodied men were rare, he was immediately offered a senior supervisor role. Barnbow Munitions also had a staff of over 100, most of whom were young ladies in varying degrees of eligibility. A perfect location for a lusty young 18 year old with a Latin predilection for a smorgasbord of young women.

So Albert, who had no appetite to go to war, was able to play football and date fine ladies; his life was just dandy.

This also suited Mami who held her Spanishness as a badge of honour at this time and maintained that she, like her home country, was neutral in this war. She had also seen bandito raids in her childhood and had no wish for any of her boys to be slaughtered unnecessarily.

Only one thing shadowed their existence at this time. Clifford had started to develop what the family referred to as 'black moods'. These were irregular up until he was 16 when they started to occur more often. Mostly they came on in the evenings with Clifford protected from his demons, secure in his home sanctuary. Clifford just hid and waited until the madness passed him by.

Mami would let Joseph Blootle know that Clifford couldn't be there and he would cover for him at the factory. Luckily most of his black moods had come over him at night and only once had he missed any work time.

Clifford could feel when a black mood was coming. He would have violent headaches, would not be able to sleep, and his mind would be filled with frightening and realistic dreams in which he would suffer horribly. Because he could sense when they were coming, his trust triangle would protect him from the effects and aftermath of his blackness. The rest of the world hardly noticed there was anything wrong.

On March 15th 1916, the routine at Mason and Family Boot Makers changed. A young attractive female, Mrs Molly Williams, started work on the floor, right opposite Clifford Hulme.

At 8.15am he looked at her and was struck with a lightning bolt. She was the most beautiful woman he had ever seen.

She was short with mousy blonde hair and her deep set eyes concentrated powerfully on the leather she was holding. Molly's face was downy soft with pink hued cheeks. She was dressed in a practical war crinoline dress of dark blue.

Molly was not going well. She looked exasperated, and as she worked her neatly coiffed hair sprung away from the hair clips to form a golden frizz around her face. She would clumsily pick at the boot leather wrenching it into place and attack it viciously with the hammer. Then she would scrutinize her work and immediately remove the tacks and start again. To add to her difficulties she was left handed and the work station was set up for a right handed person. Everything was around the wrong way for her.

The supervisor Joseph wandered past a couple of times, gently guiding her and subtly helping her out by adding a few precision hammer blows. He replaced her botched boots with ones that only had to have a few more tacks, so it looked like she had at least made some progress. Molly looked up at him and rewarded him with a relieved, appreciative smile.

When Joseph moved off she grabbed a half completed boot and finished nailing in the last ten tacks. She held it up like a premiership trophy and looked over directly at Clifford. Her voice muttered a triumphant, 'Yes I did it!' though the sound was swept away amongst the noise of the factory and she gave Cliff a friendly, beaming smile. Cliff was filled with the warm radiance that only a pretty woman's smile can create.

The conversation at morning smoko was full of the changing work environment. Five men huddled around the stove, chain smoking to relieve the nicotine urge and the icy fingers of cold. Clifford sat at the end - slightly apart.

To a casual observer he was part of the group but it was only the ritual of smoking and sipping the tea that he participated in, the conversation he always left to others.

'What we doing having a female boot maker on the floor?' scowled

Abraham Jones a nasty, cantankerous codger with a smelly coat and a nasty way of spitting phlegm out of the side of his mouth as he smoked.

'Surely this is a man's job and how can a little bit of a girlie hope to keep up,' chimed in Benjamin Sparks in agreement.

Clifford felt a surge as protective juices flushed through him. He didn't like the idea of anyone criticising his vision of loveliness. He glanced at Benjamin Sparks who he had never really looked at before. The man resembled a large lizard, licking his mean lips and drooling appreciatively. Clifford looked away, disturbed - but he kept his peace.

'Well things are tight all over. There are just no men to fill positions anymore,' explained the reasonable voice of Joseph Blootle.

'This is happening all across Leeds. With so many men going off to war, employment vacancies all over town are being filled by females.'

Joseph's reasonable words and tone calmed Clifford and he took a long drag on his cigarette to further ease the knot of tension that had formed in his gut.

'Well what's to stop them staying here and taking over our jobs. Before you know it we'll have women all over, crying when they bang their fingers. Not to mention that they'll work for cheaper rates than us men so the big bosses may be inclined to give them our jobs,' bleated Abraham Jones. 'I for one don't want her here or any more of her kind. Women should stay at home. The workshop is a man's world.'

Benjamin Sparks joined in with a saurian hiss, ' Shhh. Look she is probably no good at the job but I am very glad to have her here. I think it is great to have a pretty bit to look at when the sight of the boot I am nailing gets a bit too much like dried out cow hide.'

'If the bosses want to provide us with en-ter-tain-ment then I am all for it.' He smiled with darting, callous eyes, a furtive look that hid smutty thoughts and no honourable intent. He stretched out the word entertainment so that it sounded filthy. Clifford felt sick. Mami would have boxed his ears for what he was thinking, Clifford thought.

Joseph again took the floor. 'Don't worry men, these women know their place. When the soldiers come back victorious, they will all happily pick up their home duties like they have always done. None of them really wants to work - it is just in this time of grave need they have filled the breach. It is ridiculous to think that any of us could ever be replaced by a woman!' Joseph exclaimed.

At this comment even the pathetic, inept Abraham Jones smiled, his belief in the divine superiority of males, even pathetic ones, had been reinforced.

'Plus Molly's husband has been killed on the Western Front so she needs another chance, poor child. And you Benjamin, make sure you treat her like a lady,' said Joseph, coming down hard as the foreman, keeping the peace and maintaining decorum.

As they shuffled off back to their desks the old boot makers were satisfied. It had been explained that Molly was not a threat. Although they wouldn't actually welcome her, they wouldn't give her a hard time either.

Molly came back into the workshop and took up her seat. She had hidden herself away through the break time, afraid in case the underlying hostility she had felt earlier, surfaced causing an unpleasant scene. Plus it was not decorous for a lady to be with smoking men. She had taken the respectable alternative and stayed out of sight.

Clifford looked at her again and was again smitten, his gut was still churning and to cope he did what he always did, he got stuck into his work and took out the frustration and passion on the tacks going into the next set of boots.

Clifford had nothing against females, he loved his mother and Albert was often out walking with a lovely lady on his arm. These women had nearly all been kind to him but had not paid him too much attention and he had been able to ignore them. But Mrs Molly Williams was different. She was beautiful and Clifford may have been a bit dim but he still had all of the urges God had given to young males.

Clifford was powerfully attracted to Molly and for the first time ever he was distracted at work. At lunch time Cliff did not stay with the group; instead he moved out to the outer stove. This was a less attractive place to sit because of the smell coming across from the leather tanning sheds out the back. Cliff was already seated near the stove when Molly Williams drifted over towards him. She was female, new to the place and not really accepted. Molly could sense that Cliff too was not really accepted, they were a good match.

'Hello I'm Molly,' she started. 'I've been watching you this morning, you are so good at what you do. The craftsmanship on your boots is excellent. I feel like I am all thumbs at the moment and I don't know if I will ever get the hang of this.'

The conversation lay like billowing smoke between them. Clifford tried to search in his mind for some lesson from Albert about this one. What should he do - smile? Answer her? But he didn't want it to be over, he wanted her to stay speaking to him and he didn't know how to do this - he only knew how to stop conversations.

Clifford smiled at her and met her eyes. They were blue green and she was looking straight at him. For a while he got lost in those eyes. The rise of panic was coming from deep within him - bile was rising, his head was thumping but he also felt euphoric.

'Just answer her calmly,' Clifford determined, desperately seeking for the right key to make this work.

'I am Clifford. I have been doing this job for six years. It gets easy when you have done it lots of times.' He had answered, the words had come out. Jumbling and tumbling and finally fitting into a neat sentence that seemed to work. And just in time he remembered to smile and he remembered to ask her something. Albert had said that this was how you kept a conversation going.

'Would you like to sit down here? It's warm near the stove.'

Molly sat and she seemed to be content with silence for a while.

She opened her lunch staring at the bread and cheese on her lap.

Relief was surging over him, he had got over the first hurdle. She was sitting near him. Now for the next step. This would be the first unprovoked question to someone who was not in his triangle of trust that Cliff had ever asked.

'Why did you get a job here?' Cliff asked Molly.

Had the words toppled out too quickly bouncing into each other? Had he got them in the right order? Was his voice a bit squeaky?

Molly did not seem to have noticed that these words were in any way strange and she started to answer him in her warm and sweet, lady voice.

'I had to get work, I am on my own and have no means of support. This company was not looking for any female workers but my husband had a friend who is the son of the owner, so I asked him and he said I could have a 'try out'. I thought it would be like needle work. How wrong can a person be!' Molly's voice had a soft lilt. She sounded amused as she recalled and then rationalised her inept efforts over the morning.

Her voice then went deeper, her eyes looked down as she continued:

'My husband died a few months ago. He was shot at Ypres in October. A stupid place, somewhere in France, I cannot even pronounce it. They wrote to me after he was shot and told me it was just a minor flesh wound in his leg. I thought he would be all right. Anyway they decided not to evacuate him back here but to keep him in a field hospital at the front. Apparently the wound got really badly infected, gangrene I think they said. They chopped his leg off in early December and he died a week later. I received the telegram on Christmas Eve.'

Clifford looked as Molly sat statue like but with a small tear rolling down her cheek.

'A great Christmas Present - widowhood and destitution at 17! My parents had refused permission for me to marry so we had run away. Now they will not take me back. So now I am all alone and it looks like I had better get on with my life.'

No more words were needed. She coughed lightly, looked down at her lunch and started nibbling her bread and cheese. They sat together eating their lunch in pleasant silence, bonded by the enormity of her story. As they finished their food, they moved closer to the warmth of the stove and Cliff lit a cigarette. Both were unaware of any other workers and ignored the unpleasant vapours coming in from the tanning rooms. This was companionship and Cliff liked it a lot.

One of the supervisors walked past and commented on the two clustered near the fire: 'No hanky pancky at work you two. We're here to make boots for the trench foot inflicted soldiers at the front. So you young people need to keep focussed on your work.'

Clifford wrestled with this for a while - should he respond? No, he thought, I should do what I always do. So he stood with no more comment to Molly and he went back to his work bench and started on his work. Repetitive work, loud hammering noises stopping any conversations and dampening the thoughts swirling in his brain and the sensations flooding his body.

Three times during the afternoon Cliff looked up and saw Molly watching and smiling at him. She was going a lot better and had actually completed a couple of half decent pairs of boots. Her smiles made him feel good but he was confused; his body was giving him weird signals and he didn't know how to cope. These things were not meant to happen at work. His head thumped with frightening daydreams crowding into his thoughts.

Twice he saw the slithering snake Benjamin Sparks stop at Molly's desk and lean towards her as he spoke some vile comment. Molly did not look comfortable with his attentions. Clifford could not hear their conversation but he felt a protective urge.

When the siren went at the end of the day Clifford looked up from his last pair of boots and saw the leering face of Benjamin Sparks invading his space. He leant in towards Cliff, grabbing at his shirt near his neck and hissed:

'Back off Buckko. I saw her first and I'm not going to stand by and watch some little spic, loony ruin my chances. Why would you think that someone like Mrs Molly Williams would be interested in a little creep like you?'

His eyes were filled with dark hatred and his words stabbed into Clifford. Cliff's mind filled with red squealing and he saw Benjamin advancing on him, a giant Minotaur hovering before devouring its prey.

'Protect yourself. Destroy it!' Cliff's inner voice screamed.

There was no sanity in what came next - just innate response to blind terror. Clifford grabbed the hammer on his bench and brought it up hard hitting into Benjamin's flesh.

Immediately Benjamin released his hold on Cliff and staggered backwards. 'You bastard, you frigging lunatic, you've broken my shoulder!' Benjamin reeled back screaming obscenities and nursing his injured shoulder.

'Break it up. Break it up,' roared the authoritarian voice of Joseph Blootle, arriving on the scene in moments. He reached down and calmly removed the hammer from the quivering hand of Clifford Hulme. Clifford was still hunched at his desk; unseen horror etched his face into a contortion of pain.

'You can't hit people like that Cliff - what is wrong with you?' boomed Joseph. His voice, although raised, was trustworthy and familiar and brought him back into the moment.

In a flash Joseph had taken in the scene. Clifford was shaking and his eyes with pupils dilated were darting wildly, looking for a safe exit. Joseph's steady, strong, hands on both of Cliff's shoulders anchored him to his seat. Joseph's large body also formed an unbreachable physical barrier to keep the warring parties apart.

'What were you doing threatening him anyway?' said Joseph turning towards the angry Benjamin who was still squealing and filling the air with profanity.

'I was just warning him off Molly. The guy's an idiot,' spat back the injured viper.

'You need to watch yourself. You go threatening folk then of course they will retaliate. You may both lose your jobs over this. At the least, you will probably both have some pay docked for your stupidity. Now Benjamin get out of here.'

Benjamin skulked out of the workshop, holding his battered shoulder still. He had lost face and dignity and he would never have any luck with the desirable Mrs Molly Williams now. This fact, more than the injury, hurt him badly.

Joseph waited for Benjamin to leave. He looked at the man in front of him. He had calmed, his breathing was now becoming deep and regular and his eyes had lost their glaze of madness.

Joseph saw in Cliff's face the lovely features of his darling Rosa. He felt a powerful surge of compassion for this troubled but likable youth. He had a man's body but had not developed all the checks, balances and controls that usually come with adulthood. Joseph had sworn to Rosa that he would protect Cliff and now was the time to repay the promise.

'Look Cliff, I do not know what he said to you but you could have really hurt him. You are very strong and without control you could do someone a real damage. You need to work out how to make sure your anger doesn't get the better of you.' Joseph spoke to Clifford in a comforting manner.

'Now Cliff I want you to go straight home. I will fix things up here.'

Joseph escorted Clifford out of the building, calmly but with protective determination. Cliff staggered into the gloom making his familiar way home through the murky haze of madness and recrimination.

Sometime later, when full darkness blanketed the factory and when everyone else had left the building, a frightened Mrs Molly Williams emerged from the black shadows. This was her first uncensored experience of the real world of men. She hastily grabbed her things and timidly left the building.

She did not look back.

All Wars End 1916 - 1918
Perfect Soldier

March 15th - July 2nd, 1916

Leeds, England

The journey home after his fight was an ordeal. The approaching menace of a black mood was hovering and Clifford was deeply afraid. This shouldn't happen to him on the street, he needed to be at home in safety, not out here vulnerable and alone. Clifford was convinced that the people on the street were watching him, judging him; he believed that they had all seen the fight and they knew he had done something terrible. He shied away from people, hiding in the alleyways, freezing until the way was clear. Accusatory eyes followed him all the way home.

Clifford was shaking violently by the time he burst through the front door and Mami just had time to steer him to his bed and put the curtain around him to give him his privacy.

Cliff had panicked at work; he had hit that man with a hammer. The thud of the hammer into Benjamin's flesh had created a visceral pain and now his mind had taken up the fight. Over the next 12 hours Clifford rocked on his bed, muttering threats to foes that no one else could see. He smoked compulsively and paced the floor; sleep didn't stand a chance. Cliff's day dreams magnified the attack. He shivered and sweated, frightened by the gripping fear that had overcome him.

Mami, gently soothed him, talking him though his nightmares. She fed him broth and stayed with him as he fought his demons. Reliable Joseph came over and told his Rosa what had happened at work. He watched as his vibrant beauty was overcome with concern for her son. This was no place for a beau. Joseph left.

Albert and Young William came home, worked out what was happening and then stayed away. This level of insanity was too much for the brothers.

This attack lasted for 50 hours. This was by far the blackest mood Cliff had ever experienced and he was not able to leave the house for three days. On the last day, Clifford's periods of lucidity had increased; he was mortified at his violent response to Benjamin Spark's goading. As his sanity returned he was overwhelmed by guilt and recrimination and he thought long and hard about Joseph's words of guidance. He vowed that he would keep his anger at bay.

Albert had returned home and used the episode as a warning. Clifford needed to develop self control.

'Learn to walk away when you get angry. You can always find something to punch that doesn't bleed. You are too strong to get caught in punch ups - you'll kill someone if you land a punch. Plus look at what happens to you afterwards. This mood that struck you down came because you did the wrong thing. And you know it. So be smart Cliff and don't get violent - not ever.'

Albert himself was a keen pugilist but he kept his punches within the ring. Albert also knew when to stop punching and he never fought when he was angry. Memories of the damage his Da had inflicted on others were seared into his conscience and he worried about how this would manifest in the adult Clifford Hulme, who had been so brutalized as a child.

Young William just said, 'if you're gonna hit someone do it quick and then run away before he hits you back.' Great advice from a street fighting 12 year old.

So on the 19th March Clifford returned to Mason and Family Boot Makers fully prepared for his punishment. He walked in, sat at his work bench and started his work like he had for the last 6 years. He waited for someone to say something. But no-one did, the other boot makers looked at him, nodding a welcome back. Cliff was stunned when by the end of the day no punishment had been handed out. Joseph had promised Rosa he would fix things and he had.

Even more surprising was that the other boot makers said nothing to him about what had occurred. Perhaps there was a little more space given to him; perhaps they were just a bit more wary. The large dopey lad obviously had a temper and they didn't want to be the brunt of it. Cliff's reputation had actually improved.

The incident had caused Benjamin Sparks far more difficulty. He had returned to work, two days ago, his shoulder bruised but not broken. Before the incident Benjamin was superficially popular, but most thought he was just not a very nice man. He was too mean spirited, lazy and relished bullying others. They had all tolerated him, some had even deferred to him in the past. But the bully had been unmasked. The boot makers did give him a very rousing and quite derogatory reception. They felt he was the instigator and had deserved his comeuppance. Benjamin Sparks never spoke to Clifford again.

The only casualty from the altercation was that, by the time Clifford had returned to Mason and Family, Mrs Molly Williams had left and did not return. No-one said why, but it was generally accepted that she had just given up. Further proof that this workplace was no place for a woman.

Something else had happened while Clifford was unwell. The Military Services Act of 1916 had come into effect. The Bill had been introduced by Prime Minister H. Asquith in January 1916 and it came into force across Britain on the 2nd March 1916.

The early flood of volunteers prepared to fight for King and Country had shrunk to a trickle by the end of 1915 and the death toll was so great that the United Kingdom urgently needed replacements. Despite strict censorship on all forms of communication from within the military, the British population had started to hear the truth about the horror of the Western Front. The Parliament needed trench fodder and thus enforced enlistment was needed. Conscription meant that all single men over 18 would be forced to join up.

Albert Hulme thought at first that his employment in an 'essential industry' would protect him. Conversations with the football managers at Leeds had reinforced this belief.

'Don't worry about a thing lad. We have friends in power and great influence with the government. They'll not take you and even if you do get taken in we'll see to it that you score a nice little desk job, a long way from the bullets.'

But the country was desperate for young men and Albert Hulme was certainly a perfect example of a young man. The type of soldier the British Army desperately needed. He was fit, healthy, intelligent and athletically gifted. Plus he was 18.

On the 19th March while Cliff was returning to work, Albert received his letter telling him to present himself to the nearest recruitment office. Neither the protection of the Barnbow Munitions factory, nor the nepotistic interference of the Leeds Football Club was enough to shield him this time.

Sadly, the sour faced enlistment clerk Albert met on the 9th March in the squalid little office in Rochdale, was a passionate supporter of Manchester United Football Club and had noticed the cocky skill and prowess of Albert Hulme in the last game. Manchester United had lost; Leeds had humiliated them. The enlistment clerk blamed Albert Hulme and he was not very flattering about Albert to anyone who wanted to listen. Now the clerk was determined to do his bit for his Club and his Country. The patriotic enlistment clerk could see absolutely no reason why Albert should not go to war and serve on the front line.

Albert was declared fit and able to serve his country in an official letter that arrived at the Hulme home on the 21st March 1916. He had less than a month before he was in basic training and was destined to arrive on the battle fields of Europe by the end of June - mid summer. Albert hoped that the beautiful French ladies would have the glow of summer in their faces as they welcomed him with open arms and open hearts.

Despite not being keen to join the fray, once he was in the British Army Albert showed a great aptitude and enthusiasm for army life. While in basic training his expertise was noticed early and he was quickly promoted. Albert enjoyed the camaraderie and was popular across his outfit - but his easy going, fair manner also made him an excellent leader. Sergeant Albert Hulme was the type of leader that soldiers would happily follow into battle. He excelled at drill and took up the challenge to be first, highest and best at every task. To Albert this was the ultimate competition and Albert was a winner.

As his training came to an end, on a quintessential May day, Albert was given an afternoon's leave to say farewell to his family before he left for the Western Front. The Hulme family decided to promenade, finishing with an ice confection at Cross Flatts Park.

Mami was dressed in her finery walking beside her tall, good looking son in his smart uniform with Sergeant's stripes already attached to his shoulders. She was filled with anticipation but she had an optimistic feeling about her boy. Albert was now excited about the new adventure and he showed no fear because he felt none. Albert was indestructible. He filled the air with tales about his new chums and where they were being sent.

When it was nearly time to go, Mami dropped the pretence of proud bravery and started sobbing loudly in a totally un-English fashion. She clung to Albert, beseeching him to be safe and come home to her in a wild jumble of Espagnol-English.

After gently freeing himself from her clutches, Albert gave Young William a hug and a mock salute. The twelve year old thought his brother looked grand.

Then Albert turned towards Clifford who stood slightly apart from the others with a dejected look on his face. Albert was his anchor, his stability, the sun he had rotated around for so many years. Clifford was frightened about being cast adrift, unsure about whether he could handle the challenge.

'Now you need to step up and become the man of the family Cliff,' Albert said gravely. 'You are ready for it. Just remember to get those black moods under control. Don't worry about me.

I've been making ammo to bomb Fritz for the past two years and he must be limping badly by now. I'll be back by Christmas and I just might bring a little French Mademoiselle home to annoy Mami.'

'Now before I go Cliff remember this. You need to trust a few more people. See how great Joseph has been to you - he can be trusted, he could be in your triangle. And from what you said about that sweet little Molly from work, she sounded like you could have trusted her. There are some good people out there and you will need them. Now give me a hug and I'll be off to kill the Hun.'

And with that, tall handsome Albert turned on his heel and walked off down the road to join the reinforcements heading for the Western Front. His first engagement with his new unit was to be on July 1st 1916, day one of a brand new offensive planned to 'totally annihilate the German Army'.

The Conscription Law was to affect the Hulme Family again, two days after Albert had left. The new law allowed the Army to find their men in many ways including trawling through birth and employment records. Sadly Clifford Hulme's lie from six years ago now came back to haunt him. He was registered as being 18. He looked 18. The enlistment clerk didn't believe his mother's explanation for a moment and he was scheduled for a medical examination on the next Friday. This was only one day after the letter had arrived and involved travelling down to Manchester.

Mami was not unduly worried, she knew Clifford was unlikely to pass the examination. Mami knew about Clifford's secrets. Even in 1916 when the British Army was desperate, proven mental instability was a valid reason for rejection. Mami knew that a good doctor would also be able to discern Cliff's secrets. She thought the Army would be smart enough to work out that guns and madmen were not a good combination.

Mami had already lost her Albert, though she knew he was a survivor and would be alright. She was more concerned about Clifford. She knew he would not be all right.

Clifford fronted up to see the Army doctor on the 18th May. Dr Jacob Broderick was assessing 5 recruits at once; he was harassed, uninterested and extremely unobservant. Mami had written a letter to the doctor but Cliff was frightened that she might be telling him that he couldn't read or write or do sums. Cliff was not really keen on other folk knowing this so he kept the letter hidden away in his trouser pocket.

'Strip down to your waist.' Clifford was ordered.

This was not so good for Cliff. He didn't like the idea of taking off his clothes. This would leave him vulnerable but he noticed the other four recruits did as they were told. So he loosened his braces letting them drop and removed his shirt and waited in line with only a hint of agitation.

Clifford allowed the invasion with some degree of discomfort as the doctor cursorily examined his torso. Cliff was glad the doctor had not touched him and he was soon able to put his shirt back on; this layer made him feel far less vulnerable.

The doctor scribbled some aspects on the form and then looking directly at Clifford he asked:

'You are a boot maker right?'

Clifford answered, 'yes.'

'Do you need glasses to work?'

Clifford said, 'no.'

Once again the harried Doctor wrote something on the form.

To the standard three questions: 'Do you suffer from any diseases? Have you ever had a venereal disease? and, 'Is there any reason you shouldn't serve in the army,' Clifford answered, 'no'.

'Just fill this out then.'

The harassed doctor thrust a form in front of Clifford and turned to the next potential recruit. Now Clifford couldn't read but he could work out that there were boxes on the form that he needed to tick. He looked over at the young man next to him and ticked the same boxes - all the ones down the right hand side. Cliff always wanted to do the right thing and he certainly didn't want the doctor or any of the other potential recruits to guess that 'he wasn't right in the head', so Mami's letter stayed hidden.

And with that Clifford was accepted into the Army. His medical report had revealed him to be 'a perfect applicant in all aspects,' and was signed off by Dr Jacob Broderick of Manchester.

When the letter arrived Mami opened it slowly and read the words. She hadn't ever thought that Clifford was 'perfect' let alone 'in all respects'. She couldn't believe that anyone else thought so either. Mami cried and wailed, she could not sleep.

Rosa applied to the Military Service Tribunal for an exemption for Clifford Hulme based on mental impairment. The appeal was dismissed. She tried again showing his birth certificate and outlined the full story of how they had lied about his age to get him into work early. This too was dismissed. The panel thought that she was a desperate mother trying anything to keep her son out of the Army.

Nothing could stop the relentless process now in operation. Clifford was taken into the Army and went to basic training at Masham, on the Roomer Common on the 25th May 1916. He was only 16 years old. After a few short weeks of basic training he was declared to be a soldier; fully ready to go and fight for the Empire.

Basic training was an ordeal for Clifford but one that he managed. At 16 he did not enjoy the company of men but he could endure it. He did not let any black moods devour him. He kept his distance from groups, avoided any situations where he could lose his control and he did exactly what he was told. It was the unscheduled part of every day he found the most difficult - so he tended to keep to himself at these times.

Clifford relished the routine of the Army. He liked cleaning his rifle and polishing his boots and the boring monotony of drill was for him a pleasure because he could escape into solitary thoughts. This was the realm where he was still far more content.

Clifford was seen by his superiors as reserved but capable. His army mates accepted him. Most thought he was just a bit queer. No-one got close to him but no-one hated him either.

The best part of basic training for Cliff was learning to use a rifle. Cliff found that this was his forte and he was amazingly accurate. Once his skill was established, the brass selected him to train as a sniper. His independence, apparent lack of fear and amazing aim were wonderful attributes for this prize role.

He was fascinated by the workings of the British Enfield that he was given. The rifle had a scope, with precision lenses, perfected by the German army and stolen by British intelligence agents earlier in the war. The use of the scope increased his accuracy unbelievably. The more he practiced the better he got, and this is what he did at every opportunity. Plus Clifford, who had always been considered a bit dim, was extremely intelligent when it came to understanding the mechanics of his rifle. So in this independent pursuit and with a strong sense of self control managing his behaviour and moods, Clifford emerged as a fully trained soldier after barely five and a half weeks in basic training.

Cliff had a leave pass on the 2nd July 1916 and went home to say farewell to his mother and Young William. He had received his orders - he was heading for Egypt. Cliff was destined to become a soldier in the Mesopotamian Campaign and was being sent out to join the depleted ranks of the 1st Manchesters.

This group had fought with valour and some success over the early part of 1916 including the Battles of Dujaila and Kut. Both of these outposts had been besieged by the aggressive and desert hardy Otterman forces. This front had been a war of attrition. Often hard fought battles that were apparent successes one day, would see a withdrawal occur a few days later.

In the engagements over the first half of 1916, the brave soldiers of the 1st Manchesters had been decimated, losing 4000 men in just over two months.

Cliff was part of a group of replacements, made up of nondescript conscripts; unenthusiastic, undertrained and largely unwanted by the remaining, seasoned soldiers of the 1st Manchesters. It was to prove a very difficult posting.

But this was all in the future.

On the 2nd of July on a deceptively mild summer's day, Clifford Hulme stands ready to depart. His mother and Young William are with him on the step in front of their home. Cliff looks the part - he stands tall and proud in his uniform and he has mastered his swirling inadequacies.

The words of parting have been spoken and Cliff looks down at his fob watch - it is time to go and he is ready to leave. He is not feeling courageous but he has readied himself for this moment, determined to be bold so that his Mami does not worry.

His reverie is disturbed as a lad on a bicycle comes down the street. He is a telegram boy wearing the blue uniform of office, with smart red piping and small box hat. The lad rings his bell as he comes close to the group. The boy hands a telegram to Rosa and the world goes into slow motion.

Mami forces her eyes to the words on the telegram. She looks at the words, straining to seek a meaning from something that has no meaning. The pallor of her Mediterranean skin fades, she turns corpse like. Her screech rents the air and she falls sobbing into the arms of her two surviving sons. Cliff's trust triangle shattered.

Sgt Albert J. Hulme's name was on just one of the 19 000 telegrams sent out after that first day, the day after the battle of the Somme commenced. The number rose to 57 560 by the end of the first week in July.

All Wars End 1916-1918
Dead Eye Cliff Scores A High

August/September, 1916

Basra, Mesopotamia

The proud but bedraggled group of war veterans of the 1st Battalion of the Manchester Regiment looked on as the new recruits arrived at their camp. They had not found the first sight of this unappetising mob very welcome. These war veterans had been volunteers and were, after two and a half years of fighting numerous battles in various locations, battle hardened. They were the survivors.

The numbers in their battalion had been decimated, most had lost mates, all had lost faith that the war was really anything more than an extremely ruthless, gruelling endurance race. The tough would survive, the weak would be cast aside. But the stark reality was that the strong needed good back up and this unsavoury looking troop were not looking too promising as reliable back up.

This first impression had resulted in the old soldiers deciding that they had to toughen up the new crew and fast. The first six months was hell for the new arrivals. The conscripts, most of whom had never wanted to enlist anyway, were largely unsuited to army life. They were unenthusiastic soldiers, poorly trained and generally not very promising physical specimens.

For the new arrivals, any belief they may have had that they were prepared to make the best out of a bad situation was soon dashed by the cruel, merciless and persistent treatment dealt out to the connies (as they soon termed the conscripts) at every opportunity.

After horrific battles in the first six months of 1916, the second half of the year was a period of relative peace from the enemy on the Mesopotamian Front. Aggression from the Ottoman

Turks was spasmodic. However a strong and persistent enemy still existed, launching relentless attacks on the connies and these assaults came from within.

This is the cruel situation Clifford Hulme arrived into as a 16 year old with deep inadequacies and a heart saddened from the recent loss of a beloved brother. The only advantage for Clifford was that he never thought that he would be liked anyway. He accepted the punishments, performed the hateful chores with stoic indifference and gradually the veterans laid off him. It was grudgingly acknowledged that he was 'tough enough'.

The worst perpetrators of the harassment were Pte Arnold (Arnie) Haines and Pte William (Scratches) Crossing.

No official order had been given but Arnie and Scratches took it on themselves to niggle, demean and persecute the connies at every opportunity. Scratches was a particularly nasty brute; his nickname apparently had come from the commonly held belief that he would scratch anyone's eyes out if they betrayed him. Arnie was the brains of the operation - he revelled in creating inhuman challenges for the new arrivals.

A conscientious objector included in the group was given the worst treatment by the nasty duo. He was a devout Quaker, a gentle soul and he found the concept of treating another human being in a violent or inhumane manner an anathema to his moral principles. After only a week of being in Basra, he was found dead by an early morning patrol. His throat bore the signs of strangulation and the body was found staked out on an anthill in the desert. The Quaker's death was not properly investigated, no questions were asked but many of the connies who silently mourned his passing, believed that he had not died in vain.

The afternoon before the Quaker's death, Arnie had found that the latrine trench had not been 'covered adequately' and sewage was bubbling to the top. Scratches had dragged out a newly arrived soldier who had been allocated the responsibility for covering the offensive muck. He was forced to his knees and told to cover the area with his hands. The offending connie had desperately started sweeping sand across the offensive, oozing sewerage. Arnie had gathered ten of the connies together to witness the man's ordeal. They were then instructed to walk past him and 'kick him hard in the back' to 'teach him to do his jobs properly'.

Clifford had been in the group of observers and had reluctantly trudged forward, eighth in line, watching the men in front of him kick out brutally at the offending man kneeling on the ground. The fierce kicks connected with the victim with cruel force; as though the perpetrators where trying to ward off a similar fate happening to them.

Clifford was horrifically confronted. He didn't want to do this. Inflicting pain was wrong, but it was an order and Cliff had survived in the army so far by doing exactly as he was told. The line progressed and the desperate man tried to fend off the kicks with his hands while he still attempted to push sand over the muck in front of him. His indecision about which was more urgent, resulted in neither objective being achieved.

The seventh man in the line was the Quaker. When it came to his turn he stood absolutely still, quietly refusing to kick the man in front of him. Arnie screamed at him to: 'put the boot in'. The Quaker stood, sentinel like, a bastion protecting the man on the ground by his refusal to obey the vicious instruction.

Scratches then rounded on the Quaker, hitting him over the head with a thin cane, but still the Quaker stood his ground. Finally the Quaker dropped to his knees and started to help the man on the ground pathetically push handfuls of sand over the sewerage. This simple act, whether it came from a deep need to oppose tyranny or just from the Quaker's kindness, galvanised the onlookers.

Within minutes the other connies followed suit and eleven kneeling men were helping to cover the traces of sewage. They were joined by others. Some brought in shovels and in no time over fifty men were gathered in the area behind the latrines, frantically shovelling. These men were not all new recruits, some of the war veterans were working shoulder to shoulder with them; a combined act of unity, marking a subtle shift in the rules.

Arnie and Scratches were stunned and malevolently angry at the scene developing in front of them. They watched for a while and then soundlessly slunk from the area, already planning a terrible retribution for the brave man they now blamed for their loss of face.

The Quaker's defiant act and ultimate martyr's death marked the slow decline in Arnie's and Scratches' reign of terror. While it was not yet over, it was no longer absolute.

Some soldiers in the group folded under the persistent harassment and pressure; two suicides occurred in the first month, and at leave time the usual suspects would contemplate desertion. Sadly melting into the local population in the Middle East was really not possible so the hellish ordeal continued for most of the connies. The result of this was that the connies did toughen up and most, eventually, became accepted by the tough battle hardened veterans.

Clifford emerged from this period better than most. One thing in his favour was that he was an excellent shot. The thing that a veteran likes even better than a reliable mate as back up, is one who can 'shoot the bastards before they even confront you.'

After four weeks in their base camp, the troop had set up the monthly 'Shot Comp'. It was widely accepted that the champion Macca had this 'in the bag'. Big wagers were levied and the wily veterans expected their champion to win.

The connies had also entered into the betting with a very few, those 'in the know' who had trained with Cliff, praying that he could cause an upset. Those few, game soldiers accepted the ridiculous odds and staked their weekly wages on Pte Clifford Hulme, hoping that the underdog could achieve the impossible.

Macca was Sgt John Mackenzie, an Australian soldier seconded to the 'Manchesters'. Macca had been a sniper on the Western Front but he had asthma and the wintery, damp smog of the trenches played havoc with his lungs. The warm, dry air of the desert was far more conducive to easy breathing, so he volunteered to be one of 25 soldiers from the Australian Imperial Force lent to the Manchesters for their Mesopotamia Campaign. The group had performed with honour and great valour, however their ranks had been severely depleted. Only 9 of the ANZACs, all now present in the camp at Basra, had survived.

The 'Shot Comp' involved every soldier firing off as many rounds as he could in one minute. The target was 12 inches wide and was set 300 yards away from the firing line. Anyone who missed the target more than three times was eliminated. Using the Lee Enfield rifle with the swift bolt action and the .303 inch bullets, the skill to achieving a high score was in quickly resetting the bolt action without looking. The soldier's total vision had to be continuously focussed on the sights to achieve the extreme accuracy required.

The best scores across the army in World War 1 were between 25 - 35 rounds. To achieve anything more than 25 rounds in the sixty seconds was termed 'a mad minute'.

The regulars were confident. Macca could easily score 28 - 30 rounds in 60 seconds. He was set to go first - to set the benchmark high they thought. On this occasion Macca set the very reasonable score of 26 rounds, a bit below par but good enough most thought.

As the soldiers came up for their turn Macca's score was looking extremely safe. Most soldiers could achieve no more than 10 - 15 rounds in the sixty seconds allowed.

When the Australian contingent came in to have a go the bar was rattled a bit. Many of these soldiers had experience as snipers and when it is your life or that of your opponent, accuracy and speed become important. Three of the Diggers scored in the low 20's.

When the first of the connies lined up he could barely get one round off and hardly a bullet hit the target. Tangled hands, jangled nerves and dead fright created the worst score to be ever recorded. Hoots of derision followed as the downcast soldier made his way dejectedly back to the crowd.

Clifford was up next. He didn't take any notice of the hoots and jeers of the watching mob. Cliff lifted the rifle and felt an alliance immediately; he related to this bit of mechanics and he was in his comfort zone. On his first attempt he achieved the mad minute, firing 30 rounds in 60 seconds and with precision accuracy. The onlookers were hushed.

Only the small group of 'connies in the know' were cheering - they had made money on their bets. Moments later 'the downcast soldier' who had fired before him was clapping too. He felt Cliff's performance had vindicated him.

This spasmodic clapping soon gained momentum until everyone was giving an appreciative ovation. Even those who had lost their money, could appreciate this truly amazing accomplishment.

Cliff felt a firm hand on his shoulder. His reaction was to back away but he saw before him the warm smile and bear like friendliness of Macca.

'That was unbelievable shooting mate. I don't believe what I just saw. Where on earth did you learn to shoot like that?' Macca was unreserved in his praise, open, affable and welcoming. Cliff sensed that he could trust him immediately.

Macca was soon joined by a host of others - all wearing the slouch hats showing their affiliation to the Australian Army. The comments were loud and effusive, all derivations of: 'Great shooting. You're with us Mate.'

So Cliff became an 'honorary ANZAC' and joined this group whenever scouting patrols and raiding parties were sent out. This was his first real break, as he was often away from camp when the worst of the harassment and bullying occurred.

Now this wasn't the end of Cliff's problems. As a new recruit in the Manchesters in Mesopotamia, there were still many more travails to overcome. But it did mean that he was accepted into the sniper troop and this was far preferable to the treatment his fellow connies were being forced to endure.

The laconic Australians accepted him for what he was. He was a loner, not much of a talker but he was reliable and trustworthy. For a Tommy soldier he was a pretty good bloke.

In particular, Clifford found himself under the protective wing of Macca and his best mate Corporal Thomas Archibald Stubbs. The corporal had a violent shock of red hair so the Aussies all called him Bluey, indicative of the Australian habit of saying the opposite to reality.

Macca and Bluey conjured up the story that 'Cliff could hit a camel through the eye at 350 yards' and so they named him Dead Eye. The name stuck and so Cliff learnt to answer to his first ever nick name.

It seemed that the Australian soldiers were set on trivialising everything serious. They had immense disregard for authority especially the British High Command who they referred to as 'Brass Arse'. They spent their time making sense of where they were, by making everything into a bit of a joke.

So Dead Eye (aka Cliff), who had never before had mates, was adopted into the Aussie Diggers' group. He also had a strange, niggling sense of belonging that had never happened to him before except with his family.

This period of the war saw a series of minor skirmishes - mainly hit and run attacks. Patrols often came into contact with small groups of marauding Turks and fighting was both vicious and violent. The Turkish resistance was always fierce and the snipers were in great demand and were held in great esteem. Cliff survived quite well.

Bluey and Macca would often sit late into the night, staring up at the amazing starlight and speaking longingly about home. Cliff would sit close to them, smoking, listening but never contributing.

The lads both came from a small country town called Pinjarra in Western Australia. Both were the sons of farmers with Bluey's family growing vegetables; mainly cabbages, tomatoes and potatoes. Macca's father was a dairyman but he had not inherited the dream to take over the farm.

'Dairy farming ain't much fun,' he said, 'getting up every morning before the sun comes up. Doing the milking with the frost on everything, chilling your hands. Lugging the huge containers of milk up to the depot by lunch so it can be transported to the Perth markets. Then doing exactly the same thing every evening. The worst bit is not having any days off - not even Christmas. And cows are pretty dumb company. The only udders I want to be feeling belong to 17 year old girls.'

Macca stopped for a while, his eyes were dreamy, thinking about home. Or perhaps he was thinking of those 17 year olds, with breasts he would like to be fondling.

'Poor Dad though. When I broke the news to him that I didn't want to take it over, it hit him hard. We had this huge barney - and I went off and joined up. Both Mum and Dad were really cut up. Dad has been building up the herd for twenty years since he left the Goldfields. But my sister has a nice young man and he is keen, so they can do it I reckon.' Macca obviously loved and missed his family but this love did not extend to taking over the dairy farming life he hated so much.

'So ya really serious are ya mate about becoming a full time roo shooter?' asked Bluey.

'Too right I am. There is good money in that. Lots of women like to wear pretty fur coats and roo fur is really soft. Lots of the farmers want the roos cleared off their land too. They eat the feed that they need for the sheep and cattle.'

This conversation was a recurrent one between the two West Australian boys. Macca was a great shot - he wanted to make a living shooting, not milking cows. Bluey was more content and wanted to go home and take up his Dad's land. But he had two brothers both older than him and he didn't think he would have much of a chance.

'I heard tell that the government might open up some new land out east when we get back. I should have saved a fair bit of my army pay and I kinda fancy going further out. Perhaps I'll try a bit of wheat farming. I'll get you to come and clear out the vermin hey Macca?'

'Yeh I fancy shooting a few roos. I've certainly had enough shooting at people,' Macca replied, moving onto a much deeper topic.

'They told us that we would be doing a great thing for the Empire if we came away to fight. But how does it help the Empire shooting a Turk or an Arab who just wants us to get away from his goats or his well and leave his bloody date trees alone. This war is a bit of a farce. I would be just as upset if some Arab lobbed into Pinjarra and wanted to shoot me just because I wanted to get the cows in for milking. I can't see how what we are doing here, or anywhere else we've fought in this bloody war, helps the Empire.'

This is the way that lots of their conversations went. A bit of homesick reminiscing, touching on their planned futures, sometimes even some profound utterances. Cliff always listened in accepting silence.

'What about you Dead Eye? What is there for you when this lot has finished?' Macca asked, turning to the grave, quiet man sitting beside him. This was different to their normal conversations. Usually they left him alone, realising that he was comfortable in his shroud of silence.

Cliff turned to them slowly: 'I really don't know. I suppose I will just go back to Leeds and back to my old job making boots,' he replied.

Quite uncharacteristically Clifford suddenly felt an urge not to go back. Alfred wasn't there anymore, Mami would be happy with Joseph, William was growing up and he really didn't miss making boots. Just maybe, he might think about going to this new land.

Clifford had enjoyed listening to his two friends talk about the wilds of Western Australia. It sounded like there was lots of open space and there were loads of places where there were no people at all. This sounded like a place where he could be content.

He liked listening to Macca talk about hunting kangaroos. Now he had never seen a kangaroo but Macca said they were not too dangerous and it was not like hunting lions or elephants. This seemed to Cliff to be a pretty good life.

Over the first four months in Mesopotamia, Cliff's life was defined by the occasional sniper patrol with the ANZACs which allowed him time to listen to the yarning of Blue and Macca, interspersed with base camp army life which mainly meant avoiding persecution from the likes of Arnie and Scratches. It also meant keeping himself under tight control. Twice he had mild attacks when his black moods had threatened but he was able to shield these by hiding away in his tent until the danger had passed.

Not only were Clifford and the new recruits given a hard time from the other soldiers but the conditions they faced in Mesopotamia defied description. It was unbelievably hot with temperatures often soaring to over 120 degrees Fahrenheit and there were no sheltering trees. They were stationed in isolated, arid desert camps. Ironically, when it rained it arrived in torrential sheets of water and the camp would be flooded within minutes.

Plus God had amused himself in this land by sending regular insect plagues to torment the soldiers. When it didn't rain, the swarms of sticky flies were unbelievable, when it did, the far more menacing insect pests, their cousins the mosquitoes, drove them all crazy.

These conditions led to appalling levels of sickness and death throughout the camps. The aftermath of a deluge of rainfall that soaked everything over the Christmas of 1916 was two weeks of stifling, steamy conditions, great for mosquito larvae but horrific for men.

At least one of the million mosquitoes that sunk their proboscis into Clifford's succulent skin over that fortnight, carried the virulent amoeba Plasmodium falciparum. Thus in January 1917 Cliff came down with a particularly dangerous form of malaria, Blackwater Fever. This was to be the worst and best thing that happened to Clifford in 1917.

It was the worst because he nearly died.

It was the best because he met up with the Indian medic Dr Assem Singh Samran who along with Macca and Bluey, became Clifford's trust triangle for the duration of his service in the British Army.

With malarial fever convulsing his body, Clifford was taken to the medical tent where a harassed, over stretched medical orderly gave him a massive dosage of quinine, the normal treatment for malaria sufferers. The quinine swirling in his system reacted with the parasite infecting his red blood cells, resulting in massive numbers of them exploding. The Blackwater Fever diagnosis was easy - his urine was the colour of molasses. His kidneys had gone into over drive and Cliff entered into that mysterious, near death state.

This was not a serene state. Clifford's body was hosting the perfect storm with a full blown malarial attack, colliding with one of Clifford's uncontrolled black moods.

Dr Assem Singh Samran was the Sikh healer attached to the unit and he had seen many cases of Blackwater Fever before. He knew it often resulted in death and immediately proceeded to put into effect, a treatment plan designed to give Pte Clifford Hulme the best chance of recovery.

However he was also acutely aware that in Clifford's case the extreme headaches, bouts of uncontrollable shaking and the vivid hallucinations being verbalised throughout Clifford's delirium, hinted at some other pre-existing morbidity.

Dr Samran was the first person, other than those in his intimate family, to speculate that Cliff had a mental illness.

Over the many months of Clifford's recovery, Dr Assem Singh Samran analysed Clifford Hulme and gradually formed an opinion about his condition. Dr Samran had completed his medical training in Amritsar in India and this was augmented by the understanding of many centuries of oriental medicine.

Dr Samran had seen people who suffered like Clifford before

and he knew that various drugs and potions had been used with great effect to give relief to sufferers back in India. Recently the large, powerful and very reputable drug manufacturer Bayer, had used the oriental science to develop a new wonder drug they had manufactured and marketed as Heroin. This product delivered a small, soluble, easily digestible gram of 'safe to ingest' morphine. Dr Samran surmised that this could just be the answer for Pte Clifford Hulme.

When Clifford awoke from his tumultuous fever, he lay in an enfeebled state staring into the deep brown eyes of the good Sikh doctor. These deep eyes, contained in a darkly tanned face looked at him benignly. Dr Samran had a long rolled up beard, white clothes and a huge white turban all packaged together with a kind, sonorous voice, full of centuries of healing wisdom.

'Well Pte Hulme you have come back to us from a deep well. You have been fighting with great forces but you have won through. You will get better from the Blackwater Fever. Rest, good nutrition and some treatment for the malarial infection will heal this over time. But there is something else you suffer from too isn't there? Something about you that is different. Now I think I can help you if you tell me about the things that you keep secret. Tell me about the things that cause you fear.'

Clifford looked into the brown eyes and felt a comfort connection. He sensed that this was a man he could trust. It wasn't immediate but over the next few weeks Clifford gradually shared his history with the good Sikh Doctor. He admitted to the black moods and the evil beings that were present deep in his mind, and he told him of the things that had long lain hidden.

Dr Samran told Clifford about the little white tablets that could help Clifford to live his life a bit more normally.

'Heroin is a chemical treatment that may be able to help you with your black moods and the way your mind does not always do what it should. Take one of these little tablets when you feel the start of a black mood coming on. You can also take one when you are nervous or afraid - they will also help you feel able to cope with anger and sadness.'

These wonderful little tablets, freely dispensed to Clifford, allowed him to escape into a euphoric state and enabled him to cope very well with the challenges he faced over the next few years.

All Wars End 1916-1918
How To Catch A Parrott

May 1917

Perth, Western Australia

Myopia didn't seem to be such a big issue by 1917 and Harold had no problem with the enlistment process second time around. He had resolved to go to war and fight for his home country three years before, the shame of rejection had scorched him but his patriotism and sense of duty had not ebbed.

So on May 24th 1917 Pte Harold Eaton Smith was elated when he received his pay card instructing him:

'Pte H.E. Smith is to report for duty at Swanbourne Barracks on May 31st to commence basic training to be an engineer in the 7th Brigade, 16th Battalion.'

James' death had hit him hard but had not diminished his resolve to go and fight himself. Harold's practical mind aligned with his loyal friendship had directed him to carry though James' last wishes that he should care for his family. In fact, Harold was now the perfect 'adopted son' to the Nelsons caring for them in every way possible.

He did not seek to replace James, nothing and no-one could ever do that for the anguished couple doomed to a lifetime of recriminations and 'what ifs'. However, he was there dutifully to do the visiting, to pick up the extra workload and he was at John Nelson's right hand when he made the painful but necessary decision to quit the sandalwood company, selling out at a bargain basement price to his great rivals Paterson and Co Sandalwood.

The war had created a huge financial boon for many companies but sandalwood was not one of them. With a shrinking demand for sandalwood coming from the Oriental market, combined with the near impossibility of finding commercial ships for transport and to top it off an insurmountable scarcity of labour, the Nelsons had steadily watched their profits dwindle. For John Nelson, his heart had gone out of it.

'I just don't have the puff to do this anymore,' he said one night to Ada with a deep sigh, laced with sadness and regret. His wife looked at him with rheumy, sleep deprived eyes willing herself to give him the backing he required but unable to do so. Her own despair was so great that she had difficulty getting up every morning, let alone provide moral support to her husband in his time of need.

Harold had been there to stand staunchly by John Nelson's side when he had signed over the papers, quitting the company that was to have been James' legacy.

'Don't feel sorry for me old son,' John Nelson had said to Harold as he turned to him in the dingy lawyer's office in St George's Terrace. The ink was still drying on the papers in front of him as a thin beam of light zeroed in from the high cobwebbed window and bathed the business transaction documents in soft light.

'That signature says goodbye to my old life. We have made good money and it's time for Ada and me to create another. I am going to buy a farm out Dalwallinu way. We'll keep the Nedlands house so we will all have somewhere to stay whenever we come to town but I have the need to start again, grow things and live a new life.'

'For the last year it has just been about surviving – just going through the motions. Nothing I have been doing has been giving me any pleasure and everything I look at reminds me painfully of the past. I want to work hard physically and I want Ada to have something to do, something away from the memories, so that she too can recover.'

'I know you've got some things to do first but when you come back we'll get you and Lilly out there near us as soon as we can – it will be good to see some littlies around to let us focus on the next generation.'

Harold was struck by the enormity and all encompassing nature of these decisions and how he had the future, his own and Ada's, Harold's, Lilly's and even their future children all mapped out, with or without their permission. Harold smiled at his friend's presumption, accepting it graciously.

He reflected on James' plan to get him into the country six years before without going through the tedious and stifling lines in the Arrivals Hall. This plotting out the future for himself and everyone else seemed to be a Nelson trait and he could see some of the characteristics that he had so loved in his sadly missed friend James.

In another way this interaction had shown another amazing shift. Harold and Lilly were now a couple and this had been fully accepted by everyone. Even the Nelsons had accepted that Lillian had set her heart on another and bore him no malice; in fact if Harold had known it, they were overjoyed as they loved Harold as a son and had grown very close to Lillian over the years.

Harold had not experienced any guilt about moving in on James' lady. The instantaneous love he bore Lilly was too great to be put off by any feelings of remorse. James had died, Lilly was on the open market. Even better, James had given him permission and that was all there was to it. Harold went courting.

The dilemma had been within Lilly. She had spent almost a year mired in her self-inflicted quandary. Lilly was smitten and guilt wracked, in the throes of a full blown infatuation with one man while outwardly wearing respectful black widow's garb and adopting the behaviour of a lady bereft, mourning her lost sweetheart.

When she saw Harold she could not stand the ecstasy. She aloofly turned away and then subtly glanced back, wanting to recall his face when he was no longer there. He was the most handsome man she had ever seen. His deep melodious voice lulled and seduced her, pleading, tantalising and convincing her of his devotion. Her words spoke back harshly to him of denial, refusal to admit the surge of feelings she had for him.

Lilly was convulsed with the pain of the lovesick and the embarrassment of being discovered as a sham – mourning one man, while lusting after another. And she carried so much guilt.

Did James go to his death because of her cruel rejection? The weight of this guilt made her physically ill; riddled with shame, she was so alone in her mental anguish.

Her feelings for James had been like an infatuation or a school girl crush; just giggles, playtime and pretending. It was more about the importance of having a beau than any real long term commitment. That is why she had broken it off. She had wanted to be mature about it but it had all gone so terribly wrong.

Lilly had told no one of her letter to James requesting that they break up. So the bereaved family and friends had all deferred to her as the grieving fiancée. She had accepted this role, the condolences and the trappings of an abandoned and lovelorn widow.

The beginning of the tension came on the day of James' Memorial Service on 16th September 1915. The Nelsons had asked Lillian to sit with them at the front of the Church as befits the closest of kin to the deceased. They had also requested that their dearly beloved son's two best friends and pall bearers, Jack Parrott and Harold Smith, sit on the first pew alongside the nearest of kin.

Without a coffin the pall bearers' role was illusionary, standing to attention at the beginning of the service and reverently and silently marching out at the end. At the conclusion of the opening prayer and hymn, Harold Smith took his seat alongside Lillian Parrott.

Lilly immediately felt the firm pressure of his body against hers and she was enveloped with unbelievable sexual fission. Lilly was horrified at her physical response and lowered her eyes demurely unless someone saw the hot, red flush that inflamed her. Her black veil hid the signs but within her heart was beating, the blood rushed through her and she felt unbearable tingles – very inappropriate feelings for a sweetheart at the memorial service of her former beau.

Lilly was aghast. She felt herself to be a total jezebel, wanton, a harlot allowing herself to be consumed by inappropriate feelings while masquerading as a respectable and honourable lady. Her body was alive and tingled, her gut churned and bile rose in her throat, she shook uncontrollably.

The congregation would have all been empathising with the young lady so overwhelmed with sadness that she had lost her self control.

Harold stood to perform the eulogy. He seemed unaware of his impact on Lilly. He was here to perform a sacred role, to properly recognise his friend James and this is the task he was fully focussed on. He spoke with passion, raw pain in his voice, clear to everyone in the room the deep, profound love Harold had for James Nelson.

Lillian Parrott listened, watched and wept silently. She wept for her lost friend, she wept for her situation and she wept that she would now deny her love for Harold Smith in deference to this horrific sin her body had committed.

It took Harold twelve months of relentless and flagrant wooing to break down Lilly's resolve.

Harold had been stationed in Perth over much of 1916. With the sandalwood business declining, the Nelsons had needed their best people to organise shipping in an environment when all commercial craft had been co-opted into the navy for essential war work. Harold and his old friend Jack Parrott had been thrust into this frustrating work environment, utilising all of their charm and negotiation skills up and down the Fremantle wharf.

This location had meant that Harold, who had been gifted John Nelson's car, drove Jack Parrott to and from work at least three times a week. This gave Harold the perfect excuse to stay for an extended visit and Mrs Frances Parrott often invited Jack's good looking friend to stay for dinner. Harold rarely needed much convincing. He was more than happy to spend as much time as he could in the company of the delightful, though apparently unattainable, Lillian.

Lilly had been consistent in her rejection of his advances. However Harold was perceptive; her words said, 'no' but her body and eyes screamed, 'yes'. He was relentless.

On a crisp spring evening on the 25th September 1916, now over a year since the memorial service for James and thus past the respectable mourning interval, Harold determined to try a more aggressive approach. He was sitting on the front porch alone with Lilly. She was still dressed in black, wearing the sombre mask of widowhood and showing her customary steely resolve of resistance. Harold had been especially charming tonight, offering witty stories and anecdotes trying to get her to open up to him.

Tonight they had not had any of their usual frank discussions. He loved her intelligence and valued it when she bravely and eloquently outlined her strong, forthright opinions always imbued with an admirable social conscience. Lilly was so unlike many of the woman of the time, who were lovely to look at but had minds filled with fluff. Lilly had no intention of deferring to a husband.

'My vote,' Lilly exclaimed one night, 'will be used to express my own opinion. In so many countries woman are having to risk their lives for the right to vote. In Australia we have been lucky enough to have been offered it without a fight. And so many of my addle-brained friends are going to hand their vote to their men folk because they can't be bothered to work out what they think. I am so ashamed of them.'

Through these discussions he saw glimpses of the real Lillian; she would drop the pretence of playing the grieving sweetheart and stridently debate some aspect of improving society. Her eyes would flash and her diminutive frame would quiver with excitement. Harold loved her so.

Harold looked over at her and he was again besotted. Lilly had not grown much since she was 13, she was still short but she had a perfect figure, the result of hours of ardent tennis; Harold thought she was a perfect package. Her face was angelic with dark brown eyes, with thick lashes and her face was framed with her lustrous brown hair swept up into a fashionable loose bun. Her skin had just a dusting of freckles with a button mouth and Harold was itching to kiss her.

The time was right he thought, it was now or never. He looked towards Lilly and before his confidence deserted him, he started on the words he had been practicing all day:

'Lilly I have made numerous honourable advances to you and you deny me every time. The reason I have not taken no for an answer is that I decided on the wharf three years ago that you were the only girl for me,' Lilly started to answer, steeling herself to give yet another rebuttal, but Harold held up a finger to her lips.

'Let me go on. There are things that I need to say and you need to listen. Now, I think I know you better than you know yourself. I know what went on between you and James. And I know you carry exceptional grief at his loss but I also know that you are shouldering immense guilt. I know that you wrote to him and broke up with him and I know that this was not long after you met me. You never told anyone but he told me.'

Harold paused as Lilly let the mask of control drop from her face. She gasped and then misty tears were clouding her eyes.

'Had he known all along?' she thought. Her shame was immense, her regret profound but at last she had an ally, someone who knew about her guilt. She started to formulate some words – put off, stalling, bland words. Words to fill the void and allow her to think a way out of this one, but again Harold silenced her.

'James also knew that you did this because you had fallen in love with me. He didn't blame you for it, in fact he wished us well. It is only because he gave me his blessing to pursue you, that I have done so. I loved and admired James Nelson and I know that he loved you truly. But he has died and passed from all of our lives and his death was in no way your fault. He died in battle and he had nothing but forgiveness for you. Now your grieving for him has gone on long enough. Your debt to James is paid.'

Lilly was now staring at Harold. Tears coursed down her face and she made no attempt to wipe them away. These were the tears of resignation, acceptance and renewal. Her ordeal was over and she could move on.

'You do love me. I know it. You know it too. So now let the world know it. Miss Lillian Parrott I want to marry you.'

And with that Harold did what he had wanted to do for three long, agonising years; he pulled her to him, leaning down to that diminutive, pouting rosebud of a mouth and he kissed her. A long, hard passionate kiss filled with years of waiting, years of longing and the fervour and promise of a long future together.

Lilly said nothing, she was too busy kissing him back.

All Wars End 1916-1918
The Guns Fall Silent

Sometime in 1917 - November 11th, 1918

It was all ancient history now. Harold and Lillian were now engaged and this was accepted by everyone. Few recalled that Lilly had once been coupled with James. With this acceptance, Lilly had started to live again. It wasn't so much that love had given her a renewed spring to her step; it was more that she had accepted things for what they really were. She had stopped pretending, acting the part, living the lie and being what she thought other people wanted her to be. Oh and being hopelessly, ridiculously and ludicrously in love hadn't hurt that spring in her step either; she was positively leaping as she walked.

One night Lilly and Harold huddled together on the front porch swing, 'canoodling' as Jack called it dismissively. All of a sudden Harold gazed into Lilly's eyes. He saw in those deep brown pools his life's soul mate and contemplated how easily he could have missed out on this opportunity.

'I hope you have really learnt your lesson Lilly,' Harold began earnestly. 'You need to work out what you believe in and what you need to be. Who cares what others think? You are too strong to do what society wants, you are not afraid to say what you think. From now on start being what you think. You have lost years of your life and you nearly lost me. So no more acting the part any more - right? Be true to yourself.'

Lilly sucked in his words and let them swirl and settle. In retrospect she could see so clearly how deluded she had been and how cruel this had been to Harold. She cringed when she recalled how false she had been, and the worst thing was she had lied to herself.

'I do promise you Harold. But it was so hard – and I did so want to mourn James, but as the wonderful friend he had been to me and not as the sweetheart everyone thought he was.'

Lilly took a deep reflective breath before bestowing a 'from the heart' smile on Harold. 'And there you were wandering past me all the time making me tingle and glow in all the wrong places. It was all your fault really,' she said giggling, giving Harold a playful dig in the chest.

'Well I am glad I make you tingle and glow and I will not go into what uncalled for impulses you create in my desperate, shamelessly depraved body. It would make you blush to the roots of your lovely burnished copper hair. That knowledge will need to wait until after I make you Mrs Harold Smith.' And with this risqué endearment, Lilly did truly blush to the roots of every hair on her body and not just the ones on her head.

Lilly had accepted Harold's decision to go to war stoically and with equanimity. She knew Harold inside out and she had always known that this was something he desperately wanted and needed to do. She was not afraid for him. In fact, if anything, Lilly felt that she would have preferred to go with him.

By 1917 many of the myths of this glorious and honourable war had been dispelled. Patriotism still ran strong and there was still an almost universally held opinion that Australia had made the right decision to stand by Britain in its hour of need. But debate raged fiercely in Canberra about the necessity to supply more men to go away to fight, especially forcing people to go against their will.

The ever popular Prime Minister of the time, Billy Hughes, was convinced that conscription was necessary. This issue caused him to leave his beloved Labor Party and create a separatist party but the population and parliament turned on him and the issue was overturned.

Conscription was not just debated in the hallowed halls of Parliament; in rooms across Australia, this was the topic of the moment.

Jack Parrott who still burned with enthusiasm to go to war, was all for it. He believed he was fully recovered and still hoped the authorities would overlook his ailment.

'I would love to go and they will not take me. I think everyone who is able should be over there doing their bit. I see shirkers and pikers back here, perfectly fit and able to go fight and here they are cashing in on the good money to be made while this war is on. They are getting rich while others are dying. Those poor blokes in the trenches need to know we are supporting them and this means providing enough replacements when death or injury cuts down their numbers. I don't want to think that James and others like him died in vain. And this means making sure the Germans don't win, so I am all for conscription.'

Harold's view had not changed over the three years.

'This is fundamentally a war supporting the rights of Britain to be the predominant colonial power in the face of an aspirational Germany. I am British – it is my duty to go. For Australians, New Zealanders, Indians and Canadians and peoples of the other nations roped into this - it is just not their war. As for forcing someone against their will to go and fight, it is just not on. How can you rely on someone to give you back up in the trenches if they don't want to be there anyway? They will turn and take flight as soon as they can. It also goes against everything I believe in about living in the free world; individuals in such a society have a right to freedom of choice. I say no to conscription!'

Lillian's view was all about humanity.

'If you go to war you need to be committed to the cause and be prepared to die or be maimed as a consequence of your beliefs. This most powerful of sacrifices has to be a personal choice and cannot be forced on anyone. A conscript's army will be unable to win as they do not have faith in the reason for the conflict.'

The push to have conscription in Australia was defeated over the duration of the First World War and meant that all armies raised in this location consisted of willing soldiers.

The war that was 'only to last until Christmas' had already gone on for three long years and far too many of the local population had been touched by death. Wounded returned veterans were now a common sight and seeing these once proud youths of Western Australia now blinded, deafened and maimed, was chilling.

Unspoken by many was that some of these returned soldiers also carried unseen ailments, the secret, churning, nightmarish effects of warfare. These once carefree lads suffered from witnessing the horrific sights that no one should ever have to see. The milder cases were expressed in insomnia, migraines and long periods of silent reflection; the worst in shell shock, alcoholism and other escapist addictions.

Lilly and Harold were not naive to these effects of the war. Lilly had worked with the Women's Auxiliary and part of her war work was helping returned men assimilate, get jobs and pick up the pieces of their pre-war lives, albeit a life now minus an eye or a limb. She was well suited to this role. Lilly did not show excessive sympathy or reveal horror at the mutilations many of these young men carried. She fulfilled this role with honesty and the right mix of empathy and practical common sense to assist the depleted men get started again.

Lilly had also experienced firsthand what it is like to lose someone close to her; someone at the peak of his physical perfection and with his life just ready to unfurl before him. Still with all of this wisdom and experience, Lilly made no attempt to dissuade Harold from his course of action. Lilly knew that, for Harold, going to war was more than his duty - it was his destiny.

Lilly farewelled Harold from the Australian shore on July 16th 1917 on a bitterly cold, wet, blustery day made more bitter by the thoughts of a long separation. This leave-taking was far different from James' departure as a soldier on the first boat convoy that had left Fremantle Harbour carrying troops. This time there were no brass bands or hurrahing spectators whipped up into patriotic fervour. His embarkation was marked by little in the way of pomp and ceremony; just a few bedraggled, weather harassed dignitaries making some inane speeches that were blown away by the gale force winds. The one advantage over this departure was that parting couples and families could get up close to their loved ones before they left.

The Parrott and Nelson families were all there to farewell Harold. He was well pleased with the fondness of their words from these adopted families and friends. He reflected back on the stilted, formal and very English goodbye he and his mother had endured as he had left England six years before.

Lilly clung to him with limpet like force, draining every last physical touch from him before the inevitability of separation arrived. Her parting words had been spoken to him privately and he held next to his heart the sandalwood carved amulet she had fashioned: a red capped parrot entwined with Marri blossom.

Her intricate carving was immaculate and she had painted the parrot with brilliant green and yellow feathers and a stunning red cap. The blossoms and leaves had been fixed with resin to ensure their resiliency and the aroma of the eucalyptus combined with the sandalwood screamed 'Australia'.

It smelt of the Australian bush, and Harold clearly remembered the strong, heady fragrance of the sandalwood he had smelt on his first day in Australia. It was truly a gift from the heart and Harold knew he would be transported back to this place, and to the lady he loved, whenever he looked at it in the dark times ahead.

'A parrot from my lovely little Parrott,' Harold thought as he felt the amulet lying next to his heart.

The couple were to become even closer still over their separation, based on the extraordinary frequency of their correspondence. Both wrote daily and their letters were more than just a litany of daily events; they were filled with life and musings and the odd bit of whimsy. Of course as the mail deliveries were still just as irregular as they had been when the war started, it did mean that every mail delivery would sometimes yield 15 – 20 letters that had to be sorted into chronological order before the long awaited reading commenced. And Harold was a stunningly reliable correspondent, he also wrote to his other friends and family with astounding dedication.

November 1917

The Western Front

Some months later, a reflective Harold found himself in France at Pozières in the Somme Valley, just days after seeing his first major action, when he penned this letter to Jack Parrott.

November 27 1917

Dear Jack

Well I have finally arrived at the front and it is certainly the closest thing I can find to hell on this earth. I am sending this to you but please do not tell any details to the family, especially Lilly, as I do not want them to worry. For their information just let them know I have written and that I am well and enjoying the adventure.

The sea trip from Egypt was very rough, not a good omen I am afraid and I was very lucky that I didn't get seasick whilst on the boat. Even in the relative calm of the Mediterranean Sea it was rough and some blokes spent the whole trip retching over the side.

As we came through the Straits of Gibraltar the seas were terribly high, we were hit by a fierce storm with the full force of an Atlantic gale behind it. The waves towered above the ship smashing over the deck and covering everything with white, frothy foam. At each impact the ship shuddered from the collision like it would be shattered to a million pieces and then time and time again the plucky ship came out the other side unscathed.

When the full force of a wave would hit us we would roll and shoot forward like there was no control and then the power of the motor would snap in and the Captain would have the ship on course again ready to head up into the next wave. The supremacy of motors to conquer nature (and of course the skill and nerves of steel of the talented Captain to control the motors) had me enthralled.

Everything that wasn't properly fastened went hurtling across the room and we had to dodge flying missiles. I fastened myself to a beam and I had a great vantage point to see the full ferocity of the gale. It was really frightening but an unbelievable sight to see the ocean in full and fearsome wrath. The seasoned sailors and the Captain were amazing, they knew what they had to do and set out to do it with no thought for their own safety. Even if it meant going out on the deck with no protection except a flimsy rope in case they were swept off the boat and into the turbulent seas. And they say soldiers are the brave ones.

Some blokes thought we were goners but I felt fairly confident - and sure enough by the time we could see the French coast, things had calmed right down and ironically we disembarked on a millpond. After landing they wasted no time in dispatching us to the front.

Marching was no easy feat on legs that still felt like jelly. Some of the chums had vomited for five days straight and now had to march for hours. Still I didn't hear too much real complaining, just joking banter about our orders coming direct from Fritz High Command.

The march went from 5.15pm, through the evening and we arrived at about 9pm at the trenches - this is to be our home camp over the next few months. I couldn't see too much of our surroundings when we arrived due to the darkness. All I knew was that it was wet, cold and stank like a pile of roo carcasses. But the boys in the trenches welcomed us heartily with a hot cup of tea and a huge cheerio. I am amazed at how jolly most of the ANZACs still are after many months living in these horrific conditions and under the constant threat of death.

By the next day I could see just how awful it was - mud and filth everywhere. The land between the trenches has not a blade of grass left on it. It is supposed to be autumn, a season of stunning colours but trust me this place just has just one colour - a malignant, muddy brown. Occasionally you see a tree but these have all been blasted; twisted and gaunt they look against an angry, brooding sky ready to lay down more sleet on us poor mortals below. As I write this, I fear these clouds are now brewing up a torrent of snow just to bring more frigid misery on us.

My 'home' is a 'sandbag nest'. My bed is a corner with a coarse grey rug that I try my hardest to keep louse free. These louse love drinking soldier's blood and trust me it is truly revolting when you look down at your tender white belly and there is a bloated, blood filled bag just ready to abandon you now that it has glutinously feasted on your innards. These little pests spread the most horrible diseases; they could easily have been feasting on a corpse yesterday and I doubt they clean their mouth parts between courses.

Talking of vermin, I have to mention RATS. I have never seen so many rats - and they are really fat. These profiteers of this war are not at all afraid of humans. I will not take my boots off because Joseph Abrahams did and the rats came and chewed off his toe. I cannot imagine how I sleep every night but trust me I do, because I am bone tired.

On our first evening in the trench, we experienced a burst of heavy artillery fire – 'A Welcome from the Hun' according to the old hands. At night the shells look so pretty when they explode in the distance but when they are close it is terrifying and the sound is just deafening. You feel, see and hear the explosions and the smell of cordite mixed with putrefaction, is a constant smell we have to endure.

Snipers keep firing at our position all the time and the old hands showed us how to keep our heads down as we move around. On our first morning here one of our chaps was killed. He just woke up and forgot where he was, stuck his head up and got it straight through the right eye. Poor blighter.

Now one thing they didn't tell us at training camp was poison gas. Last week a gas bomb landed in our trench. I got a mouthful of gas before I put my helmet on and it made me vomit and I had a rotten headache. The phosgene gas comes in really steadily; it has a horrid smell and makes you choke. It is upon you before you realise that you need to put your mask on. Two fellows got caught without their masks and they were writhing in agony before we got to them. They are both more comfortable in the hospital but they reckon that their throat still feels like it has been rubbed raw. I hope there is no long term damage to their lungs.

My main job is to check the communication cables - which means going over the lines, mainly under cover of darkness. The first time I was so very scared as the shells seemed really close - there is no shelter out there and when a shell goes off it lights up the whole place like daylight so you know that Fritz can see you. Still, I have been lucky so far.

Now this sounds all very gloomy but the camaraderie in the group is great. There are lots of jokes made; though some of the humour is a bit on the dark side, which is not surprising when you think what horrors we face every day.

So I must go now. I hope everyone back home is well. It is the thought of you all back there that keeps me going when times are a bit tough.

Yours sincerely

Your friend

Harold

Six months is a long time to spend in a trench on the Western Front. Six months in such a circumstance surrounded by dehumanising conditions is equivalent to many years of 'ageing' in a normal life. Young lads don't have unspoilt minds after six months of enduring these miserable, tormented conditions.

After six months the resolute Harold Smith is far better off than most, he already had great maturity before he arrived. He also came with open eyes and was never thinking that this was going to be easy - or an adventure. Harold has proved to be a wonderful soldier, obedient and brave, ever optimistic and supportive of his mates. He has the love of a good woman and knows that sometime this war will end and that he can leave this behind him.

After six months Harold has certainly changed, but the fundamentals which made Harold Smith a good man before this experience, are still there in spades. People meeting him for the first time would be astounded to find out that this man, with the wisdom of eons etched into his face, is only just 23 years old.

Gradually the Allies have halted the relentless push of the German forces and the stalemate war is over. The group that Harold is with is now slowly inching north and east, digging new trenches and meeting new rats as they move. Over March and April 1918, his battalion helped to stop the German Spring offensive at Hamel in northern France. Harold is now an experienced engineer (sapper) working often in unprotected areas above the fortification of the trenches. This role means that he is not involved in as much direct fighting but often he is left exposed and vulnerable while he prepares the way for the combat troops.

He writes another letter to Jack Parrott.

May 15th 1918

Hi Jack

Today as I write this, it is fairly quiet but Fritz is lobbing lots of gas shells at us day and night. The word around the traps is that they are on the retreat and this is all they have left. Perhaps they will run out of real ammo soon and it will be all smoke and noise and not do us any damage at all.

I have just settled down after a lovely supper. This evening the Red Cross delivered us some biscuits, hot cocoa - and a big supply of tobacco which we all enjoy.

Our platoon Sergeant is a good bloke and although he often asks me to go over the top to check the wires he is understanding and says if I cannot do it with all the shell fire that is OK. Because he is such a good bloke it makes me want to please him so I stay up there just a bit longer to get it done, but the panic is always there, just below the surface. I'm no hero mate, that is for sure.

Lots of the officers are not so nice and they yell out orders and threaten us with all kinds of things. As if they can threaten us with anything more than the death that awaits so many of us if we do take notice of them! A fair few of the officers are real idiots; they just got their commissions from going to the right school or knowing some nob. Lots of the Aussies take the mickey out of these brutes when they are out of earshot. Some of the quips and comments are really funny and it is great to have a good laugh in a miserable place like this. I think this habit of the Australian soldier keeps us saner than the poor blighters from the other troops. I am so proud to be fighting as an ANZAC.

One late evening two weeks ago the Germans attacked us. Two men were killed from stray bullets - they were good chaps and one was only a kid, a 17 year old from Ballarat. I kept my head down and just thought of you all back at home.

It's my birthday today - I am 23. I kept this a bit quiet though, when blokes all around me will never have another birthday again. I just hope I get to come home and live to a fine old age. I can just see myself in my rocking chair, with my grandchildren playing at my feet and my sweet Lilly sitting beside me.

We are always under attack from enemy snipers, and there are some great shooters amongst the Hun. They regularly kill our men. One day I was playing cards with a bloke and wondered why he hadn't played his card; he was staring at me with a bullet through his brain. At least it was a quick death.

Still we have got some really good sharp shooters amongst our group too. Walt Smithers is really accurate. He was a roo shooter back home in Wagin and his successes are legendary; he claims he has over 100 kills. They reckon his Dad taught him to shoot when he was only five. Still with him up on duty, I sleep a bit better, thinking we are getting our own back on Fritz.

One time a trench about 100 yards from us collapsed and we had to dig out men who had been trapped in the mud. I had hold of one bloke's boot and I could feel him convulsing. It took about five minutes until the movement stopped. Three of our soldiers drowned in the ooze that day.

The days are monotonous, frightening and I just wish the whole thing would end so I can come home. It is not an adventure, it is just a slaughterhouse - with us as the dumb cattle waiting for our turn. I feel I have done my duty but how this carnage is meant to make England great I do not know.

Surely the great men who planned this conflict and have refused to end it, cannot possibly know what it is actually like. If they are aware of the hell in the trenches and they still persevere with their war games, then eternal damnation should be their destiny.

I am really homesick and I would do anything just to leave here and come home. Still I can't let down my mates, I just hope it all ends soon.

Thanks for looking after Lilly. She is a wonderful woman and very brave but I know she worries about me.

Yours sincerely

Your friend

Harold.

And nearly two weeks later Harold again wrote to Jack – this time a short note from the hospital tent.

May 27th 1918

Howdy Jack

I'm writing again so soon after the last letter because I have had a bit of a mishap. It is nothing serious but I want you to let everyone know it is all right and I am not seriously injured.

We have been at Hamel for over two months now and there has been continuously heavy firing so we needed to repair the lines in numerous places. The artillery fire was from steady to very heavy all day.

I was working with Ptes Wilson and Thomson out on lines all morning when we were forced to take shelter behind a shell crater. There was a ghastly sight of a partly decomposed limb sticking out of the ground and a skull was near me with tufts of red hair still on the chap's scalp. Thank goodness I could not see the face. The stench was horrible and I had tears in my eyes. I had the horrible feeling that this was what James must have looked like!

All that bull dust about how he was carried from the battle by his mates and interred with honour. This is our legacy, to rot on the battle field so our bones can bleach and only scraps of rotted flesh and tufts of our hair remain.

The shells were falling all around me and I thought I was a goner but I had a lucky escape that day. Some shrapnel hit me in the guts and my uniform was ripped to shreds but the belt buckle must have stopped it piercing the skin. The bruise was black, red and blue - about 9 inches by 4 inches across.

It looked like the time I was kicked in the guts by that young heifer. I lay there for ages until the medics came and got me. They took me to the hospital tent and cut off my uniform and then they just laughed. They said I had just coloured in the injury because I wanted a stretcher ride back to the trenches. I was really relieved that the wound was nothing worse.

Anyway please look after everyone and let them know there is nothing to worry about. I have survived and should be back with my outfit within the fortnight they say.

Sincerely yours

Harold

Harold spent the next fortnight, in the hospital tent. Despite the pain of his injuries he felt strangely safe and actually slept deeply, a bone weary exhausted sleep, a luxury that had not been his while he had lived in the trenches. The hospital tent was a hive of frenetic activity and Harold gazed with morbid fascination at the range of mutilation that surrounded him. He felt a bit of a shirker as his injuries were far less than most.

Harold noticed the high level of infection and was scrupulous about keeping his own wounds covered and cleaned. There were also an alarming number of soldiers in the tent who were succumbing to a very nasty strain of influenza and their hacking coughs mingled with the tortured moans of the injured meant that the tent was never quiet. Harold was witnessing the very start of an epidemic that would move across the world over the next three years and kill more people than died in the whole of the war.

Lying in his hospital bed with more time on his hands than normal, Harold was able to write to everyone including this letter to Lilly Parrott. Of course writing when lying on his back was difficult but he managed.

May 28th 1917

Dearest Lilly

So sorry but I missed writing to you yesterday. I'm afraid I was a bit caught up and guess what, I am in the medical tent but don't worry it is just a flesh wound. Now I know you will not believe this but the wound is really not serious!

After a pretty ferocious German attack we found the lines had been cut so Wilson, Tommo and I carried out two drums of cable. Two hours up there and I was getting pretty worried. It was so cold that morning with a late snowfall. I couldn't wear any gloves because I needed to feed out the cable. My fingers were chilled and I got some frost bite on my left hand, so it looks like I'll have black fingers and chilblains again.

All the time I was up on top I could hear there was pretty lively shelling happening about two miles to the north - those poor blighters were really copping it. And then, out of the blue, a huge one came down and exploded really close to us. I felt this huge kick to my guts and thought the worst.

Smoke and dust clouded everything and in the snowy light it looked really murky. I felt my stomach to see if I could feel the warm seeping of my blood where I felt I had been hit. Wilson and Tommo yelled out that they were OK but I told them I had been hit so they crawled back to safety to get the medic troop.

While I was out there alone waiting, I got out your talisman and with one smell and I was back with you. It was weird, one whiff was all it took and I felt cured. For a while I thought I must have been mortally wounded and that this was it. I thought that I was in the euphoric state just before getting to Heaven. But no, it was the power of my little Parrot's love and the sweetness of sandalwood and gum trees bringing a sense of normality to this blighted land.

Call me a bit of a dreamer but I think my little parrot lucky charm kept me safe out there. As it turned out some shrapnel from the shell had pierced me in the guts and my uniform was ruined but there was no really deep wound. The Doctor thinks the belt buckle protected me from the worst of it.

The blokes have given me such a hard time - I am now known as the biggest bludger of all time, risking bloke's lives so I can hitch a stretcher ride. All of the hilarity is meant well and Wilson and Tommo have been leading the chorus of hecklers.

Still, I have got a wonderful bruise and I get to laze back here in the hospital tent for a few days. Don't worry, I will not be looking lustfully at the nurses.

Anyway most of these wonderful ladies have had far too much of the unwanted attention of lonely soldiers. I don't think they want to be bothered by me as well – especially as my heart is well and truly in your keeping my love.

Yours forever

Harold

In June 1918, Harold's Battalion helped to halt the relentless progress of the German Spring Offensive. They continued the good work they had started at Hamel and then participated in the great Allied Offensive of 1918, fighting near Amiens on 8 August 1918.

This advance by British and empire troops was the greatest success in a single day on the Western Front, one that German General Erich Ludendorff described as '....*the blackest day of the German Army in this war*'.

Harold was involved in the fighting and he wrote to Lilly the night afterwards.

August 9 1918

Dearest Lilly

It is nearly the end of summer and I am not looking forward to another winter in this god forsaken place. Still we have largely left trench life behind and at least we get to march forward in the open air.

Your package arrived this morning and as I opened it, I blessed you a thousand times. The socks are so great. They even smell like home! Here your socks get so wet and without dry feet many of the blokes suffer from trench foot. I am so lucky to have you back home keeping me well and comfortable.

We have moved back to France. We had a long march from Belgium and it rained nearly all the way. They call this summer! Marching is with full kit so it is really exhausting.

My coat was soaked and my socks and boots squelched - I had blisters on my blisters by the time we arrived at the town of Amiens. We were able to rest up here over the day and by jove I enjoyed not having to walk. The town is largely in ruins from shelling but once must have been very beautiful. Many of the French people are still living in the houses - even though they have been shelled and are open to the elements. It is so strangely invasive seeing these people's lives, open to all viewers.

I watched one old French woman as she fossicked around our rubbish, muttering and crying while she searched for scraps. She was pathetically thin, her hair was roped and she had huge seeping sores around her mouth. It made me shudder to think of one of my own family forced into her position. I went to give her some bread but my Sergeant baled me up and pulled me back into line. He is right I suppose - we cannot be responsible for all of the poor wretches this war has produced.

Still I see so clearly that this is the real tragedy of war. It is not we soldiers who will get to leave this accursed place; it is the families who used to call this place home. They will inherit the full misery of this blasted and ravaged country.

I have just been involved in a very successful operation; they are saying it has been the most successful day of the war so far. None of us were killed and in our platoon the worst injury was Tommo's stubbed toe! You are sure to read about it in the paper (the successful operation - not Tommo's toe).

We must have taken over a mile today. We were able to walk in no man's land and no one fired back at us. Fritz is on the retreat. It is really weird going into the abandoned Hun trenches. Only a few days ago they were living here and firing at us! They have left things around that show how they lived - same as us it seems. Although their provisions look a bit better than ours. No sign here of stale biscuits or dreaded turnip soup.

I am having a good feeling that we are finally winning this horrid war. The boys are saying we will all be home by Christmas.

So keep your smile bright. I hold your little amulet as one of my most prized possessions. I smell it and I am transported home. I see your face and the day you gave it to me - with your bright, brave smile and the tears in your eyes.

It is the first thing I think about every morning when I wake and the last thing I think of when I go to sleep at night. With

all my love.
Yours lovingly
Harold

In early September Harold was back with his mates Wilson and Tommo. They had been organising a roll out of telephone cabling and were out in the open air. Their life of miserable trench dwelling was over. Harold straightened up from his work and looked around.

They were in an area of France which had previously been a no-man's land; a section of dirt that had seen bitter fighting for much of the last four years.

It was the start of autumn and Harold saw that grass had started to grow over the muddy fields. Some sparrows were hopping over the bomb craters, seeking out insects. There was a clean, newly washed smell, with no hint of carnage or rotting bodies. And as he listened he could no longer hear shelling - there was a sudden and deafening quiet that had come to the Western Front.

The War wasn't yet over but Harold was suddenly and unstintingly certain that he would survive.

All Wars End 1916 - 1918
Fall From Grace

September 16th, 1918

Cairo, Egypt

Clifford was still in hospital recovering from Blackwater Fever when his battalion was transferred to Egypt for a brief sojourn before being deployed to Palestine.

After the deprivations of their desert outposts, the war weary soldiers suddenly found the temptations of the Egyptian capital a honey pot. Illicit alcohol, gambling dens, drugs and whorehouses prospered when the fun starved soldiers arrived, spurred on by insatiable urges and with money burning in their pockets.

After two weeks, Clifford arrived to rejoin his troop landing in the centre of this epidemic of iniquitous behaviour. For Clifford saying no to these temptations was easy. He had no experience of any of these activities and he was more than happy to just stay away. His little tablets, courtesy of Dr Assem Singh Samran, gave him all the pleasure and peace of mind he needed. But he arrived to a troop already glutinously intoxicated by the sinful delights available in Cairo.

Macca and Bluey were insistent that he come with them.

'Come on Dead Eye. You haven't seen anything until you've watched an Egyptian sex show. These belly dancers sure are talented, you'll be amazed. And some of these little whores are just delightful. Cleopatra is so cute with a stunning body, deep kohl lined black eyes and her exotic perfume will drive you wild. She will dance for you, twirling her scarves, tantalising and exciting a bloke and then she will transport you to a plateau of dee-light. She really knows how to please a man. I'd like to take her home with me,' crowed Macca with a lustful gleam arising from his memory of last night's pleasures.

Bluey was just as effusive: 'Nothing is out of bounds and you can make love all night and they are still panting for more. Last night I had two of 'em at once. The Twins of Desire. They rubbed me all over with sweet oils and then licked my body giving me a right going over with their hands and mouths. I was over the moon. So how about it Dead Eye, want to come with us tonight?'

Clifford was uncomfortable. He was titillated but he'd had no experience of women and did not know what he would do if he was placed in such a predicament. Still debilitated from the Blackwater Fever, Cliff had returned to his troop on 'light duties' so he had every opportunity to retire to his tent. Carousing around the streets of Cairo would not have been an activity his good Doctor would have recommended during his recovery phase. Still his friends wanted him to come with them so, reluctantly, and with no enthusiasm for the planned adventure, he agreed.

The troop of nine ANZACs and Cliff arrived in Cairo at evening time, a golden glow bathing the filthy, teeming city with a flattering gold filter. Clifford lagged a bit behind the boisterous group, agape at the strange exotic sights all around him.

His senses were overpowered, the smell of cramped humanity layered with poverty and this all tempered by the exotic smells of spices and incense. The cacophony of noise erupting around him was conquered by the haunting voice of the Meuzzin calling the faithful to evening prayers. Clifford's only experience of the Middle East so far had been the harsh sands of the desert, army camps and isolated Arab villages, far removed from this teeming metropolis.

The mass of people and the strangeness of the place unnerved him and he looked at his companions, so relaxed and comfortable here. They swaggered like they owned the streets of Cairo, bantering with good natured bravado with the locals who questioned them as they walked.

Beseeching entreaties followed them: 'smokes - good Englees

brans', 'you come looka my shop', 'you want woman Mista', 'I give you special price'.

Hands pawed at him as he passed by desperate hawkers. 'Backsheesh, you give me money Mista', croaked an old crone with a drugged baby slooped across her arm. Clifford looked down at the child wrapped in grey, filthy rags with listless eyes and flies crawling over his face. Clifford looked away, panic was rising in him. He was flustered and anxious, so many people, all asking him questions, wanting him, looking at him and touching him. This was torment for the highly sensitive and only marginally sane, Clifford Hulme.

'Come on Mate this way.' Bluey grabbed his arm and pulled him down a side street, the strength and determination of his friend quelled his anxiety.

The noise was not so deafening here and Clifford became calmer, sailing along on smoother seas, able to take in the marvellous sights now that the terror had ebbed.

The side alley was a place of mystery – a narrow, cobbled path winding into the bowels of the city. Stores lined the narrow way, resplendent in coloured cloth, ornate oriental carpets or reeking with aromatic spices and above, towering washing bedecked tenements, housing the residents of this ancient city.

Crisscross paths were ignored until they arrived at their first 'stop off' on their night of debauchery: 'The Australian Public House, serving real cold beer.'

'This place was built just for us. But don't worry Bloke they let the odd Pom in, just as long as they behave like an Aussie,' joked Macca.

'Line 'em up Mustapha,' he called to the bar tender. The bar tender was probably not called Mustapha but he knew enough 'Englees' to respond to the request. He was a young, striking looking Arabian boy dressed in the white shift of the Egyptian male. He wore a silver ankh, the sign of an Egyptian Coptic Christian.

The troop of ten settled rowdily around a table and were instantly supplied with a round of cheap whiskies in small, smeary glasses with a snack of small, salted nuts on the side.

'The beer sure is cold but it tastes like cat's piss,' said Macca in explanation to an unquestioning Cliff who was not really concerned about what they were expected to drink.

This bar was a haven for ANZAC soldiers. A large replica of a slouch hat 'floated' over the bar. Real eucalyptus leaves sat limply in jars on the tables. Masses of comments from hordes of soldiers littered the walls, often written on the back of pornographic postcards indicating that it was not only grog the soldiers had been thinking about during their sojourns in Cairo.

Nearly all of the Australian and New Zealand soldiers had done their basic training in Egypt before being dispatched to Gallipoli or to the Western Front and a large number had stopped for a drink (or many) in the 'Australian Public House' before they had been dispatched to whatever and wherever was to be their destiny.

'Egypt is a Muslim country and they don't believe in drinking, so the bars have to be hidden away. Still they seem to be able to make the stuff just fine, even if they don't drink it themselves,' explained Macca to Clifford.

'This one didn't even touch the sides,' joked Bluey as he drained the first, banging his glass down loudly on the table as a sign to Mustapha to refill his glass.

The boys drank some draughts quickly to give them courage and then a few more because they liked feeling brave.

Clifford had just one and sipped it slowly while watching the others down whisky after whisky. The liquor burnt his throat; the tingling, warming sensation was unwelcome and he soon felt flames leaping in his innards.

Cliff again felt slow panic rising in him and he fumbled for one of his little white tablets. Immediately he was calmed, in control and able to cope with anything and he started to feel the rarely experienced pleasure of shared camaraderie. Suddenly his contented trance was disturbed by a harsh Cockney accent.

'What are you filthy blighters doing in here drinking all our grog? Probably you all need it because you would never get it up without it.' The unwelcome voice of Scratches cut into their fun.

'You piss heads had to hide out in an Aussie Pub didn't you? Thought we wouldn't find you? We have a score to settle with you blokes.'

Scratches' big barrel chest and beefcake head led the way. He was followed by the weasel faced Arnie and ten or so British soldiers, with faces vaguely recognised but unknown to Cliff. They were all liquored up and blind hatred suffused their faces. They were primed and ready for a real stoush.

Clifford never found out what the score was that they had wanted to settle or why the group wanted to fight. The Brits were already very drunk and the Australians were well underway.

No-one could say who landed the first punch or who lifted up the first chair and whether these actions were in defence or aggression but over the next ten minutes the 'Australian Public House' became a boxing ring, but with no Marquis of Queensbury rules prevailing. All protagonists were itching for a punch up and within minutes the fists flew and gladiatorial battles raged between the two warring groups.

Perhaps there was no single score to pay, years of pent up resentment gushed out of these aggrieved British soldiers. These war weary Brits had been forced to accept the cocky Australians. They had no choice but to endure their disrespectful attitudes, their sarcasm, and worst of all they felt the ANZACs were spoiled, self important and arrogant. The Australians got off the nasty, repetitive duties of camp, they were sent out on all the glory campaigns, riding out into the desert to take on the Turks while the British soldiers stayed back and dug the latrine trenches. These two groups had been forced into an unwelcome alliance on the battlefield but really never liked or accepted each other's ways. This was a battle of long hidden seething jealousies and mutual dislike.

Mustapha and his staff desperately hid things of value, but the cheap furniture was splintered and many bottles were smashed.

Clifford hid back from the action, he knew about hiding in shadows and fading into walls. He neither hit nor was hit but he knew when the fight was petering out and he moved in to get his two friends, Macca and Bluey, straightened up and pulled them out the door. That was what trust was all about – protecting the folk you care about.

'Get out of here blokes before the police get called,' yelled Macca over his shoulder as he left, stumbling next to Cliff's protective shoulder.

Macca still had enough energy to let fly with his boot at a perfectly placed set of skinny buttocks all wrapped around a broken table leg. The bottom was attached to the smashed and bloodied Arnie lying on the floor. The impact caused him to let fly with a gush of obscenities and threats aimed at the departing Australians. They left while the last shouts and thumps still raged.

Cliff could see other groups slinking off in different directions, some staggering and some limping, but the battle was over and immediate escape was now necessary. This meant that the large group needed to splinter and be absorbed into the entrails of this depraved, insatiable city.

Macca and Bluey were on a high; the surge of excitement that only a victorious punch up can evoke. They whooped and hollered and relived their exploits, glorifying their bravery and magnifying their physical accomplishments. Their excitement didn't allow them to register that blows had struck home and would by tomorrow erupt into angry red and purple welts of pain.

Bluey and Macca were also unbelievably flattering about 'their saviour,' the resolute and relatively sober Dead Eye. Cliff felt proud with the comments from his two trusted friends, mixing with the whisky and his little white tablet, making him feel invincible and ready to take on anything.

'Well there is nothing for it. Fighting always makes me feel especially horny so it's whoring time. We need to go and find some sheilas,' hollered Bluey.

'I feel a need of some Cleopatra action,' agreed Macca with a wicked laugh, laced with lewd reminiscence.

The trio set off down another lane way, singing a bawdy song, until they arrived at a street totally devoted to brothels. Ignoring the enticingly named: Lovin' Action, Passion Place and House of Desire the boys made a bee line for: 'The Honey Pot – let us fill you with sweetness.'

Bawdy descriptions of sex shows with promises of 'total pleasure, cheap price and no pox,' came from over made-up, blubbery harlots showing their bare watermelon bosoms lying limply over rolls of unappetising fat.

The sign promised whores of all nationalities but Macca told Cliff this was not really true – all he'd seen in there so far were: 'natives, but they sure come in all shapes and sizes.'

Clifford stared at the array of ladies all draped on couches and decked in lush silks. Each gave the soldiers their most endearing look, pouting, winking and encouraging the wild fantasies already rioting through the lads' minds.

'Now you get your choice. The Egyptians and the Indians like the fat ones. Some blokes go for the little girls,' explained Macca as he pointed towards two young girls probably aged about 10 but made up to look like the older whores.

'This next one is mine. I just love the ecstasy I get from bedding the divine Cleopatra.'

Clifford looked at the whore Macca had chosen. She was small and petite and did not smile but her look was alluring and she rose to come to Macca as he gestured his choice. Cliff also looked as Bluey disappeared down the hall with 'his twins'.

'Here Cliff I have chosen Tiger for you – she will give you all the growl and fight you need. I knew you'd be unable to choose - shy bloke like you. So go for it, see if you can tame the tiger!'

Cliff was in a spin. He looked at the whore Macca had chosen for him. She was smaller than most of the others with long black hair, hidden by a veil of deep brown entwined with gold thread. Her mouth was covered but her eyes looked up at Clifford and she purred at him: 'Come this way soldier.'

Tiger took his hand and led him down the hall to a curtained off enclave. The room was lavishly furnished with heavy, damask drapes and silk wall hangings, shimmering with gold brocade. A large bed occupied one corner with a small area of floor left for the promised 'exotic dance'.

Cliff stood awkwardly in the centre of the space, totally at a loss with how or what to do next. Tiger had luckily experienced it all: randy, excited first timers; experienced jaded 'seen it all before' types; embarrassed 'don't tell my wife or sweetheart that I'm here' soldiers and the worst of all the angry 'take it out on the whore' soldiers.

Tiger rapidly calculated that Cliff was a reluctant, innocent virgin. She was relieved. This one would not rough her up and if she gave him a good enough time he might give her a tip or even better he could be a return client. He could be a real money tree. Tiger led him to the bed and whispered her sweet words of comfort:

'Soldier you let me love you. You relax. Take shirt off. You need pipe first?'

She pointed to the ornately decorated Hubble Bubble pipe, packed full with choice Egyptian hashish. Cliff just nodded, words seemed useless, he was being swept along in a torrent that was not of his choosing.

'What you called?' Tiger asked as she lit the pipe, breathing deeply, inhaling the drug laced smoke deeply into her lungs. The intoxication of the hashish had originally given her the power to cope with the dislike she felt for her profession, now it gave her the reason for living.

'I'm Cliff,' answered Clifford reverting to the monosyllabic fashion of his insecure youth. He accepted the pipe and copied her actions breathing in the strongly scented smoke. The effect was heady, much stronger and harsher than the tobacco smoke he was accustomed to. And then came the tidal wave hit. Quadrupled in power in Clifford's fragile brain, already with the diminished resistance that comes with a whisky and his little white Heroin tablet.

Clifford at first felt that this head had left his body and that he had no control over his appendages, he was floating; then he felt unbelievably powerful. Cliff giggled as he felt an unbelievable sexual urge – his erection was already straining his trousers.

Tiger moved languidly across to the dance floor and slowly started moving, trance like, swirling her veils. She spun faster and faster throwing her veils one by one towards Clifford, who stared enthralled. Her scent was of jasmine and frankincense, bells on her wrists and her ankles tinkled and Cliff prepared to explode.

Then he noticed her nails, long and curved and painted red, they dripped like blood soaked tiger's claws. Tiger curved them and scratched the air with them, miming a menacing tiger roar in time with her dance. But this didn't arouse any fear in the drug enhanced Clifford, it created uncontrollable lust.

Tiger twirled faster until she was only clad in a small sheer skirt of gold see-through gauze. Clifford could see her small breasts with dark erect nipples, he could see her black pubic hair and his lust was unbearable. Her back and arms were covered with a fragile, henna tracery of a tiger in full roar. Clifford admired its mystery, felt its power and fell more completely under her feline spell.

She shimmied across the room to where he stood and led him to the bed. She took off his clothes and skilfully manipulated his erection until he felt he would surely burst. He was filled with unbearable desire. She lay flat on the bed and guided him into her moist deep parts, zones that Clifford had no real idea existed. Clifford was in heaven. He thrust into her deeply, she purred encouragement to him cooing her words of sexual excitement.

His first experience was not a long drawn out affair – he was inside her less than a minute before he felt the ecstasy of climax approaching.

As he quickened his thrusting Tiger uttered a low deep growl, feral and deeply erotic. Suddenly Cliff felt the excruciating, painful pleasure of her talons ripping down his back. He came with a thundering shudder, an overwhelming surge of relief and fulfilment.

Tiger's black kohl eyes stared into his and she whispered:

'I think I love you soldier Cleeff. Will you stay with me 'nother time?'

Clifford was all powerful, all conquering and he loved this Tigress, skilled in the art of pleasuring men. He allowed himself to be seduced over and over again until his love sanctuary was penetrated by the unwelcome sight of Macca.

'Come on lover boy. Time to get going back to camp. Surely you can't still be firing bullets after this time,' Macca said, the pretty little Cleopatra still clinging to his arm. He steered Cliff out of his Tiger's den down the smokey corridor towards Bluey. Bluey's twins were nowhere in sight but he looked bushed.

Reluctantly Cliff turned backwards to get a last look at his Tigress who had trailed behind him. She gave him her most entreating look.

'Come back and see me soon Cleeff. I love you Big Boy,' Tiger whispered the invitation just to him, using all of her feminine whiles to send him a message and seek his return.

'Sure thing – come on lover boy we're out of here,' Macca replied for him.

Just as Macca and Bluey grabbed Cliff's arms to lead him from the room a roar behind them indicated the arrival of unwanted company. Scratches and Arnie had recovered from the brawl earlier and they arrived with even more hatred and revenge in mind. They rushed at the two Australians, both with large urns in their hands.

The Aussies were caught off guard so only made futile attempts to protect themselves from the assault. The two distracted soldiers crumpled to the floor; both were temporarily out cold.

Clifford stood alone, paralysed, assessing the situation. The two angry Brits were not alone; at least five of the group had joined Arnie and Scratches. Cliff was sorely outnumbered.

Arnie then turned on him, dripping invective and hatred:

'You are worse than them, pandering to those Australian pigs. You call yourself British, hanging out with those Colonial low life scum. Now get them out of here. We've got some important work to do, giving some real loving to these ladies who have been wasting their time on you losers,' Arnie screamed at him before turning his lustful, weasel stare onto the whores who had clustered around to see what the cause of the commotion was.

Scratches was already arm in arm with 'the twins', their thoughts of Bluey far away as they whispered promises of unbelievable pleasures into his titillated ear.

'Hey sweetheart, want to have a session with a real man?' Arnie turned to the illusive Tiger. She had used the time and the distraction to dress and was again the fully covered seductress peering out from under the golden veil.

Tiger was overjoyed, two big payers in an evening was a very successful evening. She took Arnie's hand leading him seductively back to her private enclave. Tiger's curtains closed as the curtains also closed in Clifford's mind.

Clifford was gutted; the cruelty of the comments caused superficial hurt, the deep, guttural pain of full blown love followed by instant rejection was a mortal wound.

He had been cruelly spurned and all his malevolent hatred was directed at one man - Pte Arnold (Arnie) Haines.

But first, Clifford once again had to be the strong man for his friends. He carried the two limp Australian mates to the door of the brothel, propped them up and organised for transport back to the camp.

Macca and Bluey regained consciousness as the donkey cart plodded slowly back to the camp. The unquenchable Aussies awoke with revenge on their mind. They were angry, miffed and needed vengeance to settle the score. For them it was a rivalry and the Brits were one up on them. It wasn't really important; it was the principle of not letting anyone else win, even if it was a competition of minor pub brawls. They shook off the grogginess of a slight concussion, too much whisky and a heavy brew of hashish and were once again back to plotting how to 'get their own back'.

Of course if a battle had happened tomorrow, calling on the Australians to fight side by side with the British soldiers, all of these mild transgressions would have been instantly forgotten. Theirs was a scuffle of mediocrities and winning the last skirmish was about bragging rights not about survival.

For Clifford this ran far deeper, he wanted retribution. He wanted the painful death of Arnie – he had stolen the heart of his Tiger. He would extract a man-killer's revenge and for that Arnie needed to suffer exceptional pain. But these thoughts were not clear in Cliff's conscience yet. They appeared as screams renting across his mind, searing into him, his headache was breaking, his mood just teetered on blackness. The tablets allowed him to behave seemingly normally on the outside but within he was a turmoiled, gelatinous mess.

'OK you blokes, we need to devise a suitable punishment for those maggot Poms. Something untraceable to us because we're gonna be safe and sound, all tucked up in our beds,' Macca smiled. He had already devised the ultimate, untraceable and most devastating punishment.

While Cliff had been lying and dying of Blackwater Fever some months back, the Australians had been given a challenging mission. They had needed to break into an isolated fortress quietly, using just enough explosive to gain entry. The task required that they leave little trace as to how the entry had been established.

Bluey and Macca had been provided with the tools and given

rudimentary lessons in its use. Recently it had been discovered that the white innocuous and apparently inert chemical, ammonium nitrate could be made to explode and create a big bang if it was compacted and a spark applied. There were three stumbling blocks. Firstly, they needed to calculate how to make just the right size big bang for their mission. Secondly, they had to work out how to get the spark to the source without being observed. The last problem was that ammonium nitrate does not ignite easily, it needs strong heat to detonate it.

So for many weeks the Australians had a new challenge in their late night desert bivouacs. They exploded can after can of compacted crystals, blowing up sand dunes, piles of camel dung and even some unwanted red cross parcels. They were soon experts on the amount of ammonium nitrate needed and how to compact it 'just right' in the can to get the explosion they needed. They also found that by adding packed diesel impregnated cotton fibre, the spark was converted to a small fire and in the confined space of the tin can: 'Kaboom'.

For the wick they settled on kerosene soaked twine, coated with paraffin wax. It was almost fail safe, gusts of wind didn't put it out and the paraffin hid the smell of the kerosene.

Their mission had been a total success and now here was another opportunity to put this wonderful knowledge into practice.

The boys got to work as soon as they re-entered the camp. Two cans were packed with ammonium nitrate, and placed stealthily submerged under the sand, beneath the bed rolls belonging to Arnie and Scratches. These beds had already been carefully unwound offering quiet rest and safe sanctuary to their owners who would return later that evening.

The roll of greasy wick was easy to lay, just a boot mark in the sand allowed the lads to create the two channels and lightly brush over a cover of sand to ward off any observant eyes. The plot was hatched and the ambush prepared.

Of course prior to this, the lads had already made it obvious that they had raucously returned to camp, drunk as skunks, and had fallen loudly into their beds. The humps in their beds never altered throughout the next hour as the body shapes were just balled clothing; their physical bodies were busy concocting the firecracker welcome for their British foes.

A little 'welcome home surprise' for the Brits when they returned from their night of debauchery.

The plan was for a small explosion, just enough to destroy all the bedding and most of the possessions under Scratches' bed but Arnie was gifted something special, a larger cracker enough to cause some serious burns to his scrawny, unholy body.

After the diabolical plot was set, Macca and Bluey returned stealthily to their beds. They immediately fell into slumber, snoring loudly, wildly anticipating the pleasure that would come upon their early awakening when the eruptions occurred.

Clifford volunteered to set off the charge. He had agreed to light the wicks and then creep back silently to his own bed.

'Now make sure you set it off and go straight to bed Cliff,' Macca had instructed. 'Don't even wait to see if it goes off. None of this must be traced to us, so you can't be caught anywhere near the place.'

The trio reasoned that he was unlikely to be implicated. He had been a bystander at the first conflict and fairly uninvolved with the second. Clifford's wonderful skill of being unnoticed would come in handy. They were certain no-one would even remember seeing him in Cairo that evening.

And so the black night continued with Macca and Bluey snoring soundly in their beds and Clifford waiting in lonely vigil for the returning carousers. The riotous party came back to the camp at about 2am. Drunkards attempting a silent return is never a successful ploy and they tripped over tent pegs and water cans, swearing and quietly cussing their way to their beds.

Clifford waited for the deep sleep that a drunkard falls into five minutes after hitting a soft bedroll. He waited, his body in control even though his mind was in turmoil. He struck the match that would light the wicks, holding it aloft before cupping it to the two twine wicks.

The two flames along the wicks flickered, sizzling down the lengths almost simultaneously and Clifford watched, transfixed by the small lights. The previously agreed to arrangement, was that he would now race to his bed. He would then be seen sleeping soundly, awoken by the row but unable to be implicated in any way. But this great plan designed by drunks and implemented by a mad man, was never going to work.

This was where the crazed mind overpowered the controlled body. Pure rage flooded through Clifford and he picked up his rifle aiming it squarely at the tent which was just about to erupt in flames.

Clifford had the best view of the action. The explosions went off perfectly. Both Scratches' and Arnie's bedding, their tent and most of their possessions were destroyed. Screams erupted into the night air. A bit too much explosive meant that Arnie didn't surface from his tent, his severely burnt buttocks and groin area made it impossible for him to move, even though he was surrounded by flames.

Scratches raced squealing out of the tent, a stream of fire erupting from his back. His oil sleeked body, courtesy of the twin whores, plus his ill-advised movement, fanned the flames and increased the damage done.

Clifford held his rifle aloft, his favoured Lee Enfield, the 303, with the powerful Lee scope, waiting for his prey. He followed the fleeing Scratches, watched him escape into the cool night. He didn't want Scratches, Clifford was waiting patiently for his quarry to emerge from the tent.

Clifford waited, rifle cocked watching the smouldering tent. Instead of Arnie coming out, a host of supporters flooded into Arnie's tent to put out the flames and soothe his serious wounds.

Clifford was still holding the rifle steady, watching the scene roll out in front of him through the scope, when he felt a firm hand on his shoulder.

'Put the rifle down son. You are under arrest.'

Dead Eye, aka Pte Clifford Hulme, was caught red handed and would now be placed under military arrest pending a Court Martial.

All Wars End 1916 -1918
Court Martial

September 17th, 1918

Cairo, Egypt

Sometimes providence works in a strange fashion. By 3.30am, one hour after the explosion, Pte Clifford Hulme was arrested and marched back to his tent with two armed sentries standing in front of the tent to prevent any interaction between accomplices and to eliminate any chance of escape. A crime had certainly been committed but the unravelling of the enormity of it would wait until sunrise. Clifford lay on his bedroll in the grip of a severely black mood.

By 3.45am the heavens opened and a torrential downpour hit the campsite. After thirty minutes of cascading rain, the sentries were soaked through and sought some cover, but this was of no importance, Clifford wasn't going anywhere. The accused rocked and his voices screamed, his brain contorting into spasms of agony.

After forty five minutes of steady, unrelenting rain, flooding in the low lying areas of the camp was becoming serious and the camp started to gently flow. The rain water was unable to be absorbed by the soggy, saturated ground, and the rivulets gathered to form a muddy river. The sluggish, chocolate slush gathered up all the light items across the camp that were not anchored.

Part of the flotsam and jetsam that floated away on the cleansing river was: two shattered tin cans bearing traces of ammonium nitrate, one burnt match and skeletal remains of two burnt chords of twine.

When the wintery dawn touched the sky over the camp at 4.50am, an ironic watery sunrise cast its first rays on the unkempt camp. Sodden, muddied soldiers, many with collapsed tents and water drenched belongings, emerged from their shelters. To most, it had been a horror night. Even those who had not spent the evening drinking and debauching had been awakened by the explosions and the resultant commotion. For all, the last two hours had been spent in abject, water soaked misery.

Clifford's tent had not collapsed and he did not surface. He was now in the grip of a shaking, uncontrolled fever. The formerly at bay malarial infection had resurfaced again to feast on the red blood cells of the unprotected soldier. Clifford again had the amoeba Plasmodium falciparum running rampant throughout his body.

The sentries had resumed their squelchy points of duty and after doing a routine check of the accused criminal, both started to worry about his condition. They conferred and sent a message to those in command that the prisoner seemed seriously ill. The two sentries were overjoyed when the instruction came back that they were to immediately convey the sick man to the very dry and much more comfortable hospital tent.

Clifford was unconscious throughout the move and did not register his new surroundings or the improved comfort of the sentries now posted to stand guard ten feet from the base of his hospital bed. He did not rise from his fevered state for over 48 hours and the first eyes he saw when he awoke, were the dark pools of understanding residing in the kindly face of the totally trustworthy Dr Assem Singh Samran.

But prior to this occurring, a large number of developments were to happen at the army camp.

The investigation into the explosions and the possible role played by Pte Clifford Hulme needed a complete investigation with full military precision. Sadly this investigation was hampered by three things: firstly, the rain storm had washed away most of the evidence. Secondly, no person interviewed could recall a single aspect of the night which would implicate Clifford Hulme or anyone else. Thirdly, neither the suspect nor the two victims had uttered a word.

The very correct, career soldier Major Archibald Rodden was in charge of the investigation. By lunchtime he was becoming increasingly frustrated by the lack of progress. Just as he was planning to take a break for an eagerly anticipated luncheon, a dispatch was received from the British Command Centre in central Cairo. Sadly it contained some most unwelcome news.

Major Rodden broke the seal and immediately attended to the dispatch. Two groups of brawling soldiers from his battalion had been involved in a fracas in town last evening at a location known as the 'Australian Public House'.

It was alleged that a group of ten Australian soldiers had been *'peacefully drinking'* in the location when they had been set upon by a group of about ten British soldiers. The British soldiers had been, *'sorely drunk and vexatious'* according to the claim and had set upon the Australian soldiers who had *'merely responded in self defence showing no more force than was necessary to protect themselves from more serious injury'*.

The resulting brawl had caused extensive damage to the said 'Australian Public House' and an official complaint and a writ for compensation had been received at the British Command. The top brass were not pleased.

Major Rodden was asked to put all of his energies into ensuring that the culprits be found, named and punished and their records marked to show the infringement. His Company and their commanding officers were also to be rebuked for their failure to maintain control and order and admonished for bringing the good reputation of the Manchester Regiment and the British Army into disrepute.

The demands from the British Command were strident and demanding and gave little credence to Major Rodden's belief that there was major prejudice underlying the complaint. He thought the complaint was biased, vexatious and prompted by a desire for profit and not justice.

Obviously the owner of the 'Australian Public House' wanted

financial compensation. But to get it at the hands of the Australian Army, whose soldiers had been the source of great wealth for this establishment for over four years, would have been financial suicide. So the full weight of guilt was levied at the feet of the British Army and British Command was not amused.

The dispatch also included the daily papers which further reinforced Major Rodden's views on the matter. The story filled the English speaking Egyptian Dailies (the Major was not able to read the Arabian papers). The press had announced that, *'the fracas had occurred at a Tea House'* (no hint of the sale of liquor in this holy city of Islam was mentioned in these refined, religiously sensitive papers).

The journalist had obviously sought information on the brawl from Mustapha and the owners of the 'Tea House' and they had continued to paint the whole affair with their very anti English brush.

'These poor Australian soldiers, genteelly taking their tea, had been put upon by a thuggish British band of bullies....'

The attached photo was of the downcast face of Mustapha. His tunic was angelic white and his Coptic cross shone clearly, pronouncing to the world that this was a man of good Christian virtue. Such a man could surely be relied on to tell a story in a truthful fashion.

There was no mention of any second altercation happening later in the evening in any of the brothels in the City. 'The Honey Pot' had chosen to stay silent on the matter. The brothels didn't complain, the brothels didn't really exist and Allied soldiers didn't pay for sex, according to the 'public truth' of the time. That was 'the line' and the papers never printed any unsubstantiated innuendo or slurs.

The Major was flabbergasted. He knew these men, he certainly knew the Australians who were almost certainly involved and he was under no illusion that they were innocent. The Australian men were just as guilty as the British soldiers and Major Rodden intended to make them all pay, irrespective of their nationality.

Plus the Major was proudly British and a fierce defender of 'his Manchesters'; he was not pleased that his Army would take the full brunt for something that was obviously a shared evil.

However, the Major was a well read man and was also aware of the shifting politics in Cairo by the second half of 1918. Powerful locals, those steering local government and the press in Egypt, were weary of this war and were extremely fed up with the British occupation. Local uprisings with the Arabs demanding home rule and increasing unrest across the border in Palestine was making being an Englishman in Cairo decidedly uncomfortable. Brits were on the nose in this town.

After a lunch of grilled chicken with a sweet sherry that he was unable to fully enjoy, Major Archibald Rodden called in the nine Australians. This time the Major would take on the role of lead interrogator himself.

The nine Australian men sat waiting in the adjoining room as the Major returned from his unsatisfactory lunch break. There was no jocular chatter or relaxed disrespectful banter that usually accompanied this crew.

Major Rodden suddenly smiled, he had his first break all day. Every one of the nine men had the wounds of battle clearly marked on their faces. Broken lips, black eyes, swollen jaws and nasty, claret bruises covered every lad's face. He had been delivered the first nine combatants on toast.

The Major was as skilled at psychology as he was competent in directing his troops. He knew that no matter how long he questioned these men they would not 'rat on their mates'. He would get no answers from dividing them, tricking them or using either gentle persuasion or coercion. So he used the only tactic he thought just might work in this case – an honest appraisal of the facts laced with an offer they couldn't refuse.

He addressed them all at once. His voice rose up, full of authority, importance and hopefully with the right level of superior disdain this group deserved.

'You are a disgraceful group of soldiers who have brought dishonour on your Country and on this honourable Battalion. I know you went into Cairo last night and I know that you were all involved in this business up to your necks. The reality of your brawl is printed on your faces. So trust me, you will all be punished for this infraction.'

Major Rodden took a deep breath and looked around at the dishevelled, unkempt men in front of him. 'What a scruffy group of 'would be' soldiers,' he thought dismissively, amazed that any successful military actions had been achieved with these unappetising Australian soldiers. As he suspected, the Australian's all wore the same look on their faces: united, resigned to punishment but proud to be defying authority. Nine sets of eyes met his gaze, unwavering in their defiance.

'I also know that you are unlikely to name those with whom you were fighting. Your loyalty to any others who exhibit criminal behaviour may bring you some sense of strange honour but I believe it is misdirected loyalty. Still, I will not waste my breath and time on questioning you as I know none of you will 'squeal' – even on the worst of your foes.'

He again paused, facing off each individual, testing their resolve to see whether he could discern any chinks. Finding nothing, the Major went on with the tactic he had commenced, marshalling a different voice. This tone spoke of reason and his manner was more of a superior but kindly mentor and he hoped the words carried his honest intent.

'So I am privileging you with some information. The other people involved in the fight will be brought to justice too. Two have identified themselves by being so cruelly dealt with last night. The others will be easily spotted as we will conduct a strip search. If their bodies look anything like yours, we will not need you or anyone else to give us their names.'

'Their bodies will look a lot worse than this, Sir. You're looking at the trophy battle scars of the winning team,' Corporal Thomas Archibald Stubbs aka Bluey, spoke up with a beaming smile, misinterpreting the Major's comments as a friendly confidence.

The interjection from the officious and efficient British Major was immediate and loud.

'Attention. Speak only when you are spoken to Corporal. I do not invite your comment or welcome your excuse at humour. Failure to remember this will make your situation worse.'

The Major was sure he had them now. The comment showed just how lacking in guile these soldiers were. But his years of serving in a military system where rank and privilege determined rights ran strong. That a lowly non-commissioned officer would deign to think he had the freedom to speak his mind to a Major was unconscionable.

Following the necessary rebuke, the Major felt it was now time to regain their trust so he resumed his more moderate voice.

'Now I come to the part of the investigation we do need to pursue most vigorously. We need to know how the British Infantry man, Pte Clifford Hulme conducted the explosions which burnt the tents and the persons of Pte Arnold Haines and Pte William Crossing. I understand that he was known to many of you, but not really close to anyone in your group.'

'So here is the deal. You give up Pte Hulme, tell us what you know about the incident and let us proceed to a Court Martial. He is not an Australian and none of you need worry about protecting him. He is obviously guilty and should suffer the consequence of his evil actions.'

'If you agree to this I will agree to the following. You will all be fined five weeks pay for your part in the brawl. This is fair compensation for the damage you have done. However, no record of bad behaviour will be recorded against your name.'

Once again the Major looked around at the group. Their faces were still impassive, just a hint of relief on some countenances, they had expected worse.

'The really sweet part of this for you soldiers, is that if you agree to this, you can all be immediately dispatched home to Australia. The need for soldiers at some of the war fronts is less urgent now that the Allied Offensive has commenced. Sending you along with The Manchesters into Palestine could result in recrimination attacks and escalated rivalry. We need a united team in that frontier of war; I will be proposing that we need a fully British team. I have resolved that you need to be separated immediately and permanently from this Battalion.'

The Major again paused. The hook had been baited, the carrot offered. He now looked directly into nine pairs of eyes. Many eyes now glinted with hope and barely concealed smiles creased formerly impassive faces.

The one thing that every soldier wanted, prayed for and dreamed of was being offered to them and at the simplest price of giving up one man. He was offering them their heart's desire. Minutes ticked by, no one spoke. They were a team.

The Major thought as much – it was time to play his trump card.

'So I have decided that you have to leave from here immediately. You can all go home if you give me the information I need to convict Pte Clifford Hulme. Otherwise, I will personally recommend that you are transferred back to the Western Front.'

The Major's words hung in the air, festering with fear and dread. The doom words of this reviled location. This was said to a group of soldiers who had been there. They had seen the gory days of Ypres, survived the unbelievable carnage of the Somme and faced the nightmare of Passchendaele. None of them wanted to return, whether rumour had it that the conditions were improving and death tolls were decreasing or not. Plus winter was coming to Europe.

Home with glory and honour or back to the horror of the Western Front, this should have been the easiest choice they ever made.

The Major watched and waited looking at the nine soldiers agonise about their decision. As the seconds ticked by a grudging respect seeped into his consciousness. None of them broke, all stayed united.

Finally one soldier stood and gave the Major a laconic but serviceable salute.

'Sergeant John Mackenzie Sah. Permission to speak Sah', Macca stood rigidly to attention addressing the Major, who was at last disarmed by the appropriate deference and respect.

'Go ahead Sergeant, speak your piece.'

'Can I request a few minutes in private to talk to the men Sah? You will have your answer in no more than five minutes.'

The Major nodded to Macca and walked from the waiting room into the investigation room next door. He poured a sherry and wondered what the outcome would be. He took no more than three sips when a knock on the door indicated that the parley was concluded, a resolution had been reached.

Macca still stood to attention. He did not wait for permission but spoke clearly to both the Major and the seated men.

'Major, only myself and Cpl Stubbs have the ability to make this decision. None of the other soldiers know this soldier well and certainly do not have any knowledge of the alleged crime. Sadly though, although Cpl Stubbs and I know Pte Clifford Hulme better than any soldier in this battalion, and both of us will admit that we were with him for part of last night, we were not with him when the explosions happened. When we left him not long after midnight he was heading for bed as we were. So we are unable to confirm or deny his guilt. Our specific knowledge of any alleged crime or his involvement in it, may not be enough for you to convict him.'

'However if he is to be tried, no-one else in this army will ever be able to persuade him to talk about what really happened. You will need us, he will need us and this case will never be solved without us. Both of us are prepared to stay here and assist as much as possible for a successful conclusion to this case.'

Macca had spoken with passion and eloquence. The Major was

still trying to decipher what he was actually being offered. Macca now turned and with a sweep of his arm referred to the other Australian soldiers.

'Now about the rest of this group, no reasonable leader could expect them to give up the chance to go home. However, they are honourable blokes and have all agreed that the Western Front is preferable to letting a fellow soldier suffer for a crime he may not have committed.'

'So Sah, you can accept our offer of myself and Cpl Thomas Stubbs to assist you with the enquiry or we will all take our leave and pack immediately for our departure back to sunny France. So are we free to go Sah?' Macca referring this last request directly to the perplexed Major.

Sergeant John Mackenzie looked at him, with a beseeching but proud look, steel blue eyes in a rugged face. A face built to lead men into battle, what a tragedy that such a man was amongst this hopeless Australian contingent.

'At ease soldier, you are all free to go. I will think on this and give you my decision soon.'

September 18th 1918

Major Archibald Rodden did not make a quick decision following this meeting. The investigation proceeded at a snail's pace. The camp site was combed – no trace of any evidence of any crime was found. No-one had a clue about how the explosions had occurred.

Clifford's rifle had not been fired. There was no indication that he had done anything other than pick it up and look through the site. The arresting soldier had been on guard and was racing to investigate the crisis when he saw Pte Clifford with his rifle raised.

The arresting soldier had given the following account.

'I was on duty patrolling the outer eastern rim of the camp on the 17th September. I had not noticed anything unusual about the evening. Some lone groups of soldiers had returned to the camp with the last group arriving back home at around 2am. At about 2.15am I saw the explosions, the first was followed immediately by the second.'

'I thought we were being attacked so instead of running to the explosion, I immediately went to the highest ground I could find to see if I could see anyone running or looking suspicious. I saw the silhouette of Pte Hulme in his combat position as a sniper. While I watched him he made no effort to shoot the fleeing soldier. He could have just been doing his soldierly duty, aiming his rifle in case insurgents or perpetrators were spotted leaving the scene of the explosions.'

'Try not to make any presumptions Soldier – leave this to me or to the court,' instructed the Major testily, 'now continue.'

The arresting soldier had noticed nothing unusual about Pte Hulme, 'his breath smelt a bit of whisky Sir and I noticed that his hands were dirty and quite greasy. He had money in his pocket, his warrant card, matches and cigarettes on him but nothing that could have caused an explosion. He wasn't puffed or anything so I doubt he actually did the detonation. Perhaps he was just a look out?'

'Anyway, once I arrested him he said nothing in his defence. He never said what he was doing there or anything. He just went all dumb, staring at us with wild, glazed eyes like he was mad or somethin!' The arresting soldier was enjoying the notoriety and was happy to go further but the Major had heard enough.

'There's not enough to incriminate Pte Hulme in this pathetic account,' Major Rodden muttered to himself.

The other 8 British soldiers had been located and all had been interrogated. They had all admitted to their role in the brawl and had grudgingly accepted their punishment – five weeks of docked pay and no privileges for ten weeks, including no more leave.

'The Manchesters will be safely in Palestine before this period elapses,' thought the Major. 'At least we will not have continuation of the rivalry that created the brawls.'

They had been individually interviewed and none had expressed any knowledge of the explosion. Most expressed a total lack of awareness about Pte Clifford Hulme other than a general knowledge that he could shoot and that he didn't talk much. None recalled seeing Pte Hulme at the bar brawl or anywhere in Cairo on the night of the 16th September.

September 19th 1918

Early on the 19th September Major Rodden moved his investigation to the hospital tent. Enquiries from the Major indicated that Pte Arnold Haines was under sedation and Pte Hulme wasn't talking, he was in the thrall of a malaria attack, so he went first to the two sentries and ordered them to pass on anything that Clifford had said that had any bearing on the case.

The sentries were confused; their charge had said many things, mostly wild rantings. Much of this had mentioned Arnie, explosions, death threats and a tiger attack.

The first of the sentries had trained with Clifford back at basic training in England. He was one of the few who had been 'in the know' when Pte Hulme had shot his magic minute. The sentry had wagered a considerable sum on him winning – it was his first happy moment in this war, at a time when happy moments were rare and savoured. The man lying in the bed had been his triumphant thoroughbred. Sentry one had a soft spot for Dead Eye.

Both of these sentries were connies and had suffered under the torture of Arnie and Scratches. The second sentry had been the soldier so brutally dealt with in the latrine trench. Sentry two hated these two men passionately and if Pte Clifford Hulme was the instigator of their current situation then he wasn't about to assist the prosecution.

In response to the Major's questions, neither of the sentries had:

'heard a thing of relevance come from Cliff's lips.'

Pte Crossing was staked out on his hospital pallet with nasty, painful but superficial burns covering his back, the back of his neck and with blistering down the left side of his face. He was not in a good state when the Major went to see him.

His injuries meant that he had to lie on his stomach, his burnt back was covered with sticky brown ointment. Patches of burnt clothing were still attached to his skin and he resembled a partly plucked bird. The medical staff, under the direction of Dr Samran, had felt that healing would be improved with no pain relief, so he was in torment. Tears were in his eyes and answering questions civilly was not easy, so the Major abandoned formality.

Pte Crossing aka Scratches knew nothing about the explosion and he had no recollection of ever seeing Pte Hulme before yesterday. But those in pain need someone to blame, so Scratches was already sure of his guilt and he happily volunteered to be part of the firing squad.

The burnt man had no idea of how Pte Hulme had carried out the explosion and had no recollection of any reason that the accused would have carried a grudge against himself or Pte Haines.

'There just doesn't seem to be much of a motive,' muttered the Major, so he formulated this as a direct question to Pte Crossing.

'Can you think of anyone in the camp who would have a motive for this crime?' the Major asked the tormented private lying in front of him.

Tortured grimaces contorted his face but the question amused him. It reminded him of the powerful position he held in this Regiment.

'Are you kidding Major? Everyone is afraid of us two. Arnie and me keep the bastards on their toes. When they arrive they are weak, sooky fellows. We toughen 'em up. Most end up having a grudging respect for us but some are just cowards. This explosion was a coward's way. Someone who is too pathetic to fight us fair.'

The Major then went to speak to Dr Samran, however he was

unavailable to see the Major until all of his ward rounds were complete.

The Doctor was unavailable for a good reason, he had some things to put in place first. Dr Assem Singh Samran was in the British Army and thus had a duty to this most noble institution but he also had two other callings. One was that he was a passionate and devoted doctor and his allegiance to his patients was very strong. But far greater than both of these, was that he was a Sikh and had the intrinsic need to do good and make certain that no harm comes from his actions. Sikhs are bound to defend the rights of all creatures, and in particular, their fellow human beings.

Dr Samran had been a Doctor with the Manchesters for over three years. During this time he had seen many things but he found it hard to accept the number of minor injuries caused by the bullying and harassment of Arnie and Scratches. Broken arms and fingers, severe cuts needing stitches, mild burns, black eyes and bruises; this duo had created a steady stream of clients requesting the healing powers dispensed through the casualty department. Dr Samran was disarming and safe and many of these wounded men confided in the good Doctor. He knew that evil wears many faces and here it was personified by Arnie and Scratches.

But this alone had not set the heart of the good Doctor against the pair. Dr Samran was a kindly man caught up in a war that was not of his choosing. The Doctor was turned by the brutal death of the Quaker. He had related to the Quaker who had stood his ground against the bullies and when he heard the story of his defiance he had been uplifted.

'A stand against tyranny,' Dr Samran had thought. He was elated and he dared to believe that things would improve, that companionship and respect would replace bullying and discrimination. This soaring belief had been hopelessly dashed when he had been asked next day to do the post mortem on the Quaker.

Dr Samran had identified the cause of death as strangulation. He had clearly observed the brutal marks on the white, pure throat made by the beefy left hand that had caused the fatal damage. He had seen the ring mark, the indent of a snake, pressed into the tortured flesh. The ring would have been worn on the little finger of the strangler and he had seen that same cobra shaped ring on the end finger of Scratches' left chubby hand.

That same hand was lying inert on a pallet in this hospital while Dr Samran contemplated his responses before answering the Major's questions.

Standing forlornly at the post mortem table, nausea had swept over Dr Samran when he first smelt the stale urine smell that stained the front of the Quaker's uniform. The perpetrators had callously urinated over the dying man. Respectfully the Doctor and his assistant had removed the soiled uniform replacing it with another, so the man would not have to bear any more shame.

The Doctor had then delicately removed the balled underwear stuffed into the mouth of the choking man. The Sikh had then reverentially closed the Quaker's eyes and whispered soft words of encouragement and love to the soul of the man, now free to pursue his peaceful god.

Dr Samran unfolded the ball and marvelled at the arrogance of a bully who would nonchalantly ignore the fact that his name was clearly marked on the piece of man's apparel. At some stage this clothing had been worn by Pte Arnold Haines. As he stared at the lifeless body of the gentle Quaker, the Sikh reflected on the horror of his last moments and it was then that Dr Samran finally ran out of love or compassion for these two men.

A dossier of medical evidence from the post mortem had been presented to those in charge at the time. The evidence was circumstantial but strong and Dr Samran felt that it would be given due consideration and perhaps with the other evidence, a conviction would be possible. But the top officers had explained to the Doctor, that this was a particularly sensitive time with the arrival of the new recruits and exposing experienced soldiers to allegations like these, could lead to a serious erosion of morale.

There would be no investigation, no charges laid, the Quaker's death was declared to be 'accidental'.

The Doctor had been mortified at the time but on the morning of the 19th September 1918, before the Major came in to talk to him, the Sikh had started to formulate a plan. He could now see a way to achieve some form of justice for the Quaker.

Arnie had been delivered to him with bad burns to his buttocks and his groin area. The burns were red, deep and painful but they would heal. That afternoon Dr Samran resolved to treat Arnie's burns with a special ointment, an oriental salve that would provide temporary soothing relief but would cause rapid exfoliation of the soft superficial epithelial skin layers. The outer layers exfoliated as soon as they were formed, more blistering happened, more soothing salve was added and the cycle continued.

While this cycle occurred healing of another type was happening; the cells in the dermis was continuing to divide and the deeper connective tissue was healing. Without the protective layer of epithelium, hard and inflexible scar tissue resulted. Ugly chords of rigid, reptilian skin developed across his buttocks, around his scrotum and up the full length of his penis.

At discharge, two months hence from the investigation day in September, the extent of the damage would be fully revealed to Pte Haines. It would be with sincere sadness that Dr Samran would outline to the desperate Arnie that after two months of treatment, he would never be any better than this.

'The external scars may fade slightly with time but your buttocks, penis and scrotal sac will stay deformed. Luckily this can be hidden from view so you should not suffer from undue embarrassment,' the good Doctor would state in a kindly, conspiratorial manner.

'Unfortunately non painful shitting will not be possible. You will always be pushing against hard tissue. Perhaps a soft diet of bran and baby mush will make this slightly better. Now your urethra is thinned and distorted, passing urine without spillage and pain will never be possible. And there will be leakage. Perhaps you will be advised to wear a nappy?'

Then the Doctor would deliver his final sad revelation; sexual relations would definitely be out of the question.

'I am afraid your penis tissue is permanently altered. There are no places for blood to fill, so no erection will be possible. Is there perhaps a Mrs Haines and is she an understanding woman?' he would enquire solicitously to the devastated, one time man, who would be standing in front of him.

Dr Assem Samran would conduct this discharge meeting with decorum, but afterwards he would send a silent prayer to the memory of the good Quaker. The scales of justice can be made to balance in mysterious ways.

However this wondrous event would be some months in the future. By the time the Major arrived to see the Doctor it was late afternoon and these dutiful ministrations had only just commenced. However, the Doctor had given Arnie a powerful injection of morphine to counteract the pain. Lucky Arnie would be treated to the wondrous state of euphoria for the next few weeks, until any chance of him being involved in the investigation was over.

The Major first commenced the interview by asking how the three patients were doing. Dr Samran gave a brief summary:

'The man they call Arnie has deep burns that will heal with time and tender care. However, the process of healing will be painful and I have recommended that he stay under sedation. I am sorry good Major but this man will not be able to provide you with his recollections of the incident until his pain is decreased.'

'Pte Crossing you have already spoken to. He has superficial burns only and should be released within the week.'

Dr Samran was not happy that Scratches would be out amongst the men again so soon but he doubted that his capacity to do harm would be there without the evil will of Arnie. Scratches was a pawn, a nasty thug who would always do another's bidding. Dr Samran was confident that such a man would come to 'no good' but this 'no good' would not be at his hand.

'Pte Clifford Hulme is currently suffering from a recurrent dose of malaria. He suffered from this ailment only three months ago. The fever will abate but I caution you, investigators will get no answers from this patient if you question him roughly.'

'Now about this patient, I must tell you he has a very fragile mental state. He suffers from chronic anxiety and uncontrollable situations may lead to him being delusional. I have spent many hours of patient conversation with him and he trusts me. He will confide in very few people. Only people he has faith in should question him, otherwise he will retreat into himself and all you will get will be silence.'

'Clifford has no background of violence that I know of. I believe that if he was involved in any way, it was as a decoy or a passive accessory. He is a usually a gentle soul and I think someone put him up to the rifle stunt as a prank. Conversely, have you ever thought that he might have been unable to sleep and when the explosion occurred he did what every trained soldier would do. He is a sniper, he responded automatically. If he had wanted to see the death of the victims, surely he would have shot Pte Crossing who had run straight across his path.'

The Major listened seriously to the Doctor, to his appraisals of the patients and his theories. As he walked from the hospital he reflected on what he had learnt. He knew Samran to be honest and astute in his judgements and an excellent, if slightly unconventional doctor. But why was everyone trying to convince him that it wasn't Pte Hulme? If he was guilty then surely he was not acting alone, so who were his partners in crime? And if it wasn't Pte Hulme, then who had caused the explosions?'

By dusk on the 20th September he was still no closer to solving the cause of the two explosions but British Command was insistent that he resolve the brawl incident as soon as possible, so this became the priority. The explosions were seen as an internal army matter and the Major was instructed to solve this as he thought fit.

In other words no one really cared.

September 21st 1918

The cool crisp morning should have been spent on outside pursuits but Major Archibald Rodden decided that he would spend it writing the report to the British Command. He only needed two sherries to stimulate his creative thought processes.

He wrote a detailed and accurate account which involved all of the soldiers' names who had been implicated in the brawl: 10 British soldiers and the 9 Australians. His conscience demanded that they all be named. He did not mention Pte Hulme on this list. His name had never been mentioned and it never entered the Major's head that Clifford could have been out on the streets of Cairo that night.

He provided a promissory note for the reparation monies, claimable from the pays of the punished soldiers. He indicated that the British soldiers needed to have their records marked to record their crime. It rankled the Major that the Australian miscreants would not be similarly treated but he was following orders.

He indicated the punishments levied on all of the participating soldiers. Lastly, he prepared nine separate letters for the Australians, each contained his recommendation for that soldier's immediate future.

He sealed the report and poured himself a celebratory whisky which he drunk as he smoked a well deserved cigar before starting his next chore.

Later that afternoon the Major called up the Australian soldiers and, with suitable pomp and ceremony, announced his decision.

'I have thought long and hard about Sergeant Mackenzie's proposition. I find I am rather confronted by such presumption and I despair that even after four years of being shown correct military procedure, you Colonials persist in your arrogance.'

At this point in the monologue the Major turned to march to one side of the room, spun on his toe and marched back. The Australian's feared that this meant a long lecture was in order.

'In the British Army, allegiance to the Crown and the Regiment is paramount and no such insolent demand would be requested or tolerated.' This was not sounding hopeful. Eyes were downcast and feet were shuffling.

'Therefore, I have decided that after four years, your assistance in our fight is no longer required. I can see little reason to send you to another theatre of war where your disrespectful attitudes and your flagrant dismissal of authority can further erode the excellent demeanour and behaviour of our British troops.'

The Major continued his announcement, 'you will all be dismissed from duty as of this afternoon. I have your dispatch letters signed on the table. Your signatures will be required and then when the formalities are completed you will be heading back to Australia.'

'Corporal Stubbs and Sergeant Mackenzie, you have agreed to stay and assist with the investigation into Pte Hulme's role in the explosions. Your letters are included in the pile and I will ask you to sign these as well, however, I will hold these until the case is concluded.'

This last comment was delivered specifically to Bluey and Macca. The Major now turned to the group who were still attempting to decipher what his words meant to them.

'Thank you all for your contribution to your King and the Empire. Some of you have fought valiantly and you have all no doubt played a small part in what will surely now to be an honourable and complete Allied victory.'

The Major had delivered the best possible news to the Australians, albeit with the pomposity and lack of genuine appreciation that they had learnt to expect. Expressing their contribution and those of their dead mates as 'some of you fought valiantly' or even worse describing their role as 'a small part', was designed to be insulting. Still they couldn't care if the King himself had delivered a speech of eternal gratitude; THEY WERE GOING HOME.

The Major watched as nine slouch hats were thrown jubilantly into the air. Wild hoots of glee, laughter and hugs erupted from the exultant men. They lined up keenly to sign their letters kissing the signatures, tears of excitement misting their eyes.

Seven of the Australians would be transferred immediately to Aden and await the departure of the next troop ship leaving for Fremantle. The Major had indicated that a hospital ship was due within the week and that the seven able bodied soldiers on such a ship would provide great support.

The departing Australians were overjoyed but were aware that their freedom had been brought at great cost to Macca and Bluey. The two mates stayed with the Major as the seven 'soon to be civilians' spilled raucously from the room. Luckily, all leave had been cancelled – Cairo would not have been safe if this crew had hit town that night.

The Major now turned to Macca and Bluey.

'A military hearing has been scheduled for late October. Prior to this I have to establish if there is sufficient evidence to mount a successful conviction. You two soldiers have until that time to prepare a defence for Pte Clifford Hulme. All paperwork in support of the defence has to be presented to my office in writing by October 7th.'

The Major would present the case for the crown and he inferred that the circumstantial evidence against Clifford Hulme was mounting. The two mates had no legal training and no idea what they would do. What they would come up with, balanced by what the investigation had uncovered, would establish if a Court Martial was required.

October 6th 1918

The days before the deadline date had been interesting. Basically Macca and Bluey had no idea what they were doing. They had never even met a lawyer, let alone been in a court of law or had anything to do with a military court.

After some frenetic activity they developed Cliff's story. They still had done nothing about a defence.

The story they (well Macca really) had developed had been carefully transcribed by Bluey and had been signed by Clifford.

On the morning of October 6th, Bluey read it back to him:

'I had met up with Macca and Bluey in Cairo on the night of the 16th September. They had needed some help to get back to camp so I had got them a donkey cart and got them home and then they went to bed.'

'I couldn't sleep so I decided to get some rifle practice. I often do this when no-one is around, it keeps me quick. I went to the hill – you get a good view of the whole camp from there. Looking through the site I just practice the load, unload bit. When I practice I follow anything that is moving. This stops me looking at my hands. A sniper cannot do this because it is distracting and if you lose concentration you could get hit.

So I saw the others come home and followed them with my gun and then I followed the guys on sentry duty. When the explosion happened I watched it all through the sights of the rifle. I didn't see anyone running away from the tents until I saw Pte Crossing. But I didn't follow him Sir. I was looking to see if anyone else left the tent. If they did I could have shot them and maybe they were the ones who had done it. That's when I got arrested.'

'Now Cliff,' explained Macca patiently, 'we've been through this a couple of times but what is important is that it's all the truth. Now there may be just a few things that we have left out but is there any bit of this account that is not true?'

Cliff looked at Macca and he shook his head. He had been a bit worried about this but Bluey and Macca had insisted it was all right.

That afternoon he had asked Dr Samran a question:

'Do you think it's alright to keep some bits of the truth to yourself?'

'Clifford I believe in doing good things, making things better. Sometimes you do not need to tell the whole truth because telling the whole truth might hurt other people that we love. So if you tell the whole truth this time, will it hurt others that you care about?'

Cliff looked into the Doctor's deep brown eyes and he nodded.

'Let me read your statement Cliff.' Dr Samran read quietly, his turban bobbed.

'Is any of this a lie?' he asked.

Cliff shook his head.

'Well then I think it is good. This is what happened, this is all that happened. Forget any other bits because they could have just been stories your mind made up. Your mind does that sometimes doesn't it?' the good Doctor said. 'Now I want to help you too, so I have written this account of your ailment for the Major. The only bit that I will read to you now is this last bit:

'Pte Clifford Hulme is at heart a decent man with good morals. I do not believe there is any indication that he did this crime.'

The rest of the missive went on for many pages explaining the complexity of his ailments, particularly focussing on the anxiety and paranoia that sometimes caused him to behave in extreme ways. This was submitted for the trial but Dr Samran also kept a copy for his own records.

Macca and Bluey spent the week chatting at Cliff's bedside but most of the chat had nothing to do with the case. It was hard to keep the two young lads away from talking, thinking, living and breathing about going home.

They had cobbled together a couple of character witness statements. The donkey driver had signed a statement to say he had brought the three back to camp and that Cliff had been the sober one. Plus they were confident that the huge submission from Dr Samran would convince the Major.

Clifford was content. His fever was down and his anxiety under control. He had opened up to Dr Samran, not about the explosion but about his hatred of Arnie and Dr Samran had understood. When he had first come to hospital he had been given some low level morphine and now he was back on his little white tablets, and they were working just fine.

On the afternoon of the 6th October, Dr Samran had given a letter to Cliff. He cautioned Cliff that after the 7th October, he would be taken away from the hospital and that they may not meet again. He again impressed on Cliff that he had mental problems that could be controlled and that he needed to take his tablets, never too many and never too few. Just to keep his mind in control and in balance.

'Now Cliff you hold onto this letter. Any pharmacist or doctor will give you what you need if you show him this.'

The Doctor pressed the letter into Clifford Hulme's hand. It was doubtful that he ever knew its contents, but he sure got to know that it worked.

'Pte Clifford Hulme has been under my care for over two years. He is suffering from anxiety and delusions possibly caused through schizophrenia. I recommend that he is provided with Heroin tablets or an alternative with a similar active ingredient such as diacetylmorphine, for the stabilisation of this condition.

The provision of these tablets will enable Clifford Hulme to live a normal life. If he is deprived of them his quality of life will suffer.'

Yours sincerely

Dr Assem Singh Samran

British Imperial Force

October 6th 1918.'

Cliff did what he was asked. He had this letter on him until the day he gave it to a shopkeeper in Wubin, Western Australia, but that was to be many years in the future.

October 7th

At 8am at the appointed time, Macca and Bluey delivered their bundle of documents to the Major's office. The adjutant collected the thin pile of papers and the pair were dismissed.

The Major ploughed through the evidence and the investigation report first. Virtually nothing more had been uncovered since the first days of the investigation. No-one had seen anything!

By mid morning he had already started on his afternoon whisky. Things were not looking good. He stared at the pathetic offering from the defence.

The testimonies to Pte Hulme's good behaviour and character were unconvincing. The ridiculous and obviously concocted alibi was farcical.

And even the report from the Doctor was astounding in its naiveté. Obviously the doctor had his reasons for his blind defence of the accused but the Major was not privy to them. This was not the normal equitable and just report he was used to from Dr Samran.

The end paragraph was directly addressed to the Major:

Dear Sir,

At our last meeting you asked me that, if Pte Clifford Hulme was found not guilty of this crime, in my opinion would he be fit and healthy to resume duties as a private in the British Infantry. Sir, I do not think this soldier is fit to resume his duties.

I have a deep understanding of his ailments and he is mentally unstable. I would never have recommended that he would have been admitted to the Army in the first place. I recommend that he be immediately dismissed on medical grounds and that this should be granted with a full army pension.'

Yours sincerely

Dr Assem Singh Samran

British Imperial Force

October 6th 1918.

The Major read the Doctor's words and had a revelation. He saw a crystal clear solution. He could be rid of Macca and Bluey tomorrow. He could be rid of Clifford Hulme using this letter as evidence for a full medical discharge.

No-one cared about justice for Arnie and Scratches – they were universally unmourned. And the real sadness of this realisation to the Major, who valued military efficiency and justice, was that no one cared who had set the explosions and nothing but tedium would come of a Court Martial on this flimsy evidence.

So with his third whisky of the day he wrote on the top of the case file:

'No Case to Answer'.

November 11th 1918

At 11am on November 11th, 1918 the Armistice was declared across all theatres of war. The long bitter war was ended and all the boys could finally go home.

Harold Smith was having a cup of tea when the guns fell silent across the Western Front. By late November 1918, members of the AIF began to return to Australia for demobilisation and discharge. Harold was going home.

It was 3pm in Palestine and the Major had just poured himself a constitutional whisky. He smiled as he received the cable, unconditional surrender and total victory for Britain. This was excellent news. However, the British involvement in Palestine was to continue for at least 30 more years and war across the holy lands of the Middle East would still be very real, nearly one hundred years after peace was proclaimed in Europe.

Macca and Bluey were steaming across the Indian Ocean but neither of them were up on deck enjoying this most peaceful of evenings. Bluey had gonorrhoea, a parting gift from one of the 'Twins of Desire' and Macca lay wracked in a paroxysm of coughing – he had developed the Influenza. Still they were only a few days from home and the thoughts of Australia made these few days of incapacity quite bearable.

Clifford Hulme, a civilian, was sitting silently on a train heading to Leeds, his discharge papers and his powerful letter from Dr Samran were in his pocket.

When the pretty girl next to him told him that the war had ended, he smiled a dopey smile but what thoughts went through his mind remained a mystery.

The Tween Years
Lilly's Afternoon Cuppa

Early afternoon, July 21st, 1923

Wubin, Western Australia

The darkened room behind the store failed to retain any heat so Lillian Smith stoked the old Metters wood stove to the brim before sitting down to her afternoon cup of tea on a wintery, cold day in Wubin. As she sipped her refreshing brew she stared out at the rain coursing down the grimy windows. She was not happy they were unclean but she hadn't had enough time to get stuck into this chore. Some were so high that she needed her husband to help but he was so busy these days and she didn't like to bother him with this mundane job.

Lilly savoured the feel of the warming tea, wrapping her hands around the cup so she could get even more physical pleasure from her afternoon ritual.

A soft whimper indicated one of her babes was stirring. She looked over and three year old Elsie had settled again, her soft even breaths showing she was at peace. Beside her, still in the crib, baby Yvonne lay on her tummy.

'Vonny will be one tomorrow,' reflected Lilly. The birthday was just one of the things to celebrate this evening. Lillian's brief respite was a snatched and very appreciated break in her whirlwind schedule. Today had already been jam-packed as she ticked off the preparations for tonight's meal: the corned beef was bubbling on the stove, the carrots and potatoes peeled ready to be added to the pot and at the back of the stove the cauldron of pea soup was all prepared. The room was still infused with the deeply satisfying smell of the bread she had cooked. It would be a feast.

Lilly looked over at the baby; her chubby body now too large for the crib. Soon it would be necessary to collect the cot from storage at the Nelson's farm. Lilly smiled as she recalled that Elsie had fitted in the crib until she had turned 18 months. She was always a petite little one and once she started walking any puppy fat had just dropped off. Vonny was just happy to sit – still no sign of crawling let alone walking and she sure liked her food. Still she was such a bonny child, filling their life with blissful smiles and gurgling laughter. 'Bonny Vonny,' was Harold's pet name for his youngest girl.

Lilly loved her babies and the thought of them filled her with exhilaration, warmth and sheer contentment. She recalled her teenage fantasises to excel at something, to be famous or even infamous and here she was, a happily married lady with two little children. She had found her destiny and it was the last thing her 13 year old self would have thought. At 13 she had wanted her picture on the front of the paper – now she had settled for the odd inclusion under the marriages and births columns. But she had been true to her early promise to 'be her own person'. At 26 years old, Lilly Smith, nee Parrott, was happy in her own skin.

As she drained her cup, savouring the last mouthful, Lilly stood, smoothed her apron and moved to the mirror over the dresser. The face that looked back still held the same warm, intelligent brown eyes and rosebud mouth but now the hair was cut into a short bob – the fashion in the very modern 1920's. Her body was still trim despite her two pregnancies. She was thrilled that her new dress, ordered two months before through the new Boans catalogue, had arrived in the store yesterday morning.

The shot blue fabric sparkled, even in the dim light of the shuttered room. It was important to let the children sleep as long as possible so she suppressed the urge to shout out in excitement at the vision of the dress. She reverently lifted it from the bed, smelling the newness of the fabric as she pressed the soft silk to her cheek. Her finger followed the spider web tracery of silver threads that created the shimmer.

Quietly she unrobed and the new Charleston styled garment

shimmied across her body. It was lovely but so risqué. The dress fitted perfectly but it was so short; her knees felt the chill of exposure. This evening she would be wearing her tights but still her legs would be so visible. Lilly knew Harold would love it. She felt a tingle as she thought how Harold's eyes would be transfixed - appraising her, proud and so obviously besotted.

'That man makes me feel like a movie star,' she thought. 'With him giving me confidence, I can wear a dress that shows me in my undergarments. Short dresses are in fashion now so I will just need to get used to having my legs on show.'

Lilly gently pulled the dress back over her head and stood, oblivious to the cool room, clad only in her knickers and camisole. These were the very undergarments she had worn on her wedding day four years earlier. Her refection in the mirror caused her to blush as she recalled how she had naively revealed herself to Harold on the night of her nuptials. She had been nervous and frightened that day. Although she had known, with immense certainly that Harold was the one for her, the whole idea of sexual relations had her morbidly anxious.

This topic was rarely discussed amongst women in this era, but Lilly had thought she was better prepared than most. She had read a book a nurse friend from the Woman's Auxiliary had lent her, all about the sexual act. Lilly had studied the pictures and read the sterile, clinical words but this had just added to her ignorance and despair. Lilly had seen animals copulating and from their grunts, squeals and wild eyed expressions they were definitely not getting pleasure from it. Besides, Lilly wasn't really convinced that this would actually work in humans. She just couldn't see how male and female bodies would fit together.

Just prior to her wedding day, the dreaded moment had arrived when Mrs Frances Parrott, Lilly's mother, had broached the delicate subject of 'intimate relations with your spouse'. The very embarrassing, 'personal chat about what to expect on your wedding night' had to be endured and Lilly had sat, mortified, throughout the lecture. Her mother had stared, stonily at the wall, never making eye contact, as she had unrelentingly delivered her advice.

She had steered around what actually happens but she had been full of advice like: 'you won't like it but he will', 'just succumb and think of other things', 'it will hurt a bit but you will get used to it' and of course, 'it will not take very long and if you want babies this is the only way'! This guidance did not fill Lilly with any confidence. All in all, it didn't sound like this part of marriage was going to be much fun at all!

Her wedding day had been amazing. Lilly had looked at Harold a million times over the day and she knew she loved him passionately, amazingly and completely. He was the man for her. But all day, at the back of her mind (and sometimes this thought would sneak to the front) there was sheer, blind panic about what would happen that night.

But no-one had prepared Lilly for her own response. Harold had kindly retired to a different room allowing Lilly to disrobe in private. She had stripped off her beautiful wedding outfit and stood demurely in her knickers and camisole as she heard him re-enter the room. Harold had moved to her silently, bending to kiss her and gently slipped off the strap of her camisole.

At his touch, Lilly just forgot to be embarrassed anymore. She felt her body tingle with a craving she didn't understand. His touch was unbelievable and she was unbearably aroused. She just couldn't stop herself, she reached for him kissing him back, stroking his body and devouring this wonderful feeling of pleasure. It was like her body housed this other being and that being needed satiation. She behaved positively wantonly, grabbing Harold pulling him down onto her, urging him on. Her mind was a blur - the pictures from the manual didn't mention that 'the act' was also really enjoyable!

Harold had entered her, kissing her passionately and as he climaxed Lilly dissolved into shudders, her whole being feeling desire, then pleasure, then relief and then total relaxation. But right in the middle of that lovely afterglow time, Lilly felt a surge of absolute shame. The mortification of how she had let her bodily urges overpower her. What must Harold think of her!

She recalled sitting up in bed, coyly covering her nakedness that had been so flagrantly exposed minutes before. Lilly looked over at her stunning Adonis, lying spent on the bed beside her. Her face was blotchy with humiliation and streaked with tears of remorse as she started her stumbling apology.

'I am so sorry Harold. What must you think of me. You thought you were marrying a demure, chaste, virginal young girl and I have acted like someone with harlot urges. I do not know what came over me - I just couldn't stop myself. I promise I will keep myself in far better control in the future.'

Harold languidly turned to her, devouring her with his eyes, so fulfilled with pleasure he could hardly move. It took him some time before he could contemplate what she was talking about. She was apologising for being everything that he had ever wanted! When he realised what she was saying he started to laugh. It was a deep throaty, belly laugh, a laugh full of happiness and delight.

'Lill, my dearest. I want you to be just like that. Forever. I love, desire and crave you. To make love with you and have it reciprocated makes me the most contented man on earth. That I have a wife who reflects my passion is tremendous. Now I think your punishment is that I need to make love with you again and again and again. Don't you realise that the highest flattery a man can have, is that his wife enjoys making love to him?'

And with that he grabbed her strongly, pulled her back towards him and kissed her tears away.

Lilly felt the red blush of embarrassment as she thought of that first time. Once again she had let the thought of what she 'should behave like' influence her. Harold wanted her just as she was. Of course this had set the pattern for a wonderfully fulfilled physical union that rounded out their relationship. Theirs was a wonderful marriage.

Lilly quickly slipped her day dress back on. This was hardly the time to be thinking arousing thoughts. Most inappropriate. She gently placed her special dress back in its place on the bed and turned her thoughts to safer topics.

'I bet Chrissie has been shopping in Perth and she will probably have a great dress too. She might even have silk stockings to go with it,' Lilly muttered to herself as she moved over to make herself another cup of tea, eking out just a bit more private time before the children stirred.

The 'Chrissie' Lilly was thinking about was none other than her old friend and pen pal Chrissie Ayers. Only she was not Ayers anymore she was now a Parrott, Jack's new bride.

And the newly married couple were arriving in Wubin on the train this afternoon at 4.30pm. Chrissie had been Lilly's bridesmaid and Jack had been Harold's best man on the Smith's wedding day back on the 23rd of August in 1919. Jack and Chrissie had taken their roles so seriously they had ended up: attracted, besotted and betrothed, by the end of the reception. Both Mrs Parrott and Mr and Mrs Ayers had insisted that, 'a marriage in haste was not seemly' so the couple, hopelessly in love and forlorn over this decision, had been forced to wait.

Finally, on June 3rd 1923 the couple had wed. This delay had been largely at the insistence of Mr Ayers who had needed to be satisfied that John Ardley Parrott (her brother Jack) was able to provide sufficiently for his daughter. Jack's hard work and thrift had built an admirable nest egg and by May this year, the date had finally been set.

Despite Chrissie and Jack wanting Lilly and Harold to perform the reciprocal roles of their Matron of Honour and Best Man, life had got in the way. With no one to cover for them at the shop, Smith's Store in Wubin, the Smith family could not attend. So Jack and Chrissie Parrott were united at St Paul's Church, West Perth, with Rev. Holland officiating, minus the Smiths.

But now Mr and Mrs Jack Parrott were heading to Wubin to join them as partners in the store. The name had been officially changed, the sign had been prepared and was propped at the back of the store. Painted with care in precise calligraphy the words in white writing on a solid red background announced:

'Smith and Parrott General Store for all your Grocery, Haberdashery, Hardware and Agricultural Needs.'

So tonight was set to be a double celebration; day one of the partnership and little Vonny's first birthday. Lilly was so excited that Jack and Chrissie were coming to live in Wubin. She loved her brother and had missed him (even though he still treated her like a little girl) and having a girl friend in town would be so jolly.

Life in Wubin had been challenging. Wubin, a small rural town 200 miles from Perth, had only been in existence for about 8 years when Harold, Lilly and little Elsie Smith had arrived at the beginning of 1923.

Lilly thought back to that day. It had been mid January and although it was 5 o'clock in the afternoon, a hot, dusty wind scalded their faces as they left the station, lugging their suitcases along the desolate main street. Elsie screeched with tears of exhausted discomfort and Lilly felt like joining her.

Harold trudged stoically in front of them, carrying most of their personal possessions and seemingly unaware of the extraordinarily, hostile conditions. The store, with exposed scaffolding still apparent, loomed in front of them. Harold fumbled with the key to the front door. The inside of the store was dark, still and stifling. Large crates containing their household items had been delivered on an earlier train but these were dwarfed by towers of precariously stacked boxes.

The haphazard scene contained two week's worth of orders; boxes of goods awaiting sorting and organisation. This was to be the store for the people of Wubin and the surrounding district and Harold and Lilly Smith were the new proprietors. This was to be their kingdom and it would be their job to get this place in order.

'Come this way Lill. Weave your way though and come out the back and see where we are going to live.' Unbelievably, Harold's voice was filled with enthusiasm and eagerness.

'This is ridiculous,' thought Lilly with typical practicality. 'I am sulking, hot and bothered and dear Harold is still full of excitement. I must watch myself. I shouldn't be thinking of my own discomfort. I am no longer a child. This is my new life and if it is going to get any better, it is up to me to improve it.'

Lilly had pasted on a smile and had followed Harold as he lugged the first suitcase out the dark, back doorway leading to the accommodation area. Her heart sank again as she thought of her little 20 month toddler ambling through the shop with all of its dangers. She dreaded to think how she would go, heaving her pregnant body around this space over the next few months.

Harold had already disappeared into their living space behind the store. As Lilly got to the door she let out an involuntary gasp.

The large room at the back was totally unlike the cluttered scene she had just passed though. Angels had transformed the space into a homely living area. Their bed was in place, looking ever so inviting with her own crocheted rug and pillows. Elsie's cot, complete with her favourite bear was in place and her trunk, overflowing with toys, was stacked below. Elsie spotted this and let out a squeal of delight, wriggling from Lillian's arms to delight in her sanctuary. Familiar things in an unfamiliar place.

Lilly's kitchen table, draped with her favourite yellow table cloth sat beside a kitchenette stacked with plates, cups and kitchen wares. A Coolgardie safe to keep things cool and a stove to cook on, were both new to Lilly. The evening sun's rays streaked into the room and lit up a vase filled with yellow wattle and a sprig of sandalwood filling the space with its beautiful scent.

Lilly burst into tears. She turned and hugged Harold, her exhaustion pouring out in surging sobs as she gushed:

'It's perfect. How did you do this? You've been with me packing for the last week and we've been travelling for two days so how has this happened?' Her tears still flowed, but her huge beaming smile revealed that these were happiness tears.

'John and Ada silly,' Harold said, pushing hair from her face and wiping tears from her cheeks. 'I asked the Nelsons if they could come into town and get things nice. Their farm is only 20 miles to the west and they have been here all week, collecting our crates from the train and unloading them. You will find all those crates out there are empty. You've got it easy. Lots of your work has already been done for you.' Harold was beaming - his little surprise had worked.

John and Ada Nelson had taken up their farm in the area of Miamoon, west of Wubin, not long after Harold had left for the war. Farming life had been just the tonic the anguished couple had needed. Hard work and honest toil had helped them both recover from their deep and profound sorrow over the death of their only son James at Gallipoli.

The Nelsons had left their beautiful Nedlands home overlooking the Swan River, using it occasionally as a holiday home when they came to Perth. They both felt the home was too full of memories for them to be happy there again.

After their marriage, the new Mr and Mrs Harold Smith had moved into this Nedlands residence and Lilly had settled very comfortably. The home was extremely commodious but Harold was not satisfied with city life. He ached for the sunburnt vistas and the wide open spaces of his adopted country and he blazed with a passion to make his own way in life. Nedlands, with his pretty young wife and lovely daughter was nice but was never going to be a long term answer for the driven, ambitious Harold Smith!

So he had resolved to follow his dream and move to the country. Lillian, as a dutiful wife, was more than content to follow, albeit with some misgivings about giving up her city comforts.

John Nelson had alerted the couple to the possibility of building and running the Wubin General Store when the Nelsons had come to town for Christmas in 1920.

Lilly recalled the after dinner conversation:

'Look Harold, I know you want to farm. Ada and I are really enjoying it and it would be great to have you take up land out near us. But there are a couple of things you need to think about first. Farming is a risky business. The weather is fickle and can turn a good year into a bad one just like that.' John had snapped his fingers - reminiscent of the capricious nature of droughts and storms that ravaged the Australian countryside.

'Plus it is terribly expensive when you first start out. For two or three years while you clear your land, you will have no income at all. After we sold the sandalwood business we had more than enough to buy the farm, pay for the clearing, buy the necessary farm equipment and stock. But we have seen too many of our neighbours come out under prepared. The dream can turn sour pretty quickly. And watching folk nearly starve is not a good sight.'

The Smiths had listened attentively to their friend and mentor. John Nelson had continued: 'Now you have come home from the war with some savings. Plus you two are both frugal. My suggestion is to buy into a business, work unbelievably hard for a few years and you will have cash to burn when you take up your farm. Do you know who made the most money in the gold rushes? It wasn't the miners, except for a very rare few lucky ones, it was the shopkeepers!'

John Nelson's advice was heeded and over the next year Harold had purchased land in the newly gazetted railway town of Wubin and had commenced construction of the general store.

1922 had been the year Harold and Lilly had moved out to the country. They had become pioneers. The year was filled with hard work, setbacks and more disasters than successes. Harold had worked with an obsessive resolve to get things right. The place was still a construction site when they had moved in and Harold had ensured that it was fully complete, along with the out-buildings by winter. As the only shop in town in 1922, they had to provide everything: groceries, foods, drapery, tobacco, agricultural needs and of course they were the site for the Wubin Post Office. The store was fully stocked and operational by May that year.

Harold also had to service the many outlying locations and had a system of four delivery routes organised. Folk would do their orders one week and the next week they would receive their shopping between Mondays and Thursdays. Friday, was stock take and reordering day. Three young helpers had been employed, particularly to do the deliveries, but they had all proved rather feckless and unreliable. The bulk of the workload fell on Harold and Lillian. Late into the night, Harold would still be hovering over the accounts or casting a final check on the orders before they would be dispatched the next morning. The flickering kerosene lantern would cast ghostly lights into their enclave where Lilly lay in her lonely bed waiting for her husband to call it quits.

Six months ago, a godsend had turned up disguised in a most unlikely package. A giant of a man with a ghastly, disfigured face had arrived in the shop looking for work. Although Lilly had been exposed to war victims with appalling injuries, she was taken aback at the man's cruelly scarred face. However, his voice was gentle with strong traces of a soft Irish accent as he enquired if they had any work available.

Harold had been working at the rear of the shop and had instantly come to the counter.

'I recognise that voice,' he said, and as he came closer, 'how are you Charles? I last saw you as you dropped me off at the Narrogin Inne before the war. What brings you to Wubin?'

Charles Martin looked up at the man who had offered him such a warm welcome. A friendly smile crept across his face, making it look less fearsome, as he grasped the extended hand in an enthusiastic handshake.

'Harold Smith. Of course, I should have recognised the name on the sign at the front of the store. It is great to see you. And it looks like a lot has happened in your life since I last saw you too. I have left the Mill and come to Wubin and I am now looking for work locally. I am a happily married man these days and now have two babies. My wife Mabel, is a local girl and wanted to come home to be closer to her parents. You might know the Rowbottoms? Mabel's Dad is the Police Constable for the district. Who would have thought that with all of the things wrong with me, I could have found such happiness. So now the only thing I need is to get steady work. Man cannot live on love alone you know!'

Charles Martin gave them both a conspiratorial wink using his good eye. Lilly instantly had a good feeling about this man. She felt he would make a good and loyal employee.

Harold did employ Charles and he soon became their right hand man, doing many of the deliveries and taking on much of the manual labour. There was no doubt that with time his looks became less fearsome and Lilly smiled as she thought how good he was with the children. Elsie just loved him.

Lilly would still help in the shop whenever she could but little Elsie and baby Vonny, who had arrived in July, often took her away from the store. Lilly was philosophical about her life, it was busy yes, and she was often left to cope alone, but she was working alongside a man she loved and daily she could see their life improving.

Harold, known to everyone as Smithy, had been instantly welcomed in this pioneering town. He was already familiar with the idiosyncrasies of country life from his many years in the sandalwood industry. Harold loved the surroundings and relished the challenges. But most of all he loved the down to earth, unpretentiousness of country folk.

Lilly took a little longer to acclimatize. For a long time she felt that she just did not really fit in as a 'Wubinite'. She was a 'little city girl' and soon realised that she had a lot to learn about this pioneering life. Lilly had not realised she was such a town body! After discussing this one night, Harold had insisted that she join the Wubin Woman's Group. She had not been too keen. Lilly had rarely craved female company and she doubted that she would get any sensible discussion or sense of worth from this group.

Over the first few meetings she had observed them from a distance. She had been impressed at how capable these women were but she did not relate to any of them. Lilly was polite but aloof, there under sufferance. At first she had been amused at their excitement over what she had previously thought of as 'menial topics'. They raved and tittered about sewing, sharing recipes or doing craft. Lilly desperately wanted to leave the group but Harold had insisted that she persevere.

But the moment baby Vonny was born, these country women showed Lilly what they were really about. She was showered with gifts for the baby, cakes and stews were dropped off, her home was cleaned and little Elsie was whisked away and given toys and gifts to rival what had been made for Vonny. Lilly realised that this is what makes country women so special. They start with so little, they make so much and they give so much more.

As Lilly sat warming her hands on her second cup of tea she reflected on these women and how much she had grown to depend on them. She needed their guidance, their advice and the wisdom many of them had gleaned from many years of 'making do'. Lilly blushed at her former 'high and mighty attitude' and how, when she had first arrived, she had acted so superior.

'Harold knew best again,' she recalled. 'It is amazing. He is British by birth but he knows instinctively so much more than I do about relating to Australians.'

In November 1922, Lilly had accepted the challenge of making scones for the big event of the year, the grand opening of the Wubin Hall. This had been totally built by the locals, using donated and scavenged materials. It didn't look much but at least they all now had a public meeting place. Everyone was coming; there would be over 100 people in attendance including the Minister of Agriculture and other important dignitaries.

The Wubin Women's Group was of course doing the catering and Lilly agreed to make the scones. Her job was easy - ten dozen scones, complete with jam and cream. The only problem was that Lilly had never actually made scones before and she underestimated, somewhat, the difficulty of producing 'the perfect scone'.

She had jars of wonderful apricot jam (thanks to her mother who had provided her with this yummy Christmas gift) and had the cream ready to be whipped.

In the morning of the event Lilly set to baking. Her first dozen were pancake flat. Her second dozen were even worse - they failed to rise at all. Her third were totally burnt. The morning wore on and Lillian's attempts just got worse. So there was nothing for it - these would have to do.

Lilly was flustered but decided it was time to whip the cream. She had collected a gallon of fresh milk that morning and had it cooling in the Coolgardie safe. She scooped the cream from the settled milk and started to beat it. When it was nearly done she decided to give it a few more whisks for good measure. Tragedy! She had passed the point when cream is perfectly whipped and had slipped into the phase where it separates. Lilly had produced buttermilk, the cream was ruined and there was no chance of getting any more at this late stage.

Lilly packed her pathetic produce into her basket, gathered up the children and headed across the road to the Hall, already packed with an excited crowd. The tables were loaded with appetizing treats, everything looked fabulous. Lilly rapidly placed her flat and charred scones, curdled cream and saucers of jam on the table and went to find Harold.

The afternoon was a mortification, one of those days that you just want to be swallowed up. No one went near Lillian's mound of ugly, deformed scones. The rest of the food was devoured and Lilly's contribution remained untouched. She had never felt so alienated, so unable to cope.

Then Mrs Rowbottom, wife of the Police Constable went over, grabbed a scone and piled it with jam and buttermilk declaring: 'Wow these are tasty flat cakes Lillian. And the buttermilk gives them an interesting flavour.'

At her instigation others from the Wubin Women's Group had

gone over and sampled them - not with alacrity, but with a huge dollop of kindness. Some even took one for their husbands to try. There were still over 80 untouched offerings left at the end of the evening but Lilly was no longer feeling a pariah.

Lilly smiled at this reminiscence. This was their kindness and that day she knew that she was included. But what she had not managed to find was genuine, bosom buddy friendship. So when Jack and Chrissie Parrott had agreed to come and live in Wubin and help run the store. This was a huge relief.

Life would become so much easier - Jack and Chrissie would relieve the burden. But more than this, Lilly would have a good friend in town. Someone to share her inner thoughts with. Someone to laugh with and someone to trust.

This was worth rubies.

The Tween Years
Hello Dolly - Goodbye Molly

May, 1920

Leeds, England

When Pte Clifford Hulme arrived back from the war, he was one of the thousands of returning soldiers coming back to pick up the pieces of their shattered lives. It should have been so simple. Prime Minister David Lloyd George had declared: *'What is our task? To make Britain a fit country for heroes to live in.'* But despite his best efforts, issuing in a new era of social democracy, unemployment soared.

The British Government had been spending over 7 million pounds a day to wage war against Germany. After the war, the country was crippled by the need to repay its War debts. Britain faced social evolution and a changing world order. It went from a state of war, to stumbling recovery and then nose dived towards depression.

When the soldiers came home everything had altered. Their towns had changed, the people left behind had changed and they had changed. Many of these soldiers were severely damaged; physically, emotionally and mentally. The world they had left had done quite well without them. Now they had returned, expecting to slot straight back in - but the round spaces they had left had turned into square holes.

There were few vacancies for boot makers in Leeds after the war. The company Cliff had worked for had specialised in providing boots for the soldiers; after the war the demand for boots was gone and the company did not survive.

Clifford's family life had changed too. His mother had married Joseph Blootle and they had set up a happy residence. They welcomed Clifford with open arms and hearts. His home was still his home, his bed was still there, some things were just the same. But Clifford didn't live against the wall anymore and his habits and their lives rubbed. They were a couple, sharing the joys of being together, complete within each other's company. They didn't need the presence of a fully grown man, hovering on the edges of their domestic bliss.

In less than two months Clifford had moved out, an itinerant grey shadow in a country full of grey shadows. He moved into a boarding house just off the northern end of the Beeston Rd, where few questions were asked and a man who kept to himself was left well enough alone. Cliff picked up casual work in the quarries, at one of the industrial areas or down at the loading dock, or he just wandered the streets of his town. This pattern was to define Clifford's life for two years after the war ended.

Albert was now dead, his mother and Joseph were united as a couple and Young William had grown up and left home. Mami, Joseph and William remained as his triangle of trust and, even though he was not often with them, these three still guided, supported and mentored him. However Clifford was quite content to be alone, he did not seek them out so often anymore. Clifford had developed a few secrets, behaviours he had learnt in the war, that he was not comfortable sharing and to keep these secrets he needed to live separately, away from prying eyes. These secrets mainly involved the comforting use (and abuse) of his tablets and a partiality towards visiting women of dubious repute.

The tablets were easy to acquire. With the assistance of the good Doctor's letter, Clifford soon established an easy supply. Returning soldiers with varying degrees of drug dependence were not uncommon and access in the post-war years was not difficult. Supply from doctors, pharmacists and over the counter was simple. No-one tallied how many or how often a patient took pills that would, in the near future, be prohibited and officiously scrutinized.

Clifford had all he needed and he self medicated within a strict routine; rarely too many and never none at all. He kept himself 'mildly medicated' and his anxiety was kept absolutely in control.

In those early post war years Clifford Hulme was not broke. He had scrupulously hoarded his Army pay and with the careful expenditure of his repatriation pension, he lived a life of prudent comfort. He did not drink or gamble and although he was a heavy smoker, smokes were cheap. The only thing he did like to spend his money on was whores and his boarding house just off the Beeston Road, was only a block and a half from his preferred brothel.

Clifford went twice a week. He paid his money, made his choice, did 'the deed' and left satisfied. He did not stick with any one prostitute, he did not have a favourite, he was happy with variety. The brothel was happy to have Cliff as a customer; he was polite, didn't ask for 'kinky stuff' and never roughed up the girls.

This worked well until he entered the brothel as usual on a balmy May evening in 1920. The brothel was advertising that they had: *'New, Fresh Young Talent recently arrived from London'.*

With a voiceless nod Clifford indicated he was interested, when invited to view the display of new girls. He sat in the murky shadows with six other faceless men in the partially lit, smoky room as the five new ladies walked out through the curtain. The ladies of the night, clad in various states of undress, pouted, preened and displayed their wares. None of the five were young and it was doubtful that any of them were fresh. Their faces all bore the jaded look of overblown prostitutes that only dimly lit, smoky rooms can do justice to.

Shock recognition. Outwardly he did not move a muscle, he stayed motionless and silent. Inwardly he felt the rising of bile, the lurching of his guts, he was a seething mass of anxiety. Number four, wearing the name of 'Dolly Molly' on a sash that gently crossed her chest, was none other than Mrs Molly Williams. Four years ago Cliff had sat opposite her in the Boot Makers factory. He had shared his lunch with her. He had fallen hopelessly in love, even if it had only been for one day. She had been the first girl he had ever felt 'tingly' for and Molly had shared a connection with him. The connection, for Clifford, was still well and truly present.

Clifford popped a tablet and waited for the instantaneous calming that just taking a tablet could bring him. He then quickly requested number four, scared unless one of the other seedy gentlemen, had noticed that she was by far the most beautiful of the girls on show.

In reality this was not likely to have happened. Dolly Molly was not the best looking of the girls, in fact she may have been the worst. The four intervening years had not been kind to Molly Williams.

She had been working in London and the Madam had transferred her because she wasn't earning her keep. *'No enthusiasm for the job and looks like a bloated cow,'* had been part of the London Madam's reference. The downward spiral of a pretty young widow with no means of support, no skill or talent had led to the inevitability of her ending up in the oldest profession in the world. Molly had been down on her luck for the full four years since Cliff had last seen her.

At first, Molly had thought that she could do the job and remain unscathed. She hadn't minded having sex with her husband, she had rationalised. The unpleasantness of accomplishing 'the act' with strange men, could be managed and the money she would earn would get her out of poverty. She had joined the brothel voluntarily, not willingly but as a necessary means to an end.

Her first job was merely to act 'as an escort' for an 'old respectable gentleman lawyer'. 'Easy money,' she had thought. She was soon shocked out of any notion that she would be unscathed, when the old gentleman she 'escorted' brutally raped her, despite her protestations.

Early in her career she had hoped to be saved. Molly thought that a good man seeking casual sex would fall for her charms and take her away from all of this. Unscrupulous pimps, callous customers and the brutal low life that wallow in the lowest reaches of life, soon obliterated this fantasy. Her life was soon relegated to utter misery. But brothels have a redeeming feature, they are filled with women and although many of these women are mired in the depths of wretchedness, they have time for one another. Molly soon found she had friends, and these friends led her to solace. The comfort and blessed relief they introduced Molly to was gin.

Molly had gin for breakfast, lunch and dinner. The liquor replaced her need for food. It fulfilled her, substituting for love, safety and financial security. But the strict liquid diet of poison ravaged her body. Her youth had flown. Her once delicate features had puffed, her eyes were bloodshot and her lustrous hair was now lank and fell in oily curls. The neglect of her diet had resulted in her contacting scurvy so her gums bled and she had lost three teeth. Dolly Molly had no colour, no energy and no hope.

To top it all off she was a pathetic prostitute and this brothel was, in all probability, her last chance. If she did not perform here she would be relegated to the bottom level - the street whore. Doomed to performing sexual favours for anonymous men in alley ways and doorways, with no protection from the Police, the weather or from low life thugs. Dolly Molly took Clifford to her room without ceremony or hint of recognition. A bed with a faded red rumbled quilt and dirty grey sheets lay uninvitingly to the side of one claret arm chair - the only pieces of furniture in the room.

'How do you want it?' asked Dolly Molly in a dead pan voice which reflected no enthusiasm.

She was not encouraging and used no feminine entrapments to get him in the mood. The frankness of her question had a vulgarity about it that stripped the sordid act of any vestiges of dignity.

But Cliff didn't notice. He was still in a trance - his vision of this girl wasn't capturing the full essence of the gin filled hag who stood unattractively in front of him.

'Just the normal way,' answered Clifford.

Without ceremony she lay down on the bed, legs crudely wide open with the invitation: 'Come on then big boy, do your stuff.'

Dolly Molly had perfected the art of allowing her clients to complete the sexual act without any involvement on her part. She did not kiss, fondle or make encouraging noises; foreplay was ignored and after performance services were minimal. She may as well have been absent. As a result she had rarely encouraged a client to stay for a second helping or to return.

Thus it was as surprising to her as to everyone else in the brothel, when Clifford came back the next night and requested another session with Dolly Molly. When the pair arrived at the sordid room, the stunned girl, who was obviously drunk, eyed the man in front of her suspiciously.

'Why did you come back again? Wasn't last night enough for you? Don't tell me that you are actually attracted to my gorgeous body. Perhaps you are turned on by these bountiful bosoms.' She held her emaciated breasts up - displaying them like weathered, desiccated melons. At the ridiculousness of this she cackled to herself. She was now so demeaned that she could not imagine anyone could be anything but revolted at the thought of touching her. So why was he here to humiliate her further?

'I am Clifford and I remember you from years ago when you worked at the boot makers. I thought you were the most beautiful girl I had ever seen. And you were nice to me.'

This was a very long speech for Clifford. Even with the courage his tablets gave him, they still didn't give him the confidence he needed to tackle this type of emotional interchange.

A gleam of sunlight entered into Molly's gin hazed brain. A little spark of recognition, a glimmer of remembrance recalling when she was someone worth knowing. She sat heavily on the bed, and her head slumped forward. The bravado the gin offered wasn't strong enough. She had remembered.

'That's right. You had the fight with that weasel who tried to molest me and you were trying to protect me. You hit him with a hammer. I am sorry, so sorry, so very, very sorry.' Molly started to cry, she had lost her facade. She was now a pitiable, miserable sight.

With her rheumy eyes watering, she wiped her nose with the corner of her gown. She sniffed and wept, her voice faltering and embarrassed, 'and now you see me like this. Pathetic, drunk, ugly and repulsive. When you last saw me I really thought things would work out alright. But they didn't. Women by themselves don't survive, they get preyed on by horrible men and no one cares. Society casts them aside.'

Her voice rose and became more determined. She stood and opened the door.

'You should leave. All you'll get from me is the clap.' Molly's face was now streaked with tears. They streamed down her face as she heaved and sobbed. The weight of four years of desperation, fear and revulsion about what she had become, came out in those tears.

Clifford walked over to her and gently put his arms around her, rocking her as she wept. He broke his rules of not touching - she needed his protection.

When the tears were spent, he whispered to her, 'it's all right. You're safe. You did something good for me. I'll do something for you. I'll save you from this. I'll be back tomorrow night. We'll find a way.'

Molly was astounded. She had hoped for a knight in shining armour for four long agonising years. And here he was, making her a devout promise that he would save her from all of this. Was this just a cruel and malicious hoax? Could he possibly be serious? She wanted to sing and laugh and cry and shout. Perhaps a celebratory drink would clear her thoughts?

True to his word, the next evening, Clifford came back. She took him to her room and she sat uncomfortably on the bed gesturing for him to sit on the armchair. Cliff had remained standing, his tall frame stooped in uncomfortable companionship.

Last night had been a hazy memory for the working girl. Molly had awoken and thought about the amazing episode and had resolved that she would do her best to clean herself up. She had only needed one drink to get her out of bed and just another to get to breakfast. In fact she had ended up drinking as much as she had drunk every other day. But today the gin had made her celebratory not maudlin.

The paying customer looked at her and Clifford could see that at least she had made an effort. Her hair was washed, her clothes were not so soiled and her fingernails were cleaned and trimmed.

'You look lovely,' Clifford said. He bent to kiss her but years of eluding all male touch made Molly turn her cheek. She caught herself as she did so. This would not do! If she was going to capture him she must not repel his advances. She turned back to him and smiled - making certain that her right side faced him as this profile had more teeth.

She was an amateur at seduction and although she knew the mechanics of what to do, years of implementing avoidance techniques were hard to ignore.

'Do you want to make love?' she asked, attempting to purr seductively. 'You may as well, you are paying for it.'

Now Clifford was being chivalrous but he was a man, and a man who was very partial to the whole love making scenario. So he allowed himself to be seduced. Molly put more effort into the next fifteen minutes than she had for the hundreds of sessions she had endured, with countless nobodies, over the time she had been involved in this soulless business.

Clifford was conned, he thought he was in love. Sadly, he also thought these feelings were reciprocated. Various versions of this interaction happened regularly over the next ten days. They always made love. Cliff enjoyed it and Molly put on a passable act that she had liked it too. Sometimes they spoke of escape. Often they cuddled in mutual silence, content with their own thoughts. Two broken people who find communication tough.

It turned out that, what was not clear, was how Molly was going to escape the brothel. It seemed that there was some 'ownership' involved. Plus Molly had incurred debts which needed to be paid out first and the fear of retribution if these were unpaid was obviously a genuine deterrent.

But Molly was definitely on the improve. Just the thought that she might have a future was enough for her to take more care. Her appearance improved, her emotions improved and if she was ever sober enough to make a valid assessment, she would have surmised that she was happy.

Two weeks after their first encounter, Clifford asked Molly to come out with him on Sunday, her day off. There was a band playing in the bandstand at Cross Flatts Park.

Molly was hesitant. It was an unspoken rule that the prostitutes did not go out in public. The chance of humiliation, if they were recognised, was just too great. The girls tended to spend their days off, indoors.

Molly reluctantly agreed to go and with the help of her friends she cleaned herself up. She borrowed a sky blue day dress, a decent respectable outfit, perfectly suitable for a promenade in the park. Molly also borrowed a hat, a coat, an umbrella and a pair of dainty day boots.

Clifford met her discreetly at the corner and they took the tram to the Park. Molly had imbibed her normal quantity of gin that morning but she had rinsed her mouth out with lemon. She very bravely did not take any gin with her. An almost sober Mrs Molly Williams held the arm of the gentleman at her side as they entered Cross Flatts Park.

They arrived at the bandstand area and listened to the music before opting to have some ices down by the rose garden. As they walked arm in arm, they saw two couples approaching them from the opposite direction. Clifford stiffened as they approached. The older woman let out a cry and rushed towards Clifford. It was his Mami. Joseph stood woodenly to the side, giving Cliff a nod but giving no greeting to his female companion. The couple next to them was Young William and his latest flame, whom he introduced as Audrey.

'How wonderful to see you Clifford. You didn't tell me you would be here. And who is this young lady? I haven't met you before have I?' prattled his mother, filling the air with excited pronouncements.

'This is Molly,' said Clifford. 'Molly this is my mother, my step father Joseph, my brother William and Audrey.' Clifford wasn't embarrassed but he was extremely uncomfortable. He didn't like sharing the bits of his life. The 'family bit' and the 'secrets bits' were meant to be separate.

Molly was mortified. She was unused to being outside the brothel anyway. She felt her shame was painted on her, like displaying a big red P for prostitute. She felt her status as a slut was clearly visible.

Molly stammered: 'Nice to meet you all,' and turned away from them, attempting to walk on into the crowd, into oblivion. She needed a drink. She needed to escape.

But Mami was feeling particularly insensitive to other people's discomfort.

'No. No. You must come with us. We are all going to take some refreshments. So come and join with us. Joseph is feeling generous and he can buy us all cake and tea. Did you listen to the brass band? They were wonderful weren't they? You can still hear them playing from the refectory.' She grabbed Molly's arm and steered her in front, so they were walking together.

Molly felt another gin desire, this wasn't part of her plan. Clifford was her escape and now she had to work out how to deal with his family and it looked like the family wasn't going to be as easy to hoodwink as Clifford was.

The conversations continued uneasily between the parading couples. Stilted and formal and skirting around all of the issues. William didn't look much interested - he was besotted with

Audrey. Mami was just so overwhelmed that Clifford had a girl, any girl, that she would have accepted anyone. Joseph walked aloof, glancing nervously at Mami and Molly in front, and watching the agitated Clifford to his left. Joseph could read the signs and they were not looking good.

They arrived at their table and sat to drink their tea. Mami kept on prattling, oblivious. Molly had gagged when she tried to nibble on her piece of cake. Her shaking hands had betrayed her need for alcohol so she had not attempted to lift the delicate china cup a second time. Her tea sat in front of her, cooling, dejected and curdling.

Audrey giggled demurely and William mooned over his lady friend, ignoring the interplay between the others in his family. Clifford stood uncomfortably, requesting the groups' permission for him to leave to relieve himself. He needed space to plot their escape so he headed for the gent's public urinal at the back of the refectory.

Molly shakily stood up to follow him but Mami put her hand on her arm indicating that she should remain. The frail and troubled girl was full of angst at the thought of staying here, alone with the enemy.

Molly turned and met the blast of a full frontal, icy stare from Joseph. All of a sudden there it was. Total recollection. And she had no gin to provide her protection and camouflage.

Joseph had immediately recognised her from the factory four years before. The difference was, that he had not lost touch with Mrs Molly Williams.

Joseph Blootle was a kindly soul and had made an effort to recontact her some months after she had left the factory. He had arranged to meet up with an elderly lawyer friend, whom he had asked to make discreet enquiries about her whereabouts. After two weeks of investigation, the lawyer friend had told him that the lady he had been seeking was now a prostitute. She was lost to decent society and he need have no more to do with her. Joseph was placated and looked no more.

Joseph looked into her grief stricken face and read the full story of her years of pain and degradation. But he also saw her greedy, grasping efforts to secure her freedom by ensnaring Clifford. Joseph had a modicum of sympathy for her but he had bucket loads of affection for Clifford, who he had looked out for, for over half his life.

Joseph leaned towards Molly and whispered with deadly accuracy: 'I know who you are. I know what you are. You need to disappear, immediately. Permanently. And leave Clifford Hulme alone.'

Molly looked around wildly. Panic rose within her. She was terrified by the severity and the finality of Joseph's words. Clifford was away intent on his ablutions. Joseph glared at her with undisguised malevolence. She hurriedly stood up and walked quickly from the table, immediately melting into the anonymous crowd.

Molly needed a drink - a long hard drink of gin. She had no money, not even enough for the tram fare home. She walked towards the abandoned quarry area, away from the populated section of the park. She had no right to be mingling with decent people. She was an intruder, an interloper, pretending to be unsoiled.

It was late and the evening shadows were stealthily creeping over the park. Some canoodling couples were cuddled up on the seats but they were preoccupied with each other. Below her a fenced off section marked out the old quarry where an unkempt lake had formed. She could see some huddled figures gathered near a wispy, smokey fire. This looked promising. A sinister refuge, a haven for the unwashed.

She approached two old drunks slumped at the rear of a disused brick chimney. She spotted a clear bottle as one of the men raised it to his mouth, trickles of fiery, desired liquid, ambling down his scrawny turkey neck.

'I need something to drink. Can you spare a sip?' she whispered hoarsely to the first drunk.

The drunk looked up groggily, a bit stunned. Was this pretty lady talking to him? Ladies spent most of their time avoiding him, averting their eyes, smelling the clean, unpolluted air on the other side of him and pretending he wasn't even in their world.

'What will you give me for it?' he asked in desperation, rude fantasies leaping into his befuddled brain.

'A quick fuck for the rest of the bottle,' Molly said, as the need for gin overwhelmed any resistance. The decent lady of the afternoon had vanished, the craving for hard liquor had brought back Dolly the working girl. Crude talking came with the job.

The drunk did not need any further convincing. He stood up on rickety legs. Fumbling with undue haste between her legs, he hoicked up her pretty dress and entered her roughly, without any pretence of gentility and grace. Molly grabbed the bottle and drank a long, refreshing, mind-blowing gulp. One swallow, two and then three. The liquid scalded her throat and cruised through her veins, lifting her to oblivion. She hardly noticed the old, smelly, decrepit man, humping her up against the wall. She vaguely registered when he had finished and his mate took over.

Molly only dimly registered the angry phantom arise behind them both as they rutted like dogs. The phantom grabbed the old drunk and threw him violently, without mercy, down onto the grass. He flicked him off like a despised, disgusting cockroach. The drunk slunk off, nursing his pain but realising he was stealing a pleasure that was not rightfully his to have. The two drunks silently vanished into the murk, they had seen nothing and remembered nothing.

Molly tried to open her eyes but the phantom had hold of her throat. He was strangling her. Her eyes popped. She saw flashes of white sparkles, painful light. She wanted to say sorry. She needed air. She wanted to plead with the phantom but it was all too late. Her body crumpled, lifeless and rag like.

The act had been done swiftly and silently. The girl's body was rolled into the dirty lake in the quarry. Discarded rubbish. Just another unwanted, unreported and unmissed murder victim.

Joseph and Mami had followed Clifford as he searched hysterically for Molly. When he had returned to the table he had found her gone. He had left immediately, ignoring his Mami's comments that she would be back soon.

Joseph and Mami had followed him, just a few steps behind. They watched out for him, trying to make certain that he did not find the girl he was chasing. Joseph had spoken important words to Mami. He knew enough to know that the next hour would be vital.

The minders had followed Clifford as he had made his way to the unkempt quarry area in the fading, shadowy light. They had watched as Clifford had been confronted by the sight of the girl of his dreams, rutting with the drunks for gin, her agreed price for oblivion.

They stood back, silent witnesses to the outrage.

Neither Mami nor Joseph laid a hand on Molly. But they did lay hands on Clifford.

After the event, they led him quietly, sternly and securely back to his family home. Back to his trust sanctuary. Clifford went to his bed to wrestle his demons. They never spoke of Molly or the event in the Park ever again.

The Tween Years
Back To School

June 23rd, 1920

Leeds, England

Since the unfortunate demise of Mrs Molly Williams, Clifford's family had worked tirelessly to reconstruct his life and the main architect in this restructure had been his younger brother William.

Unlike his two elder brothers, William had stayed on at school. At 15 he had joined an insurance company, called the Provident Mutual Life Assurance Association, as a trainee clerk working and boarding in central Leeds.

William wasn't so little anymore and he had the charm, assurance and swagger often associated with good looking young men. He had black curly hair, coffee coloured skin from his mother's ancestors and his eyes were black and full of joy. William had made an impressive start in the Provident Company and once his traineeship was completed he moved from a junior clerk into the Claims Clerk position.

On the fateful day when the family had met up on Cross Flatts Park, William had already held his position as Claims Clerk for six months. The repetitiveness of the role frustrated him, he needed to be with people, not dealing with mundane tasks. The young 'go getter' William Hulme was keen to move into the sales arena where remuneration was founded on a commission basis. Rumour abounded throughout the company, that anyone with a gift for sales, could earn a very enviable income.

The Provident Company was a well regarded company set up: *'for the purpose of affording clients the means of making a provision for themselves in old age, for their families at their demise, and an endowment for their children.'*

The idea of life insurance was relatively new in post World War 1 Britain. Although money was short in many homes, the spectre of mortality was very real. The concern that families and loved ones could be left destitute in the event of an early death or disablement of the bread winner, was a real worry. Life insurance salesmen callously exploited this fear, signing up potential customers into lifelong commitments, with very little possibility of ever collecting a payout.

William thought he would be great at sales. He was 'oh ah' handsome, charming and talented, he related well to people and was exceptionally plausible. Plus he was not really super concerned about honesty or integrity - his own or the Company's.

On June 23rd William was bumping along on the Beeston Tram, heading out to visit his family. As the very tempting possibility of him becoming a salesman loomed, he was aware that his current very safe role of Claims Clerk would soon become vacant.

William thought that Clifford would be perfect for the role. He had the patience to stick to mundane tasks, he was meticulous and he enjoyed solitary routine. All of the aspects of the job that William hated and grated on him, Cliff would relish.

There was only one problem, Clifford was neither literate nor numerate. However, the twenty year old Cliff was a far different person than the ten year old pupil evicted from the schooling system for being dumb. Clifford did not lack intelligence. He just learnt in a different way and unless he saw the relevance for learning he just turned off. But he was very teachable; Pte Hulme, who could not read, had looked up the Enfield Rifle manual and deciphered it so that the maintenance schedule was aligned to precisely.

'Cliff can learn, he just needs someone patient to inspire him. He needs to be guided and encouraged and he needs someone to show him why he should learn stuff. Perhaps even an occasional kick up the backside wouldn't hurt him either,' William suddenly blurted out his thoughts to the suited and bespectacled Banker sitting next to him on the tram. The Banker had no idea what he was talking about but he politely nodded his encouragement to the handsome young clerk who seemed to have experienced a 'Eureka Moment'.

William was turning over such thoughts in his mind when he passed the Holbeck Public Library. A sign in front of the majestic, red brick, terracotta building announced the introduction of:

'Adult Education Classes for Returned Soldiers. Tuition in beginning reading, writing and basic arithmetic - starting on July 1. Enquire within.'

William jumped up from his seat, stunning the bemused Banker, and leaped from the tram as it slowly negotiated the next corner.

He bounded up the stairs and entered into the hushed halls of the library. The large oak desk in front of him was labelled 'Library Lending Section' and the severe librarian manning the desk glared at him disapprovingly. Even without making a sound his mere presence in the place was 'too loud' and loudness was not appropriate in a library.

With his cap in his hand he enquired about the adult education classes. The very elderly librarian looked down superciliously at him through ridiculous eyeglasses perched on her beak like nose. As she started to speak through thin pursed lips, William was transfixed by a large mole on her chin sporting three grey curly hairs that spiralled in different directions. He found her absolutely repulsive.

'Young sir. These classes are only for returned men. They are generously funded by our charitable municipality. You surely did not serve in the war did you?'

Her haughty disdain annoyed him. How could someone so singularly unattractive, be snooty? But William knew about the value of charm so, despite his misgivings, he gave her his most winning smile.

'Oh no this is not for me, it is for my brother. He served with honour and distinction in Egypt. Now he has returned to our country and he cannot secure employment. His education is a bit lacking and he could do with a helping hand. It is so unfair that someone who has given so much for his country should be penalised on his return.' William spoke in a sombre, respectful manner tapping into her prejudices and preconceptions.

'Might such a brave soldier be eligible for the classes?' he enquired solicitously.

His ruse worked and she answered in a far more sympathetic tone: 'Well yes. As long as he was born in the Municipal Borough of Leeds and he resides in the wards of Beeston, Holbeck or their surrounds. He must also have proof of his war service and be currently unemployed - although he would be permitted to pick up some casual employment. The classes are on in the evenings so he would need to commit to regular attendance.'

'My brother Cliff fits all of those prerequisites. Now how can I put his name down?'

William was keen as mustard. He thought this would be great for Cliff. Since the Park incident he had become an isolate, spending too much time sitting on the doorstep of the terraced house, smoking and whiling away time. Joseph and Mami were at their wits end. He was a grown man and too old and too big, to be just moping around.

'My niece will be running the classes. Her name is Miss Ethel Hurst - she is a monitor and may well become a teacher in time. She is sitting at the table over near the Classics Section. You should go over and fill out a form then bring it back with a one shilling deposit. We charge the fee for the loan of the pupil's equipment: slates, scribblers, pencils, pens, ink and the like. We have found that some of the men only come once and they take off with some of our stores. So the deposit is a necessary precaution.'

The librarian would have kept going and told William about the whole course if he had let her but he smiled sweetly but dismissively as he took his leave. The young Ethel Hurst would be far more worthy of his charms.

Ethel looked up from her writing as William sat down at the desk.

Ethel's chest did a little flip as she saw the disarmingly, handsome young man oozing with Latin attractiveness, in front of her. This man was gorgeous. Even though she had now experienced twenty weeks of teaching 'returned men', none of these ten fellows had been in anyway handsome or desirable. Plus her many years of imposed isolation had left her very inexperienced in interactions with men. This put her at a huge disadvantage in an exchange with the skilled and socially adept William.

William gazed at her brazenly, without subtlety or modesty. He was efficiently assessing the attributes of the librarian's niece as only a Claims Clerk can. Pale blue eyes and fine downy blonde hair captured into a bun in a very appropriate librarian hairstyle. She was dressed formally in grey with no skin showing except her hands, neck and face. He took in the pale skin of her wrist and noticed with pleasure the rapid pulse. Ethel had a pale look, with thin lips and slightly crooked front teeth. Still she had a pleasant look about her and William guessed that there was a feisty spirit all contained in this tightly controlled ensemble.

'Quite beddable,' William thought in the section of a young man's brain that is totally devoted to real or imagined sexual conquest.

'Can I help you sir? I think you may be too young for our courses,' Ethel's voice was a deep contralto, soft but melodious. She was struggling to keep her emotions in check but she met his gaze with a polite smile.

'Well the beauty in your family must have bypassed your aunt and come directly and disproportionately to you,' William said charmingly.

He was experienced in appraising women and knew just what to say to get them to say 'yes' when he decided to ask them out. William was a Ladies Man. Ethel was a bit floored with his comment and her faint blush showed that his compliment had been effective. William saw out of the corner of his eye the elderly, extremely ugly librarian approaching, so he wisely shifted the conversation from flirtatious chat to business.

'Now although I would love to talk sweet things to you all day, and I hope that I will be able to get to know you really well in the future, I have actually come to put my brother's name down for the classes. His name is Clifford Hulme and he served as a Private in the Manchester's in Mesopotamia. He is twenty and I need you to teach him to read and do some simple sums so he can get work.'

Ethel was charmed and infatuated but she too realised that her Aunt was hovering. This young handsome man with his sugary words was a ray of sunshine compared to the dour, taciturn men she had been helping. He had her from the first moment he had first looked at her.

The lovely Miss Ethel Hurst had been working at the library for over nine months and, although she was personally delighted in being in a place where reading was cherished and high learning valued, she was despairing about her life slipping away from her.

Ethel had been born in 1900 in Stockport, Cheshire, the youngest of five (surviving) children. Her father was a pastor, and her mother was worn-out by childbearing. Mrs Hurst had been nearly permanently pregnant for twenty two years by the time Ethel was born, miscarriages and the early death of eight of her offspring, had inflicted a series of callous punishments on her.

Ethel's four elder sisters were all much older and long married by the time it was decided that she would: 'stay at home to do for her mother and father as they got older'. So it was not important to educate Ethel with more than the minimum of instruction. This decision had been made without taking into account Ethel's wishes, dreams or aspirations.

Ethel, doomed to a life of domesticity and spinsterhood in the home of her aging parents, escaped the monotony through reading. Her drudgery and disappointment was only relieved by stories and her own fantastic, fantasy life. Ethel had a vivid imagination and although most who met her thought she was chaste, timid and demure, in Ethel's head she was anything but.

Her teenage years had passed her by and as she entered into her eighteenth year she had nearly given up hope of living the life she craved. There was no chance of her falling in love or being married. But by a strange twist of fate, both her parents died within months of each other and she was left with a small pension and the chance to escape. However, at eighteen it was not seemly for a young girl to be alone, she would need a companion.

Ethel was invited to live with her elderly and despised aunt residing in Holbeck, a suburb of Leeds. Invited is a misnomer as in reality this was compulsion. Ethel had no choice in the matter.

When she arrived in Leeds she soon realised that she had swapped one life of servitude for another. Her aunt was a humourless spinster who despised frivolity, engaging in laughter or games. In fact she disapproved of anything to do with being young. Her idea of an outing was a once a week church attendance. Ethel was expected to follow her example. Her responsibility was to 'keep house' as her aunt was a librarian at the newly opened Holbeck Library. The walls of Ethel's life were imploding on her.

But twelve months ago an opportunity had arisen, a junior reading clerk position at her aunt's library had become vacant. Ethel had been successful and, under the hawk eyed scrutiny of her aunt, she had come in daily to replace the books on the shelves.

This role was monotonous and there was little opportunity to meet new people. All the library staff were elderly and any form of fraternization with the public would have meant instant dismissal. But at least it meant that Ethel could leave the narrow, lonely, confines of her Aunt's house.

Three months after Ethel arrived, the library board had determined to set up adult classes for returned soldiers. These courses were well subsidised and resulted in a valuable stream of income for the library. This was used to purchase new books, under the pretext that these were necessary texts for the soldiers. In reality this was rather a scam as up to this point no soldier/pupil had completed the course to the point where they could read any of the acquired texts.

A problem had soon arisen in that, none of the existing library staff had any desire to teach. The librarians all felt far superior to the unlearned, uncouth soldiers. For the first set of courses the staff had set up a roster - doing one night each. This first course proved to be a complete failure. The librarians were old, out of touch and did not want to do the job. The soldiers stopped coming and the promised stream of income dried up with the lack of enrolments.

Miss Ethel Hurst was very keen - but her aunt did not approve. The monitor's role was to instruct returned soldiers and the soldiers were men! This was indecorous and improper. However the other library staff were very keen on giving Miss Hurst a chance to prove herself. The majority won.

Ethel's Aunt was unsure of the propriety of such a situation and vowed to accompany her niece to every evening class as a chaperone. Her Aunt's age hampered her in this role as she fell asleep after the first five minutes of each class.

Five weeks into the classes, her Aunt had given up and she now spent her evenings reading and sipping sherry. Her niece's chastity would just have to look after itself.

As Ethel had received little in the way of formal teaching herself, her mind had not been warped by the formulaic methods of the day. She had developed her own thoughts on how she had learnt and this was to be the basis of how she would teach.

The pupils who came to her classes had all failed at learning using the traditional methods. Ethel found out what they were interested in first and then taught them to read using real material about topics they were interested in. She did not use childish readers or repetitive exercises.

She showed the adult students how arithmetic could be useful using examples like betting on the horses or statistics from football games. The soldiers loved it. They learnt and they kept coming back. The first group of soldiers had been successful - ten of them had completed the twenty weeks.

When William sat in front of Miss Ethel Hurst at the end of June in 1920, she had only one vacancy left in her second course. Whether it was his charm, charismatic smile or her own sense of destiny, Ethel Hurst wrote down Clifford Hulme's name into the registry.

The summer class was full.

The Tween Years
Deliverance And Redemption

1923 - 1925

Leeds, England

Some things are just so unlikely, it is a miracle when they happen. In July 1923 Clifford Hulme was married. Some may say that Clifford Hulme was one of the least eligible bachelors in England. He was still reclusive and at times downright strange but his life experiences had mellowed him. He now knew how to get by and Clifford had found out that he did like women and the lady he was marrying was definitely a woman.

Cliff had gone through the twenty week course at the Holbeck Library never missing a night and then he had enrolled in a second twenty week course. This was 'against the rules' of course, so the second enrolment had been under the assumed name 'Albert Hulme'. William had assured him that Albert would have been pleased to have loaned him his name for such a good cause!

Ethel had proved to be an exceptional teacher. She gave Clifford manuals on guns and machinery but this proved to be a bit limiting. Then she found out that he had another real passion. He was fascinated by everything to do with Australia. Luckily, one of the board members of the Holbeck Library was a Western Australian expatriate. The Major, had been seconded to the British Infantry over the war and was still here. He had used his influence with the Library staff to ensure that he got regular reminders of home and once a month, a job lot of Australian papers was delivered.

Ethel searched though the back copies of the various daily and weekly papers: The West Australian, The Mirror, The Daily News and The Sunday Times. She would cut out articles of interest for Cliff and he would study an article a day. Many of his favourite articles were about rural life, particularly things about kangaroo shooting and farming.

By the second twenty week course, at William's insistence, Clifford was set a new area of study. He studied insurance papers. Cliff wasn't inherently as interested in these but he was cooperative. If William said he had to 'learn it' then 'learn it he would'.

This was a huge undertaking and the very kind hearted Ethel Hurst agreed to give voluntary tuition over the weekends. Ethel became a regular visitor to the Hulme family home in Beeston. Together they poured over the intricacies of the various forms, with Ethel attempting to explain the complexities of the legalese in the papers to the confused Clifford.

Now Ethel was conscientious and devoted but there was also some self interest in all of this. The reality was that Ethel saw in Clifford a chance for her own deliverance. From that first fateful day in the library, Ethel had felt an instant attraction to the magnetically attractive William Hulme.

There was no doubt that this crush had been her original motivation to spend extra time and effort on teaching and patiently guiding Clifford. Still Ethel was a realist and she knew that her charms would not be enough to capture William's wild and wandering heart for long. She could clearly see that he would be a bad bet as a long term partner. She wanted a faithful husband and he wanted every female he saw. Ensnaring Clifford Hulme was a far more cautious, prudent, long term proposition.

Cliff had a close physical resemblance to William but without the strength and charisma of William's confident personality, most people didn't see him as handsome. Ethel's Aunt had clearly been conned. She regarded Cliff as 'mildly retarded' and thus raised no objections when the proposal arose that Ethel would be offering him extra tuition. The Aunt saw Ethel's actions as, 'bestowing a kindness on one of the unfortunate' and bragged as much to the local vicar on Sundays when Ethel could no longer accompany her on her weekly church outings.

Ethel did grow more and more fond of Clifford as they spent more time in each other's company. She particularly liked his vulnerability and delighted in being needed.

At the completion of the second twenty week course, William had determined that Cliff was ready and so Cliff, with Ethel at his side, fronted up to the Provident Mutual Life Assurance Association Office in Leeds. Cliff had memorised every form by rote. William had carefully explained everything. Nothing could and would go wrong.

Clifford survived his first interview and he was offered the job. But practicing forms by rote did not indicate that he had mastered the education level needed to be an efficient insurance claims clerk. Left as an independent operator, Cliff would have been a certain failure. But Ethel only worked a short tram ride away, so every day after work, Clifford would gather his daily papers and he would stop off at the Holbeck Public Library where the very obliging Miss Ethel Hurst would carefully scrutinise his work. She would make the required alterations and the forms would be returned next day for processing. After 6 months this had become largely unnecessary, Clifford was doing it by himself.

Both pupil and instructor ignored this development, they had started to enjoy their shared time and neither wanted this to end. Ethel finally took the matter in hand when she suggested to Clifford that they go to the teahouse across the road. Despite Ethel's romantic notions, no-one was ever going to ask for her hand in marriage, so she did it herself. She asked Clifford to marry her.

Modestly, the stunned young man asked for some time to think about it.

Clifford was extraordinarily surprised. He had never anticipated that he would get married. His feelings for Ethel were much more about trust and less to do with lust.

But as William explained to him, 'look Cliff, you are never going to get another chance like this. Ethel is delightful and she cares for you. You have had women you thought you loved and look where that has got you. Go for it. Ethel has brains, she has a small pension so you will be financially secure. Plus she is really pretty. You, my big brother, have struck it rich!'

So Cliff went back to Ethel and said, 'yes'.

The family was ecstatic. Mami loved Ethel like a daughter. Joseph, the ever caring step father, was content, he had steered Clifford's welfare since the lad was only 10 years old. Younger brother William was delighted for two reasons. Firstly, he would be marrying off his fairly dim, elder brother to a charming and pretty young lady. With her by his side he would go from a liability to an asset. As for the second reason, he was not ready to discuss this just yet. William had big plans for this couple.

But they had not anticipated the difficulty that Ethel's Aunt would pose. She was adamantly and obstinately opposed. She feared losing her companion, even though their interactions were frigid and unfulfilling. She was not keen on losing her unpaid housekeeper either. The very nasty Aunt had also been secretly siphoning off the annual pension and was loath to give this up. So Ethel and Cliff continued to see each other just as much as before, but the marriage plans were put on hold until they could find a way around this impasse.

The stalemate went on with Ethel and Cliff being betrothed but the Aunt blocking their intended marriage. The rules of her Parents' Will indicated that 'her majority' was not achieved until she had reached her 25th birthday. But a benevolent god inflicted her horrid Aunt with a bout of pneumonia in May 1923. Her very selfish niece, who was by this time totally ignoring her Aunt's requests, was not at home. So there was no-one by her bedside when the last laboured breaths were inhaled through the beak like nose of the old librarian. Ethel was only 23 years old and she was now free to marry.

The couple organised for the bans to be read and, with undue haste, the wedding was planned. Ethel had inherited her parent's cottage in Stockport down in Cheshire. The Provident Mutual

Life Assurance Association arranged for Clifford to be based there and his new role would be to collect premiums. Cliff was happy with the offer of a new job. It would mean that he would be out and about more, spend time in the outside air, away from people and stuffy offices. He did not see that this job could involve any unpleasantness or could result in premium holders facing financial difficulties. Cliff just thought he would knock on the door, collect the money and be off.

Ethel was in exultant high spirits. She would be able to leave the smoky, industrial city of Leeds and set up in the more rural environment on the outskirts of Stockport. Her vivid imagination had already created a vision of her as a faithful supporting wife with a clutch of cheerful, contented children living in domestic harmony.

And William was blissfully happy. This fitted perfectly with his plans. Currently William Hulme was riding high. He was one of the best Insurance Salesmen the company had. His patch was the lower North West and he was milking it.

William was constantly on the move, visiting towns for just a few days and signing up new premium holders by the dozen. He was never involved in the second, third or fourth visit. The annual revisit, where the instalments needed collection, was often a far more complicated and less pleasant operation. This was the more troublesome part of the job. Many second visits were vexatious and needed someone less charming and more like an enforcer or debt collector. What had seemed like a wonderful opportunity when the charming young sales agent arrived, had often soured after years of re-payments. William thought that Clifford, who was a bit of an emotional vacuum, would be good at this.

William was now earning very good money. But he was also spending rather profligately. He dressed in fashionable double breasted suits, drove a forest green Morris Oxford with leather seats and had three different ladies who all thought they were the 'only one', located in different towns across his sales area.

No-one asked what story he had told the other two women when he fronted up with Monique, a French seamstress from Liverpool, to the wedding of his only surviving brother Clifford to Ethel Hurst at the Christ Church at Heaton Norris, just outside Stockport. It wasn't a large wedding but everyone who came was jubilant.

Cliff found he really enjoyed being a married man. He was married to someone he trusted as much as family. She was an accommodating, dutiful and supportive wife. She didn't even object to his secrets. Ethel had read the Doctor's letter and it seemed his explanation helped her to understand the things she had worried about. The tablets did not worry her and she even volunteered to go and get them when he was away.

Also Ethel was a compliant sexual partner - she desperately wanted children and was content to make love whenever he wanted. She was not quite as fertile as her mother had been but within the year she was pregnant. Their baby was due to be born next January.

But there was another of Clifford's secrets that he had not shared with Ethel. The reason he had not shared this confidence was that William had requested that he keep this one a secret.

'This one is just between us two Cliffy. The girls wouldn't understand. But they will certainly like the money it brings in.'

As soon as the marriage had been proposed, the super salesman William had commenced to sell policies to a range of folk within a twenty mile radius of Stockport. Now this was not unusual, this was his job, but what was different is that these policies were never entered at company headquarters. William pocketed the first instalment and kept the list separate.

By May 1924 the second instalment was due. He had carefully groomed Clifford to visit these homes and collect their second insurance premium. He had been instructed to keep these monies apart. In October 1924, William had come to visit the Stockport Hulmes, to see how things were going with the rapturous couple and to collect the earnings.

He found the couple in good health with Ethel radiant and

displaying her six month bump with immense pride. Their home had been transformed, with few vestiges of the bleak furnishings existing from her parent's time. They were the model of domestic bliss.

Clifford took William out to the garage for a smoke and some Man Talk. He handed over the 258 pounds and 16 shillings cash that he had collected over the previous few months from the 'special list'. This was a small fortune in 1924 - easily enough to fund the cost of William's new car.

William refunded him 25 pounds with the instruction that he spend it on Ethel and the new baby. It was doubtful if Clifford knew the full extent of the fraud he was perpetrating but he would have been very aware that what he was doing was very wrong. He certainly would not have thought through the consequences of being caught. Ethel however, was kept totally in the dark.

The scam worked well for another two months after William's fleeting visit.

Disaster struck just before Christmas when Clifford knocked on the door of a beautifully restored Victorian home at Marple Wood, not far off the Stockport Road. A mature, well dressed lady came to the door. Clifford introduced himself and went through his normal spiel. He was ushered into the library with the well dressed lady asking him to come in to speak to her husband.

Clifford stood rather uncomfortably in the well appointed library when a polite woman's cough indicated that others had entered the room from a back door. As he turned he saw a grey haired, elderly gentleman being pushed in a wheelchair. The man had a tartan blanket covering his knees but his top half was bedecked in the formal uniform of a British Infantry Officer.

Clifford immediately recognised the majestic profile of Major Archibald Rodden of the Manchester Regiment. The recognition was mutual and electric. For the Major, the sight of the former Private Clifford Hulme, brought back feelings of revulsion, loathing and a sense of total frustration at the case that had not been solved. This did not improve his mood.

The major bellowed, as only an ex Major can bellow:

'What in Hell's name are you doing here and what on earth do you want?'

His face was reddish purple with large thumping veins pulsing in the side of his bullish neck. The Major was apoplectic with rage and injustice. He may have appeared impotent in his wheelchair but he still had the power of his thundering voice.

The sight of his former commanding officer had momentarily relocated Clifford back to the time when he was at the mercy of an unsympathetic and ruthless Army. Back then he had been a Private, a man of the lowest rank, occupying the bottom rung of a very lofty military ladder. Back then silence had saved him. His mentors had been derogatory about those in charge including, 'Major Rotten to the Core,' as the Australians had disrespectfully referred to this angry man in front of him. But there were no mentors or trust friends here now - he was on his own.

A flood of memories surged through his mind as he struggled to regain his composure and tried in vain to work out what he could do next. The Major's response was unlike any of the scenarios Clifford had practiced.

Old habits die hard and the first thing Clifford did was to snap to attention and give a perfect salute. 'I am from the Provident Mutual Life Assurance Association Major,' he barked back, with full military proficiency and deference to rank.

This behaviour was unexpected and gave him a bit of thinking time to work out how he could launch into one of his well practiced speeches.

'And about bloody time too,' the Major roared, slightly mollified by the man's adherence to military ritual.

'Relax soldier. You're obviously a civvy these days. And it looks like you've done bloody well for yourself since I last saw you.' The Major spoke more calmly and then remembered that he was still extremely angry. So again he roared: 'Now tell me, what is your company going to do about my situation? Last year I signed a form insuring me against death or permanent disability. What do you think this is?' he said, gesturing to his wasted legs and wheel chair. 'I think this qualifies for permanent disability. The surgeon tells me I will never walk again.'

'I am supposed to be eligible for 40 pounds a year and what have I had from your company but one refusal letter after another. You bastards have refused to recognise my claim. I have yet to see one brass farthing from the Provident Mutual Life Assurance Association.'

The Major was fuming. He had a pile of letters in his hand - all bearing the well recognised seal of the Provident Mutual Life Assurance Association.

Clifford was stunned. This was not part of the plan and William had not given him instructions about this one. But Clifford was a bit more worldly wise than he once was. He knew that he needed to buy some time and the only way to buy time was to give this man money and assure him that he had been sent here to look into his claim.

His next action surprised even him. Clifford pretended he was William. Not brash, cocky, confident William but serious, concerned, 'get out of trouble', William.

'I am very sorry for this inconvenience Major. I have been sent here to investigate your claim and to fix things up. Please accept these funds as a down payment.' Clifford took out the ten pounds he had collected over the week and handed it to the Major.

'And if you would be so good as to sign here to say you have received these funds, I will make certain that the balance of the monies owing to you, is sent to you immediately I return to the office.'

This was the most professional and longest speech Clifford Hulme ever made. It was even more amazing because he had no precedent for it. He had recombined words from aspects of his role in the insurance business and they had come out just right.

It was a one off, it was perfect and he would never have been able to repeat it again!

Immediately the Major saw the money, he was satisfied that this man was genuine. Plus he had all of the paraphernalia of office including a genuine receipt book with the official mark of the company. Still the Major took the precaution of taking down agent Hulme's details. Just in case the remaining money did not follow.

A rapid and immediate exit was now essential. Politely, and with few external signs of the panic and turmoil within, Clifford took his leave and walked rapidly to the bus stop. He then made his way to the nearest Post Office where he promptly sent three telegrams, all addressed to his brother Mr William Hulme. (There were three regional offices and Cliff needed to be sure that this message got to him without delay.) The telegrams all bore the same, prearranged message:

'Client calls foul. Pls come directly to chicken coop. C'

This had all been part of the strategy - the escape plan. 'Just in case,' William had said. Clifford then caught a bus to Liverpool and took a room at a Hotel called the Hen's Roost. He took two white tablets and lay on the stark bed staring at the ceiling.

It took 8 hours for William to get the message and come to the Hotel. He was aghast, angry and mortified at what this could mean. The drive down from Manchester had taken him five hours and over the time he had visioned his wonderful world crumbling. His bid to score some extra cash had exploded.

By the time William entered the hotel foyer he had made some decisions. This needn't end in disaster for both of them. If Clifford alone took the rap, he would be able to distance himself from any crime and at least he could still earn good money as a sales representative.

William entered the room, listened to Clifford's story, chewed on it for a while and then made his pronouncement. In his most trusting voice he settled Clifford's doom, 'well there is nothing for it. The Major will not give in on this one. Sadly his policy was never registered. So what you will have to do is vanish for a while. It will blow over and you will be able to come home. I will find you and let you know when it is safe to come back.'

'It is not safe for you to say goodbye to anyone, this includes Ethel or Mami and Joseph. Don't worry about them, I'll look after them all. I have brought you a ticket on the Ormonde that I organised this afternoon, it only cost 10 quid through the Empire Settlement Scheme. The Ormonde is leaving from Liverpool and sailing for Australia. You always wanted to go to Australia didn't you? Here is 25 pounds. This will be more than enough to get you started when you arrive. Now go to sleep because you will be boarding very early tomorrow morning.'

This had been Clifford's only farewell. William left Clifford at the dock and rapidly put distance between him and the Stockport/Leeds area. He didn't visit with Ethel, who spent a lonely, confused and bereft Christmas, heavily pregnant and full of unanswered questions.

Ethel and his family in Leeds were informed by the Manchester Police who were investigating allegations of fraud and theft levelled against the former employee of Provident Mutual Life Assurance Association. No-one conducting the investigation thought to ask where the money had gone. No-one questioned why Clifford Hulme's family was left destitute when the scam would had netted over a thousand pounds.

But this all happened in January and by this time the escaping felon was steaming towards a new life in Western Australia.

The Ormonde docked at Fremantle Harbour on February 3rd 1925. Clifford never knew that his son James was born at Ethel's house in Frodsham Avenue, Stockport on the same day. Ethel had gone through the pain of a difficult labour alone - a deserted wife.

Her next years were filled with loneliness, questions and regret. She didn't know where her husband had gone until October 1928 when she finally received a letter.

While baby James Hulme was letting out his first lusty bellow in Cheshire UK, Clifford was standing at the Arrivals Hall in Fremantle, Western Australia where the Clerk had given him an advertisement from the local paper.

'New arrivals wishing to work as farm labourers are requested to make application to the officer in charge of migration in Barrack Street, or to the General Secretary of the New Settlers' League, Perth.'

As Clifford read it, he said a quiet thanks to Ethel who had taught him how to read. He missed her and Mami and Joseph. He hoped William would write to him soon and say he could come home but he was content for now, this was his chance at redemption in his new land.

Life On The Farm
Domesticity

Morning, March 29th, 1928

Miamoon, West of Wubin, Western Australia

Six foot two bodies do not comfortably stay bent into cramped positions for long, so after many hours of painting Harold Smith creakily unwound his frame. With the completion of the painting in the bedroom, the farm house was finished. He looked around at the gleaming walls and called out: 'Put the kettle on Jack. It's done. Time for a cuppa and a break I reckon.'

'No problems Smithy,' came a grunted reply from the next room.

Jack Parrott was in the kitchen. He and Clifford Hulme were manhandling the furniture back into its rightful position. While the painting had taken place it had been stacked haphazardly in the centre of each room. The lads were on a bit of a short time line as Jack's wife Chrissie, along with Lilly and the girls would be arriving later today. Harold had been cracking the whip from sunrise early this morning as he wanted the place 'all spruced up' for their arrival.

'Let's get the kitchenette in place Cliff and then we'll take a breather,' Jack huffed as he continued to slide the huge jarrah structure into its place near the stove. He then reached over and put the heavy kettle on the stove top.

'We'll need to stoke this up too. Cliff, would ya mind nipping outside and getting some more fire wood?'

Harold marched into the kitchen looking a fright, with speckles of white paint all through his dark hair. With his legs astride, he took in the scene and at last he smiled. It was finally looking like they were going to make it before the ladies arrived.

'The place will look great. Don't worry mate. Lillian will love it,' said Jack in a comforting tone. 'It was a great idea to build an 'inside out' house as the inside walls look terrific with no framework showing. And there's nothing for the spiders to build their pesky webs on. Now just think what you have achieved, you have built a four room house, got all the outbuildings up and started the block clearing all in four months. You've done really well. And this dratted weather hasn't helped you much,' Jack said while adding a drizzle of condensed milk to his friend's cup before he handed him his tea.

Harold grabbed the tea gratefully and looked morosely outside at the muddy pools, remnants of last night's rain. So much for building in summer, it had poured every day since mid February. He had wanted everything to be perfect for Lilly but the outside of the house looked like a sodden, brown mess. Still the rain had brought the grass up, unseasonably, so the hills area around the homestead looked really pretty.

'A filmy veil of greenness that thickens as we gaze,' quoted Harold softly from the Dorothea Mackellar poem, *My Country*. 'You're right Jack. This rain has made the bush look great. And at least it won't be too hot for the little 'uns. Bubby Peggy really doesn't need heat on top of everything else.'

Bubby Peggy was the newest addition to the Smith family. She had been born last July. Lilly and the three girls had stayed in Perth while Harold had come out to their new selection, 800 acres of mainly uncleared farmland 20 miles from Wubin. The property was adjacent to the huge landholding owned by their good friends, the Nelsons.

'Start small Harold,' John Nelson had encouraged him, 'the bloke before you took on too much. When you get here you will see his feeble efforts. He had barely cleared 10 acres in three years. Plus the rules are strict - if you do not clear enough land in the first year you forfeit your holding.'

Jack came over to stand by his friend and they watched as Clifford Hulme lifted the axe as he worked at the wood heap out the back. The sound of the axe fall rang out sharply dividing the crisp morning air.

'Is Cliff working out all right?' asked Jack nervously. He was only helping his brother-in-law for the weekend and they had not had any opportunity to discuss 'Harold's Project' as Jack had dubbed Clifford Hulme.

The itinerant labourer had been in the area for about three years. He had drifted in and out of work over this time, supplementing his life with a penchant for roo shooting. Rumour had it that he also just liked spending time alone in the bush. 'Cliff's gone walkabout again,' the locals would often comment. He existed on the fringes of the rural Wubin and Dalwallinu communities. He had done nothing wrong but he had not got ahead either. Quiet, not too bright, aloof and a bit standoffish, folk had not really befriended him and this had not seemed to bother him at all.

Cliff had come to the notice of Jack and Harold for two reasons. The first was that he owed them a considerable amount of money. It was the 'country way' to allow folks to pay 'on tick'. It was understood that at some times of the year people had more money than at other times. At this time the Smith and Parrott Store employee, Irishman Charles Martin, had moved up in the world and now held the position of bookkeeper at the store in Wubin. He alerted Jack and Harold to the mushrooming of Cliff's debt in late 1927 and the partners resolved to have a serious talk with him when he next came in.

The second reason was far more sinister. Clifford was addicted to heroin and he had used the local Smith and Parrott store to provide him with his drugs. This had not been too much of a problem when he had first arrived in the district in 1925. Heroin was just starting to be named as a 'drug of concern', linked with violent crimes, underworld figures and dreaded addiction. The storekeepers were not chemists but, in the absence of a pharmacy, they were permitted to dispense drugs under a Doctor's direction.

Jack Parrott had been the storekeeper in charge at the time and he had read the well thumbed letter from Dr Samran which Cliff had proffered to him to justify his request. He had happily provided the tablets with only a twinge of concern, not really considering the potent contents of the little white tablets he was dispensing.

But the world was changing. At the start of the century Bayer had nonchalantly sold heroin tablets for the relief of coughs, anxiety, headaches and asthma. Morphine based drugs had been used freely for pain relief during the war. Over the 1920's, governments around the world had become increasingly aware of the dangerous effects of narcotic drugs. The Australian Government followed the lead of the USA and Britain and laws were implemented to ban the use of many illicit drugs. Bayer had stopped production just after the war and only far flung outposts still had any stock left. Supply in WA had been reduced to a trickle.

By the end of 1927 Jack Parrott had received his last batch of 200 tablets, with a letter informing him that this drug was out of production and no more would be provided. He was also given the ominous news that, as of the 8th of June 1928, by order of the Governor General of the Commonwealth Government of Australia, The Dangerous Drugs Ordinance Act would be enforced across Western Australia. This Act deemed it would be illegal for anyone to have or supply such drugs. This included medical opium and all preparations containing diacetylmorphine, the prime ingredient in Cliff's little white tablets.

Jack read the Act meticulously. When he came to the section which stated that the punishment for contravening this Act was a fine of 200 pounds or imprisonment with hard labour for not less than one month and not more than twelve months, Jack was flabbergasted! And more than a little concerned about his involvement in the provision of a prohibited drug. He looked at the innocuous white tablets and vowed that he would have none of them in his possession by June next year.

When Clifford Hulme had come into the store on Christmas Eve 1927, Jack had asked him to wait until the store was empty as he needed to discuss something sensitive with him. The store gradually emptied as the customers finished their transactions and scurried home. Jack had started by telling Cliff that he had racked up a bill of 22 pounds and 8 shillings. Cliff had accepted this and, in a reasonable tone, had requested the chance to work the bill off. Jack was relieved. Sometimes asking people for money could be a bit tricky and their reactions were not always predictable.

Then Jack tackled the problem of the future supply of the tablets. This conversation had the most unexpected consequence. Jack had thought that Cliff would just accept the news. He had indicated that he could make an appointment to see Dr Anderson in Dalwallinu and he would be certain to put him onto some alternative therapies.

Jack Parrott was not a callous man and if he had anticipated the devastation this news would have on Clifford, he would have handled the discussion with more tact and subtlety.

But Jack found himself an unwilling witness to a demented attack. He watched while the large, quiet, reserved man started to shiver, shake and cry unbelievably. Clifford was distraught. These little tablets had been his life savers, they had given him his life back, made him feel normal. He thought back to the years before he had tablets; the black moods, the strange voices, the hallucinations and the crippling anxiety attacks.

The misery overwhelmed him and then gradually this was replaced by a seething, uncontrollable rage.

'Nooooooo,' he yelled.

Suddenly he went wild, flaying out at things around the shop. Saucepans clattered, the cash register flew from the counter. The half penny lolly box went flying so mint leaves, musks and black jacks exploded all over the floor. He punched into a bag of flour and powdery whiteness rose in turbid billows, covering everything with floury ash. All the while he screamed, a high, keening sound of animalistic pain.

Jack was inert for only a minute. He bounded from behind the counter and quickly put his arms around the panicking, angry man, locking him down so he could do no more harm to himself or to the shop. Gradually the anger subsided and Clifford reverted to weeping, miserable, heart retching sobs of pure despair. After five minutes of soothing words, Clifford was finally calm and he stared vacantly at the floor - his rage was spent.

Desperate thoughts careered through Jack's mind as he considered what he should do next. He was alone in the shop and the nearest Policeman was in Dalwallinu. But arrest seemed a bit over the top. This seemed unfair as the man had not done anything really wrong, he had just mucked the place up a bit.

The other workers had already gone home (well it was 6.30pm on Christmas Eve) so Jack led the now compliant but silent man, by the hand to the back room. This area of the shop, formerly the living quarters of Harold's family, was now empty and used only for storage. Jack guided Cliff to an unused bed, secreted away amongst the stores in a hidden corner. It was there for the delivery boys when they had to make an early start. Cliff obediently lay down on the bed assuming his coma position and started the steady rocking, an external marker for the onset of one of his black moods.

Clifford was out of tablets. Jack had intended to provide him with his monthly supply after giving him the speech but after the fearful display there was no chance he would get a tablet now. Cliff was doomed to go through the full gamut of a psychotic episode.

Jack watched for a while, transfixed by the convulsing body engaged in its own internal battle. Cliff was obviously in inner turmoil as he lay on the bed muttering. But there was no indication that he would attempt to leave the confines of his makeshift bed. He didn't like to leave him, especially in the store which contained so much but he had no choice. Jack needed help to deal with this crisis.

Jack Parrott walked back through the flour covered shop, kicking aside the lollies as he locked the front door. He looked around outside to see if anyone was watching and then quickly walked to his home, a block from the store. His wife Chrissie was inside putting the touches to the preparations for tomorrow's Christmas celebrations. As luck would have it, Harold was on the front verandah smoking. He saw the powdery white, ghost-like Jack scurrying down the street and he of course commented with a light hearted jibe:

'What on earth has happened to you? Are you hankering for a white Christmas?'

The pleasant greeting froze in the air between them as Harold saw the wild terror in Jack's face.

'You have to help me fast Smithy. I have Clifford Hulme in the shop. He went crazy when I had a talk to him about the drugs. I have to get cleaned up and one of us has to get down there with him. He's in the back room on the camp bed but I don't trust him. He could just go off again at any minute.' Jack was puffing more from cold fear and unease than the exhaustion brought about by his rapid walk from the store.

Harold immediately assumed control: 'You go out to the bathhouse. I'll get you some clothes and spin Chrissie a line. She is so busy with getting ready for Christmas she will not even notice if we do not come back for a few hours. Once you're cleaned up, I'll meet you at the shop. We'll decide what to do when we are there.'

The two friends instantly started to put their plan into action. In less than ten minutes Harold was standing looking at the anxiety riddled Clifford Hulme. Jack had already recounted the fantastic story to him and was still shaking and quite unsure about what was the best course of action. What should they do with him?

'Look, this is not so simple. I think Cliff is a drug addict and I think this is what happens when he hasn't got any access to his morphine. The Cliff we have seen over the last few years has always been under the influence of his tablets. There were lots of times blokes were given morphine in the war and some of the poor blighters got to like it too much. It wasn't just the weak willed guys; I saw big tough fellows, injured in action and put on this stuff. It got hold of them so they couldn't function unless they had it. Most of them really got stuck into the bottle when it was taken away from them. I think Cliff may be just as addicted.'

Harold was looking at Cliff but in his mind he was thinking about other soldiers he had seen, reduced to nothing and his sympathetic nature was almost certainly thinking, 'there but for the grace of God go I.'

'When did you say that doctor wrote that letter?' Harold asked of the still shaken Jack.

He had not been at the store much over the last few years. Harold had served as a silent partner while he worked on purchasing his land. It was just fortuitous that he was in town at this time as he was heading out to take up his selection straight after Christmas.

'Well, he first showed it to me when he arrived in the district. So this would have been back at least three years ago but the Doctor had written it when he was still in the war. So this means this guy has been taking these tablets for over nine years and now he has been told he can't have them anymore. I can kind of see why he went off,' Jack said, partially understanding the cause of Cliff's frenzied turn.

'So what should we do about him?'

'Well, the law would say charge him with being disorderly. But locking him up will not help him. He needs to be gradually taken off the drug or this is what happens to him,' said Harold thoughtfully.

'And it'll certainly not help us. He still owes us money. What I suggest is that we keep him here. We can take it in turns to watch him. Plus it will give us the chance to clean up the store. Tomorrow is Christmas so no-one will come in. We'll add up any breakages and add this to what he owes us.' Harold was taking control and his brother-in-law was quite happy that he was. Jack just didn't have any answers to this problem and was quite happy to defer to the ever competent and capable Harold.

'Now this man is sick. I don't hold with people being punished because of something they cannot really help. On Boxing Day, if he is all right by then, I will take him out with me - to the farm. He can work on the farm to pay off what he owes us. Out there he cannot get into too much trouble and I can pass out his tablets to him. I will start him on one a day and gradually wean him off them so by the time June comes he will be cured.'

'Are you sure about this Smithy?' Jack asked, concerned that his friend had not really thought this one through properly. 'He went really berserk in the shop. Out on the farm you will be all by yourself. What happens if he goes crazy out there?'

'I'll be alright. And Lilly and the kids will not be coming out until the end of March. By then I will be able to tell if things are under control. I will not allow them to be put in any danger. If I notice anything at all I will have him out of there like a shot.'

'There is absolutely nothing to worry about. I am a grown man and should be able to look after myself and Mr Clifford Hulme.'

So this is how Clifford came to be working on the Smith's Miamoon farm. Harold had been true to his word. He had used a kind but consistent approach to his labourer and Cliff had responded with 'dog like' affection, obedience and appreciation. He seemed to be in total control of his emotions and behaviour. Occasionally he complained of a headache, anxiety or insomnia and Harold would allocate him an extra half tablet. Otherwise the tablets would be strictly doled out, one per day.

By mid March there were 92 tablets remaining in Harold's secret stash. Harold intended to start Cliff on half tablets in early April so that by June, Cliff would be well on the way to being weaned - free of the insidious reliance on this evil chemical. By June the chemical would be illegal, Cliff would be clean and any tablets still left would be destroyed. He would also ensure the letter would be burnt. This letter implicated Jack, Harold and the store so no trace of it should be left. This plan was 'Harold's Project' and Jack went along with it, if somewhat reluctantly.

Harold had given Jack constant updates over the next few months. Only the two friends knew about the secret and had decided that their wives need never be informed.

Harold gazed out of the kitchen window of his newly finished homestead as Clifford cut wood. He had revisited this history in his mind before answering Jack's question.

'I think Cliff is going quite well. He is a steady worker and is very accommodating - and I really can't fault his labour. He has paid off the bill he owes us and is now earning steady money, so this is good.'

Harold took a long deep drink of his tea before he went on. 'But it is hard work though. He rarely says much. I sometimes feel he is watching me and I don't think he believes me when I tell him about this all being for his own good. I have tried to get him to go to Dr Anderson in Dalwallinu but he just refuses. I don't really think he trusts me. Underneath he is still pretty angry because he thinks I have taken these bloody tablets off him on purpose.'

'So what are you going to do now that Lilly is coming? Will you be able to keep it all in control when you have the family here? I don't feel too happy about you out here, coping with a mad man. It is one thing that you were prepared to have him here when you were by yourself but don't forget she is my sister. I don't want him to hurt her or the kids,' Jack blurted, letting months of pent up tension flow out.

'Don't dare think I would ever put her or the kids in danger,' Harold snapped with uncharacteristic intensity. 'If I thought for one moment that she was in any danger I would have the bloke shipped out of here in a flash. No, he is doing well. I quite like him too in a funny way. He feels like a basically good man who has had some really bad breaks in life. I started this project and I intend to see it though. I am sure when he is totally off the tablets and coping well, he will come and thank me.'

As Harold finished his tea, Clifford came through the door, his arms loaded with wood which he dumped in the wood box.

'Come and have your tea Cliff,' said Harold in a kindly tone. 'We've both had a break and you've been out working.'

'Thanks Smithy,' said Cliff. 'But can I take the rifle down to the end of the clearing. There are some roos down there. Your missus might like a kangaroo stew and I wouldn't mind snaring some more skins.'

'Sure Mate. The rifle is out the back near the water tanks,' said Harold pointing in the direction of the tanks.

As he disappeared into the distance Jack again questioned Harold:

'Now tell me I'm stupid, but you have a crazy bloke living with you. You are trying to get him off some powerful drugs that he is really keen on and you let him have a rifle. Surely that is pretty brainless!'

'It's called trust Jack. He has used that gun every day since we got here. The bloke is an amazing shot. If he was going to shoot me he would have done it in December. Plus he always makes sure we have fresh meat: duck, rabbit and kangaroo. We have no trouble with foxes and he keeps wild dogs and dingoes from the chook pens. You should hear how much of a problem the feral animals are on the Nelson's farm.'

Harold turned towards Jack and in a kindly voice he continued: 'Look Jack, I just have to have some faith in him. And you will just have to trust me. Now we have loads more work to do before the girls arrive this afternoon so let's stop chattering like old women and get to it.'

And that was where Harold's Project was up to before the arrival of Mrs Lillian Smith and her three girls.

Evening, March 29th 1928

Miamoon, West of Wubin, Western Australia

Lilly silently slipped from the children's room at about 8pm that evening. Eight year old Elsie and six year old Vonny were finally asleep. Only Peggy the baby was still awake and she was cooing contentedly being nursed by her Aunty Chrissie Parrott. Jack, Harold and Cliff were on the verandah having a smoke.

The men had been amazing - getting the home built was one thing but getting things set up and ready for them was far more than she had expected. Still there was plenty for her to do. The windows needed curtains and the house needed her woman's touch. Plus she certainly needed to get stuck into the outside, at least to get a vegie garden put in before winter.

Her two older children had been wildly excited about their new house and had run around exploring from the moment they had arrived at 3pm in the afternoon. Harold had been so proud to show his family their new home. Four spacious rooms and loads of new furniture. What with the house, the deposit on the land and the new farm equipment Harold had brought, this had really eaten into their savings. But isn't this exactly what they had been saving for?

The men had even done the washing up, so now it was time to relax. Lilly leaned on the kitchen chair near Chrissie and gently stroked Peggy's head. She was rewarded with a lovely grin showing her three shiny, white teeth.

'You look so content Chrissie. I forgot to mention it earlier but you are radiant, your skin has got a lovely warm glow. You've put a bit of weight on and it suits you I reckon,' Lilly said, admiring the Madonna like vision of her friend with the small baby.

A red glow spread across Chrissie's face as she leaned forward to Lilly to pass a whispered confidence.

'You're seeing the ecstasy of pregnancy Lilly. At last I've kept one. I'm four months gone already,' she gushed. Chrissie had endured two failed attempts over the last three years. 'Sorry, I didn't want to tell anyone too early. It is just too disappointing when it just doesn't happen. So our new little Parrott is due in very early September.'

'Oh this is wonderful Chrissie, you'll be a terrific Mum. Jack must be proud as punch. I am really looking forward to being an aunty too. I wonder if Jack has told Harold yet.' Lilly twirled in excitement. This day had already been packed with so much good news. Could it possibly get any better?

'Now let's go outside and talk to the boys,' said Lilly. 'I want to look at the wonderful night sky. There is no moon and the stars are so crystal clear out here where there are no lights.'

As the ladies approached she could hear the boys going hammer and tongs in a full-on discussion. Their conversation was a theme on everyone's lips in Western Australia in late March 1928. The state was embroiled in two horrific murder trails. The first one was the trial of a disturbed nineteen year old, John Sumpter Milner who, in February, had raped and murdered Ivy Lewis, a 12 year old school girl. Today's daily papers were filled with the triumphant news that Milner had been convicted and was to be hung in May.

The second was currently only at the inquest stage. An Irish immigrant, Nicholas Kelly, had shot a Policeman, Sergeant Alexander Mark in the front bar of Perth's Brisbane Hotel. He had been evicted from the hotel for being drunk and disorderly and had announced to everyone that he was going to 'shoot the bastard who had evicted him'. He promptly went home, got a revolver and brought it back and shot the Policeman.

The discussion on the Smith's verandah that evening, revolved around whether either of the cases should have been able to claim insanity. The defence lawyers in both of these instances had used this defence. In Milner's case it had failed as of today, despite convincing evidence from the man's employer and his doctors that the man suffered from schizophrenia and delusions.

Both of the accused men had spent time in institutions and both were drunk when they committed their crimes.

Jack believed both men should: 'rot in hell'.

'They have cold bloodedly taken someone else's life. There is no reason for ever letting someone off who has committed a crime like this. No matter what the circumstances! Both of them don't even deserve a trial. A lynch mob is too good for these scum.'

Harold was slightly more benevolent. 'Look, my view is that the taking of life is wrong. Anyone who takes someone's life has done a wicked thing. Sane men who do so, should be put to death. But I disagree with you Jack - I think this has to be the responsibility of the State and I would like to see it done humanely.'

Jack went to interrupt but Harold had the floor: 'Now I think the mentally ill who commit such a crime should be locked up for life. Society needs to be kept safe from these fellows. The only problem is proving the insanity. I pity the men on the jury. What a responsibility to get this right.'

'I wish I was on the jury,' blustered Jack. 'I'd make sure they got it right. Any soft hearted do gooder would have to cope with me telling him about an 'eye for an eye'. As for humane, do you think these scum thought of humane when they carried out their hideous crimes? Don't you think the families want to see these animals dead?'

Chrissie was usually happy just to listen and let the men speak but this case had her really riled up. Her pregnancy and her passion to have her own child had brought into stark focus the sanctity of children. To attack and murder a young girl was quite simply an outrage.

Chrissie plucked up courage to put her case: 'I think the man who brutalised and murdered the little girl has done a much greater crime. She was just an innocent. Can you imagine the grief her parents must be suffering now? I am so glad he is going to the gallows. No insanity leads someone to do a crime like this. This man is just a monster and deserves death.' Lilly put her arm around Chrissie Parrott's shoulders, giving her the moral support of another mother who shares her indignation.

Jack jumped in again, overpowering his wife and not really appreciating her female perspective on the crimes. He was livid with the injustice of it all: 'But what about the poor policemen in this second case. Who cares how drunk the idiot was, or how much he was abused as a baby. He went home, got a gun and killed the man in cold blood. The police are there to protect us. They don't need to get blown away for doing their duty. And those idiot defence lawyers are trying to get him off. Life imprisonment is too good for him.'

Lilly had listened to the passionate opinions, relishing the word play and the diversity of views this emotive discussion had evoked. She was never one to miss her chance at dipping into a debate:

'I don't think anyone should ever take someone's life. No matter what their crime. And this includes the State. I feel really sorry for the little girl's family and the family of the Policeman but executing these men just fills our need for revenge. Do you really think the day after the execution they will wake up and say: 'it's great the bloke is dead, I feel better now'? They are already doomed to a life of grief. Retribution is a poor reason for enforcing a punishment.'

Lilly was on a roll as she continued with her theme: 'Executing these men doesn't make any of us safer. Lock them away from society for ever if you need to. And if they are proved to be insane we must help them. Insanity is a disease. Plus I cannot help but worry about what happens if the jury gets it wrong. Can we give them their life back? I do not believe in capital punishment, for any reason, ever.' She was proud of her strident and well constructed argument. Harold looked at her, smiling with pride and filled with contentment. His wife had opinions and she put them over well.

'You are so naive Lilly,' said Jack dismissively, 'and after that speech it's a good reason why we need to keep silly women like you off juries. Keep the justice system safely in the hands of twelve good men I say.'

Lilly was frustrated with Jack's comments. But she had been his sister for a long time and she hoped some of his sentiment was caused by sibling irritation and that he did not really think that way. He had goaded her like this all of his life. But he was so old fashioned in his views about women and this infuriated her. She hoped that Chrissie would put him to rights but doubted it - she was so subservient.

Clifford stood to one side. He listened intently to the discussion.

But he was a man of silence. He did not say a word, so the others never heard what he thought should happen to the two accused men.

After another twenty minutes of setting the world to right, it was time to turn in. Clifford headed outside to his tent and the Parrott's had made up a swag in the lounge/dining room.

Harold took Lillian's free hand. She had the sleeping body of Peggy slumped in total relaxation against her right shoulder. She gently laid the little mite into the crib, kissing her forehead as she did so. Her first night in her new home.

And then she turned passionately to Harold, fuelled with the pent up, frustrated love of five months of separation.

'Welcome to your new home my love,' said Harold.

'Oh I am so happy to be here. Now take me to bed Smithy and you can really welcome me home,' said Lilly laughing with complete and utter abandon as she gave herself to her husband.

Life On The Farm
At The Dally Pub

Saturday April 27th, 1928

Dalwallinu, Western Australia

Newspaperman Eustace Wilkinson lovingly caressed his middy of cold beer with his three pence placed on the bar ready for the next one. He was sitting in the front bar of 'The Dally', the majestic Dalwallinu Hotel, at 5.30pm on Saturday evening watching the entertainment as local farmers, itinerant labourers and shopkeepers drank themselves into oblivion before the calling of last drinks. It was Dalwallinu's equivalent of the six o'clock swill. Eustace was less drunk than most and he watched in amusement as his sister Marjorie slaved, along with two other harassed barmaids, to keep the drunkards plied with enough beer to enable them to face the 34 long hours of alcohol drought before the bar would open again on Monday at 10am.

'Poor Marjorie,' Eustace commented to his companion, who had actually lost consciousness and was slumped onto the bar, his last beer dribbling in a slow, frothy ooze from his mouth.

'She thought marrying the handsome publican Douglas Bridges would lead her to a new life. All that has happened is she has exchanged one life of drudgery for another. And it looks like she has spent the last fourteen years compensating with an extra dollop of pudding every night to make up.' Marjorie was the former house maid at the Narrogin Inne Pub who had bewitched Jack Parrott many years before. She would not have turned his head now - she was the side of a barn!

'Still I can talk! Look at what I've escaped too. I had dreams of being a foreign correspondent, a big time reporter and here I am. Saturday Night in the Dally. Doomed to report the 'Country Roundabout' for the West Australian Newspaper. Read my dynamic writings for the latest on: bull sales, cake fairs and the latest disaster to hit the wheat crop. This week Dalwallinu, next week Northam and the week after I will report about the wondrous happenings in downtown Narrogin. Scintillating excitement in every stunning location around our state.'

His companion snorted; Eustace took this as agreement and encouragement to go on.

'What I really want to do is cover real news but nothing ever happens in any of these god forsaken, tin pot towns. I reckon you guys should all go outside at 6pm and have a big brawl. Perhaps even murder each other. At least then I'd have something to write about!'

His companion then fell off his stool, lying partly submerged in the piss trough below. The trough served as a temporary urinal, reasoning that the desperate men could not afford the time to go to the toilet, so they could relieve themselves and stay drinking at the same time.

'Your mate isn't listening to you any more Eustace. It looks like you've bored him to death,' commented Marjorie, swooping past to replace his beer and take the threepence in one action.

Then her voice mellowed as she said to him conspiratorially: 'Look this is going to get pretty ugly in here for the next fifteen minutes. I suggest you drink this and then move into the dining room. There is a better class of customer in there. Doug will call you if there is anything to report from this lot of drunken pigs.'

Eustace looked at her with mild amusement and affection. He did not enjoy the grotesque scene at the front bar with its gross display of drunk men at their worst. He had just wanted a few quiet ales, but the drinking restrictions were such, that if you wanted a drink this was the only place. He couldn't even take his drink into the dining room. So he drained his glass and headed through the saloon doors into the sedate world of the non-intoxicated.

The two worlds could not have been of greater contrast. This room had low lights and soft conversation. A Caruso record playing

'Vesta la Guibba', the Tears of a Clown, on the gramophone tried in vain to mask the loud cacophony coming from the next room.

And there were women on this side. Any woman in the public bar would have been mauled in minutes and even the drunkest man would have been indignant at their masculine sanctuary being invaded.

Eustace steered away from two family groups and a couple obviously enjoying their own company and he spotted two men sitting in contented silence, near the window at the front.

'Would you mind if I share your table? he asked respectfully, 'I am without companions and I would love to take my meal in company. My name is Eustace Wilkinson and I am a reporter for the West Australian.'

Eustace took a seat without waiting for any formal agreement from the pair.

'We would be delighted,' answered the tall, dark gentleman to the newspaperman already seated next to him.

'My companion is Mr Clifford Hulme and I am Mr Harold Smith. Now I believe we have met before Mr Wilkinson. It was on the verandah at the Narrogin Inne Hotel in Armadale at the outbreak of the War. When last we spoke you were full of boredom and desperation. You said you were sick of the place and you were dead set on running away to war. So what happened?'

Eustace was impressed and instantly recalled their distant conversation.

'It is you - I remember. We shared a smoke together and I am afraid I unburdened myself to you. Sorry about that. And bless you. You listened to me and I am afraid I did go on a bit. Great to meet up with you again. Well, my folks did stop me going to war. In fact, I didn't escape their clutches until I turned 24. Finally, I got a job at the local paper then moved to the West Australian Newspaper in 1926. So I've been working my way up since then and here you see me. I have finally made it to the job of Country Reporter. But I must admit this is not as glamorous as

I had hoped. The things I report on tend to be rather mundane.'

'Well I read the country report all the time. You may not think it is of interest but over the last five years, while I saved enough money to get my farm, I absorbed every bit of the news from the Country Roundabout. I found it really interesting and it prepared me for what I would be facing. And now I am here I am overwhelmed sometimes by isolation. We don't get to hear about things as much as you do in the City and we desperately need the country news. You provide an invaluable service.' Harold spoke enthusiastically and with deep sincerity.

This flattery was just what Eustace needed. Perhaps some folk did value his work after all? 'So what do you blokes do for a living?' he asked.

'I am a farmer. I have only just taken up my farm, 800 acres west of Wubin. Cliff works for me. I am here to get some supplies and Cliff is here to sell his roo skins. He is an excellent shooter and has done a fine job out our way clearing the place of vermin.'

Harold was answering all the questions. Eustace glanced at Cliff, who did not meet his eye but seemed quite content to let the tall man do all of the talking. Cliff glanced nervously at the pair but he made no effort to interject.

While they chatted a young maid served three piping hot bowls of chicken soup. All three of the men launched into the delicious broth before the young maid had finished informing them that: 'tonight's meal is mutton stew with brussel sprouts and there is rice pudding for dessert'.

Harold, assuming Eustace was still interested, continued on: 'We did all of our business this afternoon so tomorrow we will be heading back home to the farm. We just have to do a bit of a detour past the railway station as my orders are coming in first thing and we need to package up Cliff's skins.'

The evening conversation flowed easily and Eustace felt that Harold Smith was certainly more pleasant company than he was used to on his constant travels. Clifford listened intently, not participating but his presence was not unpleasant. It was just that, after a while, Eustace felt that he ceased to exist at all. At the end of the evening meal Eustace's sister had provided them with a complimentary port which they sipped with their last cigarettes. Cliff had declined an alcoholic drink but was eagerly slurping his hot cocoa as though the liquid would satiate some unspoken desire.

Eustace now moved onto an idea that had formed in his mind as they had conversed:

'It has been a very pleasant evening Gentlemen. I do not always like to mix business with pleasure but I would like to ask you both a favour. I am doing a series of specials on Bush Folk. What this means is that I do interviews with fellows who have followed different rural careers. I submit them for publication about once every two weeks. Now I think you have both got interesting stories to tell. So do you want to be featured in the paper?' asked Eustace.

'No, I think not,' said Harold. He was sensitive to Cliff's vulnerability and he didn't want to push things.

'I think city folk would be interested in knowing about Cliff's roo shooting. Most of our city cousins do not understand that being in the country means that we need to kill things. Even cute little animals like bunny rabbits and kangaroos. I think some folk think that the meat in the butcher's shop comes from a tree out the back of his shop,' laughed Eustace. He was keen and just a bit pushy. It was coming up Sunday and he had no stories. He must get something to send in for the Monday morning dispatch.

'So how about it Cliff? All you need to do is just answer some questions. Plus, you need to pose for a photo. This would mean shooting a kangaroo tomorrow early morning. Then you could hoist it up ready for skinning. That would make great copy - let us put a bit of shock into next week's West.'

Cliff turned the idea over. 'I'll do it I suppose. Can we afford the time in the morning Smithy?' It was the first words he had spoken and Eustace was a bit taken aback at the timbre of his voice. It was quiet and tentative but had a pleasant although nervous tone.

'Well if you want to, it's all right by me but I reckon you should do the interview tonight. And you're always up at the crack of dawn so getting a roo shot shouldn't be a problem. It would be good to see you in print Cliff. I do not think my story is very interesting tho,' said Harold. 'Perhaps leave me out of it for now and then some time in the future why don't you come out to the farm? Then you can get me and the wife and kids - the whole Smith family. My wife Lilly has always hankered to be in the paper.'

So that is how Cliff's photo appeared with the article entitled: *'A Short Expose of Roo Shooting in the Wheat Belt',* published in the West Australian Newspaper in May 1928. Eustace was pleased, Harold and the children were very impressed, Lilly was a little jealous and Clifford looked on in amazement. In his whole life, this was the only time he could ever remember appearing in a photograph. He thought he looked pretty good.

He had told his story to the young newspaper man and he had felt pretty good about that too. He quite liked the bloke. This had been one of the only things he had felt good about this year. He had even told Eustace that when he had been learning to read back in England, Ethel had used the West Australian Newspaper to teach him. Eustace had thought that this was pretty amazing.

Harold had really not told Eustace the full story of why he was travelling with Cliff into Dalwallinu. This was because it was just their business. 'Secret stuff' even Lillian did not know about.

In the last week of April the new schedule had been implemented. Cliff was on just half a tablet a day now. He had told Cliff that there were only enough tablets left to get him into early June. (Although he did have a secret reserve of tablets that he had kept very safely and secretively hidden from prying eyes.)

Harold had wanted to get Cliff away from the farm and watch his behaviour on the lower dose - just in case. He didn't want him going crazy in front of Lilly and his girls.

Cliff had been suffering from headaches, insomnia and was very anxious. He often had the runs and had lost weight, with his flesh hanging more loosely on his angular frame. Still, after his morning half tablet, he was able to cope alright and it wasn't until later in the evening that Harold heard him wake up and toss and turn in an agony of tension. The next few weeks were going to be tough.

On the trip in, Harold had tried to convince Cliff to go and see Dr Anderson. He thought that, just maybe if he could get him to go, Dr Anderson might convince him to go into hospital. Perhaps he could get him into some form of rehabilitation treatment. Harold hadn't really realised that Cliff was going to have such a tough time of it.

He had gone over with Cliff that his tablets were now against the law but something else might be available for him. Cliff listened in polite but nervous silence. He did not know whether to believe him or not. And Cliff was worried. His Auntie was put in a loony asylum back in Leeds and locked up for life. He wasn't going to tell Harold or anyone about that secret. No way would he go to see any Doctor that Smithy suggested, just in case.

As Harold steered the spring cart back into the yard at the farm at Miamoon he was getting increasingly worried about how Clifford Hulme would react when he had no tablets left at all.

Lives Unravelled
The Day The World Ended

June 22nd, 1928

Miamoon, West of Wubin, Western Australia

Harold Smith left his warm bed reluctantly, giving his still dozing wife Lilly a cursory peck on the cheek. Over his khaki work shirt he struggled into his heavy oilskin work coat, cursing to himself about how frigid these June mornings were. He left the house by the kitchen door and looked towards the faint glow in the east - dawn was still a while away. The day would be fine but with a very cold start. With his work boots on, Harold tentatively made his way across the frosty grass to the tent where Clifford Hulme was sleeping.

'Come on Mate. Time to get up. How'd you sleep?' Harold muttered in an encouraging tone as he opened the tent flap to see his worker still lying hunkered down in his swag.

Clifford Hulme's bed clothes were all twisted, the man had obviously had another terrible night. He sat up and looked out at Harold. His gaunt face and red eyes filled in the rest of the picture of Cliff's torment.

'I can't stand this Smithy. My guts are writhing and I've still got the runs something cruel. Please Smithy I just need half a tablet. You must have some left?'

'Sorry Mate. You just need to learn to get on without them. They're illegal now. I don't like to see you in this amount of pain but we don't have a choice. This is for your own good. Look, I will go in and make you a cuppa and get you some Bex. They should help a bit.'

As Harold returned to the kitchen to stoke up the fire and put the kettle on, he felt wrung out with sympathy for the tortured man. He had taken his last half tablet on the 18th June. Since then nothing. Harold had thought that the gradual withdrawal would have made it easier but he had not anticipated the physical anguish Cliff would go through.

Harold poured three cups of steaming tea. The first cup he took into Lilly who was by now awake and lying in their bed nursing Peggy. What a wonderful sight. This gave Harold a wonderful feeling of happiness that allowed him to escape his feelings of guilt and worry over Clifford.

'Here's your morning cuppa Lilly. I'll put it on the sideboard. I'm off down to the far paddock with the tractor. Cliff will be coming down later. I'll get myself some brekkie so you can stay in bed awhile. I will be back in at lunchtime. Cheerio.'

Before he left the house with Cliff's cup of tea and some Bex powders he looked in at the girls. Both were sleeping, rugged up against the early morning chill, little blonde curls scattered on their pillows and looks of absolute innocence on their faces.

At the tent, Harold bent down and handed his worker a Bex powder and water. Then he passed the steaming tea into the extended shaking hand. Cliff hungrily drunk the first and then slurped his tea noisily. He didn't thank Harold or meet his gaze.

'Do you want some porridge? I've got a pot bubbling on the stove. I reckon some good sweet porridge would be good to settle the gut pains down a bit,' Harold asked but Cliff did not reply or look up. He was a man intent on wallowing in his own misfortune.

'Look Mate, try and get yourself together. You can work up here, closer to the house this morning. Keep digging out the stumps and gather them into piles. We'll set some of the stacks alight later on. At least that means you're closer to the outhouse. Bring the rifle if you like. I'm sure you'll see some roos to shoot at. I'll see you at lunch time.'

Harold returned to the kitchen and served himself some porridge. Sweet and thick, good ballast for a day in the fields. He pushed the pot back off the heat before chocking up the fire. This would give a little bit of heat to the kitchen before his girls got up.

As Harold made his way down to the tractor he found himself thinking about Cliff and the 21 tablets he still had hidden. He had chosen a great hidey spot buried in his Lucky Strike tobacco tin in the chest of draws in his bedroom. Lilly would never look in there - she wasn't too keen on smoking and never touched the stuff.

There was no way Lilly would open that tin. It was hidden below his bundle of letters which contained a lifetime of memories, written confidences and shared secrets. His wife had never even looked at these - she was a great respecter of privacy.

And he knew that Cliff would never find this secret stash. It was in his bedroom and the very respectful Clifford Hulme would never venture into such a private place. Cliff certainly knew his place. He came into the house daily for meals but never until he was asked.

Clifford Hulme was a difficult book to read. Outwardly he was friendly and respectful but he was always watchful and suspicious. They were not friends even though they had never had a cross word with each other. Harold knew Cliff had stored up resentment over the tablets. This had been manageable while the tablets were being reduced but the antagonism was rising now that his supply had been cut off.

Harold was convinced that he was doing the right thing and he had no regrets. This was his chance to help another man through a 'difficult patch' even if he now knew he would never get any thanks for it.

However, Cliff was always very courteous to Lillian and good with the girls. Sometimes he would draw pictures and he was good at making things out of wood which he often gave to the girls. Harold felt very confident that none of his family guessed that Cliff was going through a really tough time.

He looked back at the path he had made - his footsteps could clearly be seen on the frosty grass. It would have been so easy to give Cliff just half a tablet - but his habit had to end sooner or later. And at least he was here to help him out. Harold had reached the tractor by now and he turned the crank handle to get her started. Large clouds of belching blue/grey smoke came out, fumes spilling into the frosty air.

Harold manoeuvred himself onto the hard metal seat. It was no more comfortable than it had been over the last few months. He leaned forward and eased the tractor into gear, slowly moving off to a new uncleared area. He was mowing through the mallee scrubland, flattening the bush to enable paddocks to be formed. This was a very dangerous job. He had to drive the tractor into the scrub while also looking behind to see the large roller crush and separate the bush.

He had to have eyes in the back of his head to do this properly. While he was looking backwards, branches would sweep past him poking at his eyes. He had cuts all over him after many months of this work. Still it was better than doing it all by hand as the first pioneers had done.

By lunchtime he looked back contentedly at the twenty yards of cleared paddock.

'Good morning's work I reckon,' he said as he gathered up his coat, discarded as the temperature rose to a very pleasant seventy degrees. He gathered up the empty thermos that Lilly had brought down for his morning tea and looked across his landholding, experiencing the unbelievable feeling of deep, fulfilled pride. Harold looked upward at the deep azure blue of a cloudless Australian sky and was reminded again of his long departed friend James telling him about Blue Sky days.

'You're so right James. This is when I know that I live in the best place in the world'.

He walked back across the hill towards the house, detouring close to the area Cliff had been working.

'Come on in for lunch Cliff,' he called to the hunched shape of Clifford, bent trying to shift a stubborn root from its haven deep in the rich dirt. 'Are you feeling any better Mate?'

'I'm feeling shocking Smithy. I keep getting the shakes and I must have been to the shithouse ten times in the last couple of hours. Plus my head is getting worse - it just explodes into colours and piercing lights. I have hardly done anything all morning. Sorry Mate but I am a mess. Look, if I get any worse I might just go out bush for a few days. Sometimes just being by myself helps.'

'Al'right Mate - I understand. But come into the house now. Lilly has lunch already. I'm sure a good meal will set you right.'

The two workers came into the homestead, taking off their mud caked boots on the verandah. Shrieks of: 'Daddy's home,' greeted them as Elsie and Vonnie rushed over to Harold, leaving their school work scattered on the kitchen table.

'Come back here Elsie, pack up your school books first. And you too Vonnie- gather up your pictures. Daddy and Cliff need the space at the dinner table to eat their lunch,' Lilly confidently directed her two eldest children, with her baby perched on her hip. All the while she stirred a big pot on the stove. She was a woman in full charge of her own domain.

Lilly was dressed casually in a day dress with a blue woollen cardigan and sensible brown house shoes. It was a below knee length blue and white floral outfit which had long since passed from being her 'Sunday best' to being 'around the house' wear. The whole ensemble was covered by her white pinafore apron - streaked with cooking stains. Harold thought she looked 'just perfect'.

The fashionable lady he had married had evolved easily into the farm wife - but she was a lot better looking than most of the farmer's wives out this way. Harold beamed at her with pride and with just a touch of desire. Nine years of marriage had not diminished his adoration and affection for his bride.

When the two men had washed up, Lilly placed steaming bowls of aromatic mutton stew in front of them. Piled high with potatoes and freshly baked bread, the meal was a feast. Perfect fare for a cold winter's day.

Harold demolished two helpings with enthusiasm and great praise for his wife's culinary skill. Clifford fought valiantly with his queasy stomach but despite his biliousness he still managed to eat through his serve.

'Thanks Mrs Smith. It was real nice,' Cliff said politely as Lilly took his plate and gave him a cup of tea and cake for dessert. The cake was two days old but she had added some clotted cream to make it taste fresh.

'After lunch can you light some of the wood piles Cliff? It's warmed up enough now and you should be able to get some of them alight. Later this afternoon, I'll get you to come down to the section I've cleared this morning. Some of those big roots will take both of us to shift I reckon.' Harold had shifted into work mode again as he drained his cup of tea.

'Thanks for lunch Lilly. Did you remember that John and Ada won't be coming by 'til they pick us up on Sunday morning. John's had some problems with the truck. Love you Mrs Smith,' Harold called as he walked out the kitchen door. With lunch over, the two men put their boots back on and returned to their labours.

Lilly watched for a while as Harold tramped out across the paddock; she was so proud of her man. 'Love you too, Mr Smith,' she whispered to his disappearing image.

Then she commenced to clean up the kitchen.

'My life is cooking, cleaning and organising you scamps,' she said with good humour to the girls. She had forgotten about the Nelson's truck being on the blink. This was annoying as she would miss their visit, plus she relied on them for supplies of fresh milk, cream, butter and vegetables. She would have to make do. With the washing up done she sat down to give Peggy her feed before putting her down for her afternoon nap. '

Peggy should be off day feeds soon,' she thought. 'But at least if I feed her to sleep she goes down very quickly.'

She looked over at her other two children. Vonny was still at the table eating. She had finished her own honey sandwich and was now finishing off the one Peggy had left. Elsie was silent, curled up in the corner engrossed in reading Snugglepot and Cuddlepie, her favourite book. She would happily spend every waking moment reading but she was eight now and needed to spend some time on her other subjects.

'Now Elsie, you need to stop reading your book and get back to your correspondence lessons. You haven't finished your arithmetic yet. You can read another chapter when you have finished all of your set lessons. Vonny you can take your Raggedy Anne dolly back to your bed please?' The doll was slumped on the kitchen floor, dumped and forgotten when something more important had come up.

The girls quietly obeyed their mother's instructions and the afternoon began, a copy of most other afternoons on the farm. Lilly had decided to prepare a couple of batches of date scones - Harold's favourites. A smile creased her face as she recalled her first pathetic attempt at making scones. She muttered a whispered thank you to the kindness of Mrs Rowbottom and the Wubin Women's Group, many of whom were still in the District and she now counted as friends.

She was now an excellent cook and many of their friends and neighbours fought eagerly for Lilly Smith's wonderful date scones when they joined in at the weekly social occasion. These were held every Sunday and included cricket games, tennis matches or just picnics, all held on the Miamoon Rocks. These gave everyone a great chance to get together and relax. Farming was such an isolating life.

They didn't get into Wubin as often nowdays. It was 20 miles away, and without a car, they had to rely on the Nelsons to give them a lift. Chrissie and Jack Parrott did come out once a month, and they had their deliveries and post, but besides this Lilly was alone with her family. Still this suited her fine. Lilly no longer hankered after fame, fortune or even a brilliant social life. Harold and her children were all the life she desired.

And of course there was Clifford Hulme, but she really didn't consider him much. He was just there -perched on the edges of her life. She didn't like him or dislike him - she really just didn't even think about him.

By afternoon tea time the first batch of scones were ready. Little Peggy had woken up and was sitting with Vonny on the kitchen floor. They were playing knucklebones but Peggy was too young to understand and kept taking the bones. Vonny was getting frustrated with her young sister.

'Stop it! Stop it Peggy! Mum come and get Peggy away. She keeps stealing my knuckle bones and ruining the game,' whinged Vonny, her petulant face declaring her annoyance.

Peggy wore a large cheeky grin and a face covered in grime. Lilly moved in to stop the argument, scooping up Peggy and prising the two knuckle bones from her tight fist. The baby had a wet nappy and needed to be cleaned up so she called out to Elsie who again had her head in her book:

'Elsie could you and Vonny take this down to Daddy? There are some hot scones in there too. Be sure to keep this thermos upright so it doesn't spill. Don't go too close to any of the fires. Now when you get to the tractor, make sure Daddy can see you before you walk too close. He will wave to you when he can see you. I don't want him to run over you both.' Lilly was afraid of the tractor and the large roller and would normally have gone with the girls.

'Does Mr Cliff have something too?' asked Vonny. 'He says he likes scones.'

'He is working over the other side and he said he had taken something. So don't worry about Cliff today.'

Vonny had a special, soft spot for Clifford Hulme. She had drawn a picture this afternoon of him skinning a kangaroo and hoped he would hang it up. She was fascinated with his tent and was always asking if she could sleep in the tent too.

The girls set off and Lilly watched them, Elsie serious and concentrating, determined to do this job well. Little Vonny skipping along beside her without a care in the world. Lilly could see smoke rising from the paddock and recalled that Cliff had been set to lighting some of the piles of roots. She could not hear the sounds of the tractor.

'The men must be working together to get out some of the big roots,' she thought as she took Peggy into her bedroom and started to prepare for her bath time. She brought the naked squirming baby girl out to the kitchen where she had already put warm, sudsy water into the sink. Peggy gurgled with happiness and Lilly relished this special time alone with her youngest daughter.

By the time she heard Elsie's and Vonny's voices outside she had the baby dry and in her warm pyjamas. It was late afternoon and the winter cold would come in quickly with the setting of the sun.

'Mummy we couldn't find Daddy. The tractor was there but it was stopped. And we couldn't see Mr Cliff either. There are some fires burning down there. So we have brought everything back home again. Where do you think Daddy could be?' reported little Elsie, her face a picture of concern.

'That is strange,' said Lilly looking over at the clock. It was nearly ten past five. Far too late for the men's afternoon tea now. They both would be home soon she thought, as the winter sun would be setting presently.

'Well Daddy will be home soon and the mystery will be solved I am sure.'

'First things first, I have made you both a scone and some hot cocoa, so sit up at the table and I will go and see what is going on. Then you two need to do your afternoon chores. Elsie can you feed the chooks, the scraps are near the sink. Vonny you need to bring in a pile of kindling so we can light the fire in the morning. Then we'll need to get you in the bath and get you both ready for the evening.'

Lilly walked out the back and looked across the hill at the paddock Harold had been clearing. It was a good half a mile away. She could see a man walking towards the house. He was dressed in a black shirt so she knew it was not Harold, he had been in khaki at lunchtime.

'I'm just going to see what is going on,' she called, 'look after Peggy would you Elsie.'

Lilly walked out across the paddock towards the man who seemed to be dragging himself slowly towards the house, the last faint light from the departing winter sun at his back. She could see in the distance the area that Harold had been clearing. She couldn't hear any tractor noise, in fact the farm seemed strangely silent. Even the birds were respectfully hushed. The shadows of twilight were already casting their long fingers across the cleared paddock around her. Smoke from the burning wood piles added to the murky gloom of evening.

As she approached she could clearly see it was Cliff but he was walking nervously and very strangely, like he was reluctant to deliver some unwanted news. He carried the gun nonchalantly over his shoulder. She saw his face as he came closer and her senses screamed that he had news she didn't want to hear. Cliff looked like a man in horrible torment.

'Smithy's turned the tractor over on himself. He's dead. Dead as a doornail,' Cliff said, blurting out the horrific news.

The words pierced the cold evening, slashing her life to tatters. Lilly felt life drain from her limbs and the bile of horror rising in her gut.

'No it can't be. I'll go to him.' Lilly cried, desperately unwilling to accept the words she had heard. She was gutted by the news but still hopeful that there had been a mistake, a reprieve, a slim chance that Cliff had it wrong.

Cliff grabbed roughly at Lillian's arm. 'You can't go down there Mrs Smith. He's a mess. He's been crushed, flat as a door. It's no good going down there. There's nothing you can do for him,' said Cliff. His eyes were red with crying and his body shook with emotion. Lilly fell into his embrace and she sobbed. Both bodies were bereft and sought a safe haven, something to stop them collapsing onto the ground.

Cliff had never touched Lilly before but he comforted her now, although his body was tense and shaking with the agony of recent events. Once Cliff had stopped her going down to the scene of death, he persuaded her to return to the house.

'I'll go to the Brown's and see if I can get help. It should only take me half an hour and I'll be back. You'll need to see to the kids,' said Cliff as he turned away and went towards the west fence, the boundary with their nearest neighbours.

Through her tears she watched Cliff drag himself away, walking slowly to seek help, although it seemed like help for her beloved husband would be far too late in coming.

As Elsie came onto the verandah carrying Peggy she asked: 'Why are you crying Mummy? Is Daddy all right?'

Lilly wanted to collapse into a heap and bawl. She wanted to scream and rant and she wanted Harold to come walking in the door. She looked at her kiddies and she knew she had to be brave for them first.

'Daddy has run over his foot with the tractor. Mr Cliff is going to go and get some help. Now you three have got to get ready for dinner and bed. Daddy is not going to be happy if we haven't done all of our chores.'

Lilly performed her roles automatically. The girls ate their tea and were just onto their sweets when Cliff came back to the doorway of the kitchen. He stood like an uncomfortable shadow, giving more news but not providing information that brought any relief or comfort.

'The Browns are not home. I'll go to the Nelson's place then,' he said to Lilly. His voice sounded strained and tense. The strangled voice of a man in agony. 'I'll stay outside on the front verandah, I'm filthy.'

Lilly looked up at him. He looked frightful. Wild red eyes, black curls awry and his clothes still covered in blood, mud and soot.

Lilly brought him a cup of tea and watched him smoke one cigarette and then immediately light up another.

'Do you need some dinner before you go to the Nelson's?' she asked with fear and tension entering into her voice. She had kept her emotions under tight control while she had served the children but out here in the dark, feelings of doom crowded into her.

'No,' he answered abruptly, 'I'll eat later.'

Lilly stared at him, silhouetted against the sky. Sad tears started to flow down her face and she sobbed quietly. She wished with all her might that it was Harold and not Cliff standing leaning on the post on their front verandah. She could not understand why he was hesitating, she needed him to go for help. Standing here morosely smoking wasn't helping.

'Will you go now?' she questioned him harshly, trying to provoke him into action.

'Shut up why don't you? He's dead, what does it matter if I go and get someone? It's not like anyone can help him.' Cliff's voice was crazed and angry.

With no warning Cliff turned towards her, fury blazed in his eyes. His body was tense like a coiled spring as he kicked the ashtray, spilling its contents over the floorboards. His fist lashed out at Lilly, punching her cruelly on the side of her chin.

Frustration, anger and blind rage filled his mind as he pummelled into her again and again. Punches landed on her face, splitting her eyebrow open so that scarlet blood poured down staining her apron with large drops of claret. Lilly screamed, a desperation call from a defenceless woman as she tried to shield herself from his thunderous unprovoked blows.

He knocked her in the stomach and roughly grasped at her chest - ripping the bodice of her dress. His nails scratched across her exposed skin. Lilly screamed in a convulsion of pain and tried in vain to cover her revealed and damaged breast. Cliff pushed her over and she fell violently against the exposed beams of the house. She spat out a mouthful of blood and broken teeth as she pulled herself to her knees. Her tongue was spilt and her lips were already brutally puffed.

'Please stop,' she wailed, 'don't hurt me anymore.'

Lilly was horrified and terrified. Suddenly her grasp of what had happened, changed. This man had caused Harold's accident. This anger was retribution, fuelled by revenge and blind hatred. He was not her companion, her comforting supporter. He was her enemy. This revelation made her stronger and she stopped being a subservient punching bag as she turned to face her adversary.

'What have you done?' she screamed at the mad man hovering over her. 'What did you do to Harold?'

Cliff was wild-eyed, crazed: 'I shot him dead. Through the back. They told me to. Then I shot him between the eyes. He deserved it.' Cliff mimed shooting the gun. He then roughly pulled at Lilly binding her hands behind her back with a coarse cord he had pulled from his pocket. He pulled the rope agonisingly tight giving her rope burns.

The two little bodies of Elsie and Vonny erupted onto the front verandah.

'Get away from our Mummy. Don't hurt her.' The girls squealed in unison, their high pitched childish voices, raw with fright.

Vonny raced to her mother pushing her face into her blood soaked lap, wanting to block out the terrible sight in front of her. Lilly staggered to her feet and with her hands tied she clumsily pushed Vonny back into the house behind her.

'Get back girls. Go inside. You can't do anything. Let Mummy handle this.'

And to Clifford she screamed in beseeching entreaty, 'Don't touch them. Please don't hurt my girls.'

Little Elsie ignored her mother and started punching into Clifford and he rounded on her. He slapped her face brutally and then grabbed her by the throat. Lifting her by her neck he tossed her from side to side, her body swaying like a pendulum. Her little body was no match for the brute force of a grown man with killer hands. She slumped into unconsciousness, limp and lifeless. He kicked out at Lilly as she tried hopelessly to prevent him from molesting her eldest daughter.

Cliff walked inside and callously threw Elsie onto the floor of the dining room and returned to attack Lilly again. But this time Vonny was attacking him. With all of her six year old might she hit out at the enraged man, causing him as much irritation as a mosquito. Cliff picked her up and carried her into the dining room. A large mallee root lay next to the inside fireplace, ready to be burned to stop the night chill. Clifford picked it up and crudely smashed it across Vonny's head. A sickening thud reverberated through the room as the massive root collided with the child's skull. The root sank deep into her head, leaving a crude indent exposing jagged bone and sinews. Blood gushed from the wound. Vonny, her blonde hair matted with scarlet, slumped forward like her own Raggedy Anne doll. Discarded, the child saw nothing more as she sunk into a deep coma.

Lilly staggered inside, past the wild man, over to her children. Baby Peggy was crying hysterically, teetering on wobbly steps, careering towards her mother with arms out wide. Clifford again reached the last of her children before her. This time he started strangling the baby, his large hands easily spanning the baby's small fragile neck.

Then Clifford seemed to lose patience. He hurled the baby at the wall and the toddler's fragile, delicate body bounced unnaturally from the wall. The baby's horrified shrieks fell silent on hitting the impenetrable barrier. The lump that had been Peggy, lay in a forlorn pile of bloodied pyjamas.

Lilly was frantic. She had watched the crazed abuse of her three children, unable to help and impotent to stop any further assault. Words would not form in her mouth as she tried to beg him to stop the tirade of cruelty being inflicted on her family.

Clifford was still in an uncontrollable rage as he picked her up, tossing her roughly over his shoulder and carried her to the bedroom. He flung her onto her bed. He stared at her with malevolent fury - assessing her with undisguised loathing. He slowly removed two other lengths of rope from his pocket. He then proceeded to tie her now bare feet to the posts at either side of the bed.

A muffled, plaintive cry from the room next door, indicated that at least one of the children was stirring. Clifford turned and went back into the dining room. Two large thumps led Lilly to think with despair that both children had again been hit or choked into unconsciousness.

She quietly wept at her powerless misery. Lilly had used her assailant's absence to partially prise open Harold's top draw. Somewhere in the draw he kept a large hunting knife. But with her hands tied and her legs firmly fastened, all Lilly managed was a small gap exposing Harold's private items.

Clifford same back into the room and stood, gloating above the body of his fragile and vulnerable victim. She was tied and she only had limited movement. Shame and humiliation were already overpowering her will to fight back. Only her husband had ever seen her body and she was terrified that this man was about to outrage her. Death would be preferable to living with the disgrace of rape. Lilly was defeated; hope had left as she submitted to the degradation of Clifford's abuse.

Clifford flourished a pair of large kitchen scissors and proceeded to cut off her clothing. The skirt of her blue floral dress and the nylon petticoat was divided allowing her naked flesh to be seen. The prickle of cold and embarrassment scalded her.

'You won't need clothes where you're going.' Cliff announced.

He then started to cut her knickers but again his impatience got the better of him and he crudely ripped her underwear from her. He was still shaking with anticipation and anxiety.

'Please don't,' begged Lilly hoping that her tormenter had a shred of pity and would not subject her to this ultimate humiliation.

With her last effort she implored: 'Please Clifford, just leave. Don't rape me, I beg of you.' She was humble, subservient, crushed and mortally embarrassed.

Clifford looked down at her partly naked body. Lillian's face had been punched so many times it hardly resembled a female face. Her singlet had been torn and her right breast area was red raw with the nipple bleeding. She had a broken arm and, although crudely tied, the break could be seen below the skin.

But it was her eyes, deep brown pleading eyes, asking him not to subject her to the final indignity, that haunted him. These eyes caused just a glimmer of doubt to enter his tormented brain. His internal voices told him to hurt, rape and kill her, she deserved it but those innocent, deep brown eyes begged for mercy.

Clifford took his black neck scarf off and placed it over her face blocking out the beseeching eyes. Hiding from the eyes that would accuse and make him think this was wrong. He was in control, he had the power, this would make him feel better. The voices in his head told him that this was his right.

The power of the rapist surged through him and he felt his erection grow in ugly anticipation. Clifford took down his trousers and roughly and cruelly entered into the exposed woman. He thrust himself into her unwelcoming body. He ignored her frantic begging, painful screams and hoarse grunts that descended into gentle weeping as the rape continued. Clifford didn't take any notice of the resistance of her body, how her skin crawled with the repulsion of his touch. Clifford thrust and pushed and bent to bite her breasts. This was an act of mercilessly, enforced power and dominance with no hint of kindness or love.

The neck scarf slipped a bit and he desperately pulled it back over her face. He didn't want those brown eyes looking into him. He lost his rhythm and pulled his penis from her, rubbing it between her breasts to get hard again. Then he pushed it back into her, thrusting into her again and again. He was desperately seeking the pleasure and happiness that always came from sex. But previous couplings had always been consensual - this was definitely not.

The lack of satisfaction made him push harder, more violently, taking it out on his victim. As he climaxed he felt initial relief and then there was nothing. A void. Suddenly his voices were not screaming at him telling him he had done the right thing. Instead he felt a horrible revulsion and an overpowering sense of guilt. In his head he saw Mami and Joseph and they were not looking pleased.

Clifford stood up and looked away from his victim. He must not look at her.

Lilly lay quietly sobbing and quivering with raw terror - ready for the expected end. His demons had been temporarily satiated. Lilly was preparing herself. Death would be a blessed relief after the hell she had endured.

Lives Unravelled
Lucky Strike

June 22nd - June 23rd, 1928

Miamoon, West of Wubin, Western Australia

The bedroom was fetid with the stench of repulsed sex and drying blood. Clifford turned from his victim, wanting to block her from his confused mind. The flickering glow from the kerosene lamp next door cast a quivering beam of light that illuminated the chest of draws. The draw was slightly open and he could see glimpses of Harold's private things begging to be invaded. He roughly pulled open the draw further violating the couple's privacy.

The flickering light illuminated Harold's private letters - shared correspondence full of dreams and hopes from Lilly and personal, haunting words from James. Letters that told of hope and loss and of death finally welcomed. The glow then shone on Lilly's sandalwood amulet. This charm had kept Harold safe and the couple connected throughout the war years.

As Clifford lifted it from the draw the sweet aroma of sandalwood filled the room. This was an ironic twist. This smell had always heralded safety and security. These were in short supply as Lilly faced up to her nightmare and imminent death with dread and resignation. But the scent carried with it a faint trace of hope, of happy times in the past and a chance of survival. The sandalwood smell brought powerful images of Harold back into the room and Lilly prayed for him to help her. He had been so strong, so vigorous, so confident. Harold would forgive her the indignity of this monstrous outrage. These thoughts gave her solace when all her hope had deserted her.

Clifford then spotted the tin of Lucky Strike tobacco poking out from under Harold's pile of letters. Here was the ultimate revenge. Clifford had killed Harold Smith, cruelly assaulted his daughters, raped his wife in his own bedroom and now he would have his final smoke. Gloating over his revenge on the man who had brought him all of this pain. This would finally make him feel better. His voices told him that this was only just, Smithy had taken his tablets. Smithy had made him suffer for months.

He had only made Smithy suffer for a few moments. A nice quick shot through his back had pierced his heart. All he wanted was his tablets. He just wanted to feel better. He hadn't wanted to kill him. And he was sure Smithy would have had the tablets in his pocket. But he hadn't.

When the shot had rent the cold afternoon air, Harold had not even heard it above the tractor noise. Sniper Pte Clifford Hulme had delivered a quick and fatal body shot. Harold had fallen sideways off the tractor, with the roller passing inches from the body. Cliff had jumped up onto the moving tractor killing the motor.

Cliff had returned to the body of his dead employer and had frantically rummaged though his pockets. There were no tablets. In frustration he had lifted the rifle again, with Smithy's body taking the second shot at close range. The bullet entry had made a real mess of his temple and the back of his head was obliterated. And then he had used the axe. When he had brought it down on Smithy's head, he was pleased with the red gap that had opened exposing his brain. But even this didn't make him feel right.

Cliff had then dragged Harold's body ten yards into the scrub, covered it with dead brush and then set it alight. He watched as the brush took hold, burning brightly. But it was winter and the fire didn't take, it smouldered fitfully and then went out.

Smithy's body was still there, scorched and barbecued but not destroyed. Even this hadn't made him feel right. Cliff's head was now exploding with lights and pain.

He had come across the fields and held himself in tight control when he saw Mrs Smith coming towards him. He had made up his story and had really wanted to help the lady at first. It wasn't her fault. But later the pain had got too much, his head was sparking and crackling. His thoughts exploded with vengeful scenarios. It was everyone's fault, they were hiding his tablets from him. It was a conspiracy and they all needed to die painful, miserable deaths.

And now he was nearly at the end of his plan but he still didn't feel right yet. So perhaps a ciggie would help. It would settle him down before he killed the lady and her kids. Then he would ransack the house, find his tablets and he could get out of here. Cliff sat on the side of the bed and reached into his pocket for some papers. He then opened the tin of Lucky Strike tobacco. The familiar, comforting smell of unrolled tobacco. He sought out just the right amount for a fag.

But Cliff's fingers touched something else. The recognizable feel of small tablets lying hidden at the bottom of the tin. Clifford didn't need to look down. He knew he had found the hiding place. Twenty one little white tablets lay gleaming in the faint reflected light from the kerosene lantern flickering in the next room.

With quivering hands, Cliff took a tablet and swallowed it dry. The immediate calming effect, satiation from the psychological dependence, came first. The hypnotic, euphoric relief would come later. Cliff finished rolling his cigarette, pinching the end before putting it on his lip. He struck a match, bringing the dancing light of the flame to the end of the cigarette before inhaling the deeply satisfying, nicotine laced smoke. Calm. He felt good at last.

Clifford looked over at the naked and quivering body of Mrs Lillian Smith. He knew he had done terrible deeds today but the drug was already insulating him from the enormity of his crimes. He felt in control, his pain and anxiety had subsided.

He turned from Lilly as he again dragged the very life out of the flimsy cigarette. He was peaceful, aware that things had happened but not feeling any sense of responsibility or guilt. It was like he was removed, seeing the events of the day acted out, without him having any role in any of it. It didn't really concern him.

Suddenly the stillness was broken. Clifford spoke: 'The madness has passed me by. I am not going to kill you. I will not hurt you or your family again. I will leave here and not come back this way again.'

His voice seemed far removed from the gravity of the crime scene. He did not look at the tortured female body still tied to the bed. He didn't feel sorry for her - he was devoid of any feeling.

Clifford went out to the dining room. He gently picked up the baby and brought her into Lilly, placing Peggy gently down near her. The baby whimpered softly and nestled into its mother. Peggy was going to live. After the horrific events he was kind and solicitous about Lillian's welfare. But no emotion controlled these actions, he was just doing what he always did, the right thing. This manifestation of Clifford Hulme knew the difference between good and evil.

'You'll be cold Mrs Smith,' he said as he soothingly covered Lilly with the blood splattered bedclothes and removed the neckerchief covering her face. He tenderly stroked the hair from her eyes and used the neckerchief to blot some of the blood from her cheeks. He had already covered the girls in the dining room with blankets and had stoked the fire so it blazed in the hearth, creating the myth of domestic happiness.

'Are the other two all right? Please untie me?' beseeched Lillian, sensing that something had changed. Her strength of character was growing and the need to protect her children was a powerful force. But she was still very hesitant; she had seen his fury and had the impression that he could turn again quickly. Lilly had not witnessed Cliff finding the tablets. She was unaware about why Dr Jekyll had arrived in place of the chilling Mr Hyde.

'The other two kiddies are just stunned. They can untie you when they come around. I'm going to Dalwallinu, the police will come and find you. I will leave as soon as I have changed my clothes. These are soiled from work.'

Clifford announced all of this to her in a matter of fact way. As though he was not to blame. The clothes were stained with her blood, his semen and the blood of her children and husband. These items bore testament to his reign of brutality and he glibly referred to this as: 'soiled from work'. This creature was relaxed, and was totally unlike the crazed being who had perpetrated the monstrous crimes on her and her family.

He left. Lilly listened intently. She heard the creak and gentle thump of the kitchen door indicating that he had left the house. She heard him rummaging around in his tent and then she heard the clatter of the front gate as it hit the post. Black terrifying silence then engulfed the house.

Only minutes later she heard the frail cry of little Elsie, 'Mummy where are you? I'm hurt.'

'I'm in here Elsie. Come into Mummy's bedroom. The bad man has gone. We'll all be safe now.' Lilly made sure her voice was steady and composed, exuding confidence that she definitely did not feel.

Elsie came to the door of the bedroom. The waif looked so upset and vulnerable with huge welts around her throat and her clothes dishevelled and covered in blood.

'Mummy, Vonny is lying really still and she has a big gap in her head and there's lots of blood everywhere.'

'Cut the rope and get me free first Elsie dear,' said Lilly still trying to master her own fears. 'Then I can go out and see about Vonny.'

Elsie got her father's hunting knife from the draw. She had never been permitted to touch it before and she carried it reverently.

'What happened to your clothes Mummy? They are all cut up. And you are bleeding from everywhere. Are you going to be all right?' Elsie was quivering with fear. The events of this night had been too much for her.

It took the little eight year old some time to saw through the coarse rope and as she finally cut through she was crying with frustration and effort. Lilly took the knife and hacked at the rope tying her broken arm. Every saw stroke was an agony. She managed to free her second arm and finally stood up, swaying with pain and exhaustion. Ignoring her broken arm and her smashed and aching body, modesty drove her first act. She rapidly put on her fleecy nighty to cover her nakedness and then went immediately to her children.

Weak with hurt and fatigue and still overwhelmed by shame, grief and desolation, only the innate need to be a mother made her function as she did. She treated the wounds of the still comatose Vonny and then moved on to Elsie, Peggy and lastly herself.

She grabbed the sandalwood amulet and breathed in deeply, absorbing its scent into her being. This gave her the fortitude to leave the safety of the house to collect the rifle from its place near the water tanks where Clifford had placed it before he had gone to get help from the neighbours. She returned and securely locked the doors of the house. At least she knew Cliff was unarmed.

Lilly waited in tense vigil all through the loneliest night of her life, the rifle cocked and ready in case an unwelcome visitor returned through their door.

The four Smith girls, made camp in the dining room where Elsie and Peggy slept fitfully but Vonny didn't regain consciousness all night. Elsie had put extra wood on the fire but avoided the large and hateful mallee root still lying on the floor.

Elsie was cut and bruised over her face and neck but except for a feeling of sheer terror, Lilly was positive she would survive. She had rubbed her abrasions with the bottle of Emu Oil, that her friend Ada Nelson had assured her was an effective treatment for all types of ailments.

Baby Peggy was badly injured. Her throat was purple and there was a black and scarlet blotch above her right temple. Clotted blood was forming a large pulsating, egg sized blister in the region where her head had hit the wall. Peggy's eyes were listless and she whimpered fretfully. The baby wouldn't drink and Lilly could only feed her with her undamaged breast and she felt sure this was now dry anyway.

But it was Vonny she was most worried about. She lay motionless. Shallow breaths indicated that she was still clinging to life but her eyes were sightless. Gauze soaked with iodine, lightly covered the wound on her head but exposed brain tissue mixed with blood and crushed bone gave her no faith that Vonny would survive the night. The wound oozed with a strange smelling excrement.

Lilly had given little thought to her own wounds. Her broken arm hung loosely, and she had lightly sponged the blood from her face and arms. Her major concern was ridding herself of the memory of the vile invader and she had douched her private parts with a vinegar solution. Extraordinary pain knifed through her as the solution hit the lacerated flesh and increased her blood loss. She felt her energy and her conviction seeping away. Lilly looked out of the window hopeful for the first glimmer of morning but the world was still bathed in the jet black wash which precedes dawn.

'This will not do at all,' she said to the empty house surrounding her dozing children, 'if I stay here, my children will die. No help is going to come. I didn't go through all of this so that people will come along and find the Smith family corpses.'

She painfully stood up, laying Peggy on the mat near Vonny. She gently shook Elsie by the shoulder. The little moppet opened her eyes - immediately awake and tense.

'What is it Mummy? Has he come back?'

'No Elsie, we are safe. He has gone far away now and he will not come back but I have to go for help. Vonny is really sick and I am worried about little Peggy too.'

'But won't Daddy come home soon and save us all? He must have a really sore foot if he hasn't got back to the house by now,' Elsie said, her wide eyes reflecting her firm belief that her Daddy was still alive.

Lilly felt an icy stab to her heart as she realised that none of the children knew the horrible truth. And this certainly wasn't the time to tell them. Elsie was already teetering and this reality could wait.

'We can't wait and hope someone will come and rescue us Elsie. I'm going to go and get help and if someone comes sooner, that is all the better. But you need to be really strong because you have to look after the other two until I get back. Now just give Peggy little sips of water and keep the fire going. Most importantly don't let anyone in the door unless you know them. I will be back as soon as I can. If that madman comes, aim the rifle at him and tell him you'll shoot him. Now have you got all that? I am going out now and you have to lock the door behind me. Is that clear?'

Elsie nodded seriously at her mother. No words were spoken but her eyes begged her to stay. She had never felt more alone. If this was being an adult, Elsie didn't want a bar of it.

Lilly had put little thought into her quest. She had put on her brown shoes but her ankles were so chafed from the ropes that she was not wearing socks. The thin fleecy nighty was covered by a cardigan but she was not dressed for a trek in the depths of winter through unforgiving terrain. All she took with her was a kerosene lantern, Harold's hunting knife and her sandalwood amulet.

The deep night was breaking with the sky in the east faintly the colour of aniseed in milk as she headed to the far paddock. Firstly she needed to seek out Harold.

No frost chilled the morning of the 23rd June, but wispy fog from low lying clouds decreased the visibility and added to her nervousness. The mist deposited little droplets on everything and had soon saturated Lillian's thin, unsatisfactory clothes.

She arrived at the clearing when there was just enough light to make out dark sinister silhouettes. The tractor shape loomed in front of her and she placed the kerosene lantern on the bonnet while she searched around for clues. She searched frantically for many minutes but saw no signs of the body or any evidence of any crime. The frail, flickering light did not reveal Harold's hat on the tractor seat or the splashes of blood all over the machine.

'Harold are you here? It's me Lillian. Answer me if you can hear me,' she called hopefully. But her voice sounded thin and reedy in the thick morning fog. No answering reply could be heard. Hope again left her as she realised that this quest was futile. Harold's presence wasn't here. If he had been alive she would have felt it. Harold was dead. She knew it now with depressing certainty. But another thought crowed in, deferring her grief. While she dilly dallied here, her girls lay dying.

With this powerful motivation Lilly turned and ran headlong into the dense uncleared mallee scrub. The faint glow in the east showed where the Nelson's farm should be. She would avoid the tracks - he might be on the road. Sharp boughs cut her, prickly plants pierced into her thin clothes and her feet stumbled on ant mounds and into ruts.

At every turn Lilly saw menacing shapes. The image of her feared predator was in every murky shadow and lurking behind each tree. Grazed, bruised and still bleeding from the violent rape and brutal assault, only her desperation to seek help for her youngsters, kept her going. But the reality was that the deranged and weakened Lilly was soon totally and absolutely lost.

Lilly found a granite outcrop and she made her way to the top just as the first rays of the morning brought a weak light to the wintery landscape. The mist had risen from the land and heavy cloud now layered the landscape, threatening heavy showers. Just a small patch of cloudless sky on the eastern horizon allowed a wee bit of sunlight to sneak through. Lilly looked around desperately. She had no idea how far she had come, where she was or where the Nelson's farm should be.

The sun's only ray cast a feeble, wintery beam to the north side of the granite rock. Like a beacon, the ray ended 100 yards away, illuminating a cleared track. Lilly grasped her sandalwood amulet and whispered thanks to her guardian angel for showing her the way. Tracks mean habitation. She forgot that she had wanted to avoid the road - she needed salvation and only a track would bring this.

The wounded dishevelled woman picked her way down the steep

granite rock, gingerly avoiding the slippery patches. Her foot hit the track and she again felt a surge of confidence. She would make it. The light was now all around her and a grey, drizzly rain was falling.

But her energy was slipping, she was flagging. In her head she heard a steady, motorised thumping. Lilly thought she was having an hallucination, the imaginings of a mad woman just before collapse. Into this swaying hallucination a motor truck came around the corner and slammed on the brakes to prevent hitting the exhausted woman.

A passenger urgently jumped from the truck that was being driven by the nearest neighbour, Mr Brown. Thus Mrs Ada Nelson found her much loved friend and neighbour. She was the first to clasp her beaten and battered adopted daughter-in-law into her arms. Lilly collapsed in the embrace. She was seven miles away from her homestead and had overshot the Nelson's farm by five and a half miles.

Lives Unravelled
Surrender

Late Evening June 22nd

Early Morning June 23rd, 1928

Miamoon and Wubin, Western Australia

After the attack on the Smiths, Clifford desperately needed to get away. Despite the deepening dark, Clifford's tablet had given him new found confidence and he easily made his way along the track to the Nelson's homestead.

As he walked his mind created reason from the distorted memories of the last few hours. He blocked out the distasteful reminiscences of the events within the Smith house. He quite liked Mrs Smith and the little 'uns' and did not like to think that somehow they'd been hurt. Smithy had been a good bloke too, shame he had been shot. Still, Cliff had his tablets now so things were going to be all right. He would get himself into town and then give himself up. People who do the wrong thing need to be punished. Or perhaps he might just 'go out into the bush' and wait until it was all forgotten.

He found a large rut in the road and took a long deep drink from a puddle. It had rained heavily just before he had set out, so the water was good to drink.

He could see the flickering of lights up ahead and knew he was close to the Nelson's farmhouse. He kicked the mud off his boots as he stepped onto their verandah and knocked confidently at the door.

'Who is there?' came the welcoming voice of Ada Nelson from the lounge room. She was comfortably seated near the fire knitting, waiting for her husband to come in from the wood heap before serving him his evening cocoa.

'Is Mr Nelson home?' asked Clifford Hulme respectfully.

'Yes, I'll just get him. Please come inside and stand by the fire. It's a cold bleak evening to be out on the road.'

'What's the matter Cliff?' asked John Nelson as he entered the room, arms loaded with wood.

'There's a man crushed, a tractor has rolled onto him. I have come to ask you if you can give me a lift to Wubin so I can get some help.'

'Oh my gosh. Is he all right? Our car is out of action at present I am afraid but I have a lorry we can take. Who is it that is hurt?' John fired questions at Cliff as he walked over to him. 'Is the man all right? We can always drive Ada over to look after him first.'

'No he is all right. He's at the homestead and his wife is with him. It's more important that I get in and get a doctor as soon as possible,' Cliff said with some urgency in his voice. He was pointedly only answering the questions he needed to and being evasive about things he didn't want explored.

'Look at your hand - it is a mess. Can I fix it up for you?' asked Ada looking at his bloodied right hand. Cliff had not even noticed his hand and raised it up, seemingly fascinated by the injury.

'I must have got this when I tried to lift the tractor off the bloke. Funny isn't it, when you're trying to help someone you don't always notice when you hurt yourself.'

'Here let me bind it for you. And you need to have something hot in you before you set off. You have already walked through the rain to get here and you must be chilled to the bone,' fussed Ada as she cleaned and treated his wounded hand and forced a cup of tea into his good hand. Only after ensuring Cliff was comfortable, did Ada release him to continue his journey.

The two men jumped into the old truck and set out for Wubin, twenty miles to the east.

'Why don't I drive you directly to Dalwallinu? There is no Doctor in Wubin,' asked John Nelson as they bumped along the dusty track.

'Nah, I'm going to stick to the plan. It is to get to Wubin and then someone can give me a lift from there. It's a good road and shouldn't take too long.'

'How badly injured is the man?' asked John Nelson.

'Pretty bad I think. He got crushed by the tractor. Just as well the roller didn't go over him too or he would be a goner. He was going in and out of consciousness when I left.'

'Who is it that is hurt again? I didn't catch his name,' asked John Nelson, dreading that it could be Harold, but not wanting to tempt fate by finding out for sure.

Clifford went silent, staring out into the gloom. Blinding rain came down, lashing hard on the windscreen so visibility was greatly reduced. The wipers were not up to the job and the windscreen was flooded with water.

Suddenly headlights splintered through the wash, as a car came the other way. John Nelson swerved to avoid a head-on collision and the truck left the road, coming to a stop in a ditch adjacent to the track. The truck stalled and no amount of coaxing could get it to come back to life.

'Look, I'll get myself into town. It's only a short walk from here. Thanks for the lift,' said Cliff as he left Mr Nelson and the stalled truck and headed to the east. He quickly disappeared into the dark, murky storm filled night.

After fifteen more soaked and miserable minutes, John Nelson finally persuaded the truck's motor back into life and he made the slow trip back to his home. He did not risk the longer journey towards the Smith's, as he had been assured by Cliff that there was little he could do to help the injured man before morning.

Clifford Hulme did not return to their homestead, although Ada and John only dozed throughout the long night, listening out in worried slumber.

Clifford arrived at Wubin late that night and made himself as comfortable as possible in a partially sheltered, dryish corner of the railway station. The first train went through long before daybreak and Clifford found himself at Dalwallinu just as the inky night sky became tinged with the haze of very early morning. At this moment, Lillian Smith was 25 miles away on the farm at Miamoon standing near the tractor, searching for clues about her husband's last hours.

The first urgency for Clifford was food and he was waiting at the door at 6am when the Dally Hotel kitchen opened for breakfast. His tablet had now worn off and he had awoken feeling shaky, disoriented and anxious. The man was suffering. Poor sleep, an early train journey, all compounded after the recent traumas, had not helped. And now he was becoming fretful. He needed his drug. But he knew he had to be frugal with the twenty remaining tablets and after many days of nausea, he needed food first. He had already placed half a tablet on the table to take with his meal. Just seeing the tablet on the table cloth gave him confidence.

The Proprietor of the Dalwallinu Hotel, Marjorie Bridges, sidled towards him with a plate piled high with eggs, bacon, sausages and a tomato. She also placed two slices of toast and a steaming pot of tea next to him.

'You're out and about early. It looks like you could do with a good brekkie. You don't look too well. Eat this up and I bet you'll feel heaps better after it.'

She didn't wait for a reply but instead went over to serve a tractor salesman who was reading yesterday's West Australian. Clifford did as he was told. He got stuck into the breakfast but first the life saving tablet went down. This was better than any food to get him through his day.

By 6.30am Cliff had finished and was about to take his second cup of tea when a familiar voice greeted him.

'Howdy Cliff. What brings you to town Mate?' It was the breezy, confident, happy voice of Eustace Wilkinson. Without seeking permission he had taken a seat opposite Cliff.

'Bring me a plate of your best breakfast please Marjorie,' Eustace signalled to his sister. Cliff had felt an affinity with Eustace the newspaper man. Here was a man he could trust. He liked his relaxed manner and had enjoyed the time he had spent with him last time. Clifford thought he had looked pretty good in the picture Eustace had taken of him skinning a roo. Plus he had liked how the article had made him feel important. He had even thought of sending it over to England. His Mami and Ethel would have been really proud. But he hadn't yet heard from William, so he had decided to let sleeping dogs lie and had not posted any articles.

A half smile creased Cliff's face as he nodded a welcome to his breakfast companion.

'So what brings you back to Dally? Surely you haven't got enough skins to sell already? Your last lot only went a few months ago,' Eustace had already helped himself to a cup from Cliff's pot of tea and had pinched his last piece of toast with the confident bravado of a self assured optimist.

'I'm in a spot of bother actually,' confided Cliff. Eustace felt like an ally, someone who could give him some advice and perhaps help him through the next bit. What he needed to do after this, seemed to be pretty daunting; even after a 'happy tablet'.

'I shot Smithy. There was no reason but I was feeling pretty shocking and I thought if I went shooting I would feel better. I looked around and couldn't see any kangaroos and then I aimed my rifle at Smithy and I shot him. When I went over to him he was already dead.'

Eustace stopped eating his toast. The last mouthful sat in his mouth like ash, dry and indigestible. He was absolutely stunned. This fellow had murdered someone and he was just telling him, matter of factly, over his breakfast. Even worse, the man he had murdered had been an acquaintance of his. And Eustace had really liked the bloke.

Cliff had said his piece and was staring at Eustace waiting for him to reply. In the middle of this nervous silence Marjorie served his breakfast. She was always an expert at turning up right at the wrong moment.

'Here you are my dearest brother. I hope you enjoy it. Now don't forget to settle your account before you escape this time. You seem to always have some important news story to race off to and 'oh my dear' you completely forget to pay for your food and board.' Marjorie gave him a friendly wink, but once again didn't wait for a reply. She had a room full of patrons to serve and wasn't about to dilly dally with her brother.

'Why did you shoot him?' croaked Eustace.

'I don't know. My mind was all screaming and I had felt really sick all day. I was seeing lights and there was yelling in my head. I was wanting to shoot a kangaroo but I shot Smithy instead.'

'Are you sure he is dead?'

'Yeh, I shot him clean through the back. He died instantly. He didn't suffer any pain. I went over to him and checked.'

'What about Mrs Smith? Does she know and is she all right?' asked Eustace, slowly recovering his composure and encouraging the frightened man to keep on talking. He did not know Clifford well but he recalled from last time how nervous he was and how difficult it had been to get him to talk. This time he seemed quite effusive. But this could stop at any moment.

'Mrs Smith is at home with her girls. They're all right. I told them that I would go for help. She might need a Doctor because she was really upset. I don't know whether to make a run for it or to hand myself in to the Police Constable.' Cliff delivered his story and was still weighing up his choices. 'The problem is, if I just go bush, no-one will go and help Mrs Smith. Do you reckon I should go to the Police Station?'

'I think you have already made up your mind Clifford. If you were going to run, you wouldn't be here, having breakfast and talking to me. You can't leave a lady and her littlies stranded and you wouldn't stand much of a chance of getting away with it. Murder is murder and they always catch up with you in the end. You have a better chance of being treated right if you hand yourself in,' the quick thinking Eustace replied.

'Yeh, you're right I suppose.'

A wave of relief came over Eustace as he realised that the man was fully intending to surrender himself to the law. For a while Eustace had been concerned that he would need to talk the man around, or even worse that he would have been expecting him to assist Cliff to make an escape.

'Look, I will help you. It's clear that you have done a terrible thing but it is good that you are prepared to face up to the crime.'

With this understanding Eustace suddenly felt hungry and he set into his food. Cliff sat silently staring at the table cloth.

While he ate, Eustace's head was whirring. This was an amazing break, a newspaper man's dream. Now, while he felt sorry for Mr Harold Smith, for whom he had the highest regard, the reality was that he had just been delivered the biggest scoop of his life. This could lift him from obscurity. No more covering country fairs and horse races. But he needed to move with pace and also with great care.

Eustace had already sold a couple of freelance pieces to other papers. He knew that if he did this well he could cover this, as an exclusive. There was no other newspaperman for 200 miles! He could get the full story before the others had even purchased their train ticket.

'So who else knows about this?' asked Eustace, still the supportive confidant.

'Well only Mr and Mrs Nelson - but they think a man is just hurt and they don't know it is Smithy. Mr Nelson gave me a ride into Wubin last night. Oh and Mrs Smith knows of course, I told her that the tractor had fallen on him,' said Clifford.

'Well I think you need to tell me everything. And then you need to tell Constable Rowbottom. But he will not be at the station until 8 o'clock. Now I will help you out but I have one condition.

You must never tell anybody you talked to me first. Are you all right with this? My name must never be mentioned!'

The number one important rule of a newspaper man. He needed to be kept out of it. The last thing he needed was to be slapped with a writ that would silence him. As a witness he wouldn't be able to tell the story where or when he wanted to - in the public domain, through the media.

'So we need to get you a statement organised so you say just what you have to and no more. No sense in giving the lawyers too easy a time. Let them find out all the details the hard way,' said Eustace with a cheeky grin. He was none too fond of the law. They just say 'no comment' to newspapermen. It would be wonderful to have the 'boot on the other foot' for a while.

So Clifford told his story to Eustace. He told it in a strange distorted way. Often he changed to the third person as though he had been an observer rather that actually the perpetrator. This was especially when he talked about events he was embarrassed about. His reference to the attack on Lillian and the girls was very vague.

Apparently: 'Mrs Smith had hurt herself when she had told Cliff to go for help,' and later 'the little uns had taken injury too'.

He realised that Cliff didn't want to admit he was involved in some of these things. Eustace didn't dig too much into this. This was obviously an area that Cliff was uncomfortable about discussing. Eustace felt that he could easily find out the details and the extent of their injuries later.

'Well I reckon you should just tell the Policeman about you shooting Smithy. Keep it brief. Tell him exactly what you told me first up. Don't talk about Mrs Smith and the girls. They will send a Doctor along anyway so she'll get treated soon enough. Now remember, when you have made a statement, sign it and then say nothing to anyone. They will need to charge you and then you will get a lawyer. He can take over your defence.'

'And remember Cliff. Keep my name to yourself. Good luck Fella,' Eustace said, as they walked down the street toward the

Dalwallinu Police Station. Eustace Wilkinson then disappeared, making certain he was not seen by anyone.

Constable Rowbottom saw Clifford Hulme as soon as he entered the police yard just after 8 in the morning. He had known him for over three years. He had never been in trouble before and he greeted him pleasantly:

'Good day Cliff. What brings you to town?'

'Good morning, Mr Rowbottom. I have some news for you,' Cliff said, his eyes downcast and his hat respectfully in his hands.

'What is the matter Cliff?' The Constable could sense that Cliff was troubled.

'It is rather important news, Sir.'

'Well tell me, what it is then?'

'I shot Smithy.'

'You what?' Constable Rowbottom announced, stunned at the admission and floored at the news. He, like everyone in town, had enormous respect for Harold Smith.

'I shot Smithy. Yesterday at about 5pm. I shot him in the back,' Cliff blurted out the information he had rehearsed thinking that if he got it out quickly it would be easier to relate.

'Very well, come into the office. Do you want to make a statement?' asked the Constable, readjusting from the massive shock a man feels at the loss of a friend. Now he again reasserted himself as a professional Policeman.

'Do you wish to tell me anything? If so, I will take it down in writing if you like?' the Constable said as they sat at the desk inside.

'All right,' said Clifford.

'Just tell the story in your own time. Try not to leave any important bits out.' the Constable instructed.

The statement Clifford Hulme made was as follows:

I was born in England in Leeds. In January I was 29 years of age.

I have been working for Harold Smith for the past five months. His farm is situated about 20 miles west of Wubin. Harold Smith and his wife have always treated me all right, and there has been no ill-feeling between us. I have been working as a general farm hand.

On the 22nd of June, 1928, I was working with the axe on Smithy's block. I had Smithy's gun with me. It is a 25 Stevens. I loaded it in the morning before starting work, placing it where I was working. Smithy was working on the tractor about a chain from me.

At about 5pm something seemed to go wrong in my mind, (I get funny at times). I picked up the gun, pointed it at Smithy and pulled the trigger. Smithy had his back to me at the time. He fell off the tractor. I went to him and he was unconscious. The tractor had stopped itself. I changed my clothes and went away. When I fired the shot there were no kangaroos in sight.

I returned to the house, changed my clothes and left and walked to Wubin. I caught the train this morning on the 23rd of June. I came to Dalwallinu, had my breakfast at the hotel and gave myself up to Constable Rowbottom.

This statement is true and was given by me to Constable Rowbottom voluntarily.

With that Constable Rowbottom led Clifford to a cell; he was incarcerated in the Dalwallinu lock up.

The Constable then sent a telegram to the Perth Office requesting that they immediately send up a detective. He then proceeded to go to pick up Dr Anderson from the hospital and Jack Parrott from the store at Wubin, before driving out to the Smith's farm at Miamoon to investigate the alleged murder scene.

Picking Up The Pieces
The First Day Of The Rest Of Her Life

9pm - 10pm

June 23rd, 1928

Dalwallinu, Western Australia

Brown eyes flickered under dusty lashes as Mrs Lillian Smith gradually awoke from her deep sleep. Dr Anderson had given her 'a little something' and the dreamy, narcotic effects were still flowing through her veins, easing her pain and dulling her agony. The night had set in outside, but inside the hospital ward was all officious with glowing white light. Mrs Ada Nelson was sitting by her bed, lightly caressing her hands, as Lilly turned to her.

'You're awake at last,' she said, 'Are you feeling all right?' Ada's voice was croaky with strain and worry. This had been a long and torturous day. She knew the woman before her had frightful injuries, livid bruises, lacerations and her battered face was puffed and swollen. But this was only a fraction of the hurt. Lilly Smith had been mutilated inside and out. And the worst part was still to come. When the sedatives wore off, Lilly would have to learn to live with her awful circumstance.

'I hurt. But it's bearable. How are the kiddies? Are they all right?' Lilly asked. Even in her tranquillized state her love for her children was paramount.

'Elsie is alright. She is in the next room. She will want to come and see you in a moment. She has been so brave. Peggy is stable. She is conscious but very dozy and Doctor Anderson has asked the nurses to watch her carefully. He might need to operate on her tomorrow to release some pressure. She has a big lump and the Doctor thinks it could be putting too much stress on her brain.'

Ada thought about glossing over the truth about the third Smith child. But she reasoned that Lillian was the mother and deserved the truth. She would have wanted the same if their roles had been reversed.

'The one we are most worried about is little Vonny. She has multiple skull fractures. He is still operating on her now. They have been in there for hours. They started at 3 o'clock this afternoon and it is 9 o'clock now and they are not out yet. She was in serious trouble when they got to her but the Doctor seems to think we got her in time. So all we can do now is pray and hope the Doctor's skill is enough to save her.'

The operating room was at the end of the corridor. Dr Anderson and the efficient ward Sister had looked confident and in control when Ada had poked her head in an hour ago. But the little body on the bed in front of them had looked so vulnerable and exposed.

Tears welled in Lillian's puffed eyes and found their lonely way down her cheeks. Ada gently mopped her face, Lillian's sore arm had been set in a sling and the other arm and hand was heavily bandaged. In fact, very little of Lilly had not been strapped. Earlier, the nursing staff had dealt with the multitude of untreated injuries, while she had been mercifully unconscious in a drug induced sleep.

'My poor little babies. I wasn't able to protect them. I tried but he was so powerful and violent. He just didn't seem to care. He just smashed into us without compunction. Ada I don't know if I can cope with all of this. I can't even begin to grieve for my poor Harold, this is all just so horrible.'

Ada sat with her and stroked her hand. Sometimes words make no difference. The enormity of what she had endured meant that no outsider, no matter how well meaning, could relate.

'Is he locked up? I can see him coming in through the door. I never want to see him again.'

'Constable Rowbottom has him in the lock up. He will not be out to trouble you or anyone else again. Don't worry yourself on that score.'

Suddenly Lilly went stiff and grabbed at Ada's hand. Her eyes were wild, her voice reduced to a scratchy, harsh whisper full of desperation: 'Ada he violated me. I begged him not to but he did. I will never rid myself of his stench. It was horrible, foul and unspeakable. I thought he was going to kill me. In some ways I wish he had. No-one must ever know.'

Lilly was a woman of her era. This was every woman's deepest fear and the worst sin. To be sexually assaulted was a stain that could never be removed. The horror of his crime was that it reflected as much on the victim as the perpetrator. Her honour was tarnished, her good name was soiled.

Ada felt profoundly angry. She shared Lillian's deep repulsion at the thought of her being outraged. She fumed when she recalled her kindness to the animal Clifford Hulme the night before. She could also understand Lillian's need to keep this a total secret.

'No-one needs to know about this Lillian. I am sure the Doctor and medical staff will be discreet. I will check with the Constable but I am sure that there is no reference to this in Hulme's confession. It may not be much, but I think we can hide this from the public eye. After what you have gone through, the last thing you need is to be subject to public humiliation and scrutiny.'

Ada Nelson had lived her whole life in a society where some things were better 'left unsaid'. And this was definitely one of the events that fell into this category. She would organise everything.

Lilly lay back onto her pillow. Her eyes still silently weeping, the agony of memory.

A nurse walked through the door with a cup and two more Veronal sleeping tablets. It was the pretty little nursing assistant, Maudie, who gave the medicine and the evening greeting. She merrily chatted to the two women, oblivious to their pain and distress.

'Dr Anderson has just come out of surgery. He said to pass on to you that your little Vonny is sleeping and looks far better. He had to take out a 1 inch piece of bone from her skull. The wound caused by the mallee root went right into her brain. Can you imagine it? But he has cleaned it up and she has lots of stitches. Poor little mite has had all of her blonde curls lopped off. Oh, and he said he would operate on the baby tomorrow morning if she's no better.'

Her low levels of empathy and jovial bedside manner needed work but at least some of what she was delivering was good news. At least Vonny was stabilised.

'Dr Anderson said Mrs Smith has to take these tablets and you have to go now. There should be no visitors here after 8pm you know. You can come back in at half past ten in the morning. So drink up Mrs Smith and then off to sleep?'

Maudie Black delivered all news, good and bad, with the same level of youthful enthusiasm and chirpiness. She wasn't sure that nursing was really her forte. It was too distressing and she hated cleaning up bedpans and dealing with messy, bloodied bandages all of the time. She wanted to work with young people. Here the patients were nearly all old and Dr Anderson and the nursing sister were both in their forties!

Still, if she quit working here she would have to work in the cabinet makers with her Dad, Mum and two brothers and that was far worse. Not that she minded the cabinet making but they doubled up as the undertakers. There was never any fun around her place. Her house and bedroom smelt like death and formalin. Her mother actually liked painting the faces of dead people and getting them ready for burial. She said it was respectful. Maudie thought it was gruesome.

The ladies did as they were told and Mrs Nelson reluctantly walked from the room as Lillian's eyes again closed. She looked into the room next door and saw Elsie lying sleeping on the closest bed. Next to her, in a hospital cot, lay Peggy, so totally covered in bandages she resembled a little mummy. But the third bed lay empty. Vonny had obviously not come from surgery yet. She looked down the corridor to the lighted room at the end of the ward and sent a whispered prayer that the operation would be successful.

Ada walked briskly back to the Dalwallinu Hotel where she had taken a double room for her and John. There was only one occupant as she swept through the dining room. A tall, young, good looking man was in the corner under the lamp, writing furiously. He had already covered numerous pages with words and he did not look up at Mrs Nelson. Too late for a meal, she had decided to go directly to her bedroom.

Once there she set to work immediately. Firstly, she looked at the scratchy list that she had been compiling at the hospital. Things had been added, altered and rubbed out all day. It still contained points like:

- Death notice for The West Australian. One from John and me, one on behalf of Lillian and the children.
- Send a condolence note to Mrs F Parrott in the nursing home and Mrs Smith in England.
- Visit Dalwallinu Congregational Church, meet Rev, arrange for funeral Wed?
- Arrange for order of proceedings - eulogy Jack P? Pall bearers?
- Get John to get a good suit for Harold from farm.
- Get Mrs Rowbottom, President Dally CWA, to arrange catering for wake.
- Get undertakers to make good quality jarrah coffin with red silk inlay.
- Book dining room at Dally Pub for wake.
- Arrange for flowers to be sent from Perth.

This list promised to get longer and longer. The cost was not a problem, John and Ada would not scrimp on this funeral. But, she reasoned, this was her gift. At least Harold would be sent off in style.

And then she turned to her most important task. She addressed different versions of the following letter to: Mr Jack Parrott,

Mr Brown their neighbour, Constable Rowbottom and Doctor Anderson and the nursing staff at the Dalwallinu Hospital.

To Whom It May Concern:

I would like to request, as a matter of extreme urgency, that any reference to the physical outrage perpetrated on Mrs Lillian Smith on the evening of 22nd of June, be suppressed. It is Mrs Smith's most earnest request that this is not mentioned in any statement, reference or dispatch. It is of paramount importance for the good name of this cruelly treated woman that this occurs. If this was to be published in the press or mentioned in any court case, it would create enormous embarrassment and shame for this poor lady.

I trust I can rely on your honour and discretion to ensure that this occurs.

Yours faithfully

Mrs Ada Nelson

She would deliver these letters first thing in the morning. Ada was sure that this unpleasant matter was 'under control' as she slipped into her cold wintery double bed. 'John will not be too far away,' she muttered to herself as she faded into exhausted slumber.

Immediately below her in the dining room in the Dalwallinu Hotel, the young man, Eustace Wilkinson, was desperately finishing his press report, ready to be sent to Perth on the early morning train. His first instalment of the story of the murder of Harold Smith and assault on the Smith family, would be in Monday's West Australian.

Eustace sat back and reviewed his day's work proudly. This was to be a well orchestrated release of aspects of the story. Just enough to get folk interested on Monday and then more details would be rolled out through the week in 'The West'.

He was planning for the big assault - the full expose, in the

Saturday Mirror and the Sunday Times. Eustace planned to cover all aspects: the story from everyone involved, eye witness reports, pictures from the farm, updates on the Smith family's health, Harold's funeral and statements from the local police. He had it all sown up. He would be the expert on the crime. He hoped that this would get him the prime seat in the press box at the inquest and the trial. Plus it would mean he could leave this god forsaken hole and never report on rural minutiae again.

Down the road at the police station, a harassed and tired Constable Rowbottom swore softly at the closing door. Detective Inspector Doyle had just left and was walking back to the Dalwallinu Hotel. He had travelled up from Perth, arriving at 5.30pm and since that time he had been fixing up 'the mistakes' that Constable Rowbottom had made in the investigation so far. DI Doyle thought he deserved an early night.

Constable Rowbottom was not at all happy with the overbearing, pompous and very critical DI Doyle. He had come in and ridden rough shod over all that they had done today. His pages of detailed paperwork were littered with red marks showing apparent 'holes' in the investigation. DI Doyle was a Perth bloke and was 'on the way up'. He needed this case for his promotion. He didn't care about who he would hurt in the process or the sensitivities of the locals. He wanted efficiency, expediency and a successful prosecution.

DI Doyle had wanted to see pages of interviews and witness statements all neatly written up. Constable Rowbottom had deemed that everyone was too traumatised today. No official statements had been taken. He knew these folk and he knew they were not going to high-tail it out of town. He liked these people and knew they were needing time for grief. They were not yet ready for criminal investigation and justice.

DI Doyle had been particularly critical of his decision to send the truck to pick up Smithy's body. The Constable had requested that John Nelson get the truck from Smith and Parrott's Store in Wubin and: 'Go get Smithy and bring him back to Dally.'

Constable Rowbottom hadn't wanted Smithy left out there for another night, where vermin could foul his remains and foxes and dingoes could rummage through his bones. DI Doyle was furious. He had wanted an 'untampered crime scene' to investigate tomorrow. Well, DI Doyle could be damned!

John Nelson had gone back out to the farm with Constable Rowbottom's son-in-law, the Parrott store employee Charles Martin. They had collected and reverently transported Smithy's body back into Dalwallinu. He had seen the lights of the truck go past a few minutes ago. They were heading down to the undertakers, at old Mr Black's store.

Constable Rowbottom would go over there directly, just to check the body was correctly stored. Hopefully they had got in loads of ice. There would need to be an autopsy tomorrow and Rowbottom hoped the undertakers hadn't started the 'formaldehyde and makeup' routine which they usually embarked on whenever a new body arrived. Dr Anderson would need an unadorned body to complete his forensic analysis.

Before he left the police station, Constable Rowbottom looked in the lock up at the bump that was Clifford Hulme.

'You have caused a mighty lot of grief young man,' the Constable said to the bump as he left. The bump said nothing in reply. It was deeply asleep.

The Smith and Parrott Store delivery truck was parked in front of *'Black and Son, Quality Carpenters'* as the Constable made his way down the darkened street. John Nelson and Charles Martin had just carried the lifeless body of Smithy from the truck and laid it out onto Mr Black's freshly scrubbed slab.

The body had stiffened with rigour mortis and the damage done to the head and chest had made the transportation difficult. Both bearers had unabashed tears streaming down their faces as they manhandled the corpse. They gently straightened his limbs so he looked more dignified. The two bearers had hardly spoken on the long drive; both were too caught up with memories, vengeful thoughts and recriminations. Mr Black and his sons had already started to load ice around the inert body and were making it clear that the two deliverers had done their job. Their roles were over.

Suddenly a thick emotional voice laced with an Irish accent cut into their activity as Charles Martin requested: 'Could you all give us five minutes of peaceful time with our friend please? Both of us need just a few minutes to say goodbye.'

'Certainly. Come on lads, let's give these gentlemen a few moments to pay their respects.' Mr Black subserviently ushered his family out the side door and left the two men alone with the body of Harold Smith.

By 1928 Charles Martin wore his deformed face with acceptance. It just didn't seem to matter so much anymore. But tonight the deformity showed clearly, red and livid, as he spoke his words of farewell. His face was contorted with the pain of his misery.

He spoke first:

'Smithy, you were the first Englishman I ever met who I could stomach. You listened to me, you showed compassion but not sympathy. You looked past my scars and you saw me. You helped me believe that I could have a better life and I have. When I asked you for employment you gave it to me and you kept seeing the best in me. Now I do all the books and often run the store where I used to just lift boxes. You were an Englishman who became a true Australian. And it took a gutless, English cur to kill you. Thank you Mr Harold Smith. I will miss you, to be sure, to be sure.'

John Nelson waited a respectful minute before he spoke to the body:

'Harold, I have loved you dearly. You became the son I had lost. You were strong for me and Ada when we needed you to be. Now I will be strong for you. You have left a wife and family. I will look after them and care for them until the end of my life. I will miss you my friend. Please hug James for me. I will find solace in thinking about you two getting up to all sorts of mischief in Heaven.

Goodbye my son.'

Constable Rowbottom stood in the doorway and listened to the profound and heartfelt speeches of the two men. He was even more convinced that he had been right to allow today to be devoted to mourning and recovery. The police investigations could commence tomorrow.

Ten miles to the north, Chrissie Parrott walked out to the front verandah of their home in Wubin. She stroked her distended abdomen feeling the stirrings of her unborn child. She was now in her last ten weeks. She reflected despondently on how pleased Harold had been for her, and now the child would never meet 'Uncle Harold'. Grief again welled up in her as she thought of the enormity of his death. To her, it was a tragic sorrow but she knew the loss would be far more grievous for her husband and her best friend Lillian.

Chrissie had not seen Lilly since the attack. All she had received was a garbled account of what had happened when Jack had returned from the farm at 5.30pm this afternoon. Since that time Jack had been sitting on the front porch, chain-smoking and drinking whisky. Jack was teetotal and this version of Jack as a morose drunk was frightening.

When Jack had been dropped off by John Nelson he had looked drained and gaunt. He had collapsed into Chrissie's embrace and cried, deep painful sobs of regret. Jack had travelled with the Constable and Doctor to the farm and assisted them all day with the rescue of Lilly and the girls. It was Jack who had discovered Harold's gruesomely butchered body and the impact on him had been deeply traumatic. This image obsessed his thoughts throughout that long Saturday.

He had chosen not to go back again with John and Charles to transport the body in the store truck. In a haunting voice, Jack had relayed the story of the morning to his wife.

'We arrived at about 10am and saw the Nelson's truck already at the house. We went straight down to the paddock Smithy had been clearing. We could see the edge of the scrub and the tractor just standing there off the track. Everything just looked normal.

When we got closer we could see Smithy's hat on the tractor seat and there were blood splatters all over the place.'

'I could see that something like a bag had been burnt behind the tractor but there was no sign of any body. At the rear of the roller, under some partly burnt scrub, I came across his body. It was awful. He had black soot all over him and some of his clothes had been burnt away. But it was Smithy alright. His chest was covered in blood where a bullet had come through from behind. Constable Rowbottom and Doctor Anderson agreed that this was the wound that had killed him. The cowardly bastard shot my best Mate in the back.' Jack put his head into his hands to hide his tears.

With a large sniff and a swipe of his watering eyes with his shirt sleeve, Jack continued, 'the right side of his face looked serene. There was a large gash on his forehead and the blood had streamed down from a hole above his left temple. When I looked closely the rear of his head had been blown away. The back was a pulpy, bloody mess.'

At this point Jack could not go on. He wept. Harold had been his friend, mentor, business partner and brother-in-law. In fact Harold had been the brother he never had. Jack wept for all that he lost but he also wept for the guilt that this could have been prevented. And only Jack held the secret, deep within himself, that he had feared that something horrible might have happened if 'Harold's Project' didn't work out. But in his wildest dreams he had never thought that it would be something this catastrophic.

'I know you loved him Jack. He loved you too. I hope it was really quick. So what about Lilly and the children? How were they when you found them?' asked Chrissie, full of comfort and compassion. She needed news and she needed her husband to be in control. Jack gradually mastered his emotions and painfully continued his recount:

'Well, when we got back to the house, John Nelson was in with the girls. They had arrived at about 8am and had found the three children all alone. The house had been wrecked, it was like a slaughterhouse, with broken furniture and blood everywhere. But, it was funny there were signs of normality all over too. A cold cup of tea still sat on the table and there was a batch of Lillian's scones in a tea towel on the sideboard. Poor little Elsie was beside herself. She had guarded the house since her Mum had left and was terrified that he might come back. The other two little 'uns were still out to it. They both looked near to death. I was really scared that Vonny wasn't going to make it. Doctor Anderson only took a few minutes to decide that the kiddies needed to be taken to Dalwallinu Hospital - immediately.'

'There was no sign of Lilly and I was really worried. It seemed like she had just set off by foot to walk to a neighbour's house, or perhaps even to Wubin. John Nelson told us that Ada and Mr Brown had set out early this morning to look for her.'

'We loaded the girls into the Doctor's car and we set off back to Dalwallinu. We were driving pretty slowly because Vonny and Peggy were so badly injured. Elsie just fell asleep in my arms the moment the motor started. We had gone less than a quarter of a mile when we came across Brown's truck coming the other way. They had found Lillian.'

Jack took a deep breath before continuing: 'Apparently she had been walking along the road in a daze. She was on the unused back track to Miamoon. She was over seven miles away from the farm. The moment they picked her up she just collapsed. She was exhausted and had obviously lost heaps of blood. She was in a really bad way. We carried her across to our car because Dr Anderson thought she needed medical treatment really fast.'

'Chrissie, she looked terrible. She was cut and bruised and so puffed up. I just felt so angry at the bastard who had done this to her. If that beast had been there, I think I would have strangled him on the spot. How could he do this to Lillian? How could he be such a monster to those innocent little kiddies? How could he shoot Harold in cold blood, when he had always treated him so well and really wanted to help him?'

'I didn't want him out on the farm with Harold. Even before Lilly and the kids came to live out there. I just didn't trust him, I always thought he was a bit of a loony. I saw him go troppo at Christmas time. He went really crazy and mucked up the store. And I kept telling Harold but he kept insisting that he would be all right and that he could handle it. And look what has happened! Chrissie I should have stopped it!' This last sentence Jack had shouted in a high-pitched, anxiety drenched cry. Her husband looked at her, pleading desperately for forgiveness and absolution. He was full of sorrow and tortured by remorse.

Chrissie responded with love and reinforcement. This was her man and he was in great pain. 'Look, none of this was your fault Jack. Harold was always a man who knew his own mind. It has happened and that monster Hulme did this, not you. Now I think you should just keep any hint of him being crazy to yourself. I don't want this criminal to get off from the death penalty because someone proves he's insane. He did this horrible thing and I want him to be executed for it.'

This was the last sensible conversation Chrissie had been able to have with her husband. He had refused food and company and instead had sat on the verandah meshed in a morose loop of nicotine, alcohol and grief.

He looked up groggily at her as she came through the door. He stumbled backwards before grabbing the railing. 'What do you want?' he snapped at her rudely, his voice was slurred and irritable. Any invasion into his self absorbed, guilt session was unwelcome.

'Darling I think you should stop drinking now,' Chrissie said timidly.

'Just leave me alone. You've got no idea what is best for me. How do you know what I need?'

Chrissie always deferred to her husband. He was the boss in their relationship and she had never wanted it any other way. But this man wasn't coping. She needed to put her foot down.

'Jack I want you to come to bed. Now this is not helping. You need to go to Dalwallinu tomorrow morning and identify the body. At this rate you'll be so hung over you won't be able to get out of bed. I know you are upset, but your sister needs you to be strong. I need you to be strong. Harold needs you to look after things. You are the only one who can.'

Jack was taken aback. Chrissie didn't usually tell him what to do. But her words got through the drunken haze.

'Alright then,' he muttered.

He compliantly accepted her advice and weaved and stumbled his way inside before collapsing, fully clothed, onto his bed. Chrissie wrenched off his boots and manhandled him to his side of the bed. She spent an uncomfortable night at the side of her man while she grappled with his fumes, his snoring and her own misery.

Picking Up The Pieces
Getting The Job Done

June 24th, 1928

Dalwallinu, Western Australia

Jack Parrott's hangover gave Eustace Wilkinson an exceptionally lucky break on the Sunday morning. Despite all of Chrissie Parrott's ministrations, Jack was not upright and in the car, weaving his way along the ten miles to Dalwallinu, until 9.25am in the morning. The original plan had been that Jack Parrott was to have identified the body of murder victim Harold Smith at 9.00am in the morning. If that had occurred, Dr Anderson could have done the autopsy immediately afterwards and Constable Rowbottom and DI Doyle would have been able to get straight out to the farm at Miamoon to complete a more rigorous investigation of the crime scene. But Jack was late, so all of these plans had to change.

Dr Anderson had scheduled to operate on the baby, Peggy Smith, at 10am. This was urgently needed and could not be altered. He also needed to complete a rigorous medical investigation on Clifford Hulme but this could happen at any time throughout the day. The three decided that the two policemen had to leave immediately and that a key to the station would be left in the secure and reliable hands of Dr Anderson. He could be trusted to keep the station locked and the man in the cell safe and secure. Jack Parrott could wait around until they returned in the afternoon and the identification and the autopsy could be done then.

The Constable and DI promptly left at 9.15 and Dr Anderson checked that the police station was securely locked as he returned to the hospital to scrub up ready for his morning operation.

Now the reason that this turned into a lucky break for Eustace, was that he just happened to be hovering inside the hospital when Dr Anderson returned. Eustace had been involved in spreading his charm, extremely thickly, on the very impressionable Maudie Black. In fact he was overtly flirting with her. Unbeknownst to her, Eustace was milking her for any news on the Smith children. He heard the sounds of approach and had just slunk into the shadows behind the nurse's station when the very professional Doctor arrived back at the hospital and beckoned to both of the nursing staff to follow him into the nurse's office.

'Maudie and Sister, I need to talk to you both, in private, immediately,' the Doctor said gravely. 'Firstly, I need to impress on you the need to keep anything that you have found out about the Smith case confidential. Later today we may find people from the Perth press arriving in town. They will try to find out information. They may be very sneaky. Nothing must be divulged to them.'

'It is particularly important that you do not mention anything about the grievous atrocities perpetrated on Mrs Smith,' Doctor Anderson paused for effect here. He had received Mrs Ada Nelson's letter and he approved of the sentiment and the request. This would be best for the healthy recovery of Mrs Smith. He had been able to have a brief, snatched conversation with Constable Rowbottom and they both felt that this aspect of the case could easily be suppressed without damaging the case against Clifford Hulme. They had not discussed it with the arrogant and unfeeling DI Doyle.

'Now Sister, you and I need to get scrubbed up ready for surgery on Peggy Smith. Please prepare her and bring her in if you would be so kind. Maudie, you must look after the ward on your own, and hang up my jacket please. I have the key to the Dalwallinu Police Station in there, so if you could keep my coat near you and keep it safe, I would appreciate it.'

The Doctor took off his jacket and went down the corridor to get into his surgery whites. Eustace Wilkinson smiled to himself. The smug, self satisfied grin of a man who knows he has won a big prize. Dr Anderson was just a little bit too late for the first part of his warning. Maudie had just given him a complete rundown on the progress of all of the Smiths. She had been effusive about the possibility that Elsie would be released today but was just a little bit more cautious about the serious condition of both Vonny and Peggy. Vonny was still in a very bad way and would need to be transferred to a hospital in Perth. There was every likelihood that she would not survive. Depending on the outcome of today's operation, the baby may also be at serious risk. They had not yet broached the topic of Mrs Smith's health.

Eustace worked out his strategy as he emerged from the back of the room. He sidled up towards the pretty nursing assistant making her jump. She had thought he had gone and had put him out of her mind. Maudie was working busily at the front desk, sorting pills ready for her mid morning round. She was alone, as the Sister and Doctor Anderson were already in the operating room and no visitors were allowed in the hospital until 10.30 on Sundays.

'Now Eustace, I really hope I haven't said anything to you I shouldn't. Doctor Anderson just said to keep things quiet. You will keep things to yourself won't you?' her pretty green eyes looked up, begging him to support her lack of discretion.

Eustace gave her a confident grin: 'Look Maudie, you know you can trust me. Dr Anderson meant not to tell the Perth reporters. They'll be here on the afternoon train and they'll badger you for information. So just say 'no comment'. And whatever you do, don't let them anywhere near the patients. Don't worry about me - I'm just a local man wanting to know they are all getting better. Now give me Mrs Smith's medications and I'll pop in to see her. You must have lots of other things to do.'

The confident Eustace lifted up the tray with the pills labelled 'Mrs Lillian Smith'. On the way to her room, he went into the kitchen and made her a cup of sweet tea. He also grabbed a white coat from a hook and found his camera bag and notepad before making his way down the corridor. He checked that there was no-one in sight before entering the solitude of her room.

The dozing lady before him was an horrific sight. Bruises always look worse a few days later, and Lilly had red welts, dark black and purple bruises and her face was still puffed and bloated.

At the doorway Eustace hesitated. He was at heart a decent chap and what he was about to do, violated her privacy and every sense of decency he possessed. But this was his chance and he knew if he didn't do this, then someone else certainly would. This was the dilemma of every good reporter; getting the balance between personal privacy and the public's 'right to know'.

He set up his Brownie camera, carefully facing it towards the sleeping woman. She did not flinch. Eustace coughed and still there was no response. Eustace then proceeded to take a series of photographs, quietly moving around to get the best angle to show her mutilated face. He was glad there was good light in the room. A flash would have been a dead giveaway. Suddenly he noticed her stirring and he rapidly snatched the Brownie camera and placed it in his bag below the bed.

Eustace took control by quickly filling the room with friendly chat.

'Good morning Mrs Smith. How are you feeling? I am a relieving medical student and I have just popped past to give you your tablets. Dr Anderson is treating your littlest daughter Peggy. Hopefully he will have good news for you today.'

Lilly opened her eyes groggily and they focussed on the image of the young, strange man in her room. Lillian's instant emotion was unadulterated fright. Her body withdrew, curling into a foetal position. She was not ready to face any man who was unknown to her yet. She had no trust. Her mind screamed, her pupils dilated in eyes that were wild with fear and her heart thumped loudly.

'Go away. Get out of here,' she whispered in an anxious, terror drenched voice.

'Look I am sorry. I didn't mean to scare you Mrs Smith. I will leave you directly but I do need to get you to take your tablets and

I have made you a nice cup of tea.'

His lame words were not helping. Lilly was beyond placating.

'Get out or I'll scream,' hissed the frantic, panicking patient.

Eustace needed to get out of her room immediately and he was desperate that she should not recall that he had been there. He moved rapidly down the passage until he saw Maudie.

'Maudie come quickly. I think Mrs Smith is having a panic attack. She woke to see me in her room and I think it brought back some painful memories.'

Maudie quickly followed Eustace. He was alarmed, Lillian's fear of him had been palpable. Eustace had never seen that raw dread in anyone's eyes before. He had not thought through the degree of distress his presence would cause her. He wasn't really a cad and didn't want to cause her any more anguish. He waited in the hallway as Maudie moved past him and took control:

'Here Mrs Smith, you have taken a funny turn. You take these Veronal and we'll get you back sleeping again. No-one is going to hurt you in here. We just want you to get better. Now drink this up and I'll just give you a shot to make you feel nice and calm again.' Maudie quickly jabbed her arm with a needle and her body instantly slumped back against the bed. Once again she entered into a serene, forgetful and tranquil sleep.

Maudie looked up at Eustace who leaned in nervously from the doorway. She had a bad habit of saying far too much when she was nervous. Torrents of unguarded words gushed, information that she should definitely have kept to herself.

'You must have reminded her of the bloke who raped her. She was really badly beaten up and he had his way with her you know. So not only did he kill her husband and smash up her little kiddies almost to death, but he outraged her. In her own bedroom while her kids were next door. How dreadful. He tied her to the bed with ropes and he cut all her clothes off. So she didn't even have anything to hide her nakedness. Every time one of the kiddies woke up he would go out and strangle them. He hit little Vonny over the head with a mallee root. What a horrible pig. That is why she was so scared to see a strange man in her room. I think you had better get out of here before anyone comes. Sister would have a fit if she knew you'd been in here, scaring the patients.'

Eustace gladly escaped from the ward, pulling his valuable camera bag and notes protectively to his chest. As Maudie walked with him she again had a twinge of remorse.

'Now you must not tell anyone in town about this will you? I shouldn't have let you in here in the first place. I don't want to lose my job. And I've probably told you more than I should. Doctor Anderson did say we should keep it secret. Particularly the bit about the outrage.'

'Don't worry Maudie. I won't be chatting to people around town. Now you get back to the patients. I can let myself out.' Eustace had excellent powers of recovery and had already forgotten about the sense of blind panic he had felt in Lillian's room.

'I might just come back and see how you are in about an hour. You've had a pretty difficult morning. A pretty little thing like you shouldn't have to work this hard. Perhaps the Doctor will let me take you out to lunch.'

'Well the Doctor might but my Dad would have a fit. He needs to meet and approve any gentleman suitors first. Not everyone is good enough to go courting an undertaker's daughter you know. You will need to pay him a visit and ask to take his daughter out first.'

'I just might take you up on that,' said Eustace with a cheeky wink at the chirpy little nursing assistant as she bundled him out of the hospital. She immediately turned to go back down to finish her chores.

The unquenchable Eustace hesitated on the step. He glanced back at the Doctor's coat hanging in the nurse's office and peered surreptitiously at his pocket watch. It was still only 10.20am. He reasoned that he might just have time to accomplish one more coup. But he would need to be very quick. He stealthily slid back into the hospital and went straight to the pocket of the coat, searching out the key to the police station. His fingers grasped it and he was just turning to go when a voice behind him made him jump nervously.

'Good morning Doctor. I trust you had a good night's sleep. I will be spending the day with Mrs Smith. If little Elsie Smith is to be released today, I trust one of the nursing staff will come and get me so that I can organise for her to be taken somewhere suitable,' Ada Nelson said, addressing Eustace's back. He suddenly realised that he was standing in the nurse's station and he was still wearing a white coat. Of course she would make this mistake.

Eustace realised that disguise was important, so as he turned, he let out a massive sneeze and covered his face with a white cleaning cloth. He answered in a muffled, nasal voice:

'Sorry, I have a bad cold. Yes do go through. I will let the nurses know about Elsie.'

Mrs Nelson failed to observe anything unusual about the young man; in fact he didn't even register in her thoughts at all. Her mind was whirring. She had a funeral to organise and there was a lot to do. Young men in white coats were not important.

Eustace watched her walking down the corridor and then made his escape, anxiously grasping the key in his clenched fist. He had abandoned the white coat and the makeshift handkerchief before he made his way towards the police station.

As he walked along the street, quiet on a Sunday morning, Eustace marvelled at his good fortune. He had learnt enough confidential information over the morning to enable him to write some amazing stories. Plus he had some spectacular pictures of Mrs Smith's injuries. When he added this to the explicit details Maudie had just divulged about the rape, this would be dynamite. This was the bit that Clifford had been so hesitant to tell him. The weekend newspapers would be wild for all of these salacious details.

A man was slouched on a seat in front of the police station.

The man was only a few years older than Eustace but he looked terrible. Red, bleary eyes still partly asleep, looked up as Eustace approached. A heavy night of drinking had taken its toll.

'Hello, can you help me?' asked the man groggily. 'My name's Jack Parrott. I'm from Wubin and I was supposed to meet the Police Constable here this morning to identify a body. Unfortunately I had car trouble and I'm late. Do you know where he is?'

If Jack had been less under the influence of last night's whisky, he might have recognised the young man in front of him. They had met briefly, many years ago, at the Narrogin Inne. But Eustace had been much younger and Jack had been distracted. He had been besotted with his pretty sister, Marjorie and full of dreams of going off to war. And today his mind was just concentrating on staying awake. He felt dreadful.

'I was hoping to catch up with the Constable today myself about a minor problem of my own. But I heard he has headed out to a crime scene and will not be back until after lunch. Why don't you go to the Hotel and have a rest? You look like you need it. I am going to leave a note for the Constable so I can let him know where you are too. There is no sense in either of us waiting here in this uncomfortable place.'

Jack was very relieved. This seemed like a great plan. He certainly could do with a comfortable sleep to enable him to recover. He wanted to have his wits about him before he identified the body. Smithy deserved this much at least. So he trudged off towards the Dalwallinu Hotel, trusting that the gentleman he had just met, would do as he had said.

Eustace waited until the man had rounded the corner and then he took out the key and entered the deserted police station. His first port of call was to check out Constable Rowbottom's desk. Like a good reporter, Eustace was able to quickly scan the contents of the desk without touching or disturbing the order of papers.

He rapidly read over the murder notes and Hulme's confession. He was pleased to see that Clifford's statement had been very brief, much as he had advised him yesterday morning. Then he noticed the diary and made a note that Clifford Hulme was to be charged today. This was definitely worth reporting and he would need to pose the question later that afternoon so that he had official confirmation. Apparently there was a Detective Inspector here already - DI Doyle. It looked like Constable Rowbottom didn't like him very much. There was a reference to him being 'DI Boil' under a very unflattering cartoon figure.

The other important date was in a telegram. The Constable was requesting an armed deputation to be sent to Dalwallinu late on Tuesday night so that Hulme could be transferred to Perth on the early train on Wednesday morning. This was great planning. The last train went north at 10pm and came back again at about 5.30am. This would avoid any public scrutiny and the townsfolk would be unaware of the prisoner transfer.

'I must remember to be there to record that event,' muttered Eustace as he made his way stealthily to the cell at the back of the station.

'Hi Cliff. How are you?' he asked the hunched man cowering in the darkened cell.

'Hello Eustace. I feel real sick. I've got a corker of a headache. This is really bad. No-one's given me any breakfast. Can you get me something?' asked Cliff looking haggard and needy.

'Look Mate, I'm not really meant to be in here. I just sneaked in. I can give you some tobacco though.' Eustace took a brand new tin of Lucky Strike tobacco out and piled some onto the prisoner's outstretched hand. Clifford took it and added it, furtively, to the tin he had in his pocket. Eustace wondered for a moment what he was hiding but dismissed this as an unimportant thought.

'At least if you have a smoke it'll make you less hungry. I think the two policemen have gone out to the farm. They'll be back this afternoon and I'm sure they'll get you some food. But firstly, there's something important I've come to talk to you about.'

'Have you remembered anymore about what happened at the

farm? You didn't tell me much about what happened in the house. Like what happened with Mrs Smith and the children?'

'I can't really remember much, I sometimes go a bit crazy. I get these black moods and I get really sick and have bad headaches. Sometimes I do horrible things when I am in these moods. It's like things in my head tell me to do stuff and when it's all over the voices are not there anymore. I think I hurt Mrs Smith. I might have hurt the children too. That's not good. They were nice. Even Smithy was usually a good bloke. But he wasn't being nice to me that day.'

'Why wasn't he being nice to you Cliff?'

'I was really sick that day and he had some tablets that would have made me better. Even though I asked him, he wouldn't give me any and that made me mad.'

Eustace listened and waited. But Cliff had stopped talking and just stared at the floor. This was all he was going to say. This seemed a pretty poor reason to murder someone thought Eustace; but he kept this opinion to himself.

'Doctor Anderson will be over to examine you in a little while. Don't tell him too much, say you've forgotten everything but make sure he knows you are in pain. You are going to need some sleeping tablets and stuff, so try and get them from this Doctor. It'll be pretty tough to get them from the prison doctors.' Eustace was being supportive and helpful. He needed to get Cliff's trust if he was going to get him to talk.

'Now the other thing is that you might need to let me know if there's anyone I need to contact for you. Perhaps there is someone in Australia who can be a character witness for you. Someone you can think of who will say what a nice bloke you are. And you might like to get a message out to some of your family and friends in England. You can let me know and I'll try to see you every now and again. Find out how you are and stuff. But remember it will always have to be our secret. I cannot be involved. All right?'

'Yes. Thanks. When I was a little boy I had a triangle of trust with my Mami and my two brothers. They kept me safe and out of trouble. They're all gone now. You are the only one who I can trust here.'

This was a bit too much for Eustace. He was being given an 'unasked for' responsibility. He didn't really know if he was happy about this. He had quite liked the bloke and felt a bit sorry for him but he was disgusted and revolted at the horror of his crimes. This fellow had some serious problems. Plus he was going to hang, so it made no sense to get too fond of him.

'I need to go now Cliff, be strong,' Eustace said backing away from the cell. He needed time and space to consider what had just happened.

'Bye Eustace and thanks for visiting me.' Clifford's farewell voice was muffled, a worthless echo, sorry for disturbing the air.

At the door Eustace looked back and Clifford Hulme had already disappeared, blending into the back of the cell and fading from the view of any disapproving observer.

The newspaper man left quickly; he had his story. He raced back to the hospital and quietly replaced the key without seeing any of the staff. He then nonchalantly strolled back to the Dalwallinu Hotel for Sunday lunch. It was a Sunday roast and the dining room had a good number of patrons.

'You look pleased with yourself,' said Marjorie as she waited for him to indicate that she had placed enough roast beef and potatoes on his plate.

'I am onto something Marjorie, and I am about to make lots of money and then I can leave this rural life for good. The only thing I will miss from around here, is you.'

'Well, I'll miss you too, you young scoundrel. Now, take this plate over to Table 4 would you please? That's Mr John Nelson and you can eat at his table. He is a neighbour of the Smiths and he has been helping the police with the murder. He and his wife have got a room booked but his wife will still be at the hospital. Poor things, what a tragedy for them all. And don't pester him for a story Eustace. Respect these people's privacy won't you please?' Always the big sister! Would she ever get tired of telling him what to do?

Eustace took the meals over and as he placed his plate down he asked if he could sit with him. John Nelson smiled and with a wave of his hand welcomed him to take a seat.

'I hear you were a neighbour of Harold Smith's. I met him a couple of times. He was a really good bloke,' said Eustace starting off the conversation.

'Yes, he was one of the finest. We had known him for many years and he will be sorely missed,' said John Nelson circumspectly. This man was not going to be as easy to get information from as the very naive Maudie.

'I am Marjorie's brother. She runs this Hotel and she told me that you and your wife are close to the Smiths. I know it sounds stupid, but I was wondering if there is anything I can do? I write the Country Roundabout. That means I have to work hard at the end of the week but I am pretty well free on Mondays and Tuesdays. I heard that the homestead was a bit of a mess and, if the police have finished their investigation, I thought perhaps that I could get a couple of blokes together to go out and clean it up a bit.'

'That sounds like a kind offer young man. I will check with the Constable this afternoon. If so, will you be able to come out with me tomorrow? I'll get some of the Wubin folk to help too. At least we can fix up the house in case Lilly wants to go back. Not that I think she will want to. Too many dreadful memories I fear.'

Their conversation was interrupted as Mrs Nelson entered the dining room with a shy little girl hiding behind her skirt. Ada looked flustered.

'Hello dear,' said John Nelson welcoming his wife, 'you are just in time for luncheon. This is Mr Wilkinson.' Ada Nelson nodded to Eustace with dismissive acknowledgement. She was too busy to spend time on pleasantries.

'Hello John. Yes I am really hungry. As you can see little Elsie is with us now and she really needs to be cheered up. I was hoping she could stay with you this afternoon, as I need to get back to the hospital.'

Ada turned to John and in a concerned voice she whispered: 'Lillian's in a real state today. She is really distressed. I couldn't even take Elsie in to see her. She just keeps shaking and crying. I cannot console her.'

John felt the urgency in his wife's voice as he turned to address the little girl. 'Hi Elsie. Are you feeling a little bit better? Would you like to stay here with me? We can do something fun this afternoon. Would you like some food too?'

'Yes please, Uncle John,' the little waif whispered.

'Why don't you sit down with your husband Madam. I will get some food for you and Elsie,' offered the hospitable Eustace, quite happy to leave his food only half eaten. He sensed their urgency to be left alone. He stood and went over to Marjorie in the servery.

'Can you do another adult serve for Mrs Nelson and a child's serve for Elsie Smith please?' called Eustace.

'Is that one of the little girls who was attacked?' asked Marjorie inquisitively. Not waiting for his reply she joined the cook, scullery maid and waitress as they craned their necks to get a first look at the lonely, sad little child seated at Table 4.

'This isn't a peek show,' said Eustace defensively, 'why don't you all act politely. This family will need some respect.'

'Well look who's talking! The chief invader into people's private lives,' said Marjorie cheekily. 'Mr Reporter, I bet you have been poking into everyone's privacy all day. I just hope you don't end up hurting people who have already had enough hurt.'

'I suppose you don't read the newspapers then. How do you think the stories get there? People like me bring the stories to them. It's called the public good. I don't do the crimes, I just report them.' Eustace needed to put this into words. The ethics underlying this exchange, had caused him a niggle of distress all day.

Marjorie passed him two plates of steaming roast. Eustace took them over to Table 4 and served the two new occupants.

Mrs Nelson immediately picked up her utensils. Her long hospital vigil meant that she had missed many meals. This one was very much appreciated. Elsie didn't look in the least bit interested in food. She stared at the plate with a vacant, silent daze. She was dressed in a borrowed outfit, which swam on her diminutive body. Her neck showed nasty discoloured black and purple bruises.

'I will leave you to enjoy your meals in peace,' said Eustace, respectfully taking his plate and his leave. He was intending to take it back to the kitchen and hopefully get it replaced with a brand new plate of food.

John Nelson responded, 'thanks my boy. But before you go, I mentioned your offer to Ada and she agrees that going back to clean up the place will be excellent. She wants to go out to the farm to get some clothes and personal items for Lilly and the girls. So we are planning to go tomorrow. As we only want folk we can trust, only you come please. If you were a friend of Harold's, we welcome your offer of help.'

'Yes I think it will be very timely,' said Mrs Nelson finally raising her eyes and taking in Eustace Wilkinson. She smiled at him kindly.

'We certainly need to clean any signs of that vile man out of the house. Plus I need to get a good suit for Harold for him to be buried in. I don't want him going to eternity in his blood splattered work clothes.'

Eustace left the Nelsons and the wan little Elsie. His dear sister did give him a very large second luncheon. His head was in a spin. So much had happened and he had learnt so much in such a short time. This story laid bare the very soles of these people. The ethics of his actions worried him but he sublimated any guilt with frenetic activity.

He spent his afternoon in a turmoil of writing. Eustace needed a new dispatch for the Sunday afternoon train. This would appear in Tuesday's West Australian and would be limited to Hulme's confession and the charge. He needed a statement from DI Doyle to substantiate the fact that Hulme had been charged with wilful murder. The autopsy would be done this afternoon and he knew the policemen would be back for this, so he could get their official statement then.

After that one was sent to Perth, he would drop in to the Undertakers. He was sure that Maudie would be able to get him in to see Harold Smith. A photo of the dead man was essential to really round off the report. He was sure his Brownie camera would be able to capture the essence of the story. Plus he would have a chance to pass on his respects. He had genuinely liked Harold Smith and certainly didn't wish him ill. Harold would understand his interference. This was his job!

The rest of his week would need to be carefully managed. If he went out to the farm tomorrow he was certain he could 'borrow' a couple of prize photos of the happy family before the event. Plus if he travelled and worked with the neighbours he was in a perfect position to get some excellent testimony of the aftermath of the murder.

Wednesday's paper would contain the first mention of the attack on Mrs Smith and the children. He would ensure that this would be done in a tactful, non-invasive manner. In the flurry of the funeral he reasoned this would pass unnoticed in Dalwallinu - the daily papers never arrive until later in the afternoon anyway.

Now the only problem was that, when these folk realised that it was him sending in the details to the press, he would suddenly get no more stories. So he needed to get everything he needed by Wednesday. Eustace Wilkinson hoped to be on the very early morning Perth bound train on Thursday morning. Once he was out of town he would have no compunction about telling what he really knew. No sad eyes would make him feel guilty. No nagging moralizers like his sister Marjorie to make him feel bad when he was just doing his job.

The explosive details would be revealed in the weekend press.

More people had time to sit down and read the lurid details on the weekend. And this is where the big pay cheque would come from. He would use some of the Smith family shots; these would contrast nicely with the brutal photos of the patient he had taken this morning and the corpse of Harold Smith lying waiting for burial. He even had a wonderful photo of Clifford skinning a kangaroo. No-one else would have access to a photo of Cliff.

But some folk may not be so happy that all of this was in the papers. So Eustace knew he definitely needed to be out of town before the weekend or he would be lynched as high as Clifford Hulme.

Picking Up The Pieces
Public Demonstration, Private Recrimination

June 27th, 1928

Dalwallinu, Western Australia

The heavy, wet 'thud' the dirt made as it hit the coffin created haunting echoes in Jack Parrott's brain. A handful of soil, the ultimate gift to send his dearest friend into the afterlife. Other thuds followed, poignant goodbyes from a cemetery packed with mourners. Each dollop surrendered with a private message, with no-one privy to the unheralded, premature departure of Harold Eaton Smith.

Earlier in the day Jack Parrott's resonant voice had held steady as he had delivered the eulogy in the Church. Heartfelt and sincere, Jack had carefully crafted his speech to capture many aspects of this wonderful man. He had spoken of Harold the husband, father, brother-in-law and friend. He had spoken of his achievements and his virtues. There were even moments of humour and tender reminiscences.

But what Jack Parrott had not said, was that this should never have happened! Clifford Hulme had exploded and the Smith family had borne the full brunt of his rage. And they were so terribly vulnerable. But what frustrated Jack was that this tragedy had been avoidable.

Harold had thought of himself as invincible. Time and circumstance had proved how wrong this belief was. Jack had swallowed into himself all of his rage at this travesty. He had not given voice to what he wanted to bellow out that day. His anger, guilt and frustration had been subsumed. Jack had perfect control over his emotions. Standing bravely at the pulpit in the

Dalwallinu Congregational Church, Jack Parrott gave the finest oratory performance of his life.

Jack had also not fully expressed the grief that had consumed his sister. Her anguish was too raw and far too private. Lillian had not yet spoken to Jack; the women guarding her had placed all men 'out of bounds', even her sibling. Chrissie and Ada had worked together to compose some nice words, that would suffice as a meaningful tribute to Harold.

Jack had read out these words to the assembled church congregation on behalf of Lillian Smith:

Harold,

I will not believe that you are dead. You will always be so alive to me. I will think of you when I smell the Australian bush, the rich scent of sandalwood and the first rains of summer on parched earth. I will see you when I look into your daughters' eyes and see them sparkle with happiness. I will remember you whenever I see men who achieve great things with honour and humility. I will think of you, free as a bird when I see parrots darting in the trees. I will know you are with me whenever I gather with family and friends. You have not left me and I will never leave you. Until we meet again in a happier place.

Your dearest Lilly.

As he read the graceful, humble words that so encapsulated Lillian's love for Harold, she had shown no sign of hearing or understanding. Her steady, unconscious self absorbed weeping flowed, unabated.

Lilly was not present at the grave site as Harold's mutilated body was finally interred. Earlier in the day she had painfully raised herself from her hospital bed to attend the funeral service in the Congregational Church. Her battered body was totally enclosed in black clothes, a dark veil obscured her still damaged face. No-one was granted any glimpse of her injuries. Lillian was there, but as a black shrouded shape. She was not there as a person.

The grim silhouette had been slowly, guided into the church, and had sat hunched on the front pew, supported by Chrissie and Ada Nelson. Her head had been bowed and she had quietly wept throughout the service. Respectful friends and gawking thrill seekers had all been kept at arm's length. Mourners had been asked to write notes of condolence and respect Mrs Smith's painful period of mourning and convalescence. Immediately after the service Lilly had departed. She had returned to the solace and security of her hospital bed. Thus Lilly had avoided any confrontation with the reality of the spectacle of the funeral and the public theatre this event had created.

Harold Smith had been a very popular man and he was widely known across the area. More recently as a farmer but also as a storekeeper, a machinery salesman and for his earlier responsibilities within the sandalwood trade. He had been an eager sportsman, keen on socialising and an enthusiastic participant in public works. Plus he was a 'returned man' which automatically gave him immense status across the community. But even this popularity did not explain the mass of people who packed the small church and the Dalwallinu cemetery on that cold, blustery afternoon in late June. The fame of this case had made attendance at this funeral obligatory for anyone who had known Smithy. Across the region: shops were closed, no work happened on farms, 'back tomorrow' signs went up on the doors of businesses. Padding out these numbers were folk from the press, extra police and more than a few busybodies. Over eight hundred people were in town that day and most were there for just one purpose.

Thoughtful townsfolk had skilfully separated the 'real mourners' from the others and the thirty or so folk closest to the grave were all bone fide in their grief. The solemnity of the funeral parade and the slow, respectful march of the pallbearers was a moving ritual. The lowering of the coffin had gone without a hitch.

Harold's newly dug grave was the tenth in the newly established cemetery and he was, by far, the youngest permanent resident. His eternal resting place was beneath a young but stately white gum. The Nelsons had ensured that his would not be the poorest grave site and expense had not been spared in acquiring a quality coffin. A fitting gravestone was also being prepared. Harold would lie there for eternity - but he would do so in comfort and style.

At the grave's edge the Reverend spoke solemn words about forever and the power and the glory. This was the prayer of Harold's farewell and with the dropping in of gentle handfuls of sod, the sad procession wandered slowly from the cemetery, leaving the grave diggers to complete their sombre task.

Little Elsie was the only one of the Smith children to attend the burial. She had stood stoically near her Auntie Chrissie through the solemn charade. Her face did not register her feelings, her mind was already too burdened with angst to understand the enormity of this event. Her little hand had grasped a meagre handful of soil and she had let the grains drop pathetically before turning her head into Chrissie's voluminous skirt and weeping hysterically. John Nelson had then picked up the little girl, taken her outside the cemetery to his car and back to the safety of their hotel room.

Ada Nelson had been working frantically over the past few days and one of her tasks had been to round up support to cater for the many mourners. She had enlisted the wife of the Police Constable, Mrs Rowbottom, who had organised the good women of Dalwallinu, Wubin and surrounding districts, to all bring a plate. The result was that the dining room at the Dalwallinu Hotel had tables laden with tasty treats. Even with the massive, unexpected crowd, the local Country Women's Association made certain everyone would be extremely well fed.

Marjorie from the Dalwallinu Hotel, had donated the venue. Plus she made sure that everyone had a cup of tea or cool refreshment the moment they arrived. All of the staff, plus rings-ins like her brother Eustace, were hard at work all afternoon serving, delivering and ferrying.

At least half of those who attended the funeral came along to the wake. Of course, very few of these people could get inside but the crowd was more than happy to cluster in the street. Those who had come along for the spectacle soon drifted off; they had their yarns and pictures and standing around with folk they had never met before, had little appeal.

For those who remained, the event soon resembled a social occasion, with Smithy reminisces interspersed with aspects of catching up, so important to isolated, rural folk. After an hour, the crowd's mood was buoyant. Food was eaten, tea consumed and conversation flowed. The weather, although cold with a chilly wind, stayed fine, so the outside party was not too inconvenienced.

At 4pm two things happened; both affected the mood of the assembled crowd. The first was that the bar opened. Many of the male mourners believed that they had imbibed enough tea and felt the need to consume some hard liquor to toast: 'Smithy's short but wonderful life'. The bar was soon packed, the liquor flowed and the humour turned from good natured to volatile.

The wives and children of the men who had migrated to the public bar did what they could to entertain themselves and find comfort. Lucky ones went back to friend's homes. The less fortunate sat forlornly outside the hotel waiting for their men to emerge.

The tipping point of the afternoon was the arrival of Wednesday's West Australian Newspaper. This had actually been in town since lunchtime but most had been too busy to read it.

The reports of the 'Wubin Murder' in Monday's and Tuesday's papers had been interesting but superficial. From Saturday lunchtime the country grapevine had worked efficiently, comprehensively and quickly. Everyone in town had been aware of more details than were published in 'The West' earlier in the week. But the revelations in Wednesday's West were new and explosive. The outrage on Mrs Smith and the cruel outpouring of violence against the Smith kiddies, had been suppressed. The locals had not known about this!

Now it was out and Lillian's degradation was exposed. Her shame was starkly revealed in black and white newsprint.

Eustace Wilkinson had completed this dispatch on Monday afternoon. He had felt that he had disclosed this part of the story with tact and sensitivity. As he had spent the day at the Smith's Miamoon farm with the Nelsons, he had written it while he was in a very considerate mood. He had listened sympathetically to their stories, looked at their family photographs and respectfully cleaned the blood stains from the crime scene, re-establishing the myth of a happy home. He had returned to the Dally Hotel to write his daily report and he had felt that he had done so with scant details. A reverent disclosure of the facts. He was after all, a newspaper man, and this was news. It was in the public interest that it was revealed.

Eustace watched the growing anger in the front bar with grave concern. Sometimes when you unleash a tiger, it behaves in an unpredictable way. Eustace drank his one glass of beer very circumspectly. There was no by-line under the story in the West Australian. No-one knew he was the reporter responsible for revealing these details. Still, he was very glad that he was planning to leave Dalwallinu, for good, on tomorrow's early morning train.

A copy of the paper, with the explosive revelations, was passed around the front bar of the Dally Pub as the sun set on the day of Harold Smith's funeral. Drunken men spilt their drinks over the newsprint, until all semblance of the crisp, clean story was lost. Tough, angry and fuming men became more incensed as their drinking continued. Calls for lynching and murder echoed across the bar.

The most infuriated of all was Jack Parrott. He had held it together for days, the drunken splurge of Saturday night had been a one-off. Until, buoyed by the confident bonhomie of a successful day, he had felt he should join the boys for a respectful drink to toast Harold's passing.

When the news of the paper's expose had broken in the bar he had been just sipping his second glass of whisky. He could barely manage to read the words; tears of anger, frustration and shame blurred his vision. How had this got out? Who had been responsible for this muck? How could he salvage Lillian's honour now? Someone would need to pay and his anger was directed squarely at the man responsible. Clifford Hulme had done this to his sister and he deserved to die!

As the minutes ticked closer towards 6 o'clock closing time, angry shouts reverberated across the room. Last drinks were called and the drunks drained their glasses before rolling out. The disorganised rabble swarmed, the anger condensed and there were shouts for revenge and the main call to action was to get Clifford Hulme 'out of the cells'.

A huge mob of drunk, incensed men poured from the Dally Hotel. Terrified wives and children watched as their menfolk transformed into killers. A violent, turbulent wave of vengeance proceeded down the dark street.

Shouts of: 'Lynch the bastard'; 'Why should he get a frigging hearing and a gentle death?', 'Hanging's too good for him. We'll send him to hell,' rent the night air, chilling the hearts of local families sheltering nervously in their homes.

The group armed themselves with anything that came to hand; sticks, brooms and rocks all became weapons of necessity. Windows were smashed, bins overturned, bushes uprooted. The angry mob soon arrived at the front of the Dalwallinu Police Station.

Inside the station, Constable Rowbottom had been completing his report ready for Detective Inspector Doyle to take to Perth. DI Doyle had been checking that the paperwork was all accurate and complete for the Inquest, scheduled to be held in Perth early in July.

Three extra policeman had been dispatched to the location for the funeral. They had been comfortably lounging around the station feeling justifiably content; the day had passed without incident.

The roar of the riot penetrated the station and the five policeman looked at each other with panic and apprehension. Frightened eyes met as the reality of imminent danger arose.

'Sounds like things have got nasty,' surmised Constable Rowbottom with a quiver of fear in his voice, 'I was a bit worried with this many folk in town, that things might turn a bit sour.'

'Best to get your revolvers on boys. It looks like a full blown riot,' ordered DI Doyle officiously, in anticipation of an ugly confrontation. 'Shoot first, talk later. An angry mob cannot be reasoned with.' The Detective Inspector had already stood up from his desk and was looking around for weaponry.

The local policeman was more reasoned as he tried to pacify his agitated comrades: 'I reckon we may be able to handle it without shots boys. Let me try to calm them down first. I know most of these fellas. They've had a skinful and they're just cross about their mate.'

Constable Rowbottom was calm on the outside but inside he was churning. This was his town and he felt that it was his job to keep the peace and he certainly didn't want anybody to get hurt.

'They don't know these three boys are even here,' he said referring to the three reserve policemen. 'So why don't just you and I handle it Doyle?' he asked the DI, 'you boys stay in here as back up. If we call out or if things turn violent, then come out. But hold your fire or shoot into space. These are country folk, not criminals.'

Doyle looked very unenthusiastic. In fact he looked terrified. Being a Detective Inspector meant that you didn't need to confront danger or face angry mobs too often. And this was just how he liked it. But he wasn't about to let an unimportant country constable upstage him. He needed the glory too. So he reluctantly followed Rowbottom out into the night.

The scene in front of the Dalwallinu Police Station was far more confronting than they had guessed.

Nearly a hundred shadowy, swaying figures brandishing makeshift weapons, formed an ominous wall. A steady chant of: 'Lynch Hulme! Lynch Hulme!' emanated from the seething, enraged mass. In front of the parade were two strident and angry figures.

Constable Rowbottom recognised the tall disfigured Charles

Martin and his shorter offsider Jack Parrott. At least these two were known to him. They were level-headed, law abiding citizens. They could be reasoned with.

'Jack and Charles what are you doing here?'

'We want the murdering bastard, give him to us. Save the State an expensive trial. We want to string him up,' said Jack, slurring his words.

'Give us the British pig, Rowbottom. We know he is in there. He has done his nasty crimes here so let us take our revenge - right here, right now,' seethed Charles Martin. All the anger of his own tortured past surfacing. This was his opportunity to make at least one perpetrator pay.

'Lynch Hulme! Lynch Hulme!' continued the background chant.

Glass shattered and wood crunched behind them, as some of the rioters took their frustration out on neighbouring shop fronts. A group of grim faced men had lit a fire on the street with branches and gasoline from the petrol station. They had carried fuel in buckets and had wrapped rags around sticks which they were setting alight.

'Let's burn the bastard alive,' screeched a cavorting man, brandishing two flaming rods. 'Burn down the police station.' Other men were grabbing sticks and taking off their coats to create torches in support.

'Just give the bloody cur to us Constable,' pressured Jack. 'He doesn't deserve to live. He should be damned to an eternity of hell, for what he's done.'

'Look Jack, Charles, and all of you. You were good friends to Harold Smith. This is hardly what Smithy would have approved of. He believed in justice and law,' reasoned the Constable. His voice was loud but composed; conveying reason and calm. Inside he was terrified. Two men against this crazed mob; he didn't like their chances.

'What kind of justice did that bloody animal give my sister or my nieces? Nothing we can do to him can make up for that,' screamed

Jack Parrott in frenzied anger, smashing out at the police station sign with his fist and splintering it.

This created a rush of anger amongst the group as they jostled closer to the two policemen. The two law enforcers stood solidly, united in their defiance, protecting the station door and its inhabitants. The blazing torches illuminated their brave stand but showed them to be diminished, small and assailable in the face of the crazed mob.

'Come on boys, we can take 'em!' shouted Charles Martin as he lashed out at the Detective Inspector. As the mob surged forward at the two men, the three hidden policemen fired shots into the night sky. The revolver blasts rang out, clear and decisive. The gunshots silenced the defiant cries. The seesaw tipped, giving the fully armed police the advantage. The rioters could only guess at how many police were hidden in reserve within the dark shadows of the police station. The rebels stopped in their tracks, imploding, sobriety arriving with the possibility of being shot.

Constable Rowbottom put a stranglehold on the shocked Jack Parrott and DI Doyle slipped crude hand restraints onto the instantly docile Charles Martin. 'You two are under arrest. As ring leaders you can come in and spend a night in the lock up.'

To the now leaderless and strangely subdued crowd, Constable Rowbottom spoke powerfully and calmly.

'It's all over men. Now go home, sleep it off. The man who did this horrible crime will get his day in court and he will be punished. We are the law, so let us deal with this correctly and lawfully.'

Dispirited men started to splinter off. Their bravado dissipated. They had again become farm hands, railway workers and shop assistants. Albeit rather inebriated ones. Most would rue their violent behaviour, their wanton destruction of property and their involvement in threatening the police.

One man watched the event nervously from the shadows. He had felt a fair measure of responsibility for the events of this afternoon. Had he been responsible for heaping even more misery onto this already overburdened family? Acceptance of the blame had made him feel a trifle concerned and not the least of his concerns was worry about his own safety.

But then the riot had started. The reality of again being in the right place at the right time to score a scoop that no other newspaper man would be able to report, was euphoric. This feeling overcame any sense of responsibility, accountability or guilt. The powerful surge of being in danger and beating it. Eustace was ecstatic. Enjoyment shone in his eyes, reflecting the torches of the rioters and the inner fire coming from his sense of impending triumph.

Because Eustace knew a few things that no-one else knew. Firstly he knew that he would be out of here first thing in the morning and he would carry with him the 'front page story' from today's funeral and riot. He would also take with him all the evidence he had carefully collected over the previous five days. If locals thought today's paper was volatile, just wait until the weekend's scandal rags hit the streets!

The third thing he knew was that Jack Parrott and Charles Martin were in for a big surprise. The sight that would confront them would be a big disappointment. The cell would be empty. Clifford Hulme had already been taken to Perth first thing this morning.

Eustace knew this because he had been there at the railway station at dawn to take the picture. The local lynching attempt, had never stood any chance of being successful.

The Coroner Investigates
Nobody Welcomes The Inquisition

7pm July 19th, 1928

First Day of the Inquest into the Death of

Harold Eaton Smith

Perth, Western Australia

Jack Parrott sat reflectively, on the balcony of the Nelson's Nedlands house, watching the black snaking of the Swan river wending its way towards the sea. As a teenager, he and his best mate James Nelson, had attempted with varying degrees of futility, to throw rocks from here into the river. All had fallen short, landing disappointingly in the scrubby bush below. Luckily these wayward projectiles had never landed on some hapless walker, meandering peacefully along the shoreline.

Tonight he thoughtfully stroked his glass. The day's tension was finally easing as he started on his third whisky. The former non-drinker smiled wryly as he recalled his life before this debacle. A time when he hadn't needed the courage derived from hard liquor to get through the day; or to get to sleep at night. The demon drink gave him respite from his turmoiled gut and the nauseous guilt that accompanied sobriety.

Within the house the sounds of faked domesticity had faded. The illusion that life was normal was being maintained by the adults within, until Elsie and Peggy were asleep. But this was done now and the real tensions would rise as the confronted adults would again face up to their nightmares.

'What a day Jack,' this simple statement came from John Nelson as he joined him on the balcony. He and Ada had travelled to Perth for the inquest and had taken up residence in their old home for the week. He also had a glass of whisky in his hand. Again this was unusual, as John Nelson had learnt after his son's death in the war, that liquor just defers pain, it doesn't eradicate it.

'Elsie and Peggy are down and Ada is reading them a story. Chrissie is in with Lillian. Poor thing is a wreck. She'll need a sleeping draft tonight that's for sure,' John continued.

'Well at least she is through the worst of it for a while. Though I daren't think what damage has been caused by today's public humiliation.'

'You and Ada will be on tomorrow. Are you feeling all right about it?' asked Jack.

'Yes. I think we will have a pretty easy time of it. We went over our statements quite a few times in the car on the way down from Wubin. We both recall things really clearly. I suppose we have relived that night thousands of times since, so I doubt we will have much difficulty. Tomorrow the only witnesses will be ourselves, Mr Brown, Constable Rowbottom and then the Doctor. There will be no surprises in our evidence. It was today that they all came to see. The greatest show on earth and the people we love were the main attractions.'

'It was a circus all right,' muttered Jack. 'Just getting through the crowd this morning was awful. All of those gawking, inquisitive eyes. And some of the comments they yelled at Lilly. Most were supportive but one ugly hag asked her if she had enjoyed it. Can you believe it? The cruelty and depravity of the public. It was despicable. And the way they pushed, scragged and fought to get into the public gallery, to get the best view of our degradation and misery. It was truly sickening.'

'You did really well though Jack. You had to steer Lillian in through the gauntlet of hecklers and busybodies at the entrance to the Courthouse and then get yourself ready to speak,' said John. 'When I was in business, there were times I had to appear in court on legal matters but I never saw anything like this. We've all become reluctant celebrities.'

Jack nodded his agreement before continuing on with his rehash of the events of the day: 'The funny thing was, it was thinking about Harold that gave me confidence. I was really angry when I got in through the crowd. Lillian was so devastated and she was shaking so much I thought she was about to faint but she steadied herself. A little of that stubbornness she used to have had emerged.'

John then turned his conversation to the Inquest itself: 'I thought the City Coroner, spoke well. He appeared to have a really good grasp of the case already and he just seemed wise in a sensible, prudent fashion. I just knew he would weigh things up and come to the correct decision. With the intimidating pomp and gravitas of the legalities at the opening of the Inquest, I must admit I was scared to death. You had to go on first Jack, you must have been nervous,' recalled John.

'It was strange because while the Coroner was talking, I started thinking about what Harold would do and this gave me confidence,' reflected Jack.

'He was so respectful of the law. In this regard he was very British, he admired the Western system of law and procedural justice. We had loads of debates about it. I was more into retribution and punishment - he was always clearly on the side of state administered justice. And I just felt his hand guiding me. This was his chance to achieve justice and he needed me to put my evidence forward as clearly as I could, so that he could have his day in court. He wasn't here to speak for himself.'

Jack paused, took a sip of the fiery liquid and felt the warmth flow through his system before continuing.

'I was right until the end bit when they asked me about the post mortem and the identification. That's when I cracked a bit. It was all because I had this sudden revelation about something that had worried me for a while.'

Again Jack waited theatrically. His discovery had been important and he had wanted to share it with someone all day. John Nelson waited for him to go on.

'That first day in Dally, after Smithy's murder, I had to go and identify the body really late on Saturday afternoon. I had walked into the undertakers with Constable Rowbottom and Detective Inspector Doyle. The door was locked and no-one else was there. The Doctor had done the post mortem earlier and the undertakers had re-placed the body back pretty well so that the invasive cuts and wounds couldn't be seen. But something wasn't quite right about the body. I found Harold's body at the farm and I had come out with the Doctor before he did the post mortem. He gave me a few moments in private to say goodbye to my Mate. On both of these occasions he had nothing in his pocket. Now an hour later, there was something different about him. Someone had put a tin of Lucky Strike tobacco in his pocket.'

Jack stopped talking and rolled a smoke. He smoked Capstan. He took his time with the theatre of rolling the cigarette and then handed it to John before withdrawing some more tobacco to make one for himself.

'Now in itself there was nothing wrong with this. He smoked Lucky Strike so it was a nice gesture. But who did it? I asked the other blokes and no-one knew anything. I asked the undertaker and he and his boys said no-one had been in. They had all been up at the cemetery digging the grave, so they weren't home. So who did it?'

'That may be a mystery you might never discover,' said John Nelson, not yet picking up that Jack already knew the answer to his own question.

'But I did find out, right there in the court room. When they produced the evidence photos of the post mortem taken by Dr Anderson there was no tobacco tin but the bloody photo splashed across Saturday's Mirror had the tobacco tin in Smithy's top pocket. And so the wonderful 'gift giver' was the photographer. Somehow, he had sneaked in and taken the photo between the post mortem and my identification and he had said 'thanks for the picture' with a gift.'

'So it was someone who knew how to get into the undertakers and who knew Smithy and knew what he smoked and he left him a real Judas gift. I bet the bastard got more than thirty pieces of silver for his betrayal.' Jack was now really angry as he went on, outlining the extent of the betrayal he had uncovered.

'And then I saw that snake Eustace Wilkinson, sitting in the court room with his fancy new suit, his reporter badge and press hat on. My blood boiled. I knew instantly it was him. He had pretended to be our friend, he acted all supportive of all of us after the murder and then he just disappeared. Did you notice that he vanished from town just as everything hit the press? He used everything he had collected against us. We had thought we could keep things quiet - especially about the outrage to Lillian and he let the whole bloody world know!'

John stared with wide eyes at his young friend. His expression soured as the magnitude of the pressman's treachery seeped in. This was preposterous.

'What a conniving dog. You're right Jack. That bastard, it must have been him. All of it!' Then John's voice changed as he thought through the full extent of the fraud.

'Oh no! We took him out to the farm with us on the Monday after the murder. We told him all we knew. He said he had been a friend of Harold's. Apparently he had met him years ago, before the war.' John Nelson was aghast. He prided himself on being a good judge of character. Eustace Wilkinson's betrayal of his trust had made a mockery of this.

'Yes, we had met him at the Narrogin Inne but he had been a mere boy back then,' recalled Jack.

Suddenly John recalled a piece of the jigsaw, a valuable clue, they had overlooked.

'Harold had told me all about this bloke and that he had caught up with him in The Dally pub some months back. He was the one who had interviewed Hulme and taken the photo of him skinning the kangaroo. You remember, it was featured in The West in May. The girls were so excited and we were all joking to Lillian that she was jealous because she had wanted to be in the paper. They had the cutting up on the wall in the kitchen. According to Harold, he was planning to come out to the farm and take a photo of him and the girls and do the article about them living on the farm. The scoundrel. He is nothing but a despicable blaggard.'

'And who might you two be discussing, in terms that are hardly fit for polite conversation now that ladies are joining you,' asked Ada as she swept out imperiously to join the men on the balcony. Immediately she dismissed her own query and started to let the men know about the girls:

'Both the girls have nodded off. They were waiting for their Mother to come in and kiss them 'good night' but there was no chance of her doing anything normal tonight. I have given her a double dose of Veronal so hopefully she will be out for the night.'

'She's a real mess this evening that's for sure. Thankfully she's fallen asleep now,' whispered Chrissie as she followed Ada out through the double doors. Her pregnancy was now very advanced. She had just over a month to go but what should have been a rapturous time of preparation and anticipation had been hijacked by the momentous events that had overtaken their family.

The ladies had not been in the City Court room today. She and Ada had taken the girls to complete the daily ritual; visiting the Perth Children's Hospital in Subiaco. A tram ran directly from Nedlands to the hospital site, so travelling there was easy. It was the visiting that was hard.

Three weeks after the event, Vonny was still in a pretty bad way. She had regained consciousness, and the head wound was gradually healing. Her lustrous blonde hair had been shaved off and prickles of regrowth covered her skull. Bare patches still revealed the tortuous mending of the wound. Vonny would carry a nasty jagged scar across her upper forehead for life.

The doctors now thought that she would probably survive, unless she contracted an infection but there was extensive brain damage. Vonny had forgotten how to walk, how to eat, how to blow her nose; lots of little behaviours had just been wiped out. She no longer had any speech, her facial features showed little emotion and there was very little recognition of anything or anybody. Harold's 'Bonny Vonny' had vanished.

Daily, the girls played close to her, Elsie did her lessons near her, Peggy clambered over her and they chatted, played games and talked around her. Peggy already had more words than Vonny. This was the therapy the Psychiatrist said was best. If their Vonny was going to recover then it was up to them to get her back into their world.

Lillian was not able to help. Her own fragile mental condition meant that she was not up to jollying Vonny back to reality. So Chrissie had accepted this role with an enthusiastic zeal.

By the time the Inquest started, Chrissie Parrott had been in Perth for over three weeks. She had left Dalwallinu with Elsie and Peggy on the afternoon after Harold's funeral. Doctor Anderson had grown increasingly concerned about Vonny's chances of survival and by Tuesday she wasn't getting any better so he had organised an emergency transfer. Elsie and Chrissie had caught a lift in the ambulance that had ferried Vonny and Peggy to Perth Children's Hospital and Lillian to a psychology ward in Royal Hospital in Perth.

Thus Chrissie had been out of town, when her husband had been leading the riot in the streets of Dalwallinu. Jack had been supportive of Chrissie's plan to travel to Perth to look after the Smiths during their convalescence. He was even happier when she had not been present when he was jailed for disturbing the peace!

This murder had disrupted everyone's plans with the Smiths obviously in turmoil. After the mayhem of the funeral week the Nelsons had returned, temporarily, back to their farm. They took on an organisational role plus they used their reserves of cash to underwrite the many expenses this catastrophic event created.

The Parrotts had a range of important things to deal with and they found that being store operators was no longer their top priority. Fortunately, Charles Martin and his wife Mabel were quite up to running the Wubin store and they had taken to the role like naturals. This was very lucky because, even though Jack was ostensibly back in Wubin over the early part of the month, he had been non-compos for most of this time.

After the ignoble arrest of Jack Parrott and Charles Martin on the day of Harold's funeral, Constable Rowbottom had released the two ringleaders the next morning. They had sheepishly agreed to work off any claims for damages. They had been joined by about twenty other rioters, whose own conscience's had forced them to come along and complete reparation to the town and shopkeepers. Their own regret and guilt at their foolhardy behaviour was more appropriate than any punishment the law would have doled out to them. In terms of keeping town harmony, Constable Rowbottom's lenient decision to not press charges, worked well.

By Saturday afternoon on June 30th, Charles and Jack had completed their public penance and they both returned to Wubin. They had expected that the Wubin township would be desperate for supplies after the shop had been closed for four days but Mrs Mabel Martin was a sensible lass. She had grown up watching her mother, Mrs Rowbottom, organise town events and coordinate town responses to emergencies. Responding to 'a community need' was in her blood.

Mabel had opened the Smith and Parrott Store every day and the local customers had been more than satisfied. She had even organised for two lads to do the deliveries but reordering was needed and the store was: 'very low on greens, dairy and consumables,' according to Charles' admirable and efficient wife, when the shamefaced pair returned.

On his return, Charles had slipped back into the routine and, along with his wife, he soon had the store business humming. Jack was soon a supernumerary, especially as he had started to drink quite heavily at night to get to sleep. And because he went to sleep late, he needed to sleep in quite late in the mornings. And sometimes he had to take long naps in the afternoon too. Jack Parrott, without the support of his good wife, was slipping into maudlin, alcoholic despondency.

One week of Jack's morbid sulking was about all the Martins could take and so, a week before the Inquest was scheduled to start, Charles Martin had taken things in hand. He drove Jack Parrott out to the Smith's farm, supposedly to do 'a bit of work around the place'. Jack was 'liquored up' before he went and fell sound asleep in the truck on the way out there.

Upon arrival Charles transferred the sleeping Jack into the house, checked that the cupboard was filled with canned food, took the rifle and drove off. He left Jack, isolated, marooned 20 miles from town, with no transport and no alcohol.

Charles returned three days later to a sober, very sad and sorry for himself Jack, and then the counselling sessions started. Charles Martin knew a few things about grief and despair, anger and hatred. He wasn't 'book learned' in psychology and grief therapy, but he had been to hell and come back again. He could recognise when someone was going that same way. So he let Jack talk.

Jack shared his grief and his remorse. He told Charles about 'Harold's Project' and about Clifford's addiction and his own complicity in the plan. Charles heard all about Jack's dilemma regarding providing Cliff with the banned pills and how, when he was cut off, he had wrecked the store. They even talked about Jack's feelings on the rape of his sister, how he felt public shame and embarrassment and Jack wept when he recalled that he'd been unable to protect her.

Charles gave no advice, he just listened without offering judgment or moral condemnation. In his experience, a man must find his own path but he needs mates to help him locate where the path might be.

The Jack Parrott who came back to Wubin from the Miamoon farm was not better but he was able to function again. This far more capable man was intent on providing strength to the family at the inquest. It was this more resolute man who spoke to the ladies as they came out onto the balcony.

'Good to hear the girls are settled. You are both doing a sterling job and I thank you. Now, I have had enough whiskey for this evening. I need to have my wits about me for tomorrow. Chrissie, darling, any chance of a nice cup of tea and perhaps some of Ada's fruit cake?'

He may have been more in control, but this had not come with an increase in empathy. His very pregnant wife had not stopped all day but it was in Jack's makeup to expect his wife to provide for his needs. He was the dominant husband, she was the subservient wife and this was the way of it.

'You two ladies sit down and take the weight off your feet. I'll go in and make cuppas for all of us,' said the kindly John Nelson. Greater age had provided him with both sensitivity and wisdom, traits somewhat missing in Jack Parrott.

'So what is the progress report on Lilly?' probed Jack, interrogating the now seated ladies.

'She is nearly as bad as she was in that first week when we couldn't get anything out of her at all,' summarised Ada. She had nursed her over those first, frightening days in the Dalwallinu Hospital when Lilly verged on slipping into deep despondency, or a 'comatose state of neurotic depression' as the Doctor had termed it. It was in this parlous state that Lilly had been admitted as a psychiatric patient to Perth's major Hospital in early July.

Ada continued the report on Lilly's recovery: 'I was so happy when I saw her earlier this week. She had made huge progress. Of course the physical wounds were heaps better but she was able to talk again. And she was showing interest in what was happening around her. I was beginning to think we were getting our old Lillian back again.'

Chrissie took up the story: 'Well, she is certainly shaken up after today, she was shivering so hard and wouldn't take any food. She doesn't even want to see the girls. She says that she doesn't want them to see her like this. Today must have been horrid for her and I have no idea how she got through it. We have kept her insulated really. She has not seen any of the papers and I don't think she had any realisation about how much the general public knew about the case. Until today.'

'Especially about what happened to her. For her, realising that everyone knew, was almost as bad as going though it in the first place,' whispered the sympathetic Ada. Tears of motherly concern welled in her eyes. Both women reflected for a while before Chrissie turned to her husband:

'You have done a great job Jack. Before the court, going over things with her, things that must have been horrid for you to even think about. Encouraging her to talk about things, first with you and then with John. This meant that she could get through it. I think that it was a huge hurdle for her to just speak about what happened.' Chrissie gazed with undisguised love and admiration at her husband, as she gushed out his praises.

'Thank heavens for the grace and propriety of the Coroner. He cleared the court before Lillian had to give her evidence. It was hard enough to get her in there and talking. She would have said nothing if that rabble had been in the gallery,' Jack said reflectively. 'The Coroner even let me be in the witness box with her. When she broke down, I just whispered that this was her chance to get justice for Harold. This seemed to perk her up and got her through.' Ada and Chrissie looked pleased when Jack had let them know that Lilly had been treated well in the Court.

John had arrived back with four steaming cups of tea and some of Ada's famous fruit cake. He instantly jumped into the conversation. 'We needed to get her through today. Just looking at that fiend across from us in the dock must have been an ordeal. Can you imagine how it must have felt seeing that vicious animal for the first time since the attack.'

'How did he look? Did he gloat or smile?' asked Chrissie, wanting to know but not wanting to know in equal measure. Giving voice to the morbid fascination that fires all inquisitiveness.

Clifford Hulme was still an enigma to them all. He had lived with them for so long, on the edge of their group, always present but never really noticed. None of them had really known anything about him.

'He was, well, he was just vacant. His face didn't alter the whole day. He seemed to listen but not take anything in. Like he was hearing it all for the first time. But he showed no emotion at all, no recognition and no remorse. His face looked like an imbecile,' John explained to the ladies.

'I didn't notice Lillian looking at him. I think she knew he was there but she kept her eyes averted or down,' Jack reported. 'The next real challenge for Lillian will be when Hulme speaks tomorrow. We may need to take her outside. It'll be hard for her to ignore him if he is in the witness box.'

'Of course we may find that he does not even take the stand. Just from today's evidence, I think the Coroner has enough to commit him to be charged with wilful murder. In his own statement he has admitted to this already. Plus with the witnesses coming in tomorrow morning, I think the Coroner's verdict will be easy,' John Nelson predicted.

'So what is likely to be in the papers tomorrow after today's revelations?' asked Ada.

They were all afraid of the double purgatory. They were coping, just, with the ordered process of the official justice system. This was not pleasant but they all understood it was necessary. But the parody of the ordeal being played out daily in the media was cruel and unpredictable. The hurt of the publication of stark, personal details and innuendo for all to read, was a daily torment.

'Well there were pressmen all over the place today. Shoving their wretched cameras in our faces as we came in. Shouting stupid questions at us. As if we were going to answer them! You should have seen them, filling their silly pads with notes, when Lillian was on the stand. Especially when she nearly collapsed at the end. They are vultures,' retorted the usually calm, reasoned John Nelson. He was angry, his face had reddened and his voice was tense.

'Now that brings me to an important point and this is significant for us all,' Jack said, taking control and talking with authority and conviction.

'We have discovered that Eustace Wilkinson, whom you may or may not know from Dalwallinu, has been found to be faithless. He was the main leak, worming his way into our confidence, stealing our secrets and writing 'tell all' articles for the papers. You will see him tomorrow in the court. He has a moustache these days and wears fancy suits. His evil writings have obviously elevated him and he has a front row seat in the press gallery. But don't show him any kindness. He is our sworn enemy.'

This was a pronouncement, a dictum. The ladies asked no questions and requested no clarification. The men had spoken.

At Jack's words they drained their cups, packed up and went off to their beds.

Tonight their disturbed dreams would have an enemy with two faces: Clifford Hulme on one side, Eustace Wilkinson on the other.

The Coroner Investigates
Committed To Trial

July 20th, 1928

Second Day of the Inquest into the Death of

Harold Eaton Smith

Perth, Western Australia

Murdered Man to Finally Get Justice

Eustace Wilkinson

'Never in the history of the Coroner's Court has a more revolting story been told than that narrated at the Inquest into the death of Harold Eaton Smith, which opened in the City Courthouse on July 19th. The City Coroner, Mr A.B. Kitson, listened intently to a story of the brutal murder of an innocent man, of an unspeakable outrage upon his wife and of the remorseless battering of their three innocent little children. The Court was told all of the gruesome details.

This case has ignited the public's interest like no other and many interested persons were disappointed when there was insufficient space to house them in the public gallery. The Coroner also cleared the court when Mrs Smith gave evidence. It was deemed that she was in such a parlous state that the embarrassment and humiliation would have been too much for her to have given her horrific account to anything but a closed court.

Over the two days of testimony it revealed the true triple horror, the recital of which sent shudders through those who listened. It is doubtful if any tragedy in the State's history of crime has had so many appalling features associated with it as this one.

Late on Friday 20th of July the Inquest into the death of Harold Eaton Smith returned a finding of wilful murder against Clifford Hulme. This case will be tried in early August and one can only hope that a finding of Guilty will result and this fiend be sent to the gallows.'

Eustace Wilkinson finished the lead article to top off his weekly report for Saturday's Mirror with a flourish. He was pleased with the account. This paper was the most scurrilous of Western Australia's newspapers and so needed a certain flair, with a heavy dollop of emotional rhetoric. This would suit the small minded, bigoted readers who devoured this rag: entrail eaters, muck rakers and intolerant rabble. Eustace was thoroughly dismissive of The Mirror's readership.

There was an adopted superiority to this remade version of Eustace Wilkinson, the newly instated Court and Investigative Reporter for the West Australian. Debonair man about town, dressed in a new double breasted tweed suit, sporting a fedora hat and the whole image rounded off with a pencil thin moustache. Eustace thought he looked fabulous.

Now that he was a reporter in Perth, he only needed to do the writing, he had lackey photographers to provide pictorial support. And there would be stacks of wonderful supportive photos from the Inquest and the upcoming Trial. What drama. The whole week had been full of it and with his vast understanding and knowledge of the personnel in this case, he had been in the prime position to take full advantage of it all.

Although he had reported that the case had ended late this afternoon it had actually been all over by 3pm. Too late for any reports to appear in the afternoon dailies so Eustace was again confident that he would have the first full coverage in Saturday's Mirror.

The accused had not made any comment, other than to have his official statement read to the court. The Coroner had been able to announce his findings after only 30 minutes of deliberation. This was the result everyone had expected and wanted. Well, everyone except Clifford Hulme that is.

Eustace had glanced at him in the dock. The man looked totally lost, like a little boy landed in a foreign world. Had he understood any of the court proceedings? Cliff spent two days staring at nothing, with a dopey look on his face. It was as if he wanted to blend back into the polished jarrah panelling of the dock. Did he understand the words spoken by the tortured victims? Were his recollections of this event the same as the wounded, aggrieved witnesses?

He hadn't shown any emotion when the Coroner had read out his findings. The gallery had cheered. The defence party smiled and backslapped each other. But no-one had approached the forlorn man in the dock. This man was totally friendless.

Eustace found that he had more than enough time to get his articles in for the weekend press. It was only 4.30pm now so he would shoot over to the Mirror office and then he would be free.

The inquest was complete so he had the weekend off. His mate wanted him to come down to the Railway Hotel in Fremantle tonight. They had a great Swing Session going on at the dance hall and tonight 'Harry Deluxe and the Swing Sisters' were playing. This was more like it. Real entertainment, with pretty girls who didn't object to a bit of 'slap and tickle'. You didn't see this kind of fun in Dalwallinu! The dance was due to kick off at about 8.00pm so he had more than enough time to get home, get changed and get down to the Railway Hotel in time for the first dance.

Eustace set off down The Terrace to walk to the offices of The Mirror. It was a clear cold winter's day and the frigid wind blew forcefully down the tunnel created by the tall ornate office buildings. He scurried past Newspaper House, the home of the highly esteemed West Australian, his normal Monday - Friday employer. The work he did for the weekend papers was purely contract 'on the side jobs'. He would submit a more measured review of the Coroner's findings for Monday's West Australian, but this could be submitted tomorrow morning.

Three buildings further down, a decrepit stone building housed the more seedy, editorial offices of The Mirror. Eustace felt soiled just by walking into this establishment. He passed his report over to the young clerk with a scowl and a grubby shirt, hunched behind the desk in the foyer. The Mirror published smutty stories, details of brutal crimes, divorces and scandals. Still they paid well and they paid cash. Ten pounds he had netted from his first submission. This was equivalent to a full month's wage as the Country Roundabout reporter for The West.

His sister Marjorie had been incensed when his news stories had started to come out in the press. She had written him a most aggrieved letter, accusing him of cowardice and lacking in moral fibre. In one part she had said that it was lucky his parents were dead or *'they would have died of mortification and shame'*. She had called his payments, *'his wages of sin'*. It would take a lot of sweet talking to convince her that her little brother was not the devil incarnate.

If Marjorie could see him now she might come to understand, a little pain had resulted in big gain. A new apartment in town, new clothes, a promotion and cash in his pocket. Eustace was living. At long last!

The newspaper man then left the ramshackle building and hailed a tram heading west down The Terrace. He was still mulling over the enemies he had made out of all of this. His name would be mud in many of the country towns he used to frequent. Marjorie wouldn't be alone. The venomous stares he had received this morning from the witnesses across the room showed he was persona non grata, in that camp. The Nelsons had given him a chilly reception, Ada Nelson's bitter stares dripped with pure malevolence. Jack Parrott had uttered an oath as he had passed him in the corridor. If hatred was an arrow he would have been mortally wounded.

Eustace accepted this as one of the down sides of the job. Bringing news to the masses meant that individuals sometimes get damaged. No-one is happy when their personal, private happenings are aired in public but that's the news business. Still even he, with his tough exterior, was rocked at the sight of Mrs

Lillian Smith.

In the witness stand Mrs Smith had sat, hunched and frail, fully garbed in black widow's weeds. Her face was grey, with aged skin and hollowed cheeks. Her voice was a croaky whisper, like a candle flame that a puff of wind would have extinguished. She was just a hollow shell, gutted and formless. Even now, three weeks after the attack, she seemed barely alive. Anxious, nervous and timid and Eustace wasn't so proud of himself for aiding and abetting the forces which prevented her recovery.

On the day after the murder he had assisted with the clean-up at the Smith's farm; he had used his investigative reporting skills to learn a lot about the Smith family. He had seen how they lived; admired their pioneering spirit. After the superficial signs of the violent attack were cleaned away, this home sung with happy memories.

Eustace had felt no compunction as he had invaded the Smith's personal space, viewing their photos and reading their private letters. He had even 'borrowed' a bundle of letters; correspondence between the couple over the war years. Eustace had read these the night before the inquest and he was inspired by this strong willed, passionate woman, who had so clearly loved Harold Smith to distraction. How did the authoress of these powerful letters turn into the wraith of misery who now sat in the witness stand?

These thoughts had come to plague him. He felt a slight pang of conscience at taking the letters but immediately dismissed this as 'silly emotion'. Perhaps he should try to get them back to their rightful owner? He would get through this painful case and then he would seek to make amends to this damaged woman.

Thirty minutes after returning to his apartment he was showered, spruced up and on the train heading towards Fremantle. It was only 5.30pm, far too early to go to the Dance Hall so he decided he would head past the Fremantle Prison first. Not that he wanted to wreck his night, but the thought of Clifford Hulme, alone and friendless on the night that he was committed to stand trial for murder, weighed very heavily on him. He thought he might just drop in and say 'Hello'.

Thus at 6.15pm, Eustace Wilkinson found himself standing at the gatehouse of the Fremantle Prison, requesting a visit with the accused murderer Clifford Hulme who was being held in the high security wing. Eustace was dressed to go dancing and felt decidedly out of place but this was an obligation.

An unwelcome responsibility had been placed on Eustace the last time he had spoken to Clifford Hulme. Cliff had indicated that he was the only person in Australia whom he trusted. If Cliff was relying on him, he supposed he really owed him at least one drop in visit and he doubted anyone else around the state would care. It wasn't like he could put this off - Clifford would most likely be dead in a few months. The bloke had asked him for assistance and he owed it to him to at least make some attempt.

It was another winter evening and the menacing darkness had arrived early, just as Eustace walked in through the unwelcoming entrance. No-one should ever visit a prison for the first time in the dark. The looming dark grey limestone walls were streaked with blackish mould. The prison was already seventy years old, built to house convicts and these walls had few happy stories to tell. The smell was thick, reminiscent of wet, stagnant dirt and sewerage. Every heavy iron re-enforced door he passed through shut with a reverberating clang behind him. Eustace was struck with the overwhelming, claustrophobic fear that he would never get out. Prisons are horrible places.

He finally arrived at the 'Secure Section' which housed the most dangerous men across the State. The ten minute journey into a world of unwelcome incarceration would have depressed even the most buoyant of hearts. Eustace was feeling decidedly maudlin by the time he came face-to-face with a tired, disinterested guard. Character traits which suit prison guards do not usually include friendliness, cleanliness and compassion and this guard was true to type.

'Whada you want?' he grunted.

'I'm Eustace Wilkinson from the West. Here is my press card. I'm here to see Clifford Hulme.'

'You don't have no authorisation,' announced the surly guard. Visitors meant that he had to get up. It was late and he wanted to sit here, read the afternoon paper and have his soup. Plus the bloke looked like a dandy and he didn't like toffs.

'Look Mate, I'm here as a visitor. This bloke has just received news today that he is being tried for murder. Have some compassion. Just go and ask Clifford Hulme if he will see me. Tell him it's Eustace,' he asked, slipping him a two bob sweetener - greasing the wheels of persuasion.

Eustace was persistent. The guard sensed that this fellow would not be put off. He also saw some chance for profit - often the press would be willing to pay to get some information about prisoners, particularly when they were on death row. He reluctantly shuffled off down the grim line of cells which housed the violent offenders. The occupants of these cells did not have contact with others, no exercise rights, no shared meal times and no entertainment. Their tiny cell was their world, one hard bed, one shelf, a high barred window and a pot for ablutions.

'Yeh. He'll see you but you have to talk from outside the door. I'm not going through all the bother of putting you in an interview room. He's in 16. Just walk on down,' muttered the unpleasant guard on his return.

Eustace timidly made his way down the thin metal pathway, looking in the cells at the incarcerated men. Loud shouts of abuse followed his progress. He was something to take away their boredom. Everyone had a comment. None were complimentary.

At number 16 he looked in and there was the huddled figure of Clifford Hulme, seated on his bed. Cliff stood up and made his way to the barred door, holding the rails on both sides for support. He looked sick and shrunken. His formerly tanned skin had faded and his dark hair hung lankly over his eyes.

'Hi Cliff. How are you? I saw you in court today but I couldn't come over to see you. Sorry about that. I'm with the paper and we're not allowed to go over to see the folk in trials.'

'Hi Eustace.' Cliff greeted him, his hand jutted out in a welcoming handshake. His hand lingered in Eustace's, perhaps the first touch of another human he had felt for some time. Even Cliff, who usually avoided touch, craved some contact after his experiences.

'Are you feeling all right?'

'Na. I'm always sick. I get headaches all the time and I keep vomiting up my food. And this place is not nice. Can I get out soon?'

'Well, not really Cliff. You see today they decided that you did kill Smithy and that means you have been charged with his murder. Did they explain this to you?'

'Yeh. They did. But I thought if I handed myself in, things would work out,' Cliff said plaintively, 'but they won't will they?'

'No they won't Cliff. You'll go on trial now. That was what the Coroner decided in Court today. If they find you killed Harold, they will hang you.'

Eustace let the horror of these words sink in. Cliff looked downcast - the full weight of this thought made him slouch lower against the bars. Hope left him. Receiving news of your imminent death, in a place where the gallows were less than 50 feet away, was truly terrifying.

Eustace shuffled his feet, feeling very uncomfortable. Why did he get the job of explaining this to him? Perhaps it is because Cliff doesn't have any faith in the world and unless someone he trusts explains something to him, he doesn't take it in. He was like a small child. A very dangerous, unpredictable child, capable of violent and despicable acts. Eustace was clearly aware that he was dealing with a volatile but also very vulnerable person and he was filling a very necessary but unpleasant role. Cliff needed to know the truth but he also needed something to believe in and this too could only come from someone he trusted.

'You have already admitted that you shot Smithy. So this makes you guilty. Your only chance of getting off is to claim insanity at your trial. Do you know what this means?' Eustace asked, continuing on in the unsolicited but essential role as interpreter, mentor and counsellor.

'That's saying I'm a loony right?'

'Well, yes. But you have said all the way through that you don't remember doing these horrible things. So if you get your lawyer to prove you were insane when you did it, you might get off. It is true that you don't remember doing these horrible things isn't it?'

'I saw lights and my head hurt. Something snapped in my brain and told me to do those things. But I know it was bad. I remember some of it. But I don't think I did it. I just wanted my tablets. I have hardly any left now. The Doctor in here is quite nice. He has given me stuff to help me sleep and other pills that calm me down a bit but they are not like my old tablets.'

'You'll just have to take the stuff the Prison Doctor gives you. Save the rest of your tablets for when you have to go to court and special times. Now with your trial, you have to tell them everything about your headaches and stuff. Tell them about other times when you have done bad stuff or been sick in your head. Tell them why the Doctor gave you these tablets in the first place.'

Eustace felt that Cliff needed to be honest and open with his lawyer. It was his only chance.

'When did you first get the tablets and did the Doctor say what was wrong with you?' asked Eustace.

'Way back - in the Army, after I got Blackwater Fever. Some blokes got hurt in an explosion and I got caught aiming my rifle at one of the blokes and they were going to kick me out of the Army. Doctor Samran was really nice and he understood. He gave me these tablets and wrote me a letter so other doctors would give me the tablets. Now they won't give 'em to me anymore. That's why I got cross and why I went loony and now I feel sick all the time. When my trial comes up, will you please help me Eustace?' asked Cliff, with desperation creeping into his voice.

'I can't Cliff, I work for the paper. Remember what I said, it has to be a secret that I come to see you. But you'll get a lawyer. Let him know about the strange things that happen in your brain and about the Doctor and everything.'

'Who will my lawyer be?' Cliff asked.

'The State will give you a lawyer. You need to trust him and tell him what you have told me. He will be working hard to get you off.'

'Now did you think about who you wanted me to contact for you?' asked Eustace, wanting to be able to share the load of being the only person Cliff could trust.

'Well there's no-one in West Australia who will say nice things about me. Not now. Only you, oh, and I would have asked Smithy or Mr Parrott but that's no good now. I had two friends from the war, Macca and Bluey, but they are both dead now. I looked 'em up when I first got here.'

So no character witnesses. Eustace was again overcome with this man's total aloneness. He had been in Australia for over three years and had no-one who would vouch for him, except the man he had murdered and that man's brother-in-law. Clifford Hulme existed, but he was unimportant to the world. Who would cry at his passing? No-one it seemed.

'But I need you to let my family know back in England about all of this. Don't tell them yet. Wait until after this is all over. Mami and Joseph will be pretty cross at me for doing these bad things. I know right from wrong and I shouldn't have hurt Smithy. He was a bonser man. And I have a wife. Her name is Ethel Hulme and she lives in Southport. She probably has a little child by now. I want you to let her know that I love her and miss her. Oh, and tell her I'm sorry I wasn't a better husband.'

Eustace realised that he was once again being given an unasked for burden. It seemed that he was to pass on the unwelcome news to the family back at home. These words would be hard to write. Still, as a wordsmith this was his skill. Words to upset and inflame or words to commiserate and console.

'I will do all of these things for you Cliff. But don't give up hope yet. You have a trial coming up. We don't know what the outcome will be.' Eustace wanted to leave and he needed Cliff to have some hope.

'And there is one other thing I really want to do Eustace and you have to help me to do it.' Cliff looked up at him with piercing, pleading eyes. Eustace was pensive but intrigued.

'What is it Cliff?'

'I want to say sorry to Mrs Smith. To her face. I can't remember doing any of the things that people say I did to her. But it happened. I know it happened because I saw it. And everyone says she's hurt really bad. She is a nice woman and I am really sorry if she got hurt. And I didn't want the kiddies hurt either. I listened in court and she seemed really upset. I need to tell her that I am really sorry.'

Eustace was overcome by this one. How was he meant to respond? The perpetrator of this callous, inexplicable crime wanted to apologise!

'Why don't you write her a letter Cliff? Let her know this in a note. She would find this easier. She is a pretty sick woman at the moment and I don't think she would like to come into a prison.

Suddenly Cliff became animated. He grasped the rails and looked desperately into the newspaper man's eyes.

'Nooo,' said Clifford adamantly. 'This is the only thing I really want. I don't mind being hanged. I don't even mind being locked up in this horrible prison for ever. But I need to say sorry to her, Mrs Smith needs to hear me say this. If she doesn't hear me say sorry she'll not be able to get better.'

Cliff then turned away and lay face-down on his bed, he had nothing more to say to Eustace.

The snappily dressed newspaper man gradually turned away. He retraced his steps. Once again his passing caused jeers and rude oaths to erupt from the bored occupants of the cells. The surly guard was still slurping his hot soup as Eustace passed with a silent nod of thanks.

Eustace found his way out of the prison. Heavy doors opened and with every unbolted door the air became easier to breathe. In ten minutes he was out and he looked up at the inky night sky dotted with stars. An infinity of freedom with not a lock or wall in sight. A prospect Clifford Hulme would probably never experience again.

Eustace made his long, lonely way home to his apartment. Going dancing just didn't seem like such a good idea anymore.

The Trial
Twelve Good Men And True

The Week of Clifford Hulme's Murder Trial

Early August, 1928

Perth, Western Australia

Eustace Wilkinson was resolute and determined as he sat down to complete his first news report on Sunday August 5th, the day before Clifford Hulme's trial for murder commenced. This was his week to make a name for himself. This major news story would appear in every newspaper across Australia, and Eustace was in the box seat to deliver a comprehensive summary. And to reap the rewards.

The West Australian

Hulme Trial to Commence Today

Clifford Hulme, a farm labourer, who is currently in Fremantle Prison on remand, will be tried at the Perth Criminal Court for the wilful murder of Harold Eaton Smith. The crown prosecutor Mr A Wolff will conduct the prosecution and Mr Frank O'Dea will represent Hulme. Nine witnesses have been subpoenaed by the Crown and the hearing is not expected to last more than a day.

It was a lazy Sunday morning in Perth. Eustace was back in his fancy apartment overlooking the old Barracks building, off St Georges Terrace in Perth. The young man about town had just returned from the King St Cafe where he had taken a coffee and walnut cake. Coffee was a new sensation for Eustace. He considered it a wonderful drink and Eustace had no doubt that it was more than a passing craze. A cup of coffee really made you feel alive, far better than tea in his opinion.

The reporter had finished his Court alert for tomorrow's West Australian but he was ready for more. He had some time on his hands and was consumed with the complex thoughts swirling through his mind. This week would throw up some interesting news topics, but he needed to stir up the public's imagination, get the case on everyone's lips. And he also wanted to tackle a topic he had begun to think about more and more recently. Thus he also penned this opinion piece for publication in Monday's paper:

The West Australian

How will Mrs Smith and the Little Smith Girls Get Justice?

This week Clifford Hulme, will face court, charged with the wilful murder of Harold Eaton Smith.

But Mr Smith's wife and family were also subject to horrific abuse. How will this wrongdoer be punished for these crimes? Mrs Smith was cruelly beaten and outraged, in her own home and in the presence of her children. Even worse, this outrage occurred from someone she trusted. Little Elsie Smith (8) was beaten and had the horror of looking after her mother and her badly injured sisters, after the event. The six year old Vonny Smith's head injuries were so severe that, even today, she is still in hospital recovering from the damage to her brain. Baby Peggy, was callously flung against a wall and was very lucky to survive.

Although these abuses were made public through the press and have now been officially recognised in the Coroner's Court, there is no chance for these four victims to see the perpetrator punished. The criminal assaults and aggravated rape charges do not form part of this week's court case.

Sources close to the Smith family, tell sad stories about the transformation that has occurred in this family since this crime occurred. The physical injuries were dire and are of course taking their time to heal. The financial impact has been huge, as this little family has lost its breadwinner. But it is the emotional impact that has been catastrophic.

Those who knew Mrs Lillian Smith before this event, have reported that she was a happy, confident and very contented wife. Mrs Smith joined in eagerly with the community and was socially very popular. She had a keen intelligence and was not backward in stating her opinions, which were nearly always kindly, reasoned and modern in outlook.

The Smith's marriage was said to be based on mutual respect and trust and their close relationship was maintained robustly over the war years with 9 years of their marital union to be celebrated this month. This couple should have grown old together, enjoying their hard earned wealth, their offspring and each other. Sadly this will never happen now.

The Mrs Smith who has emerged after the attack has little resemblance to this carefree lady. She is anxious and introverted and is scared of her own shadow. With her good name shattered and her future destroyed, Mrs Smith's life has quite literally been ruined.

Public opinion is strongly of the view that this man will be hung for the crime of wilful murder. If so, death will be the ultimate punishment and no further allocation of penalties will be possible. But does this mean Mrs Smith and her daughters will feel that the crimes against their persons, were never taken into consideration? How will the death or permanent incarceration of Hulme help Mrs Smith recover what she has lost? The criminal will be dead but she will have to live with the memories of what he did to her and to her children for the rest of her days. Alone and destitute. Our society needs to help this poor lady and her children.

Eustace Wilkinson

By Sunday afternoon, Eustace was still filled with nervous anticipation. This would be the week that would make his career. At lunchtime on that day, he had made a second 'friendly visit' to Fremantle Prison, just to give Clifford Hulme some confidence. Surely he needed at least one supportive friend before he faced the worst ordeal of his life! This time he had travelled during the day time when the bleak forbidding surroundings of the prison were less oppressive.

By the time he was safely back in his home, Eustace had persuaded himself that it was permissible to use some of the 'strictly confidential material' he had discovered during the visit. He was prepared to pull out all stops to get this last news report in before the trial started. This story had to pique the reader's interest. He opted for another opinion piece. This one would tap into the prejudices rife across the community. Logically, it wasn't likely to hurt Cliff's chances, as this would be revealed in the paper at the same time the real life drama would be rolled out in the court room in Perth.

The West Australian

Insanity Plea to be Explored in Murder Trial

Early information has been obtained that in the murder trial starting in the Perth Criminal Court today, the accused Clifford Hulme will be pleading 'Not Guilty' - claiming a mitigating plea of insanity. The very experienced defence lawyer Mr Frank O'Dea is expected to ruthlessly explore all avenues to enable his client to escape the gallows. This, despite the accused Clifford Hulme already making a statement admitting to the callous, cold blooded murder of Harold Eaton Smith.

Sources from within the Defence team will argue that many of Clifford Hulme's behaviours may be explained if insanity can be established.

This is the third plea of insanity made to the courts this year.

In the first case a jury found John Sumpter Milner guilty, the Executive Cabinet upheld this verdict and the sentence was carried out. This case wrenched the heart of the public, as it involved the vicious rape and murder of Ivy Lewis, a 12 year old school girl. Clear evidence was presented to the court of Milner having past psychiatric episodes and employer testimony regarding the accused's unstable mind prior to the heinous crime being carried out. In this instance the decision makers were not swayed and declared Milner sane. The death sentence was carried out on May 21st.

Similarly, in April this year a jury of twelve men took little time to determine the guilt of Nicholas Kelly, accused of the murder of Sergeant Alexander Mark, an innocent policeman discharging his public duty. Kelly was shown to have had a disrupted upbringing including extended periods of care in boy's homes and as an adult he had a diabolical record of alcohol abuse. The premeditated nature of this crime led to the public having little sympathy for this evil criminal. In this case the Executive Cabinet did commute the death sentence and Kelly has been sent to an insane asylum.

There is little doubt that Mr Frank O'Dea will be buoyed by this more recent case and will try to draw parallels between the two cases. Of course if the Defence do their job well, the jury may be convinced that Hulme is not of sound mind and they may impose a verdict of not guilty by virtue of insanity. It is hard for any person to contemplate that the horrific and brutal acts against Harold Smith and his family were not carried out by a mad man. Even if the jury finds him sane, the State through the Executive Council can reverse this decision as they did in the Kelly case.

However, the public of Western Australia wants consistency in our courts. One is hard pressed to see why one callous murderer gets off while another is hung.

The plea of insanity is a difficult one for juries to wrestle with. Firstly, there is a great temptation for perfectly sane, but evil men to claim insanity if it means escaping the hangman's noose. Secondly, the defence needs to show that the accused was insane at the time of the crime. The man in the dock may be having a lucid period and look perfectly normal at the time of the trial. Only experts can determine such complex matters.

Sadly, even when a criminal is shown to be insane, this does not alter the horror of their crime and surely this means that they should face the same punishment as a sane person? Lifetime incarceration in an asylum seems like a soft alternative to death by hanging.

One can only hope that whatever the outcome, Mrs Smith and her family are comforted in the knowledge that the public's condemnation of this fiend is universal. The public will only be satisfied if this

criminal is sent to the gallows.
Eustace Wilkinson

Monday August 6th, 1928

The press bench in the Criminal Court had been packed on Monday morning as reporters filed in to cover one of the most notorious crimes in Western Australian history. Eustace had taken his time to dress that morning. His hair was combed back and greased with a little tonic, he sported a new silk shirt with a claret red bow tie and the whole ensemble was set off by his pride and joy, his new two toned shoes in brown and white. Eustace looked and felt both handsome and urbane. He was in total control and this was going to be his day.

Unlike the other reporters, Eustace just focussed on the parts of the trial that had to do with the claim of insanity. He reasoned that the details of the crime had already been extensively documented (thanks largely to his exhaustive efforts over the last month). Readers were now more interested in new testimony.

And of course they were in a frenzy of excitement and anticipation. Everyone had an opinion about the possible outcome.

The testimony at the Criminal Court on day one of the murder trial went until 4.30pm. Eustace had notified his paper that his report would be delivered by 5pm. They had held the print run, knowing that his work would be exceptional. Reports of this calibre ensured that this newspaper held onto its phenomenal market share.

The editor was already pleased with him and by tomorrow he would be ecstatic.

The West Australian
Hulme Pleads Not Guilty of Murder
He Admits the Shooting but Claims he was Insane

Terrible, tragic and intensely sad was the story told to the Chief Justice, Sir Robert McMillan, and the jury in the Criminal Court today, when young Englishman, Clifford Hulme, was charged with the wilful murder of Harold Eaton Smith, a 34 year old farmer of West Wubin on June 22.

The murder was followed by a savage outrage on Mrs Smith and horrific abuse of her young, defenceless children. Perhaps never before in the history of Western Australian crime has a woman spent such a night of horror as that experienced by the wife of the murdered man.

The Criminal Court was crowded, women making up a fair proportion of the gallery. Many disgruntled folk had to be turned away when the public gallery was declared to be full. At times during witness testimony, the gallery had to be silenced. The Chief Justice was particularly harsh on the making of public comments when Mrs Smith gave her heart rending account.

Hulme in the Dock but Chooses Not to Take the Stand

Clifford Hulme presented a lonely figure as he sat motionless in the dock. He stared uncomprehendingly at the proceedings, with a remote look on his face. In the dock, Hulme kept his eyes focussed downwards, deliberately averted from Mrs Smith's face! The young, sad looking man of 29 years, appeared tense and uncomfortable with his surroundings and uneasy about the battery of eyes which played upon him. The accused was poorly dressed with greasy and unkempt hair. Hulme's voice was almost inaudible when he pleaded not guilty. Mr O'Dea explained to the court that Clifford Hulme had elected not to take the stand.

Admission of Killing

Prior to opening the Crown's case, Mr Wolff made it clear that the question of Hulme's sanity at the time the crime was committed, was the main question for the jury's consideration.

'There is no dispute on two main facts in this case,' he said, 'firstly that Smith was killed, and secondly, that he was killed by the accused.'

Mr Wolff had theatrically pointed to the man in the dock. 'You have to give your serious consideration gentlemen, to the mental condition of the man in the dock.'

Having made this preliminary observation, which drew audible exclamations of surprise from the gallery, such as 'he admits it,' Mr Wolff then outlined the Crown's case, which relied heavily on the testimony and findings from the Coroner's Court.

The Defence Claims Hulme's Brain Went Wrong

Mr O'Dea for the Defence, said Hulme, would not dispute many of the facts of the case. Hulme had already made an admission that he had murdered Harold Smith. What the defence was attempting to establish was that Clifford Hulme was not sane at the time of the murder.

Mr O'Dea read a statement from Clifford Hulme to the Court:

'I have been working for Harold Smith for the past five months. Mr Smith and his wife have always treated me all right, and there was no ill-feeling between us.'

'Mr Smith and I were scrub rolling and he was about a chain from me. My head was really hurting all day. Suddenly red and yellow lights flashed in my eyes and I dropped the axe, grabbed the rifle and pulled the trigger. Something in my head had told me to shoot. Something had gone wrong in my brain. Smith had his back to me at the time. He fell off the tractor and I went to him and he was unconscious. There was nothing that could be done for him. I then changed my clothes and went away. The next thing I remember was sitting on the roadside drinking water out of a wheel rut. I tried to reason things out and heard a voice saying: 'You've shot Smithy, you've shot Smithy.' I went to get help and Mr Nelson gave me a lift to Wubin but the truck broke down and I walked the rest of the way. In the morning I handed myself in to Constable Rowbottom.'

Mr O'Dea paused to point out to the jury that the accused had voluntarily handed himself in to the police before continuing with Hulme's statement.

'I do not remember seeing Mrs Smith after the shooting, but I must have returned to the house, because when I 'came to' I was wearing my best clothes. The next time I remember seeing her after the shooting, was at the Court. This is all I remember.'

The Defence Attempts to Establish a Lifetime of Psychiatric Disturbances

Mr O'Dea went on to claim that Hulme has had a long history of taking 'turns' and he had found learning difficult and had only learnt to read and write as an adult. Mr O'Dea admitted as evidence, psychiatric tests showing that Hulme had sub-normal intelligence and a low level of 'emotional accordance'. Mr O'Dea indicated that there was family history of insanity, with a relation on his mother's side having died in a lunatic asylum in England.

Mr O'Dea revealed to the Court that Hulme had suffered from Blackwater Fever while serving with the British Infantry in Mesopotamia. While in camp in Egypt, Hulme had been implicated in an incident that documented Hulme having a psychotic episode. A military inquiry had dismissed the case and had not proven any wrong doing on the part of Pte Clifford Hulme, however, he was given an early discharge on medical grounds.

Mr O'Dea provided an incomplete Army Doctor's report which allegedly indicated that Hulme had shown symptoms of mental incapacity. However, as this had no covering letter, it was deemed inadmissible as it had no official British Army authentication. The jury was directed to disregard this evidence.

Mr O'Dea explained to the Court that while at the Smith's farm, Hulme had regularly taken himself into the bush alone to deal with his moods. Sometimes these lasted for two to three days and Hulme had no memory of what went on while he was away.

Mrs Smith Tells her Harrowing Story

Mrs Smith was the first of the witnesses to appear. She was dressed in sombre black and her quiet, soulful eyes mirrored the tragedy of a wrecked home and shattered dreams. She presented a frail, forlorn appearance as she told her tragic story.

The sympathies of everybody in Court were with her as she spoke of Hulme's lustful outrage upon her and her children. In broken sentences, she bravely revealed her night of horror. Her brother, Jack Parrott, was permitted to be with her in the witness box, as she recounted her nightmare. Three times her voice faltered and she was at risk of collapse, however, each time she was able to compose herself and continue her distressing story.

Mrs Smith told the court how she had been turned upon and bashed. She haltingly described how she had been tied hand and foot throughout her ordeal. When released by her daughter Elsie, she had sat up all night to protect her girls. She expected any moment to hear the footsteps of the monster returning to exact further toll and reek further damage on her once happy home. She relayed to the Court her actions in the early morning when she had set out to find her husband and then had walked over seven miles in the bush to get help. Through it all, she knew her husband had been brutally murdered.

Short Cross Examination

Mr O'Dea asked very few questions and gently probed the delicate Mrs Smith. He confined himself solely to matters which might have a bearing on Hulme's sanity.

In reply to questions from Mr O'Dea, Mrs Smith said she had treated Hulme in a kindly manner and had never had any reason to doubt him. Her husband had also had great regard for the man, whom they had welcomed into their family over the six months he had been at the farm. Hulme had never made any improper overtures towards her, in fact he had been respectful and polite and had been good to the children. He was trusted and allowed every latitude.

When Hulme told her that her husband had been accidentally killed, she had believed him and turned to him for comfort and support. Prior to this chilling night, Mrs Smith had not noticed that Hulme was abnormal, however he had been ill and her husband had indicated that he had suffered from headaches and insomnia. She had not witnessed any of his black moods.

When Hulme turned on her, his nature and behaviour was quite out of character. After the attack when he had returned to her room saying that 'the madness had passed him' he had been far more like the Hulme she was used to. He had seemed to care for her welfare but by then she was too terrified of him to accept his offer of support.

Little Elsie Smith's Account

Brave little Elsie Smith won hearts across the Court room when she took the stand, bravely recounting her recollections of that horrible day. The waif is only 8 years old but she spoke with the conviction and bravery of a much more mature child. Mr O'Dea did not ask Elsie Smith any questions.

Other Witnesses are Cross Examined
The Police Accounts

Mr Wolff for the Crown, then took the floor. He commented on the fact that there were too many unfilled blanks in Hulme's story. Hulme had made no mention of the brutal happenings after the shooting and prior to his departure from the farm. Constable Rowbottom had indicated that Hulme had quite spontaneously volunteered information about where to find the rifle and Smithy's body. Mr Wolff contended that this proved that Hulme's memory was quite clear and there was nothing wrong with his mental condition when he could remember details such as where he left the rifle. The weapon had been found by Mrs Smith exactly where Hulme had said he left it.

Constable Rowbottom told the Court about finding the body, indicating it was exactly as Hulme had recounted.

In response to Hulme's demeanour he replied: 'On the day he handed himself in, he seemed extremely agitated. He was aware that he had done something wrong and clearly felt remorse.

I had always found Hulme quite normal in the three years I have known him. He seemed a quiet, law abiding chap who kept to himself.'

Detective Inspector Doyle had charged Hulme and believed he was perfectly sane at the time but he was excessively nervous and complained of a headache and a stomach upset.

Doyle pointed out that there had been serious flaws in the police examination prior to his arrival and that evidence could have been tampered with or missed.

The Neighbour's Testimony

In reply to Mr Wolff's cross examination, John Nelson had said that Hulme seemed normal when he accompanied him in the motor truck.

Following Mr O'Dea's question, Nelson confirmed that Hulme had been agitated and evasive. He had known him for six months and had found him to be a hard worker. He described him as: *'quiet, simple and pleasant'*. He had never seen any sign of insanity, moodiness or depression.

Jack Parrott is Declared a Hostile Witness

When Jack Parrott was on the stand he indicated that he had known Clifford Hulme for over three years. He had suggested that he worked on the Smith farm to pay off debts that he had accrued at the Wubin store, jointly owned by Mr Parrott and Mr Smith. Mr Parrott revealed his deep dislike for the accused. He had not witnessed any turns and had no knowledge of the accused being unwell but had said he was sometimes *'moody and taciturn'*.

Following Mr Wolff's questions, Mr Parrott had indicated that he thought Hulme was:

'Perfectly sane and fully aware of the terrible crime he had committed. Hulme was given friendship, opportunities and support by Harold Smith.'

The witness believed: *'Hulme cold bloodedly and maliciously planned this brutal attack. He is now feigning illness in a futile attempt to avoid the gallows'. The Defence stood to declare Mr Parrott's views were 'speculation' but this was not upheld and Mr O'Dea then declined to cross examine Mr Parrott.*

The Country Doctor Presents Medical Evidence

Dr Colin Anderson, of Dalwallinu, detailed the injuries to the murder victim and to Mrs Smith and the Smith girls. The Court Room Gallery gasped when they heard about the extent of the brutal injuries. The photos of the injuries were shown to the members of the jury and many strong men were shown to blanch and look discomforted at the sight of such horrific damage on innocents.

Dr Anderson confirmed that, to the best of his understanding, Hulme was not drunk or under the influence of any drugs at the time of the crime. He was not aware of him being a drinker or habitually using medication that would have affected his sanity.

The witness, who was once in charge of the mental ward of the Perth Public Hospital, said he examined Hulme in the gaol at Dalwallinu, and considered him normal at the time of the examination. Hulme had indicated that he felt quite ill and could not sleep, but Dr Anderson indicated that these symptoms would be expected in someone after such a traumatic event. He declined to express an opinion as to Hulme's sanity.

The Crown Presents an English Doctor's Certificate of Good Health

Mr Wolff stated that in 1916, Hulme had been accepted into the British Infantry. To allow him to do this he had to pass a medical and a Doctor's Certificate was shown to the court signed by Dr J Broderick, of Manchester. This certificate disclosed that Hulme was normal in every respect.

Mr Wolff indicated that this brought into doubt any evidence of medically proven, psychotic events in Hulme's past.

Doctors In Court

Seated at the Barristers' benches, and following the evidence with close interest, was Dr Bentley, Inspector General of the Insane and Superintendent of the Claremont Asylum and also Dr Kerr, the Fremantle Prison Doctor. Significance was attached to their appearance in Court owing to their contradictory testimonies at the Kelly Murder Trial. (Kelly had shot and killed Sergeant Mark). The two doctors had come into conflict on the question of Kelly's sanity. Dr Bentley had argued that Kelly was insane, while Dr Kerr contended that he was sane and the jury in this case, had supported Dr Kerr's view. However, after being sentenced to death, Kelly was reprieved. Speculation in the gallery was rife as to the stands these two medical men would take in regard to Hulme's sanity.

Medical Testimony Presented

Dr James Bentley said he had studied Hulme on three different occasions and was satisfied that Hulme was insane at the time of the murder, although he was not satisfied that he was insane now. He came to his conclusion because:

(1) there was no motive for the crime;

(2) an unnecessary amount of violence was used as the deceased was struck after death;

(3) uncharacteristic violence was used against the children and

(4) the violent sexual assault was at odds with the accused's stated moral attitudes.

'Periods of memory loss frequently follow malarial infection and Hulme has suffered from Blackwater Fever, a severe form of malaria,' claimed Dr Bentley.

Dr Kerr, the Doctor from the Fremantle Goal said he saw the accused immediately after his admission. He had questioned him about hearing voices. Dr Kerr said that at the time he examined him, he had no delusions, however, he had requested tablets to make him 'feel normal'. Dr Kerr felt that the accused had subnormal intelligence. Hulme had complained of sleeplessness, anxiety, nausea and headaches.

He did not feel that anyone could definitely state what the accused's mind was like when he committed the crime. He did not think that the insanity was a pretence but he thought that the loss of memory probably was and that this may have been due to shame and embarrassment. These emotions are characteristic of a sane man who regrets his actions. Dr Kerr thought that he was normal enough now to feign insanity and that Hulme is perfectly normal now. Dr Kerr's testimony was the last to be presented to the Court.

Summation

The Chief Justice (Sir Robert McMillan) indicated that Mr Wolff (for the Prosecution) and Mr O'Dea (for the Defence) would be given opportunity to sum up their cases tomorrow and then he would give his summation before the Jury would retire to consider their verdict.

Has the case for the Crown established that this is a simple matter of a hideous crime committed by a sane man who deserves to be hung? Or has the Defence established, beyond reasonable doubt, that the accused was insane at the time of the murder. People across our nation are nervously anticipating the jury's decision.

We will all know tomorrow what fate awaits Clifford Hulme.

Eustace Wilkinson

The Trial
When Fate Is Determined

Early August, 1928

Perth, Western Australia

Late on Tuesday afternoon after the Jury had made their momentous announcement and the Chief Justice had pronounced Hulme's doom, Eustace Wilkinson sat at his typewriter and hastily completed the dispatch for tomorrow's paper.

West Australian

Hulme Sentenced To Death

A jury of 12 trusted and true men, rejected an insanity plea on behalf of Hulme when the murder trial was concluded at 4.30pm on August 7th. A listless and morose participant in the trials, Hulme's face showed little understanding or comprehension when he learned that he was to die.

The afternoon session had been harrowing. Eustace had seen euphoria on some faces, relief on others but the face that haunted him, as he wrote this dispatch was the troubled face of Clifford Hulme. The lost, confused face of someone who is not really aware of what has just happened.

'A reporter should not get involved,' Eustace berated himself as he typed. His eyes were watering. He kept seeing Cliff's lost, bewildered face as he was led off by the prison guards, back into custody, back to face a grim and very short future.

'This man deserves death. He may seem like a sweet, misguided innocent but think what he did. How can I sympathise with someone who did those things. I was a witness to the smashed body of Harold Smith lying on the slab. And what about the images of Lillian Smith the day after her attack, her face bruised and battered, lying in petrified isolation in her hospital bed. What kind of monster does this to a woman? Why on earth do I feel sorry for him? No-one else does.'

This was Eustace's mindset as he continued with his report for tomorrow's paper.

Speedy Justice All Over in a Few Hours

The law is generally considered to be a slow and lengthy process so when it was announced in Monday's West Australian that this case would be all over in less than a day, few believed this would be possible. However, the murder trial of Clifford Hulme was conducted in a record time of 6 hours and 20 minutes. The evidence was shorn of all but the most pertinent of details with most witnesses occupying the witness box for periods of less than 10 minutes.

With all of the witness testimony completed the day before, the case reconvened at 2pm on Tuesday. The summations included a powerful 20 minute long address by the Crown Prosecutor in which he evoked many of the more brutal aspects of the case. He urged the jury to consider the horrific nature of the crime and find the accused perfectly sane and thus guilty.

This was followed by the closing appeal by Mr O'Dea which lasted fifteen minutes. O'Dea gave an impassioned plea to the Jury to give due consideration to the possibility that Hulme was insane at the time of the murder.

The Judge commenced his summation at precisely 2.45. Sir Robert McMillian directed the Jury thus:

'I have listened in the court to many terrible stories of crime but never to one which equals this in horrible details of killing, brutal assault and unspeakable cruelty to children, one still a babe. Yet all of these were actually done by the accused man. However, this court is not considering these horrendous acts. The murder has been admitted to. This court is only concerned with matters of the accused's sanity at

the time the crime was committed. It is not for the Crown to prove that the accused was sane at the time but for the Defence to establish insanity. If you feel that this has been established, you must return a finding of Not Guilty.'

The 12 grim faced men then retired to the jury room to commence their serious deliberations. There was no hint as to their private thoughts as the men filed out of court.

After an hour's retirement the Jury returned - still with stern, inscrutable faces, that gave no clue of their decision. The foreman stood and gravely announced that the Jury had found: '

Clifford Hulme guilty of the wilful murder of Harold Eaton Smith and accepted no mitigating circumstances of insanity'.

The Chief Justice in sentencing Hulme to hang said: 'The only question was whether you were sane or insane at the time of the murder. The Jury have found you were sane and all that remains for me to do is sentence you to death.'

When asked if he had anything to say, Hulme shook his head with barely a perceptible motion. He looked down dejectedly as he was led from the court.

Only if the Defence feels they have grounds for appeal or if the Executive Council commutes the sentence to life imprisonment, will this man escape the hangman's noose. Unless one of these events happens, Clifford Hulme will have less than a month to live.

Eustace Wilkinson

Wednesday August 8th 1928

On the Wednesday morning Eustace awoke late. He had slept fitfully, with vague images of the characters in the drama he had been documenting, fleeting in and out of his dreams. This anxiety annoyed him. Nagging concerns about how Clifford Hulme and Mrs Lillian Smith were coping, were not welcome. He wanted to feel self-assured, confident and buoyed. He had completed some great editorials over the week and the bosses at the paper were very pleased with him.

As he shaved and dressed, Eustace programmed his day. He needed to get down to Mr O'Dea's Chambers this morning, to ask if there was any chance of an appeal of the judgement. The Lawyer's rooms were just off King St, so Eustace happily realised that he could combine this visit, with a morning coffee at the cafe next door.

He had already sketched out an article outlining a fund raising drive to assist Mrs Smith with her recovery. Eustace would have liked to have sourced some quotes for the article, perhaps from a local supporting the appeal but he felt that his reputation in the Dalwallinu and Wubin locations was tarnished and he didn't fancy his chances of any polite interchanges. So the article would go in without any local commentary. This needed to be approved by the editorial staff ready for tomorrow's paper:

West Australian

Appeal for the Battered and Destitute Mrs Smith

Now that the trial of Clifford Hulme for the horrific murder of Harold Smith is complete, it has been revealed that the dead farmer's family have been left in awful circumstances. Ruthlessly robbed of her husband and her home, with three tiny children to raise, Mrs Smith's plight is now desperate.

The Miamoon farm had only recently (last December) been taken over by Harold Smith (dec). Under the rules of the New Farm Ownership Scheme, land is forfeited if the first annual subscription is not made and the clearing quota is not met. As this will not happen now, sadly the farm and their significant investment, will be lost to this family. It has also been revealed that very little of the plant and equipment on the farm was paid for and the family's extensive insurance policies were all cancelled prior to their take up of their farm.

The sad and sorry circumstances of this discovery is that Mrs Smith was not aware of the cancellation of the insurance policies or her dire financial situation. Mr Harold Smith was an astute and competent financial manager and she had always deferred to him in these matters. There is no doubt that, if this exceptional man had not been murdered, this family would never have been reliant on public charity.

Luckily Mrs Smith still has a half share in the Wubin Store, co-owned with Mr J.A. Parrott, Mrs Smith's brother. Otherwise, she and the children would have been left totally destitute.

An appeal has recently been launched, aimed at raising funds for the widow and her children. The aim is to raise sufficient funds so that the community of Wubin can construct a Boarding House business for the widow and her children to run. Land has already been donated for this purpose. This business will be looked after by trustees in the interests of Mrs Smith and her children.

Interested persons who wish to make a contribution, are encouraged to make contact with The Wubin Sporting Association c/o Wubin Post Office, or members of the public can make donations via the West Australian. Donations of over 10 shillings will be printed daily in this paper.

The West Australian Newspaper has kicked off this appeal with a very generous offer of 25 pounds. Let us all get behind this worthy cause.

Eustace Wilkinson

The newspaper man gathered this article and the morning post as he headed out into a crisp August day to the law firm of 'Carroll and O'Dea Barristers'. At the hushed law office, Eustace directed all of his charm at the attractive young lady with fabulous blue eyes, seated at the front desk.

'Good morning, is Mr O'Dea in please?'

'I am sorry sir, Mr O'Dea will not be available for the rest of the week.'

'Would I be able to book an appointment to see him early next week then?'

'My apologies sir, but Mr O'Dea's secretary is also not available and I am not able to make appointments in his absence. In fact, everyone but me is out to lunch and I am filling in for today only. I am afraid my expertise and knowledge of the firm is limited and I am just here to do the mail and to take messages.'

'That is a pity. By the way you have absolutely amazing eyes. Like the colour of a fresh spring sky.' Eustace let the flattery sink in before he continued with his honey covered tongue.

'I am Mr Wilkinson and I am from the Clerk of Courts. Apparently there is a letter being prepared regarding the appeal for Clifford Hulme. I was passing this way and thought I would come in personally and see if it has been completed. If so, I can take it back and lodge it this morning. This would bypass the official lodgement fee of 5 shillings. Perhaps you could look through today's outward mail and see if it has been prepared?'

'Well I don't know if this is accepted practice but you look like you have an honest face. Here is the mail ready to go. Would you like to have a look through, as you will be able to recognise it more quickly than me?' The sweet, gullible little receptionist had an open and trusting look on her face as she handed Eustace the mail. He quickly scanned the mail and found immediately the one he was after.

'Can I please open this, I will be able to tell immediately if this is the correct piece of correspondence.'

Not waiting on a response, the crafty reporter quickly opened and scanned the letter then replaced it inside the envelope and handed it back to the bewildered receptionist.

'This doesn't seem to be it. Obviously it has not been done yet. Well, I'll be off then. Thank you for your kindness.' Eustace gave her a bewitching smile and he quickly left the building.

As he stopped at his favourite coffee house, Eustace reflected on the momentous contents of the letter he had just read. Eustace slowly sipped his hot coffee as he contemplated this latest discovery. This was yet another of Cliff's chances gone. Best to get this message out as soon as possible rather than let another faint hope remain,

Eustace reasoned as he quickly handwrote yet another article for Thursday's paper.

West Australian

No Appeal Planned for Hulme

After yesterday's verdict of 'Guilty of Wilful Murder', The Chief Justice sentenced Clifford Hulme to hang. It has been revealed today that the lawyers are unlikely to appeal the verdict. Sources have indicated that all avenues have been fully explored and there were no grounds for appeal. Now, unless the State reverses the sentence, Hulme will be sent to the gallows.

Eustace Wilkinson

Now Eustace turned to opening his own mail. Three reminders for monies owing were stuffed offhandedly into his coat pocket. The fourth letter was handwritten and he could tell from the flowery writing on the envelope, that it was from his sister Marjorie. This would not be good. Another barrage of insults he predicted. So it was with a great deal of reluctance and trepidation he opened this letter.

Dearest Eustace

No, I have not forgiven you and I am still and constantly angry with you, every time I open a paper. I read your articles and I cannot believe you write with such flagrant disregard for the good feelings of the people you are discussing. Still, this is your chosen occupation and it is your conscience and you have to deal with it in your own way. This is not the subject of my letter.

I am offering you a chance of redemption. Here is your opportunity to do a good deed. If you do so, I just may consider forgiving you for the reprehensible behaviour you have demonstrated of late.

Your sister Elizabeth is in some trouble and needs our support. Of course this will need to be done with the utmost discretion. Now

I realise that you are not overly fond of Elizabeth but this is of no account, you are needed.

Elizabeth, as you realise, made a very good union with Mr Collins some years ago and two fine children have arisen from that union. Mr Collins has provided exceptionally well for Elizabeth and she has lived an opulent and pampered existence. They are considered important dignitaries in the township of Geraldton, where they have made their home. I can only say that I have envied her on many occasions, as her life certainly did not require her to work long hours, as I have had to do all of these years. Still, I am not complaining as my marriage has brought me great happiness.

Now this next part of my letter is a trifle delicate and I need to choose my words very carefully. About five years ago, Mr Collins determined that he would have no more intimate relations with Elizabeth. I was never privy to why this decision was made but I had heard that it was a convenient and mutually agreed to arrangement.

Four months ago I received a distressed letter from Elizabeth as she had found herself with child. Mr Collins is, of course, not the father. Elizabeth has not indicated who the father of the child might be and I have not asked for this confidence.

Mr Collins has very decently and considerately opted not to divorce our sister. In fact he has been more than reasonable, agreeing to take Elizabeth back into his household after the birth. However, he will have nothing to do with the child and he has insisted that it be offered for adoption. A resolution I totally agree with. Having a baby that is the result of a scandalous liaison in the household would be untenable.

Six months ago Elizabeth was sent away to Perth until after her confinement, so no-one is aware of her condition. Luckily the two children are both away at boarding school and are not home to witness their mother's shame.

Now here is where you are required to step in. She is currently housed in a boarding house in Claremont, just off Davies Road. This is a respite home for wayward women from affluent families and is very discreet. But for the birth she is booked into Rosalie Private Hospital in Subiaco. This place is very exclusive and will only accept married women.

So what you need to do is to accept the role of 'pretending to be Mr Collins'. You will need to visit with Elizabeth in the boarding house, acting appropriately. And you will need to be in attendance at the hospital when Elizabeth goes into labour. (Not that I am asking you to be a witness at the birth of course! But you should be waiting enthusiastically and nervously in the father's room.) This will mean that her good name and honour will be preserved in case anyone questions whether she is a married woman. The expected date for the delivery is late in August or very early in September.

All of the other details, including the adoption and Elizabeth's return to Geraldton after the birth, have been organised.

So 'Mr Edward Collins', I expect you to immediately go and find your 'good wife Elizabeth' and start acting as a concerned, expectant father. I hope to hear from you, that you have at least been able to perform this duty with discretion. You are on your honour as a Wilkinson to carry out this duty fittingly and prudently.

Yours sincerely

Your ever loving sister

Marjorie.

Eustace was stunned. He was also just a trifle amused as Elizabeth was certainly not Eustace's favourite relative. She was very egotistical and there had never been any room in her heady world for an irritating younger brother. As a young teenager, Elizabeth had always been a bit wanton and headstrong. She was sent away from home frequently for flirting and for engaging in the odd dalliance with the customers at the Old Narrogin Inne. For a while there was talk of her being placed in a convent. When her parents had been offered the opportunity to marry her off to one of her father's cousins, they had leapt at the chance. Mr Edward Collins was very rich but he was also very old and very boring. Eustace and Marjorie had teased her about this mercilessly, they both felt that she had got her just desserts.

Now this had come up. It was certainly unexpected but it gave him an excuse for a wonderful day trip and this would ensure that he would not spend the time pondering recent events. Eustace needed something to distract him from morosely and repetitively worrying about Lillian Smith and Clifford Hulme. He determined to immediately travel to Claremont to visit with 'dear sister Elizabeth', whom he had not seen since his mother's funeral three years before. He sincerely hoped she was not as vain and obnoxious as he remembered her.

After a brief detour past Newspaper House to drop in tomorrow's articles, Eustace was soon on the train heading toward Claremont. The train trip went without incident and the young man found himself heading towards Davies Road, just after noon.

Eustace passed the walled show grounds and took a shortcut across the oval, home of the Mighty Tigers, the team from the Claremont Football Club. As he did so, he noticed a very happy looking man approaching him. The man was in his sixties and was strangely dressed in khaki overalls. Eustace reasoned that he must have been a groundsman at the oval and wondered as he approached whether he was going to be asked to 'get off the grass'.

'Excuse me kind Sir, have you the price of a train ticket on you? I am afraid I have no coins on me at all,' the man asked Eustace in a lilting Irish accent. As he spoke he opened out his pockets to show that he had no money on him.

'Here's sixpence, that should be more than enough?' said Eustace feeling very generous as he thought the fare would be no more than twopence.

'Oh for sure. I be only needing to go to Fremantle. It's a wonderful day to be out and about and happy and free. Top of the day to you Sir,' he said tipping his hat with polite deference.

The reporter thought nothing of the exchange and soon arrived at the large, rambling, turn of the century house with a sign high above the portico proclaiming the residence to be a *private guest house*'. Large bay windows looked into a calm, ordered garden of rampant honeysuckle and recently pruned roses.

Eustace had been practicing being Mr Edward Collins, a very respectable banker from Geraldton, as he rang the bell and entered the sombre, austere foyer. A table with a stern sign, *'authorised persons only beyond this point'*, stood in front of a long, silent hall. A large bosomed lady, dressed efficiently in a senior nurse's outfit approached:

'Who are you and are you after someone in particular Sir?' she asked, oozing with superior competence and proficiency. Her badge proclaimed her to be Matron Stark.

'Hello Matron, I am Mr Edward Collins. I am here to see my dear wife Elizabeth who is a resident in your good establishment.'

Matron Stark was not fooled. No-one in her establishment had a real husband or was here without some scandal. But she was more than happy to keep up the pretence.

'Certainly Mr Collins. I will lead you through to her. No gentlemen are permitted to be with the ladies without a staff member close at hand and we request that you refrain from speaking to any lady other than your own dear wife. You can either meet with her in the front garden where you will be left in some privacy or you can meet in the sitting room. Obviously you cannot enter the private rooms of the ladies. Follow me please.'

Eustace smiled at the strict propriety of the place.

'Pity they didn't have these rules in the girl's lives some months earlier and they may not have found themselves in this predicament,' he muttered quietly to himself as he followed the large Matron into the garden. Eustace only waited a few moments before Elizabeth waddled in to join him. She was not bearing this pregnancy well. Her previously attractive face was blotched and puffy and her hair was starting to turn grey. Plus she looked like a whale. Obviously food had been her solace.

'Hello dear. Lovely to see you,' the polite Mr Edward Collins greeted his 'wife'.

'Thank you for visiting me,' Elizabeth said demurely, watching through heavily lidded eyes as the Matron left.

She immediately grabbed Eustace's hands. 'My oh my, I have got myself into such a predicament. I am so miserable. I just want this horrid pregnancy to be over. If I could cut this hateful child out of me tomorrow then that is what I would do. I hate it. I had such a lovely life and then this happened. It's truly dreadful.'

'Well my dear. I am here to play my part. I will visit with you over the next few weeks and I am happy to play the role of the excited father at the hospital.'

Elizabeth looked into Eustace's eyes and spoke to him urgently: 'I do appreciate it. Now did Marjorie mention that you are not to tell anyone, I will be mortified if you do. No one must ever find out about this! Mr Collins is already so angry with me. I cannot stand him. He is such a self righteous, pompous pig. Still, he has agreed to take me back in and for that I am really grateful. If he didn't I would have been ruined.'

'I gather that the other party is not concerned with you or the offspring?' Eustace asked, not able to contain his natural inquisitiveness.

'He was married. It's over. It should never have happened in the first place. But it does make me so angry. We only had a dalliance for about eight weeks and then I find out I have a problem and he just leaves me to sort it all out. It's always the way. Men play and women are left to pay! I don't want to ever talk about him or think about him again.' Elizabeth was determined that this part of her life was over and it was only this accursed pregnancy that stopped her moving on.

'I am here to support you my dearest wife,' replied Eustace, his tone decidedly sarcastic. His view of his sister as egotistical and vain remained unchanged.

Elizabeth then looked disapprovingly at her younger brother and she said acidly: 'Now, if you are going to play this role, you had better dress the part. Important bankers wear conventional suits and they certainly don't wear two toned shoes. And that moustache will have to go.'

'Hey hold on Elizabeth. I will do some things but this pencil thin moustache is my pride and joy. This is my lady killer. No, I will not take this off for anyone.'

Their banter continued as they chatted together amicably but they found themselves needing to raise their voices. Outside the walled garden there seemed to be a large increase in traffic noise. Soon they could hear sirens and whistles and, although their conversation was important, the distractions outside soon caused them to fall silent.

Suddenly the Matron came onto the verandah looking harassed. Something had disturbed the serenity and order of her establishment.

'Excuse me, Mr and Mrs Collins, you must immediately join with us in the sitting room for an important announcement'.

The couple followed the amply, proportioned Matron into the sitting room where six nurses in starched uniforms and about fifteen young girls showing various sized pregnancy bumps, were gathered in nervous groups. At the front of the room was a concerned looking Police Sergeant. He looked decidedly discomforted in this purely female domain as he started to speak:

'Good afternoon ladies. I do not want to startle you, but at around 12 noon today a patient escaped from the Claremont Insane Asylum, which as you know is less than half a mile from here. So we have launched a massive police search across the area. The missing man is dressed in the khaki uniform of the Asylum.'

The policeman shifted his feet uneasily and stroked his chin nervously as he went on: 'Now the reason there is a massive hunt for this chap is because he is Edward Nicholas Kelly, whom you may have heard of. He is a convicted killer and was under sentence of death earlier this year. This was commuted to life imprisonment in an asylum. He gave the guards the slip when he was being taken back to his room after lunch. If you see him do not speak to him. He may appear very friendly but he is extremely dangerous. If any of you see him, immediately contact the police.'

'Sergeant this is not acceptable,' came the harsh voice of the Matron. 'I am looking after very vulnerable girls here. This man is a convicted killer. We have had 8 escapes from that institution this year. Most were low security, so there wasn't any fuss, but this is different. The security in that place needs to be looked into. Outside the high security central wing, you can just wander all over the grounds and no-one ever asks you who you are. Good law-abiding folk live in this suburb and we cannot be held to ransom by crazed madmen who could attack us in our beds at any moment.'

The very embarrassed policeman took responsibility for the Matron's complaints: 'I am so sorry Matron. I will arrange to have one of my officers patrol outside these premises until the man is caught.'

The Matron moved into organisational mode, 'girls, you are all confined to your rooms. Your meals will be served in your quarters. Do not open your windows or doors to anyone but the staff. There will be no visitors until this man is caught.' The ladies looked crestfallen but dutifully left to do as they were told. Elizabeth was included in this obedient group who filed out with heads bowed.

'Mr Collins you must leave now,' the Matron snapped at Eustace. He was promptly bundled out of the establishment along with the frazzled policeman.

Eustace was amused. He thought about telling someone in authority that he had seen the escaped man earlier in the day. Perhaps he should notify them that he had seen him heading towards the train station? They may even be interested that he was planning to go to Fremantle and searching around here may be rather futile. But, he reasoned that this knowledge was his and need not be shared. Eustace made his way back to the railway station, through multiple checkpoints and road blocks.

All the way home he was compiling his next story. Once again he had been delivered a story on a plate. He was in the right place and at the right time. Here was his story for Friday's paper. It was only when he had got to the end of his article, that he realised that this would have momentous implications for Clifford Hulme's chances of clemency.

August 10th 1928

Prisoner's Escape

Life Sentence Man at Large

The people of Perth may have thought that Edward Nicholas Kelly would be safely locked up, away from the public, for the rest of his days but at noon on Thursday, Kelly, who is serving a sentence of imprisonment for life for the murder of Police Sergeant Mark earlier this year, escaped from the Claremont Mental Asylum. The residents of Claremont and Graylands now cower nervously in their homes as this dangerous and deranged killer wanders loose. Kelly gave warders the slip while being taken back to his room after lunch.

A local spokesperson, who is very critical of the Asylum security, stated that:

'Once Kelly had escaped from the secure wing at the Asylum, he would have just been able to meander out of the grounds with little fuss. The security at this facility is decidedly lax. He may have been able to wander down the road and catch the train to any area of Perth, where his many friends and associates would doubtlessly offer him sanctity. An inquiry must be launched about the security of the Asylum, with 8 escapes having happened in the past year.'

Policemen across the metropolitan area have been searching their districts. Even detectives and mounted policemen were engaged in the search. Anyone travelling in the Claremont area will need to go through numerous checks but perhaps the deadly killer has already fled this area?

Kelly was last seen wearing the khaki uniform of the Hospital for the Insane and a cloth hat, however he may now have found more suitable attire to enable him to better blend into the population. Kelly was still at large late on Thursday evening. After the Executive Council granted a stay of execution, Kelly was transferred to Claremont Asylum in April this year.

This escape must create serious misgivings in the Government Executive Council as they consider the sentence of death passed this week on Clifford Hulme. Surely they would not dare to commute this sentence if there was any chance this hideous criminal could be allowed to escape, like Kelly has. The safety of the public cannot be assured if our Asylums are not guarded like fortresses.

Eustace Wilkinson

Fires Within
The Shop Burns

16th August, 1928

Perth, Western Australia

Happy sounds and smells of breakfast filled the Nedlands home; Lilly was feeding baby Peggy small soldiers of toast dipped in egg yolk. Her arm had mended and except for light scars at her hairline, most of her physical injuries had healed. Now that the public drama was over, the former ebullient, confident young lady was returning too. Every day there were just a few more glimmers of her previous indomitable spirit arising.

Jack Parrott was sitting at his normal patriarchal place reading out random pieces from the paper and making sweeping comments of antipathy or approval.

'They've caught Kelly. Apparently he was at large for a whole week. He led the police on a fine chase.' Jack then silently read on for a minute before announcing:

'This is amazing! Apparently he, '*handed himself in at the Claremont Asylum with a large jovial audience present. He organised with the Police to hand himself in at 10am yesterday but he actually turned up at 9am. So he managed to pose for a photo and gave autographs first.*' This makes a mockery of the law and our police. That scoundrel Eustace Wilkinson managed to get the scoop again. That blighter seems to be living a charmed life, while everyone he writes about spends the rest of their life in purgatory.'

Jack put the paper down in disgust. He was still consumed with anger and the reporter was often the brunt of his venom.

'Please watch your anger, Jack dear. The children are present,' crooned Chrissie as she placed a cup of tea near him and removed his empty plate.

'Well at least this debacle with Kelly has had one positive outcome. The Executive Council have indicated they will not be reversing the Court's decision. Hulme will definitely be hung. They will set the date soon. This must bring you some satisfaction Lillian.'

'Nothing about this whole sorry period of my life brings me any satisfaction Jack. I don't want to think about the death of any man. In fact I don't want to think about that man ever again,' Lilly retorted, some of her old fire flashing in her eyes.

'Sorry Lilly. I didn't mean to upset you,' Jack said in a kindly but rather paternalistic fashion. He had morphed into a very protective older brother, guarding her against the world. In fact, protecting Lillian and his family was the only thing that seemed to interest Jack Parrott at this time. The trial was complete and Chrissie's confinement was still over two weeks away so he was at a bit of a loose end. The Nelsons had returned to their farm, Chrissie and Lillian were fully engaged in recovery, home duties, visiting Vonny and parenting, but Jack was becoming superfluous. He hesitated to return to Wubin, worrying that the girls might need him but he needed to go and both Chrissie and Lillian had been gently persuading him to leave.

'I am all right Jack. You need to stop worrying about me, I'm getting stronger every day. In fact you need to stop worrying about all of us. It's time you started to live again. Why don't you go back to the shop?' quizzed Lilly.

'Well Charles and Mabel seem to be able to cope perfectly well without me. They have sent a large order through yesterday which I think I might go down and supervise. But I feel a bit 'betwixt and between'. What do you think Chrissie? Do you think I should go back to Wubin? I'm worried that the baby might arrive early and I will not be here to support you.'

'You should go Jack, you need to get back to work. Or perhaps keep exploring the idea of setting up a second shop in another town. You were talking about that before all of this happened. Lilly is more than willing and happy to come with me to the birth. Fathers are no use at a birth anyway, it's not like they can come into the birthing suite. Lilly has been through it all herself three times and will give me all the advice and support I need. But if you plan to come back by the 1st of September, you should make it anyway. So go and supervise the order and make your mind up. I will pack you a case and you can decide over the day. I will miss you but we are able to cope without you. So if you are not home for dinner this evening we will know you have gone.'

Chrissie wanted the best for her husband, but she too was getting a bit tired of Jack following her every move. She needed a bit of space, plus it would be lovely to sleep alone for a while as her body was so huge that sharing a bed had become uncomfortable.

Jack gave her a thankful smile as he grabbed the morning post. The first letter he opened made his brow crease as he pondered its contents.

'What is this Lillian?' he asked shaking the letter. 'It's an invoice for a new blue hat and a dress from Boans. The charge is 22 shillings.'

'Yes Jack. I went and purchased it yesterday and have left it at the store for some readjustments. The hat is coming from Sydney but it will be ready next week on the 23rd. That date is my Wedding Anniversary and I thought that would be a good day to come out of mourning.' Lilly stated with a hint of stern resolve in her voice. She bravely met his gaze, challenging him to disagree with her actions.

Jack stared back at her with his mouth open. His face had become mottled with red blotches and his moustache bristled.

'This is preposterous Lillian. How can you think of such a thing? Your husband has only been dead for two months. What will people think if you are seen parading around in blue. You have been outraged Lillian. This is a public humiliation, you have to consider your reputation. This case has made you public property. You also have to consider what the public is going to think of all of us too. I cannot condone such selfish and frivolous behaviour!'

Everyone in the kitchen stared at the irate man in stunned silence.

Jack was livid. Chrissie gathered up Peggy and ushered Elsie out of the room. This was a private matter between Lilly and her brother.

Lilly turned to face Jack and in a measured but infuriated tone she replied:

'You do not need to lecture me about what was done to me and taken from me Jack. I know what crime was perpetrated against me. I have thought about it every moment for two long months. But I was the victim. The humiliation was not public but it was intensely, invasively private. I did nothing to deserve any of this. And I am not going to live in an embarrassed, self imposed exile for the rest of my days!'

'But you have not thought this through Lillian. The public will not forgive you, they will see this as you being wanton and uncaring. And this is an insult to Harold's memory. Surely you should retain your mourning period for at least a year!' blustered Jack.

Lilly bit her lip, hot tears stung at her eyes.

'Jack, it is because of Harold I am doing this. When James died I strictly adhered to the rules of mourning, wearing black for a year and a day and not participating in any unseemly activities. This was seen as the correct thing to do and society was satisfied. But while I was doing this, I was not being true to myself. I was not mourning James and I was killing myself. Harold took me aside and explained this clearly to me. He was the one who told me to be true to myself. I will miss Harold desperately until the end of my days, but wearing black isn't going to fix this. Next Thursday is my 9th wedding anniversary. This was the happiest day of my life and I will celebrate it with a blue dress and a new blue hat. If you do not want to see this wanton display, I advise you to be in Wubin.'

Lilly let her words sink in as she turned on her heel and left the room. Jack sat with his mouth agape for some moments before he too pushed his chair in and went to find Chrissie.

Loud ranting could be heard until, after about ten minutes, Jack Parrott, carrying the suitcase Chrissie had packed for him, left the Nedlands house. The house settled back to a normal day routine but with a strained and uncomfortable backdrop.

The ladies went as usual to the hospital and spent the day with Vonny. The middle Smith girl was making gradual improvement and already her words were returning. Lilly joked that by the time her hair had grown long enough to put it into pigtails, she would be back to normal again. Of course they all knew that total recovery might never happen but the family was determined to be optimistic.

Jack did not return that evening and Chrissie and Lilly did not discuss the argument or Jack's departure. They had both wanted Jack to go and start work again but Chrissie would never have sanctioned such an angry farewell. She had attempted to appease him before he had left but he was far too angry at his sister. Jack had set himself up as Lilly's moral arbitrator and Lilly was not the compliant, subservient victim he wanted her to be. Jack thought that Lilly was ungrateful and just plain wrong.

There was a wall of unsaid difference between Chrissie and Lilly as they went through the domestic routines that evening. When the children were in bed, both Lilly and Chrissie could think of very little they wanted to say to each other and both retired to their bedrooms just after 8.30pm; although sleep did not come easily to either party.

It seemed that they had only just closed their eyes when a loud banging on the front door announced the arrival of a very late visitor. With bleary eyes, both tousled women stumbled to the front door at 1.30 in the morning in response to the angry knocks. With the trepidation that always accompanies a late visitor, Lilly enquired who it was before slowly unbolting the door. Two police officers stood on the front step.

'Good morning ladies. My apologies for waking you at this unseemly hour but we have some extremely important news for you. Is the man of the house in?' asked the first policeman in a grave voice.

'No, he is away at present. Would you care to come into the sitting room?' asked a very nervous but still polite Chrissie.

Once the small party was settled, the policeman began again, 'are you Mrs Parrott and Mrs Smith and were your husbands the owners of the Smith and Parrott General Store in Wubin?'

'Yes that is correct,' answered Lilly, nervously picking up the past tense in the reference to the store ownership.

'Well I am afraid we have some distressing news for you. Last night the store was totally burnt down and has been completely gutted. No remnant remains.'

Both women gasped. The full realisation of what this meant would come later but the shock of losing this huge part of their lives caused both to be jolted to their cores.

'I am sorry to be the bearer of bad tidings but we have even more disturbing news. At least two persons were present in the store at the time of the fire. One was a male and is now deceased, the other we think may be female. She sustained horrific burns and has been conveyed to the Dalwallinu Hospital but will be transferred to the burns unit at Perth Hospital as soon as this can be arranged. The accommodation unit behind the store was saved and at least one adult and two children were in this location and they are said to be safe.'

Lilly was the first to regain her composure and asked the question she knew haunted both of them.

'Do you know who the dead man is?' she whispered, her voice scratchy with tension.

'Well, no complete identification has occurred as yet and this may take some considerable time as the body has been horrifically burnt. Apparently the victim was carrying a kerosene lantern when he bent down to close off the fuel tanks. The lantern tipped over and the whole place just went up in a fireball explosion. The poor man didn't stand a chance, he would have died instantly.'

'They also found the burns victim quite quickly. Some brave man went inside the burning building and carried her out. He is a real hero. Early accounts seem to indicate that the burnt lady could be Mrs Mabel Martin. Tomorrow, when it is light, an investigative team will be sent up and they will have a better chance of checking if there was anyone else inside.'

The policeman gave the account in halting sentences. The two women sat on the couch - their hands clasped in miserable solidarity.

'My husband was in Wubin from yesterday lunchtime. He owns the store so he would have been there. Do you have any idea of where he is or whether he is the dead man?' Chrissie asked bravely, voicing this fearful thought that had gathered in both of their minds.

'Look I am really sorry Mrs Parrott, we just cannot tell yet. Of course we will have more idea in the morning when some of the eyewitness accounts get to Perth. At present we have just had a series of telegrams from Dalwallinu. As you know, your shop housed the Post Office, so there is no communication possible from the town. We need to wait until we get the first report from the local investigating policeman and that will come in by train.'

'What we can do is pick you up at 7 in the morning and take you to the East Perth Railway Station. Then you can be there with us, when the early morning train comes in. At least then, you will know as soon as we know.'

Five long painful hours away. This seemed an eternity to the two fretful, agitated ladies whose fantastical minds were imagining horrific scenarios. They sat together on the couch, whiling away the slowly passing hous and waiting for the return of the police car. Lillian had decided that Chrissie would go to the station and she would stay with the children. She watched Chrissie anxiously, the stress could trigger an early labour, but by dawn this at least, seemed to be averted.

They passed the long bleak night with repetitive muttering of comforting phrases, re-assuring each other that the dead body would not be Jack's. It wasn't until 5.45am that the first grey streaks of dawn appeared in the eastern sky.

'Go up and get dressed Chrissie. I will make us both a cup of tea,' said Lilly, 'just remember that the worst part is waiting. We'll know soon enough for good or ill.'

The policeman was true to his word and the police car was waiting in front of their home an hour later. So an exhausted, anxious Chrissie was waiting on the platform when the old steam train gushed and wheezed its way into the station. She and the policemen were focussed on the goods section, reasoning that any police dispatch would be arriving via the mail car. Thus they had their backs to the small party of weary passengers who alighted at the East Perth station.

This group were clustered around a stretcher carrying the badly burnt body of Mabel Martin. Dr Anderson walked attentively nearest to the stretcher, monitoring the patient. Her mother, the indomitable Mrs Rowbottom, guided her two sleepy grandchildren towards the waiting ambulance. She had spent a life time coping efficiently with community emergencies but the personal trauma of this one defied even her ability to keep going.

One of the stretcher bearers was her husband, Constable Rowbottom and he had the grim task of carrying his horrifically injured daughter. The waiting ambulance staff walked hurriedly over to the stretcher, loaded it gently into the waiting ambulance and the small party quickly got into the front. The second of the stretcher bearers bent down to gather up his small suitcase and them made his way gingerly over to Chrissie and the waiting police.

His agonised voice disturbed their concentration.

'Chrissie my darling what are you doing here?' Jack Parrott croaked. Chrissie wheeled around at the familiar voice, screaming with the ecstasy of sheer, unrestrained relief.

'Oh Jack you are safe. I had hoped and prayed that it would be so,' and then her voice softened as she croaked, 'Does this mean that the dead man is Charles?'

'Yes, I am afraid so. That wonderful, kind hearted and brave soul has died, may he find peace in death. He was born Seamus Martyn from County Cork in Ireland and may his soul be released to dwell back in that beautiful green land. Still, he died instantly. It's Mabel we are all concerned about now, as she has burnt to within an inch of her life.'

Jack now turned to the waiting policemen, 'I am Mr Jack Parrott and here is the Police Report outlining the circumstances of the fire. Constable Rowbottom completed it, however, he has gone to the hospital as he is related to the couple involved. I was a witness to the accident and I am quite prepared to help in any way with your enquiries. However, at present I ask that I be allowed to go home, as I have had no sleep and I need to settle affairs at home first. I will be heading back to Wubin in the next few days. I was the owner of the store and will need to meet with the investigators.'

Jack reported this to the policeman in a matter of fact but exhausted tone.

'We will drive you and your wife home immediately Sir,' said the Police Sergeant, empathising with the brave man standing in front of him.

So by just after 9 in the morning, Jack and Chrissie returned in the police car to Nedlands and were met by a whirlwind as Lilly raced towards Jack as he got out of the car. She had seen his profile as the car approached and the hours of fear and dread were suddenly discarded in her enthusiastic embrace.

'Be careful please, Lillian,' he announced with the joy of reunion in his voice, as she rushed into his arms, nearly bowling him over in her excitement. 'I have some injuries that I need to take care of you know.'

This was the first he had mentioned his burns. He had spent the time in the car holding hands with his relieved and thankful wife and outlining aspects of the accident to the police. The second policeman had taken down his statement as they drove along.

The recount Jack told the police was as follows:

'I arrived in Wubin just after lunch on the 16th August. I was warmly welcomed by Charles and Mabel Martin who had been running the store exceptionally efficiently since the tragic death of my brother-in-law and partner in the Smith and Parrott Store, Mr Harold Smith. His untimely death occurred in late June.'

'The store had traded normally all afternoon and I worked alongside Charles. At about 4pm Mabel came into the shop to report that her mother, Mrs Rowbottom, had agreed to stay for the evening and so Mabel was able to look after the front counter until 6pm. This gave Charles and me a good chance to review the last two months of trading.'

'At about five to 6 Mabel popped her head in to say that she was just about to close up. Her Mum had made dinner and she suggested that I should go home to get changed first as I was still in my soiled, travelling clothes. She asked Charles to see to the fuel tanks.'

'Charles and I walked out and he went over to get a kerosene lantern. We had only installed the fuel pumps three months ago because of the increase in the number of cars in the region. This had proved very popular and fuel had become our biggest seller. We had developed a very strict system of turning off the fuel every night, for safety.'

'Our home is only three houses down from the shop and I was walking towards my front door when I felt the heat of the explosion. The sound of it was deafening. There were two more explosions as the underground tanks ignited. When I first looked around, the flames were all out the front where the fuel pumps had been. There was just a solid wall of flame, red, yellow and green but with huge billows of black smoke. I couldn't see Charles. After the second explosion the shop front burst into flames. It just erupted. I ran back up the road towards the store but the heat was so intense I couldn't get very close. I ran around the back and yelled to Mrs Rowbottom to get the kids out

of the house. They had their accommodation in the back room, where Lilly and Harold first lived when they moved to Wubin.'

'Then I tried to get into the back of the store but the entry to the shop is through a very narrow door and I couldn't open it. Some type of suction from the fire had wedged it shut. The flames were all over the front but the back still looked all right. I was really worried about Mabel. I hadn't seen her and she would have been at the counter when the tanks had ignited. I smashed the small back window and climbed in, landing just behind the counter. I found Mabel collapsed near the back door, the poor thing hadn't been able to get out. The fumes all around were black, nauseous and choking and I knew I had to get the poor girl out of there and into the fresh air. I couldn't use the window so I just went at the door with all my might. The first time I just bounced. The second time I charged it and it splintered. I went back to get her and carried her outside. That first breath of fresh air was sheer joy.'

'But I am afraid I was too late for Mabel. She was conscious as I lay her on the ground, her clothes had been burnt and her arms and legs were charred. Her beautiful face was red and bleeding and her skin just sloughed off. She asked about the kids and her Mum and I told her everyone was safe. Luckily she had lost consciousness before I could tell her about Charles. He was the love of her life.'

'Anyway that was about it. The whole place burnt to the ground in less than an hour. Our shop, our dreams and our memories. But worse than that, the fire took away our good friends. Charles is dead and poor Mabel has such bad burns, Dr Anderson says she has little hope of surviving. He has had her under sedation but he is afraid she has lost such a lot of skin and her lungs are badly damaged too. The Rowbottoms are beside themselves. Poor Constable Rowbottom had to complete the report and he must feel absolutely devastated.'

Jack had to tell his story over again to Lilly when he was safely at her side in the dining room. This time Lilly was attentive and no remnant of the old animosity remained. Over those long hours when she had been afraid that Jack had died, she had agonised about the harsh words spoken just before their parting.

Not that she wanted to take them back, Lilly still felt exactly the same way. Why did her stubborn brother always want to dominate her and put her down? But she loved him and was overjoyed that he was safely home.

Fires Within
Putting Out The Flames

Evening, 19th August, 1928

Perth, Western Australia

Mrs Ada Nelson took her role as surrogate grandmother very seriously and promptly arrived in town on Saturday 18th August to take two of her grandchildren, Elsie and Peggy Smith, back to the Nelson's farm for the remainder of the August school holidays. This was a huge relief to those left in the Nedlands house. The opportunity for Lilly to handle the after-effects of the shop burning down along with Chrissie's delivery and Clifford Hulme's execution, without her children, was a godsend. Her middle daughter Vonny was still making good progress but she was hospitalized and daily visits were not obligatory.

News from the Wubin store disaster was not good. The shop had been razed. Nothing of their venture remained and the financial implications for the already impoverished family, would prove disastrous.

As the astute doctor had predicted, the seriously burnt Mabel Martin, did not survive for more than twenty four hours. Some in her bereaved family actually expressed some sense of relief when the full extent of her injuries were revealed. She would have lived a scarred and painful existence. It was planned that she would be buried along with her husband on the 21st of August in the Dalwallinu Cemetery.

Jack Parrott had not returned immediately to Wubin. His arms and face were crisscrossed with superficial but painful burns and he was suffering from bruising and exhaustion. Jack had also sustained bad cuts from climbing through the smashed glass of the back store window and his shoulder was severely strained. The Doctor had recommended a few days of bed rest and Jack complied grudgingly. He had never been a compliant patient and now he was fretful, thinking of the ever increasing torrent of worries overcoming his family.

Jack had re-arranged his meetings with the investigative policemen and the insurance agents for the days after the funerals of Charles and Mabel Martin. Jack would represent the family; Chrissie was too far gone in her pregnancy and for Lilly, the pain of her recent bereavement, was still far too raw.

Some momentous dates were set for early September. The Court had set the date of Clifford Hulme's execution for Monday, September 3rd and Jack was determined to be back in Perth by then to support Lillian. He also wanted to be there for Chrissie, as her due date was the 4th September and Elsie and Peggy Smith were coming back to Perth on the train on the 5th September.

'September will be a time of rebirth for us all. A bad life taken and good one given - this will give us all a real sense of renewal,' Jack had reasoned.

So on the evening of the 19th August only three residents remained in the house and one of these, Chrissie Parrott, had indicated to Jack and Lilly that she needed to have an early night. Her pregnant body was starting to revolt; she had late term oedema and the swelling in her feet created thumping, painful spasms by the end of each day. She was irritable, tired, uncomfortable and just wanted the whole thing over and done with. And she still had two more weeks of this discomfort to go!

When Lilly walked out onto the balcony she found her brother looking morosely into his glass of whisky. He spoke without turning: 'Chrissie has had enough of being pregnant and she has started to take it out on me. She just snapped at me when I asked her to massage my arms with burn cream. Would you mind doing it please Lillian? I'm actually feeling relieved that I'm leaving tomorrow.'

Lilly picked up the salve and rolled up his sleeves. She gently dobbed the cream onto each wound and then slowly rubbed the cream onto his arms. She was taken back to a time when she had rubbed his emaciated body to prevent bed sores, after he contracted the debilitating illness that had stopped him from going to war.

'Fourteen years ago I did this for you Jack. When you had brain fever. Mum and I didn't think you were going to make it. It was a harrowing time.' Lilly was suddenly struck with a vision, skinny Jack was coming out of the honeysuckle covered outhouse. His painfully thin body was distressing, but at least he was upright, and at least he was alive!

'Now I am going to let you into a little secret Jack Parrott. I was actually pretty glad you didn't go off to war you know. So many of our young boys didn't survive from that first lot. Look at the agony the Nelsons had to go through when James died?' Lilly reminisced.

'Yet you seemed supportive when Harold went away to fight. Why didn't you try to stop him?' asked Jack in retort, enjoying the soothing feeling of friendly fingers penetrating his skin. It seemed to ease the pain and itch of the healing process of his thousands of little injuries.

'Well I wasn't happy about it but his mind was made up. I didn't try to stop him for the same reason I wouldn't have stopped you from going. I believe that people have a right to tread their own path. Friends and family can only guide them and be there for them when it proves a bit of a wayward road. Plus, did you ever try to stop Harold when he wanted to do something? That man was 'not for turning', that's for sure.' Lilly said, laughing about her late husband's stubbornness.

Jack hesitated. He certainly knew how stubborn Harold had been. So much of this current mess wouldn't have happened if Jack had been able to get him to change his mind.

'Yes, it seems strange all this time later. What was the use of that silly war anyway? I really don't know. Look at this cream, made by Bayer, a good German Company,' Jack said, reverting to the safer topic about the futility of the war.

'Lots of German companies did well out of the war, but I think the German people suffered greatly. That is the way of wars: companies profit, people endure.'

'Yes, we were all filled with patriotic fervour. I felt less of a man because I didn't go. I was scared that someone would give me a white feather or call me a coward.' Jack remembered the passion and zeal of his adolescent self which had driven him and the humiliation he had felt when he was rejected.

'You have always been a bit too worried about what people might think Jack. Who cares about public opinion. I don't. It's being happy within yourself that matters. So are you happy within yourself Jack?' Lilly asked as she gently rolled down his sleeves, looking searchingly into his eyes. The strong bonds of a sibling communication were being re-established. Paring away the distractions that had pulled them apart, here they were, brother and sister again, united against the world.

Suddenly Lilly was looking into his very soul. Jack's eyes grew misty, his Adam's apple bumped dejectedly in his throat. Jack and Lilly had not been this close for many years.

'No I am not happy within myself Lilly,' Jack's voice was rough and raw with emotion. 'In fact I am terribly and agonisingly unhappy with myself. If you really want to know!' Lilly misread the enormity of his confession: 'Oh Jack that sounds very melodramatic. Why on earth are you not happy, you are just about to become a father?'

'Don't worry about it Lilly,' Jack replied, catching himself before he said too much.

'Now that will be enough of that Jack Parrott. I can tell when you have something that you need to share. So out with it!' Lillian stated, but her intrigue was laced with disquiet, she sensed that something was coming that she was not prepared for.

Jack thought deeply before he responded: 'Well if you think you are ready for it? I am going to tell you some secrets and they are really hard to say and they will be very hard for you to listen to. I'm only telling you because you seem stronger now. You were always the strong one in the family you know. I only gave you such a difficult time because you always bounced back. It made me feel strong and powerful to put you down.'

'Well that probably made me more resilient in the long run anyway,' Lilly laughed, 'now back to these secrets, if they are causing you pain, you must tell me.'

'You may not be so keen on calling me brother after I share these burdens with you.'

'You are so sensational Jack. As if I would ever not count you as my brother. So tell me your worst. I am ready.' Lilly was still in control, apprehensive yes, but she was sure that she was ready. How bad could these secrets really be?

'You are not to interrupt me Lillian. Just sit in silence and let me talk. And at the end you can make comment or you can just leave if you want. I doubt that there will be anything positive that you are going to want to say anyway.'

Jack's voice was now low and measured: 'Now the reason I feel bad is because I am cursed, I have sent two good men to their deaths. And I am about to condemn another to death and, despite him being the worst kind of evil, I even worry about the wisdom of this!'

Jack had started the saga. Lillian thought this seemed over theatrical but she had promised him silence so she let him continue. These deaths had happened but how Jack could feel that he was responsible had her fascinated.

'The only two other men who knew this story are now both dead. One was Harold, the other was Charles Martin and now I am sharing it with you because it is only fair that you know the facts. The hell you have gone through is because I kept things secret. You just said that you believe that people have a right to tread their own path and friends and family can only guide them. I have worked out my path and it is to tell you the truth. Once you have the information, you can work out what path you want to tread. Whatever you decide, I will not stop you.'

Lilly still felt that Jack was being histrionic and was accepting blame for events that, in truth, none of them had ever had any real control over. Still she let him go. If her brother was unfairly blaming himself and she could absolve him of blame, this would be a successful result.

Jack looked at her with sad, apologetic eyes and slowly made his pronouncement: 'I know Clifford Hulme is insane, or at least he was insane when he murdered Harold and attacked you and the girls. He was suffering a psychotic attack and he had no medication to lessen the impact and I did nothing to help the Defence discover what I know, in fact I prevented it. I said the opposite in court. I have committed perjury.'

Lilly took in a sharp inhalation. This was certainly not what she expected.

'Clifford Hulme is a drug addict. He is hopelessly addicted to tablets which are based on a drug that resembles morphine or heroin. He suffers from a mental condition that was diagnosed as a type of schizophrenia. A doctor in the British Army diagnosed this many years ago. He prescribed Cliff tablets that stopped these 'moods' and allowed him to live a normal life. I know all of this because I used to procure these tablets for him and I gave them to him for three years. While he was on these tablets no events happened, that I was aware of, and Clifford lived a normal life. It was only after the tablets were withdrawn that Clifford's pre-existing mental condition came back and that is when these horrific things occurred.'

Jack took a long, deep drink of his whisky. Perhaps he hoped the bitter, mind numbing liquid would give him the courage to go on. Lilly stayed silent. This was explosive and unknown to her, if she spoke up she was sure Jack would clam up. Still, she was now feeling very uncomfortable. Perhaps she wanted him to stop telling her these things. Perhaps she was not yet strong enough to handle these things and her mind would slip back into the zombie like trance of a month ago.

Lilly let Jack continue: 'I know all of this because I have read the Army Doctor's report. Cliff does suffer from 'black moods', and while he is in these moods he does bad things. I know because I have seen one and I know he has no memory of what he has done when he recovers. His brain does hear voices and they tell him to do horrible things. I have watched him going through one of these moods and seen him convulse and argue with these voices. And I have seen how all of this is suddenly fixed when he takes one of his little white tablets. The Defence team tried to tell the Jury about this but they had no proof. There was no-one who had witnessed one of these moods. Well, Harold and I had and I never said a thing about it.' Jack gulped loudly with the pain of his admission.

'Last year the Australian Government banned these tablets so I couldn't get them for him anymore. When I told him, Cliff went crazy and wrecked the store. So Harold came up with a scheme to help him get off the tablets. He thought he was being kind. You know how he was, always keen on helping out people who are down on their luck. I called the scheme 'Harold's Project'. Harold took Clifford out to the farm and steadily decreased how many tablets he was given every day.'

'When you and the girls came up to live at the farm, I quizzed Harold about how safe you would be but he got really angry with me. He felt that everything was under control but I was really worried. By mid June, Cliff had been taken off all of his tablets. That is why he was sick and had such bad headaches. The 'black mood' that came on him that day was much worse than the one I had seen but I have no doubt that is what happened. He did do those horrible things but he was insane when he did them. It was the demon inside Clifford Hulme which the tablets kept satiated that did those horrible things and Harold and I let it happen!'

Jack's voice was reduced to a hoarse whisper as he continued with his gruesome confession, 'Clifford had spent his whole life coping with the effects of his black moods. Then in the Army, a kindly doctor comes along and gives a name to what he suffers from and provides him with tablets and a letter. This letter lets Cliff be totally normal for ten years and then we take his tablets off him! Cliff isn't that smart. He didn't think we were being kind, he hated us because we took away his chance to be normal. He just thought we were monsters.'

'Now you are probably cross with me already but it gets worse. I stole the cover page and two of the pages from the Army Doctor's report; that made the evidence they bought into court inadmissible. They didn't even have the Army Doctor's name. I had taken the parts out which proved their case. I just wanted Clifford Hulme to die because of what he had done to you, to the girls and to Smithy.'

'But I know what was in those pages and that is why I cannot sleep. The fire that burnt down the store has taken away those pages for ever. They are now destroyed so no-one can ever see them. But I know - they are in my conscience.'

Jack took another deep drink. He had stopped looking at Lilly. Meeting her eyes after his admission of this betrayal would have been too much to bear. Lilly said nothing, she was past words and had moved to an area where swirling, colliding thoughts were crashing into her brain. She had moved into a brain storm; the screaming 'what ifs'.

'After Harold's funeral, Charles Martin saved me when I made the first catastrophic decision to drink myself into oblivion. He did not offer moral judgment but just implied that I was taking the coward's way out and I have always been a bit worried when people call me a coward. He also sat with me and listened as I talked and I ranted and he led me back to rationality again. So I came back and helped you through the inquest and the trial. I was strong for you and I protected you but I was a bit late! Every time I looked at you, I felt like a sham. I could have saved you from rape and the children from abuse. I knew back in January that this could happen and I DID NOTHING.' Jack shouted.

Jack stopped and lit a cigarette, sucking it angrily and then letting the smoke swirl before continuing.

'Now over this period I did do something, secretly. I found and contacted the British Army Doctor, Dr Amran Singh Samran. He is now the head of Psychiatric Medicine at the Edward IV College of Medicine in Singapore. He wrote back to me saying he clearly remembered Pte Hulme and the sadness he had felt at the sorry turn of events. The Doctor was quite prepared to come to Western Australia, to examine the accused and to testify for Clifford Hulme. He indicated that advances have been made in this field over the last two years and he was certain that Clifford would now have a better diagnosis and that there was a good chance he could be stabilised with long term treatment and care.'

'Dr Samran even provided a document that he had prepared in the Army which outlined Clifford Hulme's medical condition. This was the evidence that enabled him to be granted a medical discharge based on his mental instability.'

'This letter arrived before the inquest but I kept it secret. I took it to show Charles Martin, before he died last week and we talked about all of this. He knew a few things about hate and revenge. He said that he understood and would not pass judgment on me if I did nothing. The evil things that were done to Harold, to you Lillian and to the wee lasses were very personal. But he also knew what was on those pages and what Dr Samran had said.'

'Charles advised me that one man cannot tread another man's road to hell, he does this all by himself. But he also told me that, if it was him, he would use the Army Doctor's letter to get Clifford Hulme a stay of execution. If the Defence had known about the documents or if Dr Samran had been asked to testify, the Jury would have come down with an insane verdict and Clifford Hulme would not have been sentenced to death. And if he was placed in an Insane Asylum he would now have careful monitoring and medication that would ensure that he does not do something like this again. Now the fire has taken the Doctor's second letter too, it has all been burnt along with the wonderful Charles Martin.'

'I have memorised the original covering letter and this is what it said:

'Pte Clifford Hulme has been under my care for over two years. He is suffering from anxiety and delusions possibly caused though schizophrenia. I recommend that he is provided with Heroin tablets or an alternative with a similar active ingredient, for the stabilisation of this condition. The provision of these tablets will enable Clifford Hulme to live a normal life. If he is deprived of them his quality of life will suffer.'

It was signed by: *Dr Amran Singh Samran, of the British Imperial Forces on October 6th, 1918.'*

Jack had recited the letter - burnt into his memory. Finally Jack turned and looked at Lilly and his look was haunted and disturbed.

'Now this is not the worst thing Lillian. There is something that I did not tell Harold or Charles. Before I sent Cliff out to the farm, I had secured another batch of tablets. Here they are, 200 little white tablets. Enough for at least two years. Do with them what you will. These would have saved Harold's life, stopped you being raped and prevented little Vonny from being brain damaged. I have sat on these for six months.'

'So I give them to you. I just do not know what to do with these or with any of this information. You have always been the strong one and I am asking you for help. You choose. I will testify to all of it. Even though I have committed perjury, the truth is now more important to me. I am so deeply ashamed and so totally sorry for all of the evil that I have done.'

Lilly sat for a while in horrified silence. She looked at the little white tablets, ghostly in the moonlight. Just one of these could have kept Clifford's demons at bay. She would have had a husband still. She wouldn't have been viciously raped. Her girls would not have been assaulted and Vonny would not have brain damage. These men had conspired to keep these secrets from her and they had ruined her life.

Restorative Justice
Lillian Hardens Her Resolve

23rd August, 1928

Perth, Western Australia

Pottery. The appropriate gift for a 9th year wedding anniversary. Well, probably in the strictest sense, both partners should still be alive before a couple should be eligible for a present. Still Lilly had decided to overlook this technicality. She stared, enraptured, at the cute little pottery vase with the pretty red capped parrot on it. And the parrot was perched in amongst eucalypt blossoms. It had just shouted at her to be purchased when she had seen it in Boans yesterday as she had picked up her hat and dress.

'See Harold, you are gone but never forgotten,' she whispered to her unseen but ever present friend. 'And today I intend to remember you. You always liked me in blue so the tut tutting busybodies can mind their own business for a change. I'm coming back to the world of the living.'

Lilly had put on her new blue dress and her hat and she breathed in deeply before leaving the room. 'I'll need you beside me. This will take some courage,' she said to her husband's spirit as she went out, determined to recapture her former sense of self belief.

After Jack's unbelievable revelation, Lilly had spent days in deep concentration. She had taken long walks, pushed herself ever harder into her domestic chores and kept frenetically and crazily busy. What she didn't do is discuss any of this with anyone.

Jack had left for Wubin on Monday morning and Lilly had been polite but aloof, giving him no hint as to what she would do with the information. Her brother left, anxiously wondering and more than a bit distressed, at how she would respond to the burden he had dumped on her. Their relationship had altered, irrevocably changed, with Lilly being most definitely ascendant.

The only person Lilly had discussed this with was Harold. In her head, while she took long strenuous walks along the river bank, Lilly had turned the thoughts over and over. She had gone over her grief, berated the world for the unjustness of the situation and re-lived her horror at how the men she had most trusted, had all been responsible for her nightmare.

By Tuesday she had forgiven Harold and he had guided her in determining what she would do now with her new knowledge.

'What doesn't kill you, makes you stronger. You are only being given this information because you will be able to use it for good. Don't punish the men who kept things from you. They were all following their own conscience and now you need to follow yours.' These quintessentially Harold's words had come to Lilly as she walked along the muddy sands of Matilda Bay, staring out at the waterbirds cavorting over the beautiful expanse of the Swan River.

This hardening of resolve had led to her first steps of defiance when, on Thursday, she had cast off her mourning clothes. It felt so different to wear something with colour and as she looked into the mirror she practiced a smile - and she saw her own dancing eyes looking back at her. She swanned confidently into the kitchen where Chrissie was waddling uncomfortably over to put the kettle on the stove.

'Lilly you look lovely. The colour is superb but you have lost so much weight, you're as thin as a pin. Still you look so much better and you have a new glow lighting up your face. I am glad Jack is not here though, he certainly wouldn't approve.' Chrissie had been aware and supportive of the plan and was happy to see Lilly looking more positive after her anxious, driven week.

'Come on Chrissie, we're not having breakfast here. I'm taking you down to the Tea Rooms at Matilda Bay and we're going to have breakfast in style. I need to talk to you about a few things that I am planning to do and I doubt whether my brother will be happy about any of them. You look like you are ready to burst and you shouldn't be on your feet at all. I'll go up and get your hat for you.'

Chrissie was given no opportunity to object. Lilly had organised for a taxi cab from the newly formed Swan Taxi Company to pick them up at 9am and the car was right on time.

At the tea rooms the ladies were given a polite, although reserved greeting by the head waiter and ushered into an alcove off the spacious balcony. Pregnant women were rarely seen out in society, so modesty decreed they be placed away from the public gaze. The river was a deep blue, dotted with a few sail boats and sunlight glinted cheerfully on the dancing waves.

The ladies perused the menu and relished the scandalous extravagance of dining out. Lilly reasoned that her discussions could wait until after they had eaten and was concentrating on her breakfast when Chrissie's soft but urgent cry broke into her thoughts:

'Oh no,' gushed Chrissie in horror, her face stricken and ghostly white, 'I have wet myself.' When Lilly looked down, the beautiful polished wooden floor under Chrissie was flooded with rivulets of water.

'This is terrible, I can't stop it Lilly, my under clothes and dress are completely soaked. How am I ever going to get out of here and back home; I am so embarrassed.'

'You're not going home Chrissie silly girl, your waters have broken. We are going to the Rosalie Private Hospital straight away, you are having your baby,' said Lilly gleefully taking control.

Lilly rushed over to the embarrassed head waiter who went to organise a Taxi Cab for the two ladies. He also hastily arranged for a privacy screen to be placed around Chrissie and shifted two tables of shocked and unimpressed customers to other parts of the restaurant.

By 11.30am Chrissie was settled in her birthing suite at the very discrete private hospital; this luxury provided thanks to the generosity of the Nelsons. There was no sign of any contractions yet but the experienced midwife assured the ladies that they would be sure to start soon.

'All your signs are good Chrissie. This is it. Just the birthing bit to get through and you will have a bonny, bouncing baby. Now I am going to leave you for a few hours. The midwife said you will not have your baby until I get back. We are so close to Vonny here so I will just go over and see her for half an hour and I need to go home to get your birthing bag. You haven't even got a night dress with you.'

As it turned out Lilly returned to the hospital just after 3 in the afternoon, bearing Chrissie's suitcase and a bouquet of tulips and daffodils that she had purchased from the green grocer on the corner. True to the midwife's prediction, Chrissie was now definitely in labour and was experiencing mild, but regular contractions. These were still about ten minutes apart and the pain was not causing her any major discomfort.

What was creating her more distress were the loud shrieks coming from the lady in the birthing room next door. This woman was begging for pain relief and had been shouting obscenities with every contraction from the moment she had entered the hospital not long after Lilly's return.

Mrs Elizabeth Collins was not prepared to go through the ordeal of giving birth to an unwanted child without causing discomfort and embarrassment to as many people as possible. By 4.30pm harassed midwives provided Mrs Collins with anaesthetic in the form of ether and her cursing and screams were gradually reduced. The complication of this course of action was that her labour would be seriously prolonged as Mrs Collins had not yet entered the stage of labour when her own efforts were not required.

Having heard these interchanges reverberating down the corridors and coming through the walls, Chrissie vowed to Lilly that she would try her best to handle the pain with decorum. However, by 7.30pm Chrissie's labour pains were causing her extreme discomfort and the nurse recommended some ether.

'We will only give her a small amount and she will be able to get a few hours sleep. Her delivery is still a long way off,' the nurse had said to Lilly. 'You can take a break too, perhaps you should go and get yourself some dinner. Or you could go down to our Father's Room at the back. There are some comfortable chairs in there and you may be able to get a bit of sleep yourself, it could be a long night.'

Thus Lilly found herself entering a large, well appointed room at the rear of the rambling hospital. This room was built for comfort and long stays and included large leather lounge chairs, a day bed, a book case complete with books and newspapers and was dominated by a long, central jarrah table.

Lilly was not alone in the room, a tall, strangely dressed gentleman was at the table and was writing furiously. The man was quite young and attractive but he was dressed in a rather dated manner in a suit that would have been more at home on John Nelson and a homburg hat like her father had loved to wear! He was sporting a well trimmed, short beard and a full neat moustache.

The young man stood straight up when she entered the room and looked at her in an embarrassed, rather uncomfortable fashion, as though she was familiar to him already and their interaction had not been a pleasant one.

Lilly entered the room with feigned confidence, although in truth she was feeling a little bit nervous about entering the Father's Room, supposedly the bastion of male privacy in this very female establishment.

'Excuse me. I am sorry to disrupt your work. The nurse sent me down here to have a rest as my sister-in-law is sleeping. She has been sedated so there will be little happening in her birthing room for some hours.'

'Please come in, you are certainly not disturbing me. I would appreciate someone to talk to. I have been here for many hours already and I fear that I may be here for many more. The reports are that my wife will be many hours before she gives birth.'

Eustace Wilkinson responded, trying desperately to act normal.

But this situation was anything but normal. Here he was in the room, attempting polite discourse, with a lady whom he had offended so grossly. Still, she seemed not to recognise him. But that was perfectly understandable, he had seen her in the hospital and in court but she had not been in any state to recognise him. Plus in this ridiculous outfit he doubted if even his close kin would know it was him.

'Your wife must be the lady next door to our room. She does not seem to be having a very easy time of it,' Lilly said kindly. She had interpreted his discomfort as embarrassment over his wife's unseemly and petulant display.

'I apologise if you have been disturbed, Elizabeth has not suffered in silence that is for sure. However she has now been anaesthetized and hopefully the birth can continue without her having any more part in it. I am Mr Edward Collins and I already know that you are Mrs Smith, am I right?' As Eustace talked he felt he was gaining control over his initial turmoil.

'Yes I am Mrs Lillian Smith and I am afraid that my fame extends further than I would wish. I am here as the companion to my sister-in-law, Chrissie Parrott, who is having her first child. The father, my brother Jack, is away and he is not scheduled to return until next week and so will miss the birth. I have been by her bedside all afternoon providing her solace, support and of course my advice. It must be far worse for you as a potential father; birthing must be a lonely and fairly boring vigil when you are denied any real involvement.'

'Well I must admit that it does take a long time but this has already been a real eye opener. Men are never allowed to know much about all of this 'woman's only business'. My wife has already had two children but I was not involved in these births. Now, I wonder if you can explain something to me as I am a little confused about what is going on and the nursing staff are too busy or they feel it is not seemly for me to know. I thought it was just a matter of coming into hospital and pushing the baby out.

What is going on and why is it taking so much time?' Eustace was indeed disturbed by her presence but his natural inquisitiveness forced him to ask some questions that had perturbed him over the last few hours. He wanted to know what was going on!

Lilly was a bit disconcerted by this inquiry. Polite men didn't ask such questions and polite ladies certainly didn't respond, particularly to men they did not know! Still, Lilly had never been overly worried about decorum so she launched into an explanation.

'Well Mr Collins to understand this you need to know a little about a female's anatomy. The baby lives in the womb over the pregnancy but it has to travel down a very small narrow passage called the birth canal to get out into the world. But before the baby can start its journey, the womb needs to open to the size of the baby's head. This is the first stage of labour and this is what your wife and Chrissie are doing at present. The contractions are causing the womb to open. It can take many hours and it is very painful. Once the womb is fully open, the real action can happen and the two ladies will push their littlies out.'

Eustace was taken aback by her candid response but very appreciative as this had confused him all afternoon. He had asked the nurses but none of them had given him more than a rudimentary and most unsatisfactory explanation.

'So if they give the mother ether can this still happen? Won't the drugs make the womb sleepy too? Doesn't she have to be awake and active for the process to work?'

'Well I'm not a medical person but I think it's like your heart - it still beats when you are asleep. This is like the womb, it can still do its job when the mother is not conscious, I think. But they do like the mother to be fully awake by the time she gets to the second stage of labour. This is when she needs to push, so hopefully she will be fully recovered and ready to go for this stage,' announced Lilly.

'Thank you for your frank and clear explanation Mrs Smith. It would help if they let us fathers know a bit more about the mysteries of childbirth and then we may be a little more sympathetic. It all sounds very confusing and complicated and I had no idea it was so painful. The sounds alone are very distressing and I doubt that I would want to be much closer than this!'

'Well I have gone through three births and while they were not pleasant, the joy and happiness which comes from the birth of a healthy baby makes it all worthwhile. They always say that when the baby is born the memory of the pain of labour is immediately wiped away,' said Lillian wistfully recalling not only her beautiful girls but the painful reality that, for her, there would not be any more children.

'I am afraid this will not happen in Elizabeth's case. She does not welcome this child. This has not been a happy confinement and she will have no joy in the birth. So for her the pain feels like a curse, which perhaps explains her bad language and evil temper.'

Eustace was verging on dangerous territory here, but he was discomforted. He knew he was sworn to keep his sister's secret but this lady was quite disarming and he already felt a trust with her. Of course he knew this was ridiculous, as Edward Collins a casual liaison could be formed, but as Eustace Wilkinson he would be reviled.

'That is so sad for both of you. Are you looking forward to the birth? It will be a double tragedy if neither parent is celebrating the arrival of the child. I am sure the baby is excited to be arriving and I doubt that it is the babe's fault that the mother is cross with her pregnancy.' Lilly's sympathies were clearly on the side of the baby and the way she said it, made Eustace think that she was absolutely right.

'You are so right. Actually, I am very excited,' he said and he was. All his uncle's juices were flowing. He had not had anything to do with Elizabeth's older children and Marjorie was childless. This was the first 'little Wilkinson' he would know and he was definitely delighted about it. Playing the father surrogate was really getting under his skin.

'Now it is still terrible if the mother is not pleased but do not despair, when she looks into the face of her little babe she will bond. Mothers always do. The baby will start to suckle and Elizabeth will just love it, don't worry,' Lilly had answered with certainty.

'Sadly this will not be happening. Elizabeth doesn't want to even see the baby after it is born, she has already made plans for the babe to be adopted. She is quite content with the family she already has and will return to that household after the birth. There are private aspects regarding the circumstance which produced this child, that brings her heartbreak and shame. I am afraid she will never accept this child.'

Lilly looked at Eustace with shock, registering the significance of his words. They awoke empathic chords from her own tragic experience.

'Look Mr Collins, you clearly knew me when I first walked in, so you must know at least some of my story. This may seem rather presumptuous of me as I do not know Elizabeth's circumstance and it may have no resemblance to my own, but I feel qualified to speak on this topic. As you may know I was cruelly abused and subject to an outrage so I know the full horror of having an unwanted sexual encounter. Now this has brought me and my family shame and the dreadful memory of it makes me shudder with revulsion. But I can honestly say, that if I had become pregnant from such an event, I would still want to see the child loved and brought up in a happy family. It is not the child's fault. Now an adoptive family may provide this loving home but what about if it didn't, or one was not found. I could not stand by and watch any child born of my loins, be brought up in an institution or become a Ward of the State purely because of the sins of the parents or an unspeakable episode.'

Lilly had spoken with eloquence and compassion but it was the subject she had spoken of that was truly disturbing. Eustace was shocked to his core, ladies in this era did not speak about rape. She had endured this awfulness and still had enough concern to seek a positive result for any child that resulted from such a hateful act. Her quiet, wounded, unconquered dignity was simply astounding.

'You are obviously an amazing lady and I am swayed by your words. I do not want to see the child adopted either, I suppose I had not thought this one through properly. Now I will let you into a small confidence, Elizabeth is actually my sister and the real Mr Edward Collins is not the father of this baby. That is why I am here to provide support and to preserve Elizabeth's reputation. No-one in here must know this, so I will keep my real name from you for the moment. So what do you think I should do?'

Eustace hardly noticed that he had broken his sister's confidence. His allegiance had definitely shifted and Marjorie and Elizabeth would not be pleased but keeping this secret from Lillian just didn't seem right in light of the sincerity of her recent disclosure.

Lilly responded: 'It is of course, not really my decision but if it was my sister's child and for some reason she could not or did not want to raise it, then I would. After all, it is your blood and this young babe is your family but I will leave this to you and your conscience. You will know what to do when you look into the baby's eyes. I will bet that you will not be able to give it away - you are far too kind hearted. But you have the added hurdle that you are a man and such decisions may not be so easy for you to take. Either way, your family may not be too happy about it!'

Lilly could so clearly see the proper path and had no hesitation in pointing it out to him. And he knew she was right. Eustace sat for a while in shocked silence, contemplating this interaction and weighing up what he should do.

Suddenly Eustace took stock of himself, this wasn't meant to be happening. They were engaging in a conversation which would imply they were lifelong confidants not recent acquaintances. Lilly was oblivious to the real worries and concerns that Eustace harboured. He knew Mrs Lillian Smith intimately, even though he had never really met her until today. He had been her unauthorized biographer making public the most private aspects of her life; he had even stolen her love letters. He had dredged through her past, exposed her shame and raked mud over her name.

And now he was talking to her, having normal conversations, very intimate ones at that and he was petrified unless she should find him out. He was the Judas who had sold her out. But the worst part of all of this, is that Eustace found himself to be totally smitten. This self composed and attractive lady in front of him was absolutely delightful.

Should he continue to have conversations with this charming but seriously wounded lady? He had already shared that his name was fake but he knew he was on borrowed time. She may not recognise him, but Chrissie Parrott most certainly would. Or worse still, if the father-to-be Jack Parrott arrived, he would not only recognise him but he might do him some form of serious injury.

Eustace Wilkinson was at a loss, totally disarmed and not capable of making any wise or astute decisions when a nurse came to the door with a large parcel wrapped in newspaper.

'Excuse me, are you Mr Collins? This is the fish and chips you ordered earlier from the shop down the road. A boy has delivered it and here is your change Sir.'

The nurse handed over the large package and a mouth watering aroma arose from the paper wrappings.

'Can I eat it in here please nurse?' Eustace requested politely.

'Please yourself Sir. Fathers do all sorts of things in here while they are waiting for their littlies to be delivered. Just make sure the left overs are thrown in the bin so we don't attract rodents if you please,' the nurse replied as she turned to leave.

The large package lay on the jarrah table and the scent which wafted around the room was irresistible.

'Would you care to share some of my fish and chips. It is not the most high class meal but it's certainly tasty. Plus I have over-ordered, I thought perhaps Elizabeth might want some but she is not allowed to eat and I would be happy to share with you,'

Eustace said betraying his affection.

'That is a very kind offer Mr Collins, thank you so much. I have been so busy that I have not eaten all day and I am starving. Sharing a meal with you will be wonderful.'

Ignoring their burning fingers, the hungry pair were soon savouring the enjoyable meal of mouth watering portions of hot fish and salty chips, all doused with vinegar. The food was delicious and more than satiated their hunger. Both licked their fingers and devoured the tasty offering that had been delivered all wrapped in Monday's West Australian Newspaper.

The fatty residue oozed into the newsprint but could not obscure Eustace's daily opinion piece in which he had waxed lyrical about the varying types of executions currently being used across the world. Eustace had clearly explained the advantages and disadvantages of the various Government sanctioned methods currently in use: firing squad, hanging, stoning and the new method being introduced into the USA, electrocution.

Eustace saw the oily words and his shame and mortification grew. His words were greasy, his intention slippery and he felt complete humiliation in the face of this virtuous, wronged lady.

He quickly gathered the soiled papers and rolled them up to remove any reminder of their meal and more importantly his venomous pen. The food had satisfied their hunger and Eustace was desperately seeking a way that he could wriggle out of his dilemma with some honour, when Lillian suddenly turned to him:

'Mr Collins or whatever your real name is, this may seem impertinent as I have only just met you, but I already feel we have a bond of friendship. I am in need of male assistance. There are some things I really want to do but I cannot do them alone and I cannot ask any of my family or any of my acquaintances to help me. For them it would be too personal. Will you help me please Sir?'

Lilly was about to take a huge gamble, she did not know this man at all. He was a complete stranger but she was determined to go down a particular path and for this she needed a male accomplice. In the world of 1928, the road she wanted to tread was barred to women, even strong minded ones.

'Mrs Smith I do know your story. I know it well and before I go on any further, I want to pass my sincere condolences on to you for all of the misfortune that has beset you and your family. You have suffered loss, calamity and heartbreak. Most families do not have to face in a lifetime what you have had to face in a few months.'

'I have watched you from afar and, having now met with you, my heart is wrenched by the anguish and suffering you have undergone and I admire your courageous recovery. Your dignity in the face of adversity is amazing. Any other woman would be still confined to her bed, letting others take the lead and accepting the charity of friends, family and society.'

'Now I see in front of me a lady all dressed in blue, no longer wearing widow's weeds and showing a quiet but determined sense of resolve. A vision of loveliness but also a vision of great strength. I do not know what you are going to ask me but I vow that I will assist you in any way that I can. What is it that you want me to do for you?'

Lilly took a deep breath relieved at his reply. Most men would have reprimanded her sternly about her unseemly behaviour and putting herself at risk by trusting a total stranger. This man had taken her on her word and she liked that.

'Somehow, I need to get inside Fremantle Prison and speak to the convicted murderer Clifford Hulme. There are questions I need to ask him and there are things I need to tell him. And it has to be very soon as his execution is set for Monday week. I have no idea how to organise such a thing and I have never been anywhere near the prison let alone sought to go inside it. But there is a constraint. No-one can know, not ever. Not my family, not the lawyers and definitely not the press. Can you please help me to do this?' Lilly Smith asked, her brown eyes beseeching him.

'I hate to ask you to help me but it is very important and I do not know who else to turn to.'

Eustace was absolutely floored. In his wildest dreams he had not expected this and, as his heart did a little jump, he resolved to help her achieve her goal.

Restorative Justice
Two Babes

24th August, 1928

Perth, Western Australia

Just after midnight Lilly gave Chrissie's hand a comforting squeeze. She was now in the pushing stage of her labour and Chrissie Parrott was putting in every effort to get her baby into the world. The ether had long since worn off and the mother was experiencing every sensation; she now clearly knew why it was called labour and she certainly knew how much it hurt.

With Lilly at her side and the experienced midwife shouting for her to 'push hard,' Chrissie entered into another long, painful contraction. She gave it all she could and then the midwife announced that the head was crowning. Everyone in the birthing room relaxed, entering into a latent period before the next push, everyone that is except the little baby Parrott. The baby was keen on coming into the world at once, mid-contraction and just squeezed out, all slippery and mucousy, right into the pan at the bottom of the bed.

The nursing staff scrambled to rescue the babe and with a huge 'hurrah' placed the little wriggly, girl baby onto her mother's chest. The baby took a life starting breath of air and instantly was suffused with a rosy pink glow and she let out her first yowl as the medical staff cut and tied the umbilical cord.

Lilly was weeping excitedly as she watched the euphoria flooding Chrissie's face.

'You've done it. Well done Chrissie, you have a lovely, healthy baby daughter. Now at long last I am an auntie and Elsie, Vonny and Peggy all have a little girl cousin. Jack is going to be so pleased and I am so proud of you.' Lilly gushed, ecstatically happy, however she was also mindful of the midwives and the medical staff at the end of the bed. A successful birth is only declared when the difficult next stage is achieved and a lot can still go wrong. Still all looked normal and no-one seemed to be panicking, so Lilly started to relax.

Over the next hour Lilly stayed by Chrissie's side, watching as the babe was cleaned and started to suckle. By just after 2am the nursing staff had taken away the infant and took Mrs Parrott down to a nursing ward and prepared her for a well deserved sleep.

'You are free to go Mrs Smith, I think this new mum will sleep well for the next few hours. You may like to go to bed in our visitor's room where you too should get some sleep while you have the chance,' said the competent and kindly midwife.

'Thank you so much, you're right and I am very tired, but before I go can you tell me how Mrs Collins is progressing? I was speaking to her husband earlier and I know he was very concerned.'

'Her labour is not going so smoothly. Even though she has had two previous births she is most fractious and has shown little regard for herself or for the baby. She has demanded both ether and chloroform in large quantities. She seems unwilling to experience even the slightest discomfort and the birth has proceeded very slowly. She is now entering the second stage but in her drugged state she will not be able to push, so the little baby will need to be delivered by forceps. The child must be quite lethargic from all of those drugs and hopefully this will not affect it too much. We have called in a Doctor to do this birth as it could be a very problematic delivery,' announced the midwife, speaking with just a hint of annoyance at the mother who had shown such little regard for her new offspring. This midwife was passionate about babies too.

Over the long hours at Chrissie's bedside, Lilly had been contemplating her discussions with 'the man whom she now knew was not really Mr Collins'.

What did she know about him? Almost nothing. So why did she trust and like him? Most men of her acquaintance did not relish talking to women and certainly didn't accept them as equals in a conversation but this man had. Lilly had warmed to this. Something about this gentleman made her feel good, accepted in a way she hadn't felt for a very long time.

Now she was not fooled, this in no way paralleled how she had felt about Harold, her soul mate and the love of her life. Their's had been a sacred union and Lillian knew that no-one would ever replace Harold Smith. No, this was more about a trusted friendship and she felt a sense of fun when she was with this gentleman. And fun had certainly been missing from her life of late!

She had asked the spirit of Harold whether she could depend on 'the man whom she now knew was not really Mr Collins' and he had indicated 'yes' so this was a positive sign. Plus she had realised who he reminded her of - he was the very essence of James Nelson.

They were unlike in looks, James' hair had been red and his colouring was pale with dusty freckles; this man had darker tanned skin and brown wavy hair and was much taller. But there was definitely a similar devilish glint in both of their eyes and that charismatic smile would thaw an iceberg. That was pure James. But the characteristic that was most similar was that he possessed a carefree, almost flippant nature that concealed a serious, kind heartedness.

As she walked to the visitors' bedroom she hesitated, Lilly felt that she had no right to feel so exhilarated about her new niece when her new friend must be despairing about the chances of his sister's child. She turned and retraced her steps to the father's room, where a reading light showed that the man she knew as Mr Collins was still awake.

'How are you? It is nearly 2.30am and you are still hard at work, it must be important material that you are working on. Have you had any sleep at all?' she asked the man who was again bent over his papers.

'Oh hello. I hear your sister-in-law has had a little girl. Congratulations. How was the birth?' Eustace looked up and gave her that wonderful smile.

'Yes they are both well and thankfully asleep now. The little girl seems healthy and weighed in at 7lbs and is nearly 20 inches long. It was fascinating to watch the birth. It is very different when you are giving birth than watching one. Somehow it seems to explain our reason to be on this earth when you see the miracle of childbirth. The giving of life is just such an amazing gift,' Lilly said, still overwhelmed with the euphoric feeling of the night.

'And does the little Parrott have a name yet? I hope they are not going to call her Polly,' joked Eustace.

'No, not yet and don't laugh. I used to get called Polly all the time when I was a school girl. How is Elizabeth going, have you had any progress reports?'

'It has not been an easy delivery apparently. They have kept Elizabeth sedated throughout the birth. The Doctor is in there now and the nurse told me that they would have news for me any minute. They are worried as the baby is showing no vital signs or movement but they are hopeful that the cold air at birth will jolt it back into life.'

Lilly went over and put a comforting hand on the man's shoulder. His voice was harsh and scratchy revealing his worry about this development.

'You know the stupid thing is that a still birth would be just such a perfect solution to this whole debacle. Elizabeth and her husband would be perfectly satisfied with such an eventuality. So why does it feel so horrible to contemplate?' Eustace spoke with misty eyes and a heaviness in his chest. 'Still that is something I have no control over at the moment and I am sure the medical staff are doing everything possible.'

'They are very competent, you must have faith that things will work out,' soothed Lilly, sharing her new friend's sense of despair and helplessness.

'Yes, you are right,' Eustace answered before changing his stance and tone, becoming more in control and firm.

'Now I need to talk to you about the other matter we discussed some hours ago. I said I would help you so I have outlined how this can happen. Now Mrs Smith, I do have a price for this. You must not ask me who I am or why I can do all of this. I promise you I will reveal this information to you by the end of the night. I have my reasons.'

Eustace had spent many hours on this and he knew, if and when Lilly discovered his true identity, she would have nothing more to do with him, so he needed to remain incognito for a while longer at least.

'Well, I suppose so but I don't understand all of this subterfuge, I am trustworthy you know!' Lilly retorted with a hint of annoyance, 'and I also cannot understand how you can organise this type of visit here and in the middle of the night? Plus I have a price too, I need to be given a name to call you as saying: 'the man I now know is not really Mr Collins,' is too much of a mouthful.'

Eustace smiled at her response. She certainly was no longer meek and passive, that's for sure.

'Well for the time being please call me Edward, as that is close to my own given name and I will call you Lilly if I may as the very formal, Mrs Smith seems inappropriate. Secondly, I know I can trust you, I have never doubted your trustworthiness. As I have said, you will understand about all of this later.'

'To answer your other question, I can organise this in the middle of the night in Subiaco because I am one of the only people across the State whom you could have asked, that has the skills, knowledge and contacts to arrange such a visit. Our meeting was astoundingly fortuitous. You see, I said I know your case very well and that is, unfortunately, very true. I also know Fremantle Prison and the schedules in the prison and the best times to visit. I even have a contact within the Gaol, a very unsavoury guard whom I have no doubt, can be bribed to set up a private meeting. Now for two other reasons it is lucky that you asked me to assist you. The first is that you wanted it kept strictly secret and I can promise you that this will never appear in the press. Even if we are caught, this will never be reported. And the last and perhaps the most important reason, is that I know Clifford Hulme and as you know, he is unlikely to do this for anyone who doesn't know him.'

Lilly stared at him, this was incredible. Her mouth gaped open in amazement.

'How on earth do you know that man?' she whispered, dislike and distrust tainting her tone.

Eustace ignored her question and proceeded to place the first piece of paper on the table in front of her. It was headed: 'Prison Visit' and contained a time line and a series of contacts and organisational procedures. Lilly focussed her full attention onto the plan.

'Now this is what I suggest. I am aiming at this Sunday, 26th August - weekends are always less busy and the best time to visit will be late afternoon or early evening when all of the normal activity at the prison is settling down. There will be no-one there who is not an inmate or prison staff at that time. The prisoners are fed at 5pm and are locked down by 6pm. The guard change is at 8pm, so I suggest that the meeting could be arranged at 6pm without attracting too much attention. Will one hour be enough time?' Lilly responded to his question with a soundless nod.

'To make it even more likely that you are not noticed, I suggest that you dress in male attire. Can you borrow one of your brother's suits and perhaps have a hat over your hair. It will need to be pinned up. When we are inside the Gaol, I will do all of the talking until we are in the interview room. A woman's voice would make the prisoners go into an uproar.' Lilly was stunned into silence, listening transfixed as Eustace laid out his tactics.

'You had said your brother will be still away and Chrissie will still be in hospital, so are you sure that you will be alone in the house on Sunday?' Lilly's head gave a bob indicating to Eustace that he was perfectly right in his assumptions.

'All right then, I will pick you up at 5pm on Sunday. I will have a car at the end of the street near the bushy scrub on the river side. Just go out like you are going for one of your walks and carry your camouflage outfit, you can get dressed in the back of the car on the way. We do not want any nosey neighbours noticing anything strange.' Lilly's mind was whirring: how did he know where she lived, how did he know she went on frequent walks? How was she meant to get into men's clothes in the back of a car? This was all rather disquieting.

'Now when you get into the interview room inside the prison, I may need to leave you and organise things, so you may be alone for a little while. Be prepared, the prison is very frightening, especially at night. When the interview is over we will leave, and you will be at home and safely in your bed by 8pm. When Clifford is in the interview room he will be manacled, so you will be perfectly safe. If you feel scared or you want to leave at any time you must say so and we will go immediately. You have thought this through properly haven't you? Coming face to face with your attacker will be extremely confronting,' Eustace finally asked Lilly.

The lady in front of him had so recently been a victim and the physical and emotional damage had been horrific. Eustace had seen what this had done to her and he was concerned that he was again to be the agent of her undoing if he assisted her with this foolhardy plan.

'It is not something I want to do but it is something I need to do,' Lilly said defiantly. She clearly recalled the last two months where her existence was ruled by nameless fear. Was she ready for this, probably not, but this time line wasn't of her choosing. Lilly stared at the page in front of her and said nothing more of her thoughts to Eustace.

'Well if everything I've outlined is suitable to you, I will go ahead and organise it all. If anything is to change I will slip a note into your mailbox.'

Lilly was still listening intently as Eustace continued: 'Now there is one other thing that I need to tell you before your visit. Clifford Hulme has already requested to see you too, so there will be no doubt that he will be willing to meet with you. Perhaps, if I am permitted to give you counsel, he should be allowed to say his bit first. He is not very talkative as you know and I am afraid if the matters you relay to him are too upsetting, he will retreat into himself and not be able to speak at all.' Lilly nodded her tacit agreement.

Eustace took the top piece of paper from the pile and placed it in his top pocket. He was not prepared to leave any documentary proof of their arrangement. Lilly didn't need any written reminders, it was all committed to memory.

Now she turned on him and her acerbic response was crammed with pent up frustration: 'Now Mr Edward or whatever your real name is, I am very grateful for your exceptional work but I am filled with a mass of seething questions. How on earth do you know so much about me and how is it that you know everyone from my case so intimately. Do you work for the Defence law firm and is this all a conflict of interest for you?'

Lilly had made a very shrewd guess and Eustace was again amazed at her keen intellect and her ability to make the links.

'Well here goes,' thought Eustace, resigned to the inevitability of discovery, 'I had better let her know sooner or later.'

'No I am not a lawyer, but yes, I have been involved in your case from the very beginning. In fact, I knew your husband Harold and I admired him greatly. I first met him many years ago before he was married to you and I knew Cliff before all of this happened too. But the next piece of my admission about my role in all of this, is less pleasant. So before I let you know who I am, I need to say something to you. I have not behaved with honour and I'm sincerely and humbly sorry for any distress I have caused you. My behaviour seemed perfectly reasonable while I was carrying out my role. I believed I was just doing my job and if I didn't do it, someone else would. Now that I have met you, I must admit I really admire you and I am truly and utterly sorry.' Eustace bowed his head, preparing himself for his confession when a voice interrupted his thoughts.

'Excuse me Mr Collins. You have a baby son. Would you like to hold him sir?' the midwife handed him a tightly bound bundle. Both of their minds were immediately distracted and eyes were instantly transfixed onto the newborn, as Eustace reached out for this most precious of packages.

Tiny blue eyes looked out from a scrunched red face with cruel dents on the sides of his little head showing the angry marks of the forceps. The little baby pushed its clenched fist into its mouth and hungrily sucked, searching for nourishment. He showed little sign of the reported lethargy and seemed perfectly and supremely normal to Eustace's untrained eye.

'He is beautiful,' cooed Lilly, her maternal instincts flooding over her. Eustace was speechless, this was the most astounding thing he had ever seen in his life.

Suddenly another voice cut into the magical spell that had enveloped all in the Father's Room, 'I am so sorry Mr Collins, there has been a mistake. The midwife did not know about the post birth instructions.' An efficient, officious nursing sister walked in and held her arms out for the baby.

'And what were these post birth instructions?' asked Eustace with strident defiance, refusing to hand the little bundle over to anyone.

'It says here quite clearly that the baby is not to be presented to the mother or the father and that it is to be removed for adoption immediately after it is born. I have the birth certificate here and will fill in the date and place of birth as instructed, but the parental names will be left blank. The adoption agency will arrange for a suitable name. Now if you will be so good as to pass the child over, we will take him out and a bottle will be prepared for his first feed. If you are giving the child away it is not advisable that you spend any time with him at all. This just ends in regret and grief from my experience.'

Eustace was not swayed by the nursing sister's experience and in a voice that didn't welcome any contrary opinion he requested: 'Lilly would you be so good as to read what is written on the paper in front of you on the desk. This should clarify the matter.' Eustace stood back, still unwilling to hand over the young baby to anyone.

Lilly reached over and took the piece of paper from the table and read out loud in a strong even voice:

To Whom it May Concern

I declare that I am the legal father of the child born on the 24th of August 1928 at Rosalie Private Hospital in Subiaco, Western Australia. Any previous instructions about this child in relation to my relationship with it, are null and void. The mother has relinquished any claim over the child and her name is to be left off the birth certificate. As the sole parent and guardian I would like to instruct Rosalie Private Hospital to seek out a wet nurse for the child as I would like to have it breast fed and raised in a warm caring family as close as possible to this location. I intend to raise the child in my home and will collect it as soon as I can arrange suitable quarters for the child and the nurse. I have attached a promissory note of 20 shillings as a deposit to ensure that this happens.

Yours sincerely

Eustace Wilkinson

The nursing sister looked stunned but accepted this more recent information as it certainly sounded legal and was thus fully acceptable. Lilly went pale and then blushed in a mixture of shock, shame and total animosity. His name hung in the air between them, a name that Lillian could not forgive and would never forget.

Eustace turned to Lilly with the young baby still perched comfortably in the crook of his arm.

'I profoundly apologise Lilly. This is why I couldn't tell you who I was, I knew how you would react. Our agreement will still hold and I will do everything as I have said and after this you need never see or speak to me again. But I ask one more thing of you, if you please. I need to complete the birth certificate and I need you to witness it. Sister could you please fill in the following parts on the Certificate:

The baby is a boy and his name is Harold Wilkinson. I am the father and my name is Eustace Wilkinson and my profession is a Reporter.'

Lilly did as she was asked and then she left the room. Her reply to him as she left the room was easy:

'No comment,' she stated with venomous disdain.

Restorative Justice
Secrets Shared

Sunday 26th August, 1928

Perth, Western Australia

A shiny black and green Buick was waiting at the end of the street as Mrs Lillian Smith, dressed to lock out a cold and blustery afternoon, approached and slipped unobserved into the back seat.

'Good afternoon Lilly, you are right on time. This is it - are you sure you want to continue?' the driver politely asked his passenger.

'Yes I am sure,' the response came in a clipped fashion, not encouraging any further conversation.

The fancy car, on loan from the Editor of the West Australian, changed easily into gear and Eustace was soon cruising down the Fremantle Road. His passenger was mute and stared noncommittally at the passing scenery, but he was determined to keep up a steady stream of chatter.

He spoke of many random things including: the weather, public events and most importantly the progress of young Harold. This baby was, apparently, the most unique individual and everything just amazed Eustace who was spending an inordinate amount of time at the nursery in Rosalie Private Hospital. He explained to his apparently disinterested passenger that a wet nurse had been organised, a local lass who had lost her own babe. With two other young children to provide for, she was quite happy to drop into the hospital and give little Harold his three hourly feeds. This wonderful lady lived in Leederville, not far from Eustace's flat and was perfectly happy for this arrangement to continue when the baby would come home. The newspaper man was full of his plans which he shared enthusiastically with his silent passenger.

Eustace now proceeded to let her know that he wanted to start writing a series of articles on parenting and social mores and that he had dropped into his offices on Friday afternoon with this news. His Editor had accepted this with some amusement but felt it was probably just a passing fad and he would soon tire of this and return to investigative and court reporting. Still he had been happy to loan his car to Eustace, especially on the promise of one more article on how Clifford Hulme was preparing for his approaching execution. All of this Eustace related (except for the part about the article on Clifford Hulme) while Lilly remained aloof and impassive.

'So how are you going getting changed in the back there?' Eustace asked in response to the muffled sounds of undressing and redressing coming from the back seat.

'I'm nearly done. Look, I asked you to do something for me and you are doing it. We do not need to converse you know,' rejoined Lilly, not willing to relinquish the many months of built up animosity. She was still angry and one good turn and a charming smile, didn't reverse months of churlish behaviour.

'Well I beg to differ. You see, I promised you that after this visit you would never need to see me again. So this means I have about three hours to prove I am actually a very lovable sort of fellow. And I doubt that once we get inside the prison, I will get much opportunity to impress you with my wit or scintillating conversation, so that is why I am piling it on so thickly now,' Eustace went on, ignoring her hostility.

He was not just being stubborn. Eustace realised that this was very challenging for Lilly and he was attempting to make her less anxious by being flippant. To give her something to be angry with, he was offering himself up as a target!

'I wish you would just be quiet. This is hard enough without you prattling on,' stated Lilly, but Eustace sensed that she was less tense and frigid, his strategy was working.

'Well I'll be silent soon enough. We are nearly there and you can wager, I will not be chatting much once we get inside. Now don't forget, if it gets too much at any time we will leave.'

They had now arrived at the southern outskirts of Fremantle and as he spoke, the large dark grey, looming walls came into view, dwarfing the Buick and casting long shadows into the already gloomy, late afternoon.

'We'll park here and walk. This side street is well away from the normal parking area.' Eustace left the car and went quickly around to open the car door for Lilly. In her independent frame of mind, she had already opened the door and so they collided. Both instantly reversed back in embarrassment at the unwelcome touch (well it was for Lilly) that had resulted. When they parted they appraised their co-conspirator and both were rather taken aback at the other person's appearance.

Mrs Lillian Smith, had been transformed and although small in stature, she carried off being a young man perfectly. She had found one of Jack's old suits and, after some deft needlework, it fitted her to perfection. She wore a grey newsboy's cap which fitted over the neat topknot of her hair and, except for the fact that she looked a trifle too pretty, she looked every bit the dapper young gentleman.

Eustace also looked far different from his alias, Mr Edward Collins, of two days earlier. The beard and moustache had gone, his hair was cut and pushed back in a modern style and he was now wearing very contemporary casual clothes. Smart trousers, a grey waistcoat and a dark sports coat without padding. He looked very well turned out as he gave her his most disarming smile.

Eustace recovered quickly and offered the encouraging words: 'Come on, this way. You are travelling as Frankie Smith. Now remember, do not speak until you're in the interview room. And Lilly - all the best. I hope you get what you came for.'

The pair now made their torturous way into the unwelcoming fortress. Lilly felt intimidated and overwhelmed; he offered his hand as a platonic comfort and she gratefully accepted it. She was terrified. This place was horrific, a claustrophobic tomb of a place which permitted no light, no joy and definitely no hope. She endured the journey by just concentrating on putting her feet one in front of the other. Lilly listened as Eustace greeted people and made arrangements, and after his conversations doors opened, only to close behind them with foreboding finality.

'Is this the young Frankie Smith who wants a chat with our gallows bait?' enquired a swarthy, filthy guard, speaking in a guttural coarse voice and all accentuated with a loud throat clearing spit. The guard was seated in an old, dirty armchair tucked into a cranny littered with newspapers, discarded cups and food wrappings. Lillian looked up and saw behind the nasty looking man's hidey hole, a long corridor of cells with heavy iron doors.

'It is. Now hopefully you have organised everything as we discussed. I want Frankie to just be able to sit in the interview room, he has a gentle constitution and I do not want him upset. We will not be walking past any prisoners. You get Clifford to come to us. And here is the money we agreed to, half now and the rest when we leave. I will give you a bonus in a week's time once you have proved your total discretion. This is all clear isn't it?'

'Anything you require, Sir. Now come this way if you please,' he indicated with a mock bow. The smirking guard led them to a dank room with four chairs and a central table. A weak gaslight cast eerie lights which cavorted over the damp walls. The guard was pleased, he had been well paid and this bonus was more than he earned in a whole month. Lilly moved inside and perched uncomfortably on a chair, willing herself to stay calm and trying to prevent the rising bubble of vomit that threatened to erupt from her at any moment.

Eustace stood protectively at the door and waited for the guard to return. He was very concerned about this interview. For a start he had no idea about what the two wanted to talk about but he was also aware of Clifford's parlous mental state. He had nearly run out of tablets with only one half tablet remaining. Yesterday, Clifford had asked Eustace if he should keep it to calm him on the day he met his executioner or take it on the day he faced Mrs Lillian Smith. Eustace had been unable to advise him.

After ten long minutes, loud metal clanking indicated the prisoner's approach and with painful manipulation, the guard led the manacled Clifford Hulme to the seat on the opposite side of the room from Lilly. He chained his leg to a large shackle on the floor of the room and with a cheery: 'well, have a wonderful catch up,' the repellent man left them.

Eustace looked into Cliff's eyes and he knew immediately that he had taken his half tablet. The newspaper man had been a regular visitor to Clifford Hulme's cell since the sentence had been passed and he had watched with sadness and concern his drift into morose, moody despair interspersed with manic terror. But this version of Cliff was controlled, his eyes had no wild insanity dancing in them and his demeanour was restrained. This at least showed how much he wanted this meeting.

Lilly slowly raised her eyes to look into the eyes of her oppressor. She had steeled herself for this moment and was prepared for a flood of hatred and revulsion and she knew she might even panic. But she was not totally prepared for unexpected feelings of deep pity and sympathy. This pathetic vestige of a man in front of her raised no feelings of fright, she felt superior and she knew she would be all right. She suddenly realised that she would get through this.

Eustace started the conversation: 'Hi Clifford. This is Mrs Smith, she is in disguise because women cannot come into the prison as easily as men. Now Mrs Smith has agreed to come and meet with you. She has said you can say what you need to say first and then she wants to tell you a few things and ask you a few questions. So do you want to start?'

Clifford swallowed hard. He had practiced and practiced this and he hoped that the words would come out alright. He remembered the lessons from his youth: look at the person and just put the words together, let them flow and it will work.

He looked straight at Lillian and with his eyes fixed on her face he began: 'Mrs Smith I am really sorry for what I have done. I shot Smithy and he was a really nice man and I know he was just trying to help me. And what happened to you was horrible and I hurt the little girls too. And I love those little kiddies and I am so very sorry.'

Clifford took another deep breath: 'I couldn't say this to you in court because there were too many people there and this is none of their business. I only want you to hear it. The lawyer was right, there is something wrong with me, I am a loony. I have been like this all of my life and my family knew it too but they tried to hide it. I have nasty demons in me and when I am having a turn they yell at me and make me do bad stuff. I can keep them in control most of the time but sometimes they come out. The demons came out that day. Now what I wanted to tell you was, that I used to have these little tablets and they kept me in control but they had run out and that is why I went mad. But I know right from wrong. I know that what I did was really, really bad and I deserve to die for it. But I am so sorry I can't undo all the horrible stuff that happened.'

That was it, Clifford just wanted to say sorry. Eustace looked over at Lilly as she stared back at the apologising monster who had caused her so much grief. The cold stone room remained in deathly silence for an agonising minute as Lilly took in what Clifford had said. Eustace shifted his feet uncomfortably, wondering how she would respond and Clifford looked down at his feet, in complete submission.

Then Lilly began to talk - her light female voice sounded so light and brittle, alien in this male only environment. Her voice started softly but got stronger as she gained confidence.

'I am not going to forgive you Clifford, you have caused me far too much pain. But it was brave of you to apologise and I thank you for that. Now, I too wanted to see you for a number of reasons.'

She felt a wave of vomit rise in her and she stopped to take a series of deep breaths. Lilly called on her inner strength to keep her going when she felt the waves of weakness threaten to overcome her. She just wanted to escape from this horrid place but this unpleasant duty needed to be completed first.

'I know you were insane when you did those horrible things to my family and me. My brother Jack Parrott told me about your turns and he told me about the black mood you had when you wrecked the shop. He saw what you were like when you went into a mad rage and he watched you going though your fit, listening while you argued with your demons. That is when Harold and Jack had decided they would help you. Harold felt sorry for you and you repaid him by shooting him!' Lilly let the full horror of this situation sink in before she continued.

'I know about the white tablets and that your supply had run out. These tablets were now illegal to buy and the Government would have put Jack in prison if he kept giving them to you. You thought Harold and Jack were just being cruel to you. Harold tried to help you get off them but he didn't know how sick you were or what you would do when you ran out.'

Cliff had his eyes down but he was listening intently. Harold and Jack had explained this to him but he hadn't believed them when they had said it. But this time he believed her words - Mrs Smith had no reason to lie to him.

Lilly continued: 'Now we found out about the Doctor in the Army who prescribed the tablets to you in the first place. Jack wrote to him in Singapore and told him about your case and what had happened. The Doctor is now the Head of Psychiatry at the University there and he was willing to come down and testify for you in court. In the letter he wrote to Jack, he explained that you suffer from a mental problem called schizophrenia and that this problem can be looked after in mental asylums these days. Jack Parrott knew about these things but he didn't tell anyone in court because he was too cross with you for what you had done. He is ashamed about keeping these things secret and now he has told me everything.'

Eustace listened, mesmerised, this story had been far deeper than he had realised or the court had explored. Both the Prosecution and Defence had only scratched the surface. This family had held the keys to the Defence case and, of course, they had not been willing to hand them over.

Jack Parrott had said, under oath, that he had no knowledge of Cliff's moods and that he did not believe Clifford Hulme was insane. Now, after Lilly's admission, this was blatantly untrue and they had the hidden evidence that could have proved it. Jack would have known this when he stood in the witness box. He had committed perjury and would be jailed if this was disclosed. Just how far did this family believe in the pursuit of truth and justice and at what cost to them?

Lilly kept speaking. She now spoke clearly and with great authority, she held all the cards:

'Now the hard thing about all of this is that if it had been revealed in court, you would have got off the murder charge. Still they didn't know all of this but now I do and I have to decide what to do with this information. Do I take it to the lawyers and the Government and try to get your sentence commuted to life imprisonment in an insane asylum? Or, do I let the sentence be carried out?'

Lilly was inviting Clifford to choose his destiny! She took a deep breath and considered the fate of the prisoner in front of her. She held his life in her hands and this interview would help her make her choice. Eustace kept his silent vigil but he was bursting with questions. This was amazing, the entrails of the story underlying this horrific crime, were being revealed in pornographic detail. Eustace was a voyeuristic spectator watching the two major actors determine what should happen, without a judge or jury or a newspaper in sight.

'To help me make this decision, I have to know something. After you attacked me, did you find something in the draw in my bedroom?'

Lilly paused and stared at the man in front of her. He had

struggled with some of her words but he clearly knew what he was being asked.

'Yes, Mrs Smith, I found Smithy's Lucky Strike tobacco tin.'

'And that tin had some tablets in it, didn't it, and you took one. That is why your mood changed that night wasn't it? The tablet controlled your demons and you came back and tried to help me, is this right?' Lilly asked, having already made the link regarding the reason for his mood change.

Clifford was now crying, large tears were flooding down his guilt wracked face. He had sublimated these memories and now the realisation of the horror of his actions and being forced to confront his behaviour, was a torment. This interview was forcing him to admit to things he had kept hidden. This would allow him to finally be free, more surely than if someone opened the prison gates and let him out.

'I know right from wrong Mrs Smith and the demons in me had done horrible things to you. What I had done was very, very wrong and then I saw the littlies. I had hit little Vonny with a mallee root and crushed her little head. She was always my favourite. Elsie pulled back from me with hate and fear on her face and I realised what I had done to her. And baby Peggy wasn't breathing, just lying on the floor so I covered her up and brought her into you. When I looked at you I realised I had hurt you so badly and you wouldn't look at me either. The tablet had stopped the screaming voices and made me be me again but I could see how much I had hurt you and I was embarrassed. There was nothing I could do to make it better. I just wanted to get out of there and that is why I ran away. I could have sent help earlier but I couldn't tell the Nelsons or anyone, I was just too ashamed. So I just tried to forget about the bad things and made stuff up so I had a story.'

'It wasn't until I talked about it with Eustace and he said I had to hand myself in and get help for you, then I knew what I had to do. So I went and handed myself into the police because running away wasn't going to help. But I still did all those things so I need to be punished. I know I have to die.'

This restatement of events made Eustace's actions sound more virtuous than they really had been. As he recalled it, he had not been guided by any honourable intentions. He had been shocked by Clifford's admission and more than a bit excited about getting a story. This realisation now made him feel mortified, so Eustace was pleased that Clifford's version of his role in the whole sorry episode had been expressed in a rosy light.

Lilly seemed oblivious to this as she went on, 'with or without your demons you have committed some horrible acts Clifford. You killed my husband Harold and he had only wanted the best for you. You shot him in the back and that was a cowardly act. I will never marry again, Harold was the love of my life, so you have doomed me to a life alone. You assaulted my daughters and could have killed them. Vonny has brain damage and will never live a normal life. And what you did to me was unmentionable. Do you realise what that type of crime does to a woman? It is unspeakable. You have to confront how much you have hurt me. You have to take responsibility for the damage to all of us, just saying it was the demons in you, does not face up to the reality that it was you who did this crime.'

Lillian spoke with vehemence and fervour. Every word stabbed into Clifford, making him realise how much he had wounded this brave lady and her family.

'I am sorry, I am sorry, I am so sorry,' wept Clifford, his shoulders cavorting and heaving with the agony of realisation. He had profoundly and fully accepted his guilt.

'Clifford have you ever done something like this before?' Lilly asked, still unwilling to let the agonized man go. Her bearing was proud, almost regal and she allowed no compassion or sympathy to sway her from her course. Eustace marvelled at her strength.

'Yes Mrs Smith, I once killed a lady in England and I've had some bad turns when I've hurt other people too,' Cliff replied, snivelling in abject misery.

'I thought so. I was wondering if your attack on my family was a one off or if you had done something like this previously. Now when you hurt that lady, were you on your tablets?'

Clifford squirmed at the frankness of her question but never faltered in answering her truthfully:

'Yes Mrs Smith I was, but they were not strong enough to stop me. I loved her and then I found her giving herself to two drunks and I got so angry. The demons in my head yelled at me and I strangled her. Sorry to talk about stuff like this in front of you Mrs Smith. My family covered it up and we never talked about her again.' Clifford's polite apology for referring to this distasteful act may have seemed astounding when his own crime against Mrs Smith was considered but this was ignored by everyone in the room.

Both Eustace and Lilly felt the profound impact of this admission; Clifford Hulme had killed before. A life lost, a protective family hid it from the world and no-one was ever aware of it. This is the point when Lilly realized, with instant clarity, what she needed to do.

'So this was the hardest part of my decision Clifford and I needed to know this before I decided which path to take. If I take proof of your insanity to the lawyers, we may be able to defer your execution and they may be able to put you in a mental asylum. This would mean that you would live but you will still have your demons in you and at any time they could get out.'

'You killed that lady in England even though you were on your tablets. You could kill another man just like my beautiful Harold. You could hurt other little girls like Elsie, Vonny and Peggy. Or you could hurt another lady like you hurt me and that is something I couldn't stand. I cannot take this risk. Do you understand this Clifford?'

'Yes Mrs Smith. I don't want to feel this guilty ever again either. I understand that I have to die to get rid of the demons that might hurt other people. I know this but I am still really scared and I don't want to be hung.'

'This is part of your punishment Clifford. It is the only way you can stop your demons hurting someone else. Now, how many tablets have you got left Clifford?'

'None now Mrs Smith. I had a half tablet but I took that before you came in. I wanted to be me when I talked to you and I didn't want the demons to come out and have them shouting things in my head, while we were talking.'

Lilly realised that he had used his last tablet to prepare for this meeting. Rather than save it to cope with his own death, he had taken it for her and she was not without compassion.

'Clifford I cannot allow you to be let off. The burden of keeping this a secret will go with me to my grave. The risk of you re-offending is just too much for me to bear but I will give you these, they will ease your final week and help you to face your executioner calmly and with some dignity.'

Lilly took the bottle of tablets out of her top pocket and walked over to the manacled prisoner. His face lit up with gleeful pleasure when he saw what she had in her hand. The little brown bottle sparkled in the gas light as she unscrewed the lid and gave the manacled Clifford the bottle and a tablet which he swallowed whole. His face and demeanour was instantly transformed. He slumped against his restraints, with that familiar dopey look on his face and his body was no longer tense and anxious.

'I wish you well over your final week and I hope in death you find peace and serenity. I said earlier that I cannot forgive you but this was too harsh. I can see you were not in control when you did those things and, although you have taken so much from me, I wish you absolution. With your death you will be free and your demons will be gone. So remember this as you go to the gallows.'

'Now Clifford can I ask you one other thing before I go? When you found the Lucky Strike tin there was another thing in the draw that I want back. Harold had kept a bundle of my letters in there and they went missing. Did you take them?'

'No Mrs Smith. I didn't see them.'

Lillian looked deflated, she was hoping that Clifford could provide her with this last link to her husband. Still, momentous decisions had been made at this meeting and she was now certain that her decision was, morally if not legally, the right one.

'Eustace the interview is over,' she said dismissively as her head dropped into her hands. She was spent.

Eustace went outside to call the guard who returned immediately to take the prisoner back to his cell. Clifford went without complaint and without looking back.

He had fulfilled his last role in life, to give his most profound apology to Mrs Smith and she had helped him to face up to his evil memories and actions. He knew his Mami would want him to face up to his punishment like a man, and this was all the freedom he needed. Now he could die without regret and the tablets would ensure he would be totally anaesthetised to any pain or suffering.

Restorative Justice
Father's Day ... Is Over

Early September, 1928

Perth, Western Australia

The note in the letter box had been cryptic but interesting and more than a little tempting. It said:

'I feel I still owe you so much and I have come up with a plan to repay my debt. If you would be so kind as to join me this Sunday. I will pick you up at 11am at the end of your street.

P.S. Dress for the outdoors. E.'

It was attached to the following clipping from Friday's West Australian:

Father's Day

Some traditions that have been borrowed from overseas have proven to be very popular in our own country. The concept of having a special day for fathers has really captured people's imagination and this year it will be celebrated in households across Australia on September 2nd. The tradition of Father's Day can be traced back to the ruins of Babylon where there is a record of a young boy called Elmesu who carved a Father's Day message on a card made out of clay nearly 4,000 years ago. Elmesu wished his Babylonian father good health and a long life. Although there is no record of what happened to Elmesu and his father, the tradition of celebrating Father's Day has remained.

Some years ago, Miss Sonora Dodd, a loving daughter from Washington convinced Americans to take on the tradition. President Woodrow Wilson approved of this idea in 1916 and President Calvin Coolidge supported the idea of a national Father's Day too in 1924 to, 'establish more intimate relations between fathers and their children and to impress upon fathers the full measure of their obligations'. Now it has caught on in Australia too, so Happy Father's Day to all Dads across Australia. What are you doing for your Father this Sunday?

Eustace Wilkinson

One week before, as Lillian sat in the back seat of the Buick on the way to Fremantle Prison, she had clearly indicated to Eustace Wilkinson that she didn't want to see him anymore, but this man was proving to be both unquenchable and very persistent. Plus the prison visit had subtly changed their association. The words which had been spoken and the decisions taken had been momentous and Eustace had been a witness to Lilly's final and fatal resolution. This shared experience had moved their relationship to a different plane because Eustace knew Lilly's secret. He knew why she had defied a value close to the core of her existence. Lilly had resolved that she would not act to save a man's life.

There was no conversation in the car on the trip home from the Gaol. Lilly was utterly exhausted and Eustace was, for the first time in his life, totally bereft of suitable words. When the car had arrived back at Lilly's Nedlands home it was shrouded in total darkness.

Without being asked, Eustace had turned off the car and escorted Lilly in, her shattered body leaning on him heavily, requiring his strength, forgetting that she had previously spurned his offers of help and friendship. Eustace acted decorously and supportively as he led her inside, made her comfortable and then put on the kettle.

With just polite utterances, Eustace had established that Lilly needed a sleeping draught and had found a packet of Vernonal on her bedroom dresser. Within ten minutes the exhausted woman had looked sleepily across the table and had declared that she needed to go to bed but had asked if he would stay the night downstairs as she feared to be alone. The children were still with Ada, Jack was in Wubin and Chrissie was in hospital: Eustace was on sentry duty.

Early the next morning, a slightly embarrassed but much recovered Lilly had come into the lounge room where the newspaper man had spent an uncomfortable night, sleeping disjointedly across a lounge chair. As he opened a sleepy eye she placed a steaming hot cup of tea on the table beside him and announced:

'Thank you Eustace. I do appreciate what you have done for me and thanks for staying overnight. I am afraid you have had a very uncomfortable night. I did need someone to be with me last night. I thought I was strong enough to get through the interview with Clifford but I didn't realise how emotionally drained I would be. So my sincere thanks. Now I have prepared a towel and some soap ready for you. The bathroom is out the back. You probably need to freshen up. By the time you are finished I will have made you a hearty breakfast.'

Eustace gratefully took her up on her offer and went out to the washhouse to complete his ablutions. Cold water on the back of his neck and a dampened flannel re-freshened him and along with some deftly applied rose water and a comb, he felt spruced up enough to join Lilly at the kitchen table.

A soft boiled egg, along with three thick pieces of toast and butter and all washed down with freshly squeezed orange juice, almost compensated him for his very uncomfortable night.

'Thank you Lilly. That was delightful. Now I really must check again whether you are all right before taking my leave as I must get the Buick back to my Editor. I am afraid he will be a bit cross as I promised to return it last night,' said Eustace sheepishly, weighing up what sleeping-over might have cost him.

'Yes, I feel a lot better this morning. I am expecting Jack back today so I will not be alone again this week. Once again my thanks Eustace. I was so angry with you for revealing my life to the public, it never occurred to me that you could be such a reasonable chap.'

Lilly was all bustling efficiency as she cleared the breakfast plates. She went on, 'Actually you are quite tolerable. You have shown your immense integrity with this act of kindness. Now I have been thinking about your profession and whether I really believe that all reporters are despicable and loathsome and I have concluded that some are and some are not. I suppose if we all were permitted to keep our confidences all the time, then the newspaper would be very short and if we didn't want to read these stories, then papers wouldn't sell and reporters wouldn't have jobs. So we are all at fault. I suppose, I have discovered that reporters are humans, just like the rest of us.'

Lilly gave him a forgiving smile. She had rationalised her former disdain and Eustace was hopeful that this was almost an olive branch.

Lilly went on: 'I am extraordinarily thankful for your actions in arranging last night's meeting. The complex organisation, the establishment of the contacts and the bribes must have been exorbitant and I don't think I had realised just what I was asking. What you have done for me is priceless and without you this could never have been accomplished.'

'This has all made a huge difference to me. Because I confronted Clifford, I stopped being a victim and for the first time in two months I now don't feel afraid any more. There are no sick feelings in my stomach and I actually feel perfectly well. I needed that interview to make my decision and to move on. But most of all I needed to meet Clifford Hulme again so that I could make him face up to what he did to my family and to me. Now he can die with dignity. This all makes me proud and strangely at peace.' As she spoke she smiled and a whimsical, satisfied look came over her face. The peace was short-lived however as she abruptly stood, collected Eustace's coat and ushered him out the door.

'You must go now Eustace. I will now count you as a friend as you have repaid your debt to me, however, I am not sure you will be welcomed by anyone else in my family. I would not like to see what might happen if Jack was to arrive home and find you here, so you must leave immediately. I may not see you again so good bye and good luck. Oh, and Eustace, enjoy your wonderful time with little Harold. I am so proud of you for making the decision to keep him with you and I am sure it was the right one.'

With that Lillian Smith bundled him out and closed the front door, quietly but definitely, on the young bemused man standing isolated on the front step.

September 2nd, 1928

Six days later, on Sunday morning, Lilly had just returned from her morning walk when her eye was distracted by something in the letter box. She hastily scanned the note and quickly raced inside to dress. There was only ten minutes until Eustace would be there to pick her up. Luckily Jack had already left for the hospital to visit his wife and new baby daughter. This was a great relief to Lilly, as she was unwilling to explain where or with whom she was going.

The reality was she didn't know herself and so the first question she asked Eustace as she entered the Buick (this time she was comfortably seated in the front) was: 'So what is the great secret then and where are we going?'

Eustace was ready for her: 'We are going to Kings Park - that part is easy. It is a beautiful day for a picnic but there is a bit more to it than this.'

Lilly had already noticed that for the second day of spring, Mother Nature had spoilt Perth people with a magic day, a deep, cobalt blue sky with only a brush of light, wispy white clouds.

'Harold used to call these Blue Sky days. He used to marvel about them and said he could never recall them occurring back in England. So, Eustace, you must tell me what is the real reason for all of this.' Lillian turned to the driver showing her expectation and excitement, like a little girl waiting for her Christmas present.

'What? You don't want to just spend a lovely day out with me without a reason?' joked Eustace as he pulled the car around a sharp corner, taking a short cut to the Park through the grounds of the University. His companion just rolled her eyes so he was encouraged to say just a little bit more.

He needed to drag out the explanation until he arrived to make the most impact.

'Before I tell you why, I need to give you a bit of background. Firstly it is Father's Day and because I am a new father, I have asked my nurse to bring young Harold out for his first outing. They are catching a taxi and will be meeting with us around 12 noon at the tea rooms.'

Eustace was now turning the car into the southern end of Kings Park, the still undeveloped native bush part. Conversation was difficult as the Buick bumped and lurched along a bush track heading steadily upwards to the central area.

'But we have another job to do before then. Do you know much about the history of Kings Park?' asked Eustace, still stalling for time.

'Well not really. I've been here lots of times but look, stop stalling and tell me what I need to know and then tell me what you have planned,' Lilly begged, her inquisitiveness starting to get the best of her.

The car had now turned into a more ordered area, the stately May Drive, with the plantings of trees honouring the soldiers killed in the Great War. The road was wide and in good condition and the trees, which were not all thriving, had commemorative plaques.

Eustace slowed the car down and parked as he spoke authoritatively:

'If you notice these trees, rows of Plane and Oak, were planted in 1919 to commemorate our fallen soldiers in the Great War. Now, sadly, many of these trees have not prospered. The soil up here is just too sandy and I don't think they like our summer heat. So come with me please Lillian,' Eustace led the way to a sad area where two trees had died and a large empty space existed. Lilly saw two deep holes had been dug.

She looked down and there was a plaque near the first hole:

Pte James Nelson
Killed Gallipoli
3rd August 1914
Fighting for his Nation

'This is James' spot and his tree has died, how distressing,' Lillian said, turning towards Eustace who had walked into the bush and was retrieving a well grown eucalypt tree in a pot.

'Yes James' tree has died and I thought it was fitting that we plant a new one for him. Now James was a true blue Aussie and he shouldn't have an Oak tree or a Plane tree. I think he should have a true Australian Eucalypt tree. This will grow and flourish in this location. Now I believe he liked red, and I think he really liked your 'Rosie Red Hat' so I have chosen a red flowering gum for him.'

'Well this is a lovely thought Eustace and I really appreciate it but how do you know about James or what he liked?' asked Lilly, wondering just how come Eustace knew anything about James Nelson at all. The information had certainly not come from her.

She watched as the newspaper man took the red flowering gum from the pot, placed it in the hole and started compacting the dirt around the sapling.

'Just wait and I will explain everything Lilly. Now come over here to this hole. This tree was planted for a very unsavoury character by the name of Pte Archie Smoots. No wonder his tree died, by all accounts he was particularly nasty. Now I reasoned that the last thing James would have wanted was to spend his eternity next to Pte Smoots. You see this rogue stole your red hat and wouldn't give it back to James, even after he told him that it had come from his sweetheart. So I have organised for another tree to be planted somewhere else for Archie Smoots. A new tree is to be planted here for another soldier who James would have liked to be near for eternity.'

Eustace went back into the bush and retrieved another eucalypt tree and a polished brass plaque. The plaque was marked with the following inscription:

Pte Harold Eaton Smith
Served on the Western Front
Killed from the after effects of The Great War
While Building His New Country
22nd June 1928.

'This tree has white flowers and is particularly attractive to the red capped parrot. It is the Marri or the Red Gum and it should also thrive in this location. I can imagine it in a few years time, strong and proud, inundated with gum blossom and alive with squawking, cavorting parrots.'

By this time Lilly was now weeping unashamedly as she watched Eustace plant the gum tree. The emotion of seeing Harold's plaque and the true significance of the choice of tree was truly poignant. Lilly was speechless as Eustace directed her to complete his plan:

'I have some gifts on the back seat of the car to place at the foot of each tree; could you please go and get them.' Lilly walked over to the car, appreciating the break so she could wipe the tears from her eyes. She walked back carrying two large bouquets; one was long stemmed red roses all done up with a red ribbon and the other was a large clump of sandalwood blossom. The second bunch had been sourced through a friend from out past Dalwallinu and had been procured with great difficulty.

Lillian immediately placed the roses near the base of James' tree and the sandalwood under Harold's.

Once the wreaths were in place Eustace said reverently:

They shall not grow old while we are left grow old.
Age shall not weary them, nor the years condemn.
At the going down of the sun and in the morning,

We will remember them.

Both Eustace and Lilly then bowed their heads and said quiet words of remembrance.

'This is my gift to Harold, a place to be mourned. His grave is a long way away and his family may find it easier to travel here to speak with him. Plus he can get up to some fun with his old friend James. I understand that they were a formidable pair of larrikins.'

Eustace then turned to Lilly and said solemnly:

'For you Lilly, my gift is 'The Cover Story'. You can bring your children here and just say: 'Daddy died from the after effects of the War.' Clifford Hulme was certainly an after affect of war. You need never tell anyone the grisly and gruesome facts of Harold's death and you never need to refer to what happened to you or to your girls. May this be a comfort to you, that you will never need to publicly speak about this episode again.'

'I needed to give you this gift as I was the instrument of revealing all to the world, and now this is the mechanism to cover it over again. Only Elsie will remember any of this, the others are too young and even Elsie's memories will fade with time. They can visualize their father as a brave and valiant soldier, buried far away, but celebrated amongst our war heroes. This can be 'The Story of our Daddy the War Hero' for your children and your children's, children. This is my Father's Day present to the Smith Family whom I have wronged so grievously.'

'I have had permission from the Repatriation Department of the AIF and Harold's name has been included in their lists. They made the plaque up for me and gave me permission to replant the trees, so don't worry, it's all legal. Registering Harold's death as a War related casualty, also means that you will be eligible for a pension and some allowances, so your circumstances may not be so dire.'

By now Lilly was crying unashamedly. Large sobs of emotional tears were cruising down her face as she leaned protectively and trustingly on Eustace.

'There is one other thing Lilly and much of it you may have guessed already I am afraid. I knew about all of this because I have read Harold's letters - even some of his private letters from James that I doubt you have ever read.' Eustace looked demurely into Lilly's eyes.

The apologist continued: 'I maliciously stole these letters from you and now I hope by this act, I have partly repaid my debt. This is one of those despicable acts that I am very ashamed of, so here are your letters. I am humbly and truly sorry.'

Eustace took the shaft of letters from his coat pocket and handed them to Lilly who clasped them protectively against her breast slowly looking up at him.

'When I asked Clifford if he had taken the letters and he denied it, I knew that you had taken them. It was just a matter of time before you plucked up the courage to return them to me. You are right, it was despicable and cowardly to steal them but by this action you have shown that you are also capable of great good. So thank you, sincerely for my gift and Harold's gift.'

Lilly looked at the crestfallen man in front of her and suddenly realised she could totally and completely forgive him. He was her true, albiet flawed, friend. She bestowed on him a radiant smile.

'Now we need to get to our Father's Day luncheon because your nurse will arrive soon with young Harold and I need a cuddle. Don't forget I have not had much experience with little boy babies, so this is particularly special.'

Lilly's face still bore an immense and satisfied smile. She was ready to start living again.

Monday 3rd September

At 8am on Monday morning, Jack Parrott sat with his sister Lillian Smith, his hand solicitously placed on her knee. He marvelled at her self-possession, he was consumed with gut wrenching turmoil but she was calm and determined. Lillian sat in silence and watched the Swan River wind its way relentlessly towards the sea.

At 8.05am she muttered:

'It is done. May God have Mercy on his Soul.'

Eustace Wilkinson walked from the prison at 8.10am with tears stinging his eyes and a painful lump in his throat. He had attended Clifford but had not stayed to witness his death.

Along with Cliff's few meagre treasured possessions, Eustace carried two letters: one was addressed to Rosa Kujawski and Joseph Blootle of Leeds and the other was to Mrs Ethel Hulme in Stockport.

Both letters were strokes of genius, Eustace thought, in which he had explained that Clifford Hulme had been executed but that in death he had been stoic and valiant, accepting his guilt and making a full apology and reparation to his victims.

He had teased out the best points of this whole sorry incident and perhaps brought comfort to the few people in the world who had actually cared about Clifford's death.

Before Eustace had left Clifford Hulme that morning, he had read him the letters and then reminded him that back in England he had a child and that yesterday was Father's Day and because of the time difference it was still Father's Day over in England.

Clifford had smiled his dopey smile and said: 'I hope the little child, I don't know if it is a boy or a girl, behaves itself and is smart like Ethel. Thanks and goodbye Eustace.'

And with that he had sat back on his bed and waited for the guards.

Eustace had also completed his article for tomorrow's Western Australian Newspaper. He intended to drop this into the office early, for the rest of today he just wanted to go and look into the eyes of baby Harold Wilkinson and celebrate the joy of life.

The West Australian

Tuesday 4th September

Murderer Executed

Hulme Goes Quietly to the Scaffold

Yesterday morning, in a peaceful manner, Clifford Hulme, who last month was convicted of the murder of Harold Eaton Smith, was hanged in Fremantle Gaol. Prior to the execution that took place shortly after 8 o'clock, the condemned man spent some time with his spiritual adviser.

It was reported that Hulme's demeanour was quiet for several days and that the approach of his last hour did not appear to unduly affect him. The previous four executions in Fremantle Gaol attracted a small crowd at the Gaol gates, but yesterday the gates were deserted. The Chief Secretary supplied the following official statement yesterday afternoon: 'The death sentence was executed on Clifford Hulme today. The proceedings were decorous and orderly and without special incident.'

Hulme gave no explanation, taking the reason why he committed these horrific acts to his grave.

Hulme's last words, in reply to the usual inquiry, were: 'I have nothing to say, thank you.'

Eustace Wilkinson